Far Modulus

Modulus Series, Volume 2

Science Fiction by
RTRomero

ISBN: 978-0-9898689-1-4

Also by RTRomero:
Modulus, volume I of the Modulus Series
Barefoot in the Temple, poetry
Volume III of the Modulus series, "Moduli Beyond" will be published
Summer, 2018

Cover Art by Luca Oleastri of Bologna, Italy

Connected Star Systems and Moduli

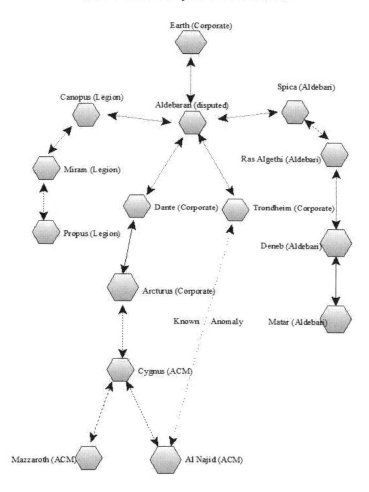

Far Modulus

Contents

Chapter 1: Harden

Seven days out from the Al Najid planetary system, Paul Harden adjusted course. His right hand was healing nicely, but it still ached. Tibs had cut him badly. His thumb still felt stiff and weak. It bore a pink scar, but he could now use it without serious discomfort. The ship's automated medical station had functioned as it should, given the cost. At least it didn't bother him with unwelcome questions and counsel.

His launch was more a yacht than a utilitarian naval vessel. Harden was not a man to prefer function over form where both could be bought. His impoverished youth in the streets of Paradiso left him with a fierce appreciation for luxury.

The blue disk of his modulus shone ahead, stark against the star-filled blackness of the interstellar void. And it *was* his modulus, after all. Nobody else knew it existed. It had never been seen by another living soul. The modulus was a week's travel beyond the orbit of the outermost planet of Al Najid system, well beyond all areas normally traveled.

His accidental discovery of this modulus, years earlier, had been a fluke. Now it was one of his last remaining personal possessions. Paul Harden wasn't a sharing kind of man. Sharing is for codependent people, for the herd, in his view.

A modulus is a great ring made from refined modulinium. The modulinium ring tames the violent energy of a spatial anomaly, where widely distant places in space overlap. What seems straight and regular in space actually bends, in the continuum.

Those who built the modulinium rings were gone. They were otherwise unknown. Whoever they had been, they left behind them fourteen moduli between habitable planetary systems. The modulus Harden now approached was the fifteenth.

Harden felt impatient. Beyond the calm blue aperture of this modulus drifted the wreckage of an alien spacecraft. Harden had discovered the wreck years earlier, shortly after he found the modulus itself. What a day that had been.

The derelict ship had already yielded great wealth to him. Over the years, Harden had salvaged artifacts of a technology more advanced than that of humanity. Some of the advances resulted in his 'inventions'. Marketing those designs had launched and nurtured his career. Armor composites, crystalline conductors, and improved capacitors were three patents he owned and licensed to manufacturers. The devices he patented had been carefully selected. They couldn't be too advanced. He wished to avoid drawing too much curiosity, and his restraint paid off handsomely.

Reducing alien technology to humanly intelligible schematics does require a measure of genius, and Harden could rightly be credited with that. The advances he could adequately describe and depict were not always ones he felt he could get away with claiming. Harden patented the designs and marketed them without breathing a word of their real origin.

He kept secret the most significant pieces of salvage. The best of the stolen technology was too advanced to share with anyone. Much of it, he admitted to himself, was beyond his understanding.

Harden believed he had to incrementally introduce what he did understand of the technology. He released his derivations to create transitional steps. To do otherwise might have revealed suspicious leaps of understanding.

Harden was not so vain as to imagine he could bluff his way through the questions of any real scientist. Questions would lead to other questions, and require answers that would reveal more than he intended to share.

When he gained control of Celine Interstellar's corporate research assets, Harden isolated his technical teams to keep his secrets. It was for their own good. Harden was prepared to silence them completely if it became necessary. Uncontrolled revelation might easily have jeopardized his monopoly over the alien wreck. That would curtail further acquisition of power.

His measures had worked until his enemies stole some of his more advanced, unreleased technology. One of his cruisers, the *Pyotr Velikiyer,* had been defeated, and its technology had been salvaged by his enemies at Al Najid. Harden was dismayed by that memory.

That was all over now.

Now he was a hunted man. He had to assume that the rest of his 'inventions' had been compromised. His technicians were no longer under his control. Most of his secrets were surely in the hands of his corporate rivals.

Harden's eyes grew hard. Most of his secrets were lost, yes. But not all.

When Harden was unfairly judged a criminal, instead of acclaimed as the hero he was, his fortune and all of his documents had been confiscated. His possessions, including his patents, had been parceled out to his competitors.

Harden shook his head in disbelief that the government of Earth, the Corporate Board, had so readily betrayed him. The elite, the people in control of Earth, had betrayed him for the sake of political expedience. The Corporate Board, after all he had done for them, after all he was willing to do, had shifted their responsibilities onto his back while taking everything they could seize of his possessions.

Betrayal is a very bitter fruit.

He knew that his downfall was due to that meddler Tibs, the Aldebari, and to Steve Holbrook, the blue collar lawman who had survived the destruction of Perry. But the worst of them all was the traitor, Martin Avery.

Avery's personal holdings had given him access to Celine Interstellar's Board of Directors meeting when Harden had to gain authorization to use a nuclear device. He had to have a way to make enough modulinite accessible to supply Earth's massive need, and the Directors could vote to make one of Celine's nukes available to him.

Avery was the weasel who secretly recorded the meeting. Avery was the traitor who gave that recording to the Aldebari, information that any real patriot would have kept secret. He had betrayed Earth for the sake of petty personal revenge. He gave the Aldebari sensitive details of the plan to secure a supply of modulinium that would be adequate to the desperate needs of the home world. He betrayed humanity out of pure greed.

Avery's company, Antarctic Continental, had lost their bid to solve Earth's overpopulation. The job was rightly assigned to his own company, Celine Interstellar. Celine had the shipyards to build the transports that would be needed.

Avery's fantasy 'solution' would only have compounded Earth's problems. They would still require more modulinium than could be found without sacrificing the planet Perry, and now that Harden had done the hard part, Avery intended to steal all the glory for himself, the bastard.

Harden clenched his jaw and balled his fists. The damn meddlers didn't recognize that solving the problem of overpopulation was more important than anything else. No sacrifice is too great if it means the preservation of the species. What they thought of as victory was in fact a setback. They had no vision. In their ignorance they didn't know that fighting him was fighting against humanity.

Humanity's survival is, without doubt, the correct imperative to work toward.

In study after study the numbers showed that within just a few years the Earth's population would become unsupportable. The massive, complex supply infrastructure that fed humanity would break down, unable to feed everyone. Those who grew hungry would have no recourse. They would grow lawless and civilization would crumble. Damaged by unrest, the infrastructure would fail, unable to feed anyone. Food that did make it beyond the wealthy orbital cities to the Earth's surface would be wasted at the distribution hubs. People would starve. Unable to breach automated defenses they would be killed, and those who weren't would eventually starve or be eaten, or both.

Unrest and starvation would be inevitable. Civilization planetside would be lost, and the dark age that followed would be blighted with cannibalism, disease and chaos. Knowing the chronic opportunism and avarice of the Legion and the Aldebar, when the moderating influence of Earth was lost, war would ignite all across human space until even the great orbital cities of Earth, the pinnacle of human achievement, would also be lost. Humanity would be reduced to hunting/gathering tribes feeding on the carcass of civilization, and probably one another.

Those were the stakes, as Harden saw them.

The meddlers were fools. Their judgment of him was blind to consequence. Whatever has to be done to preserve humanity is fully justified, no matter what.

Moral and ethical "*issues*" are vacuous compared to survival. The purpose of morals and ethics is to mediate civilization, but without civilization they are pointless.

"Fools!" he said sharply. The medical station sprang to life, trying to analyze his outspoken word. Harden rubbed his forehead: he was talking to himself.

The medical station said. "Please rephrase your query."

Harden glared at the machine. "Is idiocy contagious?" he asked the artificial intelligence, causing it to search its database fruitlessly. Harden realized he was obsessing, but in his frustration he chose to relish it.

It wasn't as if breaking the planet open had been a casual choice. There had been no other practical way to obtain the resources he needed in time to save Earth's humanity. To install gravitics, the necessary inertia dampening systems, and shielding systems strong enough to withstand the fury of spatial anomalies, he had to obtain and refine vast quantities of modulinite. It would have been his superhuman task to transport enough people to relieve Earth's chronic overpopulation. But the meddlers had made the survival of Earth's people nearly impossible, now that he was isolated and stripped of power.

No one else could have done it. Only he had the technology needed for the mass migration to reach new and distant planets suitable for habitation. The frontier planets wouldn't accept enough immigrants to avert the disaster. He had to either find new planets, or gain political control of the whole frontier: Impossible in the time he had.

No, he had to have enough modulinium to get the job done. That was the missing piece in his plan. The ore was available in the quantity he needed, but it had been too deep to extract by normal means from the crust of that stubborn, backward planet of farmers.

Modulinite is an ore that was first found adrift near an anomaly in space centuries earlier.

Three-dimensional space appears regular and continuous to us, but in fact it is irregular. Locations can overlap, even between very distant places, and where this happens there is imbalance in the energy states of the two locations. Sharing an anomalous volume of space manifests as a sphere of violent energy. The imbalance is so great that it taps into dimensions other than space and time. Specifically, the violence of an anomaly opens the source dimensions related to gravity and inertia. When nickel-iron asteroids pass through such an unmodulated spatial anomaly, their iron is transformed into modulinium.

Impure modulinium ore is called modulinite. Modulinium can be refined from modulinite ore in vacuum, and it has unique properties. When excited by specific electrical frequencies, modulinium can affect otherwise constant natural forces. Artificial gravity and inertia dampening are two technologies enabled by modulinium.

The planet Perry had presented a unique opportunity. At the genesis of the star system, while the planet was still cooling, and before the seas and atmosphere formed, the planet's orbit had passed through a spatial anomaly. Much of the iron in the planet's cooling crust became modulinite.

Harden had learned of this when on a survey mission in the system. When the discoverer he had been assisting died, Harden kept the old man's knowledge as his own secret.

No other substance was so valuable. He had used Celine Interstellar's assets to begin mining Perry's rich modulinite ore, but the project had come to a standstill when a vein of modulinite was exposed to oxygen in the mineshaft. Local law enforcement, primarily Steve Holbrook, began to interfere and cause problems.

When Harden and his company were later tasked by the Corporate Board to productively solve Earth's problematic overpopulation, he had needed unrestricted access to that modulinite. He had to obtain it quickly. To accomplish the mission, he had used his influence and his company's resources to set off a nuclear device high in Perry's atmosphere to amplify a powerful electromagnetic pulse, deep into the planet's surface. The energy was amplified at the frequency required to trigger inertial conduction in the raw modulinite.

The pulse frequency lasted only as long as the four deployed emitters survived the event, which turned out to be only a few moments. But in those moments, the pulses energized the modulinite's inertia-dampening property in the planet's crust. Vast deposits of the ore, deep within the crust of Perry slowed suddenly, while the rest of the planet continued moving in its natural orbit. The planet ripped itself apart. The cataclysm exposed the planet's unique deposits of modulinite ore to the vacuum of space, where it could be mined with minimal exposure to contaminants, in particular, oxygen.

The resulting deaths of a half million settlers weighed heavily on Harden, but their sacrifice had been necessary. A half a million people gave their lives to save eighteen billion other people, the people of Earth. The loss of life bothered him most because the Aldebari captain, Tibs, and the surviving Perry sheriff subsequently interfered with the mission. The opportunity was lost. The meddlers had wasted the sacrifice of all those people, and that was criminal.

Harden sighed, and squared his shoulders. Some things just have to be done. No one else would bear his burden. People were in denial about Earth's swelling overpopulation, as if ignoring anything would make it go away. Harden felt as Atlas must have felt in mythology: a titan bearing the responsibility of the whole world. By rights he should be the hero of the age, but instead he was maligned by idiots.

He paused, hardening his jaw, seething. *Idiots!* He would have his revenge. He would have his revenge *and* he would save humanity as well, despite them all.

Harden knew he had to rebuild his assets quickly if he was to pull victory out of defeat. He knew exactly what he had to recover from the alien wreck. He knew exactly who he would sell it to. The Legion would pay any price he named for a sufficiently advanced weapon system.

Harden recognized reality. He no longer had the time or infrastructure he needed to disguise his salvage as his own design. He was glad he had refrained from registering the location of the modulus ahead of him, but he no longer had time for such subterfuge.

His Legion buyer would realize the value of the weapon system, but he would also learn it was of alien origin. When that happened, the revelation of Harden's alien wreck would also become inevitable.

He resolved to sell the location of his modulus as well. It would not remain a secret much longer anyway, so he might as well monetize the location. His short-term profit must be maximized to offset the loss of monopoly. It was a business cost he would have to absorb, but the net gain meant a rebirth of his former power. He would engineer miracles.

He was obsessing, he knew. But this mattered. It was a one shot deal. It was make, or break, and he had to get it right.

Harden would never rebuild his influence subtly now, not after being exposed by that damned Perry sheriff and the recording provided by Avery.

He would sell the main armament of the alien derelict and the location of the modulus. Together these should easily bring enough money to buy an entire squadron, and *this* time Harden would not settle for a scrapyard filled with obsolete ships. He would buy the best warships on the market, and he would negotiate for professional crews.

Then he could do what must be done to enable Earth's inevitable diaspora. Tibs and Holbrook would try to stop him. He had to be ready for that. Saving mankind was the right objective, but it would also give him an opportunity to exact his vengeance. His was the path toward Mankind's salvation. It would cement his proper place in history.

Harden's launch passed through the calm blue modulus while he mused. His communications array went completely silent. The transit placed him instantly beyond communications range with humanity.

He had never taken the time to work out exactly where this modulus led, but he had to be near the galactic rim. More than half of the space around him was populated by only the dimmest motes of light in the intergalactic darkness. Under sufficient magnification, those motes of dim light would resolve into galaxies. Few stars of the Milky Way were farther from the galactic core than he was now.

The derelict ship was a bright speck of white against the darkness ahead. Its hull was starkly lit by the local sun. Almost as soon as Harden emerged from the modulus he spotted it. There weren't any visible stars beyond it. To one side was the nearest planet, displaying striated umber, sienna and cream colored atmospheric bands.

Harden adjusted course slightly and began slowing for the rendezvous. Historically, all other moduli led to systems with habitable worlds. An inhabitable planet in this system would surely be among the first destinations for his colony ships. It was certainly unclaimed, because nobody but Harden knew it would be there. Nobody would have to negotiate the politics of the exodus... except that, now, this system would surely be claimed by the Legion when he sold them the location of the modulus.

But no matter. Once he had the ships he needed to seize the modulinite of Al Najid, there would be no limit to the number of planets available to him, and to the people he would save.

For now, all that mattered was what awaited him in the wreckage, just ahead. He need only reach it, salvage the alien weapon system, and return back to Al Najid space. Once there, the most worrisome difficulty would be to pass unrecognized through the

Al Najid/Cygnus modulus. Then he would make way to his pro-
spective buyer in Legion space.

The alien wreck had been abandoned and left adrift. The
damage showed all the signs of a battle in space. Harden had no
idea who the combatants might have been. Such details were
now irrelevant. It was a lesson he wished he could share with
those who opposed him. The combatants here might have been
different species, or different factions of the same race. What
mattered was the opportunity the wreck presented, not whatever
illusion led to its ruin.

The alien hull was broken open to the void on one side, but
the weapon he had in mind to recover was partly housed in a nacelle mounted on the end of a stanchion. The rest, its core, was
integrated into the hull.

Harden knew the labor ahead of him would be exhausting.
Normally he would have disdained the work as beneath him, but
this wreck was his alone. There was nobody around to see him
perform manual labor. In fact, he felt almost eager to get to work,
but he felt hungry. He would need to eat before he exited the ship
to work.

Harden turned to his ship's small but well-stocked galley. A
packaged meal required hardly a minute to reconstitute and
warm. Before long, he was eating as he looked at the derelict
ship on a portable viewscreen, considering where to begin.

Chapter 2: Recovery

It had taken hours to uncouple the weapon from its housing, disconnect the optical conduit to the aperture gimbal, and extract the core from its casing, which was integrated into the hull. Now, finally, it was decoupled and loose. Harden breathed heavily, recovering from the exertion of trying to move the five- meter-long weapon core. He secured a long tether between the device and the hull, just in case a serious misstep sent the massive device adrift.

Not for the first time, he wished he'd had the foresight to bring an anti-inertial field generator, to make his task easier. He was certain he was due a break. First, he had to let the weapon move enough to clear the mounting bolts, and then stop its motion evenly, so that the weapon core would be in the right position for the next step. Timing the moment when he should begin countering the weapon's impetus, and gauging how hard to apply resistance and where to anchor his body against the hull was a matter of estimation. The amount of force his muscles could apply was too variable.

He didn't have more than a ship's most basic maintenance tools to work with. He hadn't planned this recovery expedition, after all. He had been compelled to it unexpectedly when his cruiser was seized, and he had to abandon ship.

Weightlessness doesn't mean an object is without mass. Exert enough force to move something and it will retain that energy and keep moving until it is stopped by the same amount of force against the motion. On the other hand, once an object is stationary there is no appreciable gravity to undo all the work invested. Leave something hanging relatively motionless in space and it will stay there. This conveniently allows a worker to take a break when needed.

After applying enough pressure to give the weapon motion, he then had to apply equal countering pressure to stop it, once it was clear of its mounting.

Finally, Harden was satisfied that his efforts had been well applied, and the weapon was stable and free of obstruction. After watching the weapon for a moment to ensure it was motionless, Harden allowed himself to relax. He had to admit the exertion felt good. He reached over and switched off the bright portable lamps he had been using so he could gaze awhile on the stars, while his respiration returned to normal. His throat was a little dry, so he snagged the water sip inside his visor with his tongue and drew a quenching pull of the cooled liquid. Space suits are expensive enough to make small comforts important.

The stars in the galactic half of his panorama were simply glorious. He had to avoid looking toward the local sun because that would polarize his visor and block out everything less brilliant. But if he shaded his visor with a gloved hand, half the universe appeared filled with a vast treasure of bright, starry jewels. Harden turned to look the other way. The other half was empty darkness, lit only by the faint dust of unimaginably distant galaxies. They were so far away that, vast as they really were, very little of their light reached him there, on the very edge of the Milky Way.

There was a dull, unexpected flash of light out where there shouldn't have been anything. Harden disbelieved his eyes, thinking he imagined it. Then there came another flash, slightly larger this time. Harden strained his eyes to see, then spoke to his system's artificial intelligence: "Increase visual magnification, three". The suit complied. He could now see some kind of object incoming, extremely fast, and another bright flash of light. This time he saw the flash briefly envelope the approaching object. An energy shield, he thought. The object was a starship, and it was moving at great speed. "Decrease magnification half" he commanded. The suit systems complied.

It was indeed a spacecraft, but he had never seen it's like before. He couldn't quite make out what was chasing the first ship, but something was shooting, making the strange ship's defensive shield flare. The ship being chased looked flat, a pentacle in shape, like a star. It looked like it might pass close by.

The pursuing ships were sleek, angular in design, and looked similar to the one he was salvaging. Harden realized they might spot him. They were going to pass close by his exposed location.

Harden yearned to hide, but there was no shelter that he

could reach in time. His position was exposed, and his ship was just hanging out there in the void next to the derelict alien ship, completely visible. Harden thought his best chance at avoiding detection would be to just hold still, and not draw attention to himself. Maybe motionless he wouldn't be noticed. He felt relief that he had turned off the bright work lights to stargaze.

He didn't consider that the heat from those lamps would still glow brightly in infrared.

"Magnification neutral" Harden commanded his suit, but before his vision could resolve the ships were past him, out of his view. They had passed quite close to his launch.

It was a dilemma. Harden urgently wished to flee the area just as quickly as he could. His heart was pounding. His nerves felt jumpy. He was nervous and fearful. What he had thought was a secluded, unknown region of remotest space was unexpectedly a field of combat in some unknown alien war. He smelled the scent of his own fear in the closely regulated atmosphere of his suit and it bothered him.

Yet he hesitated. He didn't want to leave without what he came for. Harden didn't know if he would ever have another opportunity to retrieve the alien weapon. Without it, his ambitions would be futile. This salvaged alien weapon was needed to fund all of his long term plans. He had lost everything to the Aldebari and to his competitors on Earth. He had to rebuild his assets if he intended to lead humanity to settle new worlds, turning overpopulation into a strength rather than a weakness. Successful, he would become known among men as a savior. The political power that estate would yield him should be godly. But without this alien weapon's technology, his path to destiny would close.

Such an extreme reward seemed worth some risk. The potential outcome attending success rationally outweighed a potential threat that might never materialize. The aliens were surely intent on their running battle. They hadn't even slowed, after all.

Yet his nerves were tense. His body was alert with alarm. Harden felt an urgency that almost overwhelmed him. His heart hammered insistently that he should flee now, while he still could. Yet his intellect was self-assured and analytic. He determined that he must control his fear. His visceral reactions were just chemistry, a primitive hormonal response to an unexpected threat. He needed to guide himself with his mind, in an act of will, and not merely react to the prompts of animal urges.

Harden situated himself to begin pushing the heavy weapon until it began to noticeably move toward a spot directly across from his waiting launch's open hatch. Then he pulled himself along the weapon to get ahead of it. He waited at his intended receiving point impatiently. He braced himself, just where he could begin to stop the weapon's ponderous transit. He knew it would be hard to slow and stop the mass of the weapon before it crushed him against the bulkhead. Thinking ahead, once he did have it stabilized he would angle it toward his launch's cargo bay, and then push it across the intervening space. He would have to pull himself along it again out there, so that he could slow it to a stop in the cargo bay before securing it. Then he could close the cargo door, and he would get away, back through the modulus to human space.

The sensation of danger was very hard to ignore. It irritated him. More than once he rethought his decision, but each time it was even later. He sensed that there wasn't enough time. His anxiety about being discovered by the aliens kept him committed resolutely to his plan as the most efficient path to success.

As time inexorably passed, Harden's fear mounted. He resisted the urge to push the weapon faster. He knew it would take all of his strength already to stop it in the right position. From where he waited he could see his launch, cargo bay open to the vacuum, perfectly situated not twenty meters away. There was still no sign of any alien activity, and he began to feel a spark of hope that he would get away, and his risk would be rewarded.

Finally, the big weapon arrived where he could reach it. With his feet on a bulkhead he began to resist its slow forward motion, steadily pressing upon the massive metal surface with all the strength he could impose.

Periodically his endurance was overcome. Then he had to let

his muscles briefly rest. In those intervals he hung onto the inexorable weapon, allowing it to press into him until he mustered his endurance to start resisting again. Finally, he had the weapon stopped in a good position to turn for the final push, out into his waiting cargo bay.

The next step would be to carefully pivot the weapon so that it might fit into the waiting cargo bay when he pushed it across. Measurements told him it would fit. It would be a slow ride, but he would stay with the weapon while it moved across the gulf. He would pull himself to the far end, then push off into the cargo bay where he could stop it, and then secure the massive weapon core.

Beyond the open cargo hatch of his launch something caught his eye. A speck grew bright and became larger, until it resolved into an approaching starship. It did not appear to be of human origin. Mouth falling open, Harden realized he should have tried to escape when he had the chance.

The alien ship grew immense and bore directly toward him. Sparks of electricity arced between the weapon he had meant to salvage and the hull of the derelict ship. He remained frozen in place. While fear informed his hormones of impending catastrophe, his mind casually surmised that the electrostatic charge was a side effect of powerful sensors. Incongruously, he heard his own odd, nervous laughter. His stomach lurched in alarm. He felt a surge of adrenaline in his legs and back, and he trembled with an urgent need to move. His body responded chemically to his fear, but it was as if his racing mind had slipped out of gear. His feet seemed stuck in place. Harden could not respond to the need to get away. Panic gripped him and escalated. Where could he go? The closer the starship came, the larger he realized it was. It was much too large.

Paul Harden was caught.

Chapter 3: Visitation

Steve Holbrook gazed down on Kyle's pale face. His friend's head was propped on the starched white linen of a thin hospital pillow, his hair clean but tousled. The hospital gown covering his chest and shoulders was a pale cornflower blue.

Steve's former deputy was now the chief of security. He had been badly wounded in a boarding action, aboard Harden's cruiser weeks before. Now he was recuperating on medical leave, and Steve had temporary duty filling in for him at his old job.

Kyle was engrossed in a news event that was being broadcast and rebroadcast through the moduli across human space from right there on Perry Station. Images of a recently discovered alien mummy were recorded and relayed through the Al Najid/Cygnus modulus, and beyond by communication relays that would receive segments of the broadcast, transit the modulus, and retransmit the holocast on the far side to the rest of human space.

Communications signals cannot transit through a modulus, even by wire. The modulinium of the ring that tames the wild energy also scrambles and absorbs digital signals. Upon transit, communications and other digital systems must reboot. Even neural synapse activity in the human brain is momentarily confused during transition. While that is happening humans don't notice the lapse, and never remember it happening. Evidently harmless, people no longer worry about it.

The wounds Kyle sustained aboard Harden's heavy cruiser had been too severe for first aid to more than stabilize. His life had been saved by young Bobby Morrison's quick, correct response and the timely application of direct pressure. An emergency medpack had kept his body from shutting down in shock.

In a chair next to his bed Kyle's fiancée, Lian, held his hand. Her clear, serious eyes were often on Kyle, but even she was distracted by the imagery and narration of the news report. Lian was Aldebari, one of the people who rescued Steve, Kyle and the other Perry pilots from their destroyed fighters' lifepods after their planet had been destroyed.

After their rescue, and the construction of Perry Station was well underway, Kyle and Steve witnessed the destruction of an Aldebari research station that had been studying a spatial anomaly in the Al Najid system. The research station had been the site of Lian's residence and her duty station.

They had been aboard the *Jade Temple* when it emerged from the Trondheim anomaly to return to the Al Najid system. On system entry they saw Harden's heavy cruiser unleash final destruction upon the Aldebari facility. Kyle feared for the safety of his sweetheart.

Fortunately, as it turned out, Lian had been among the refugees who were evacuated to Perry Station.

Most of the early losses in that battle had been material rather than lives. Combat spacecraft are equipped with lifepods. Lifepods will detach from a badly damaged spacecraft to speed the pilot to the nearest refuge.

Unfortunately, many pilots ultimately died in the battle anyway. The research facility had a very limited supply of reserve fighters. When the supply was exhausted, their lifepods stranded the pilots there without a means to escape. When the station was destroyed, any pilots who were stranded there were lost with it. They died after defending the evacuation, but their sacrifice had saved many, including Lian.

The holovid broadcast that engrossed the three friends documented the examination of a mummified alien, recovered from its small spaceship. The scout ship bore advanced technology that fascinated the engineers who were attempting to understand it. Scientists consequently wrestled with newly uncovered implications for what they thought they understood about the universe.

When Perry Station announced the discovery of a mummified alien, premier exobiologic specialists from across human space were invited to examine the specimen. Most who could respond arrived quickly.

Engineers and physical scientists examined the hardware of

the alien ship carefully, while the exobiologists and a leading forensic expert carefully examined the alien's remains.

The alien ship's computers were challenging to even locate.
Suspected information systems defied attempts to access them.

Major news organizations also arrived in force. These media
companies competed to make the presentation of dry, painstak-
ing scientific processes more lively and entertaining. Speculation
and banter are generally inappropriate to science. 'Enhance-
ments' that embellish more popular media narratives annoy
academicians, but the public was enthralled. The media will always package information with an eye toward marketing.

Less popular, official accounts of the forensic proceedings
were cerebral, filled with specialized jargon. They were less
laced with speculation and conjecture. The average viewer over
the HoloNet found it difficult to endure the facts unenhanced.

Analysis of the alien's remains showed it had been a female
biped, approximately the size of a human. She appeared to be
both reptile and bird.

An intricately articulated ornament, like a metal-scaled hood
or cowl, was carefully removed from her head and from the back
of her long neck. It revealed feathers from the crest of the alien's
head, down her back to the tail. Similarly, feathers covered the
outside of her arms and thighs. Her face and forehead displayed
reptilian scales. She had a lizard-like tail with feathers, but was
scaled, smooth as a snake belly, on the abdomen and the tail's
underside. Above the eye orbits, on the creature's high forehead,
the scales gradually lengthened and articulated into bird-like
plumage. Her shriveled eyes were set forward on the skull,
suggesting that she'd had good depth perception. The eyes
were dehydrated and shrunken beneath closed lids.

Holographic still images were magnified to focus on the tear-
ing and shearing teeth of a carnivore. They were partly concealed by pale, gently curved, and broadly scaled lips.

The alien's hands boasted opposable thumbs. The thumb and
fingers looked powerful, but the structure of the hands seemed
slightly at odds with the design of parts of the ship where there

were handles to grasp or buttons to press. The hands were covered in fine scales. Ultrasonic sensors revealed retractable claws rather than human-like nails in her spatulate fingertips.

Extraction of the dried corpse from the alien craft had been a delicate and time consuming operation. The scientific community voiced dismay that the ship had been carelessly contaminated by the 'amateurs' who first opened it. At the same time, they were ecstatic that the alien ship was there at all, that it was whole, and it was open.

And there was the alien specimen to examine.

Humanity had known, since the discovery of the first modulus, that there had been at least one previous species capable of space travel. Who those may have been opened constellations of speculation, and became the subject of many works of fiction.

When explorers found no other verifiable sign of intelligent aliens, the questions and fears that initially swept the Earth faded into a kind of popular myth. Those who subsequently traveled space seeking any sign of an alien civilization wondered why, among all the planets people found and settled, there was no other evidence of non-human sentient life more advanced than Earth's dolphins.

Almost everyone who could was viewing the proceedings or reading text feeds about the investigation of the alien. Fear and hope rippled through humanity with each revelation, and reflected conjecture back from the fringes. How old was the dead alien? Were there more aliens out there somewhere, alive?

The banter of newscasters did seem to have the effect of muffling the shock of discovery with chatter. Their talk partly mitigated hysteria in some quarters. Talking heads lent an air of normalcy to whatever they discuss, even where the subject is outlandish.

A news commentator reassured his audience with the long-held opinion that a civilization advanced enough to travel the stars would surely be at least as enlightened as humanity. As a lawman, Steve had seen enough of the dark side of mankind to find that thought less than encouraging.

"Well, I'm glad to see that you're on the mend, Kyle." Steve offered to his friend, thinking he should either get back to the office or call it a day and go pick up his kids. "When do you start physical therapy?"

"Already begun, Steve." Kyle replied. "I want my life back to normal. The doctors say physical therapy will be my route back. Laser pulses are much less messy than kinetic rounds, but I'll still have scar tissue to overcome. Laser wounds have their own drawbacks when it comes to healing. How are your kids?".

"Kathlyn and Stevie are doing okay." Steve responded with a smile and some introspection. He looked down at the palms of his hands, troubled. "They miss their mom, naturally, but we're talking about it." He looked back up at his friend. "I think they're slowly coming to terms with our situation." He looked over to Lian. "It would be easier in some ways, I think, if we could know whether she really is gone. I don't think she survived, but we don't really know."

Lian's eyes were sympathetic and clear. Steve continued, "The chief investigator for Oberon security told me a house fire consumed most of the evidence there may have been. No human remains were found there. Neighbors reported that a small craft landed briefly before the fire. That's how they must have taken the kids and Pat away. Cygnus Command spotted it, but failed to check on the landing. The investigation into why *that* happened is inconclusive so far. Officially, they are attributing the oversight to a lack of training. That doesn't sound right to me, but it is better than blaming it all on some sacrificial lamb I suppose."

"The kids, naturally, want their mother back so we can be a family again," Steve concluded with a weary, almost despairing tone. "I don't think I'm as good at nurturing them as Sandy was. I'm at a loss as to how I should try to work it all out with them. I'm hesitant to encourage their hope for Sandy's return, but I don't want to kill that hope, either."

The three friends were quiet for a few moments. Some problems don't have easy solutions. The holovid news droned on, a background noise repeating the same information they had already heard a dozen times.

"Maybe you and the children should visit a counselor, Steve. Who do you have watching them?" asked Lian.

"We should see a counselor eventually, Lian," Steve admitted. "For now I'm trying to keep things simple. I want to give them some time, maybe not crowd them. I don't want to push things unnaturally just to make my life more convenient. They're back at the education center for most of the day, now that I'm working regular hours again. Since Kyle here," he gestured toward his friend, "decided to be a lay-about."

Kyle grunted in protest.

"The educational staff keeps an eye on them while they study their coursework on the net. I'm thinking I may help a group of parents on the Station sponsor another history elective. We've already subscribed to a very good Oberon school for their technical content, and we have a few decent general ed teachers on call here at the Station, in case the kids need assistance. I'm mostly concerned with which view of history we're going to get. The versions told by Earth, the Legion, and the Aldebari are from different points of view, but I don't think we can afford all three."

"Don't underestimate your influence, Steve. I remember how important my Dad was to my education." Lian assured him. 'Teach them what you know about whatever they study. I remember one of my favorite things was listening to my Daddy read to me before bed."

"Wait! *Listen!*" exclaimed Kyle, pointing toward the holodisplay.

Initial forensic procedures were in progress on the mummified remains of the alien pilot. The examiner scanned the body torso using a medical sensor. Her very first pass located an unnatural object embedded under a faintly discolored rupture in the pattern of the creature's scales, where its ribs should be. The examiner observed aloud for the record that the image of the object appeared to be of a projectile of some kind. Steve was intrigued. A fletchette? A bullet?

The presiding medical examiner was assisted by select exobiologic specialists. Her voice was detached and professional, and her observations were laced with medical jargon. After reporting the presence of the projectile, the examiner's voice could no longer be heard clearly in the newscast because of speculative chatter among the media commentators.

An embedded projectile implied direct interaction with someone or something else. It was the probable cause of death for an alien found alone aboard her starship.

Steve felt intensely curious. While the examiner worked carefully to extract the object from the creature's torso, her assisting specialists took desiccated tissue samples from the mummy for laboratory analysis.

Lian turned her inquisitive green eyes from the broadcast toward Steve and asked him "Has there been any sign of Harden?"

Nobody was pleased that Harden had escaped. Although the *Jade Temple* should easily have been able to intercept Harden's launch, one of the measures used by the boarding party had scrambled the communications system aboard Harden's heavy cruiser. Uploading that virus was one of the first steps they had taken after boarding. Once the boarding action was complete and they were victorious, however, the computer virus they had used to disable communications also prevented them from transmitting warning of Harden's escape until it was much too late to catch him.

The seized cruiser's data banks held the engineering schematics for the Captain's launch that Harden had used for his escape. It was more of a yacht than a launch, but at least they knew what to look for. Unfortunately, it hadn't turned up yet, anywhere.

"No sign." Steve told her. "He didn't show up on sensors, according to the Legion base out on Al Najid V, and Harden hasn't passed through the modulus to Cygnus. Our patrols have been alert for him. We are requiring visual range inspection for all ships prior to transit. We aren't relying on transponder signals anymore. He has to turn up here at the station eventually, because there isn't anywhere else for him to go."

Harden had shown himself adept at using false transponder

signals to hide his movements. He had spoofed transponder signals before, and he would surely try it again. But in the meantime, the man had vanished completely.

Steve had to go get his children and take them home from the education center. He needed to prepare supper before they could eat. Like Kyle and Lian he was fascinated by the unfolding alien autopsy, but practical life is necessity.

The facts about the alien would be revealed in due time. There was no rational need to watch it live, but it took deliberate effort to pull his attention away from the constant feed of speculation. With an act of will he took his leave.

If the education center had to attend the children after hours he would be charged overtime. Lian gave him a brief hug and he shook hands with Kyle in farewell. Kyle told him to stay out of trouble.

The education center was a complex of large rooms toward the center of Perry Station. It was warm, clean, and well lit. Around a carpeted central area where the children could run, play games and exercise, a ring of rooms was furnished to provide a space of learning. The common area was crowded with children playing together. Around the periphery, students either studied, or at least appeared to study.

A large room to one side housed a daycare for children who were too young to use the digital network unattended. One of its walls displayed a digital forest scene that looked quite real, despite an unnatural abundance of animated animals cooperatively playing together. Even very small children were rapt, enchanted by how the animated characters found solutions together for things they could not solve alone. Social interdependence was consciously programmed into them from early childhood, and would perpetually influence their adulthood.

Every able adult on the station was employed. Almost all of them worked the same hours. A working citizen with children could use the education center to care for them. A continued influx of immigrants meant the education center would have to be expanded soon. Already Perry Station's governing council was debating plans for a second education center.

Once children graduated as young adults, they would enter compulsory military or civilian service with the independent ACM Alliance.

The alliance was comprised of the Al Najid, Cygnus and Mazzaroth planetary systems. With their service, new citizens gained experience, made contacts and gained a source of income. They also earned the privilege of life-long learning over the HoloNet, funded by the Alliance. Maintaining this regimen helped scale the ratio of government to population and filled the demand for professionals, managers, specialized technicians and skilled workers in all industries and trades as well as civil service.

Productive interdependence was a necessary cultural adaptation for people on Perry Station, and it was expected of emigres. The relation between productive behavior and social virtue was considered a measure of personal liberty.

"Daddy!" Steve's son spotted his dad and raced to him, amazingly quick on his little legs. Steve couldn't help but smile.

"Dad!" Kathlyn followed her brother and ran toward Steve with a more graceful lope.

"Stevie!" laughed Steve, sweeping his son into the air in a wide arc to hold him in the crook of his arm. As Steve brought him in the boy fit naturally to his hip, his small arms circling his father's shoulders. With his other arm Steve bent down slightly and hugged his daughter in welcome, kissed her cheek, and took her hand to turn toward the elevator. "How was your day, Kath?" he asked her. "What did you learn?".

His son laid his cheek on Steve's shoulder and his eyes grew distant. The boy stroked the cloth of his Dad's tunic, feeling the smooth fabric in his young fingers.

Kathlyn announced matter-of-factly that she had been awarded a star on her math quiz. Steve was appropriately impressed and he commended her. Immediately Stevie perked up, sat upright, and declared proudly that he also had a star. Kathlyn imperiously disputed her brother's claim. Stevie haughtily denied her dispute and tried to reach into his backpack to retrieve the evidence, but his positioning prevented ready access. With a squirm he signaled his father that he was ready to walk and Steve set him down. Immediately the boy withdrew an electronic tablet from his carryall pack and thumbed to where he had drawn a series of pentacles using a stylus. The earlier five-pointed drawings were not terribly star- like, but the later ones were noticeably improved.

"Well done, son!" Steve pronounced with great seriousness, and little Stevie turned righteously from him to Kathlyn. "See?"

Kathlyn was, of course, quite severe in her sisterly countenance, not troubling herself to point out the obvious difference between a star her little brother had drawn and her prestigious and official performance award.

Having established the legitimacy of his claim, Stevie was again ready for a ride and held up his hands to let his father know he should be picked up. Steve comfortably complied.

"Shall we stop by Mary's to see if she has anything for our supper?" Steve asked them.

"Yes!" both children urged in unison, dispute abandoned.
With an epiphany young Stevie suggested "Ice Cream!"

Mary Stirling was the proprietor of a small food and kitchen appliance shop on the way to Steve's quarters. The shop was in the oldest retail district on Perry Station. She was clearly fond of both Steve and his children. For each child she held out a mildly sweet and salty glazed cracker imported from a bakery in Oberon, largest city in the Alliance. "Hi, Steve!" Mary greeted him with a smile.

"Hi Mary. We were just discussing the matter of tonight's supper." Steve explained.

Steve winced slightly as his son chomped the cracker loudly next to his ear. The boy seemed to revel in making noise, and Steve set him down on his feet.

"We have some new freeze-dried soups from Earth and fresh eggs from Arcturus, but they are pretty pricey. We also received a carton of more reasonably priced frozen shepherd's pies from Paradiso. They were flash frozen and are ready to bake in the culinary unit we installed for you last week. If you follow the directions they'll have a golden, delightful potato crust. I tried one, and I liked it."

"Okay, well, how big are the shepherd's pies? Would two of them be enough for the three of us?"

"Well it really depends on how hungry you all are but I think probably, yes."

Steve looked at the price thoughtfully. Not bad. "Okay we'll take two, delivered with a half-liter of your chocolate chip ice cream." Steve decided. The children perked up at that news.

Mary was a pretty woman approximately Steve's age. She had a clean look and she smelled wonderful. She had shown hints of personal interest in Steve in the past, but their relationship was little deeper than that of shopkeeper and customer. She reminded him of his late wife, and he feared she might develop issues with his line of work.

"You haven't been eating enough fresh vegetables, Steve. We have some good butter lettuce, cucumbers, and tomatoes in from hydroponics, and I just received a shipment of dressings from Earth. I recommend the garlic vinaigrette. Do you still have some green onion?"

"Yes, I have a couple of them left. Have you been following the alien autopsy?" he asked in diversion.

"Of course I have, Steve. Who hasn't? Nobody talks of anything else." Mary noticed his gambit to evade a discussion of vegetables. "I have a holovid in back. Sometimes it's hard to leave it, even when I hear a customer come in. Why do you ask? Has something else turned up?"

"No, I don't know. I was watching a little while ago, when they found something inside the alien, a projectile, but then I had to go get the kids. Did they ever say what it was, exactly?"

"It was a large stone arrowhead, Steve." She answered. "Can you imagine?"

"An arrowhead? And how large is 'large'?" he asked. A fletchette or a bullet he could imagine. If the creature had come into contact with humans in space then the rest of humanity might never have known, assuming it eliminated whomever it had met. But an arrow is primitive, an unlikely weapon for a spacefarer.

"They didn't say exactly, or not that I recall. The news just described it as 'large'. The scientists are sending it to a lab either on Oberon or maybe Earth for analysis."

Steve felt dissatisfied. The information was incomplete. He turned back to the practical matters that he needed to handle.

"So... for tonight we'll have the shepherd pies, which I assume contain vegetables, a salad for more vegetables, and a dessert of ice cream then. Chocolate is a vegetable isn't it?" Steve joked. "Thank you as always, Mary. Where would we be without you? We should be home in about fifteen minutes. Then we can take delivery."

Mary smiled at him. "Alright, Steve. And chocolate would be a nut, just like someone I know. I'll have my guys deliver the order to your place when they can fit it into their rounds, but after you're home."

The only planet Steve could imagine where the alien might have been wounded by an arrow was Earth. The other worlds humanity had settled had no native sentient life. If the alien had been wounded on Earth, yet died from it in space here in Al Najid system, then it had to have come through the modulus. The distance between the several moduli between Al Najid and Earth meant it had lived wounded for weeks, unless it's ship was much faster than anything humanity had. Or it may have transited the anomaly from Trondheim system, although that did not seem likely. But where had it been trying to go?

Steve felt his son's little hand tugging on his and looked down. Stevie was looking up with serious eyes. He balanced on one foot and was swinging the other wide. The boy whispered "Dad, your wrist is blinking." Sure enough, the 'message waiting' LED was flashing on his wrist-com.

"Thank you, son." Steve smiled to his boy. Kathlyn was quietly focused on reading the headlines and descriptions of available teen magazine flash downloads on a kiosk that was obviously designed to appeal to young ladies. He looked back at Mary. "Okay, so I suppose our business here is done for today. I should get these kids back home and fed."

"Okay, Steve. But don't be a stranger. Come back soon."

"Bye, Mary. Come on, Kathlyn."

Kathlyn tore her eyes away from an image of a teen idol and dutifully came toward her father's side. She diverted slightly to accept Mary's hug. Then Mary opened her arms to little Stevie who let go of his dad's hand to accept.

"Come back soon, you three." Mary invited with an open smile for their father.

"Count on it, Mary." Steve smiled back and he took the hands of his daughter and son. At the doorway he gently held his children back and observed the plaza outside the shop. He noticed details in the environment, scanning for anything unusual. Not long ago a corporate assassin had nearly killed him, right here on Perry Station, quite nearby. His mission to recruit technically proficient settlers from Earth had been in some ways too successful, and an illicit bounty had been placed on his head. Steve believed Paul Harden had been behind the contract, but he couldn't be sure, and the contract might not have been canceled. Harden had probably not been acting alone, and the assassin still hadn't been caught.

The way looked clear. He smiled to his children and led them home.

Chapter 4: Identity

His name was Genevieve Trent. The mirror said he had laughing green eyes and soft, light brown hair tending toward blonde. He noticed an imbalance in the mirror and adjusted the pads that gave his body the appearance of feminine hips. He wasn't sure how long this disguise would last, but it had been fun.

Building a new identity is more involved than just changing apparent gender, name and restyling his hair. For him, it was an art form. Asserting a fictional history, a new legend, on an isolated space station with a finite, well known population was time consuming. Genevieve had painstakingly engineered his new persona's arrival, and had matriculated immigration as if a new arrival without ever leaving the station.

The assassin had grown fond of Genevieve, but Security seemed tighter than ever. Every move he made incurred increased risk. Every effort to increase his anonymity, to hide his identity, was also an opportunity for error. Yet, remaining the same too long incurred risks as well.

Civilians have it easy, simply remaining themselves, letting history fall wherever it may without a real care, never having to deal with complicated fictions and ever-multiplying environmental variables that could mean recognition from a previous incarnation. Living a disguise is challenging. Truly, while it is better to keep everything as simple as possible, sometimes simple is not good enough.

Not only had his contracted target failed to grow careless but, if anything, the station's security measures had grown even more rigorous. The security chief was in the hospital, but Gabriella, his meticulous office manager, seemed to oversee everything. She was too good. She apparently never slept, she was astute, and she had connections all over the station. If there was gossip in the salon, or drunken words in the bar Gabriella or one of her people was there on top of it, taking notes. Overt security operations ran too well. Genevieve saw it as a sure sign that covert security operations were also respectable. Those covert operations had to be out there, but so far they remained impenetrable, which itself effectively neutralized the assassin.

Worse, Holbrook did not get in Gabriella's way while standing in for the Station's security chief.

The greater portion of any successful operation is preparation, and most of the rest is a matter of coordination. Preparation empowers action. Genevieve's previous efforts to make an example of Holbrook and escape had depleted his supply of weapons-grade propellant, but the news emerging from the recovery of the alien gave him an idea.

Chapter 5: The Aldebari

The *Jade Temple* was in atmospheric dock at an Aldebari naval station, deep within a metal-rich asteroid field circling the giant binary star system called Spica.

Apparently the two stars once had their own planetary systems, but proximity had drawn these together, resulting in what must have been a series of cataclysmic planetary collisions. Those spread mineral-rich debris across the binary system. Like all systems served by a modulus, there remained a habitable planet, but the hazardous frequency of meteoric bombardment, coupled with an Aldebari reluctance to reside at the bottom of a gravity well, left that planet uninhabited.

There had been too many Aldebari pilot casualties in the assault on Paul Harden's heavy cruiser. The fallen had assisted in a boarding action by the *Jade Temple*'s Marines. It was a ship-to-ship assault.

The Marine commandos were well trained in shipboard firefights, but Tibs and his pilots had been out of their element.

Under the command of Lieutenant Ishi Matsuo, the assaulting Marines had worked their way aft toward Engineering. Tibs led his debarked pilots forward, toward the command deck.

The pilots were trapped in a crossfire at an intersection of hallways, where there was no cover. Casualties had compelled Tibs to surrender.

A four-man point team led by Steve Holbrook had avoided the crossfire and was able to penetrate up to the command deck in time to rescue Tibs and young Bobby Morrison, who had been caught trying to reach and neutralize Paul Harden. Bobby had been attempting to avenge his parents.

Now, young and untested Aldebari pilots were graduating from the Aldebari Naval College into the junior ranks of the *Jade Temple*'s pilot squadron. The renown of the ship was enhanced by the reputation of her commander. Gaining a commission aboard the *Temple* was prized among Aldebari pilots.

Tibs diligently tried to read his new pilots' personnel files. He kept notes on their family, factional affiliation, and personal interests. To command his men and women well, he needed to understand them. For them to serve to their full potential they should have personal reasons to believe in the mission of the *Jade Temple,* as a matter of their own self-interest as much or more than for any idealistic sense of duty or, even, career path.

Tibs had found that ideals and abstract notions of long-term gain can be too easily eclipsed by immediate self-interest. If he could find ways to promote their real interests in readily understood terms, then they would more reliably promote the interests of the ship and their shipmates. Tibs believed his was a proactive leadership style.

Yet the news feed from Al Najid, and now from Earth, were terribly interesting distractions. Tibs had always wondered why there had been no truly intelligent alien species on any of the new planets that mankind discovered. He believed similar planets should have produced similar life forms, but his expectation was invariably disappointed on all discovered worlds. There were native species of fauna, to be sure, but it seemed that evolution for each planet stopped with small animals.

Initial findings from the analysis of the projectile that mortally wounded the alien were intriguing. It wasn't widely known, but his intelligence sources on Perry Station informed him that it wasn't just an arrowhead that had been recovered from the alien, but the stone point of an atlatl dart. It had still been attached to part of its shaft, and that shaft was made of mahogany.

Mahogany is the wood of a tree native to Central and South America.

In ancient times, an 'atlatl' was a throwing stick for a small spear. That type of spear is called an atlatl dart. The throwing stick was notched to hold the dart as it was thrown. The atlatl multiplied the leverage of the hunter's arm, enabling him to fling the dart with great force. This prehistoric technology predated the bow, but was used worldwide long after the bow became hunters' ranged weapon of choice.

Tibs sighed quietly to himself. He had so much to do. He knew that trying to satisfy his curiosity now would be futile. Good answers always spawn more questions, but while the matter of the alien was unquestionably important, it didn't strike him as urgent. He needed to attend to his crew. There were other practical and immediate issues requiring his attention as well.

Yet he wasn't getting his proper work done. It was necessary that he should understand his new pilots. He was having trouble focusing on that task while confronted with this hunger to know more, especially when the alien appeared to have a connection with ancient humans.

Tibs recognized that his worry over getting his work done in fact compounded his problem.

His wrist-com was blinking. His eyebrow rose a notch as he saw it was a text from young Bobby Morrison, who should be down in the junior officers' quarters. Bobby's message initially did not help him to focus on the job at hand. Bobby had written:

> *"I'm thinking that if we draw a line from the Al Najid Modulus through the discovery location of the alien ship it may describe the axis of a cone of probability, given we wish to discover where the alien was headed. That axis and the circumference of the Al Najid modulus as a section should define the most probable search vector, beginning at the apex of the discovery location."*

Bobby was a bright young man who had joined the crew of the Jade Temple after being orphaned by military action near the Al Najid modulus. His passion for mathematics was matched by his skepticism. He also had a terrible knack for getting himself into impossible situations that he somehow always seemed to resolve... at least so far.

Tibs sent an encouraging reply:

> *"Good thinking, Robert. I'll run this by the Admiralty to see if we may investigate. I think it will*

*move quickly: Well done. I'm wondering about
some related information from our agents on
Perry Station. The alien was wounded by an atlatl dart, from Earth, probably millennia ago. The
shaft was made of mahogany. Let me know if
your further research suggests any other insight."*

After sending his reply to Bobby, Tibs reflected that possibly the search for the alien's destination might also uncover where the escaped criminal Harden intended to go. Coincidence can be significant.

He attempted once again to clear his mind and focus on his present tasks. Bobby's hypothesis united Tibs' insatiable curiosity with what he really needed to do. Congruence of interests lends focus to thought. To discover the truth, he had to get his ship's compliment fully operational. Taking care of the crew meant efficiency for his operations. This would give greater weight to any proposal submitted to the Admiralty that the *Jade Temple* should seek the alien's destination. Instead of idly wondering as a dreamer, this practical purpose finally drove him to action.

Tibs called up the dynamic status of the *Jade Temple* from the shipyard's mainframe to verify his impression that maintenance and repairs were nearing completion. The resupply of the ship's store of munitions and other supplies were well underway. He opened a new document on ship's letterhead to begin a proposal to the Academy admiralty to search Al Najid space, mentioning Bobby's idea and reasoning. He set reminder deadlines for himself to discuss the matter with Elder Pilot Lu and Master Kinkaid. Then Tibs sat back in his chair with a refreshed mind to study the personnel folders of his new pilots.

~

Bobby Morrison reread Tibs' reply and turned his attention to the Aldebari HoloNet to research the Aztec atlatl. He had guessed from the description of 'an arrowhead' that the creature had been wounded on Earth, but he had not expected the details that Tibs had shared with him.

It was a great honor to be on first name basis with the senior authority on the *Jade Temple*. Even so, to also be entrusted with information from Aldebari intelligence assets on Perry Station was extraordinary.

On reflection, Bobby's privilege was an affirmation. It was a consequence of the choices he had made since Steve Holbrook rescued him from the wreckage of his parent's defeated gunship. An orphan, Bobby was learning to seek and obtain what he needed, and to understand the reality of life in space, away from his previous life under the control of corporate Earth. He enjoyed his apprenticeship. Tibs' sponsorship and tutelage had developed his appetite for conversation, especially with his mentor.

Bobby focused on his research with a sigh. There was so much to learn and understand. But, as Tibs was fond of saying, it is more important to form and pose good questions than it is to identify an expedient answer.

Bobby was intrigued to learn that many of the atlatls found by archaeologists were decorated with a feathered serpent motif. Such decorative images were thought to be associated with the Aztec god Quetzalcoatl, the 'plumed serpent'. For Aztecs, the image of Quetzalcoatl later became human in form. Earlier depictions represented the god as looking more like a dragon.

Bobby diverted his research to find out more about Quetzalcoatl. He learned that the Aztec were not the first people to worship the plumed serpent. Before the Aztec, the Toltec people worshiped a plumed serpent in the eleventh and twelfth centuries. There were even earlier artifacts discovered, dating from the first century. And there was a stone carving of a feathered serpent found at an ancient Olmec site, thought to be from 900 B.C. The idea that the alien may have provoked the myth of Quetzalcoatl grew compelling.

Chapter 6: Captive

Paul Harden was awake, naked and exposed. He lay immobile upon his belly atop a slab that looked and felt like ceramic, or perhaps dense plastic. His eyes were drying in the breathable atmosphere, but for some reason he couldn't blink. His drying eyes exuded moist tears to try and compensate, and the wetness was a welcome relief. The wetness gathered into blurred drops and dripped straight away, down to the smooth gray floor below his face. His forehead rested on a cushioned bar. When his tears dripped, his vision momentarily cleared into focus as the drops fell away. They didn't spatter when they hit. The way his tears struck the floor suggested it was made from some kind of porous material, almost like cloth.

When he had first been brought into this room, his captors had set an articulated assembly of cool metallic plates, like vertebrae, onto the back of his head and neck. He felt the device probe and test, adjusting its grip smoothly. He didn't at first realize what was happening. The device moved what felt like smooth disks around on his scalp. The metal disks slid around on his skull and neck, and then down his spine to the middle of his back. Gradually the movement of the disks became almost as relaxing as a massage, but then Harden found he could feel nothing whatsoever, not even the pressure of his chest and belly on the cushioned slab. He couldn't close his eyes. He grew mentally and emotionally frantic when he could not escape the impression that the device was somehow reading his memories, and sharing them with his captors.

For no apparent reason, his mind raced to his earliest childhood memories, some of which he recognized. These were buried memories, long forgotten, and now uncovered. Disturbing memories.

His memories spooled from his mind unbidden. Somehow his mind was focusing not his conscious thoughts, but on his memories, his recollections. His conscious mind could not divert his memory to other things, but he could direct the focus of his active thinking. Inexorably his memories unreeled before his mind's eye like a holovid. He was compelled to recognize that the experience was completely out of his control. He sensed that his memories were being browsed by the bird- lizards in an extreme invasion of his privacy.

One of the creatures took samples from his flesh and blood within his field of view, from his left arm. Then it used a chemical solution to mend the wound left by the biopsy, leaving only a faint scar. Harden hadn't felt anything.

The reptiles didn't bother to learn his language. Instead they directly experienced his memory through the interface of their technology. The feathered lizards conferred together in unintelligible warbling and burbling, punctuated with whistles, clicks, and chirps. They sounded just like birds on Earth. Harden couldn't more than occasionally see their feet in peripheral vision. His face was held up by a curved and cushioned tube, like a cradle that left his nose and mouth free to breathe and which allowed his tears and sinuses to drip away to the floor. He could hear and smell his captors. They were faintly pungent.

He had seen them earlier. They were the size of humans, but were bipedal lizards with feathers. But now he only saw their feet when they came close enough.

The reptiles cooed musically when his memories displayed a crowd of people. Then his memories blurred ahead, faster than he could track. Harden caught glimpses of personal events that triggered conflicted emotional reactions. His had not been a pleasant childhood.

As he watched his own history unfold, he felt his horror increase. He was a helpless witness to the violation of his innermost secrets, yet his anger was silently impotent. His anger, a sentiment that defined who he was, didn't even seem to exist, and its loss frightened him more than anything else.

When his memories slowed to approximate real time again, it was during a visual recollection from the first time he had seen Earth from space. The bird-lizards seemed agitated. They actually reversed his memories twice to view the Earth, as seen from orbit, specifically over the eastern coast of the isthmus connecting North and South America in the western hemisphere. Then his memory sped again, forward to a sequence that revealed a densely populated city on Earth. He thought he recognized it as Caracas, in the continent of South America.

The tour of his memories stopped, as if the aliens had seen enough. He heard his captors stalk away from him on the padded floor with their bird-like gait and left him alone there, on the rack and helpless. Their footsteps and warbling conversation grew faint to his ears. Their feet had been almost noiseless on the floor despite their claws, but he noticed the quiet when the padding sounds were gone.

Harden's face still rested in the cushioned cradle, and his eyes still dripped tears onto the floor. His skull, his neck and upper back were still encumbered with the articulated electronic machinery. He was still unable to move. His muscles simply would not respond to his will. At least they left him able to breathe. His heart continued pumping. Harden wondered whether it might not have been better had his heart simply stopped. He knew his desire for life was as strong as it ever was, but he felt growing despair of regaining volition.

Harden was deeply afraid. He was well beyond thrashing in futility within his mind. He was focused on trying to move, even to blink. In his heart he was beyond despair. He was aghast.

He had seen their teeth. They were carnivorous. Harden had no way to defend himself. He was filled with helpless dread. He had been left with no vestige of dignity. He had been allowed no chance to refuse. There could be no heroic denial, and the unraveling of his memory proved that there were no secrets he could keep. He did not even have the excuse of pain to shelter his self-respect. What these creatures wanted, they simply took from his mind, with no more consideration for him than Harden might afford to a vegetable on his fork.

There was a tingling sensation from his right leg. Harden felt a spark of hope. Maybe whatever had been done to him was wearing off? Then he felt that tingling sensation in his arms and chest. Then his left arm spasmed and jerked, but the spasm subsided.

Like a puppet on the strings of an inexperienced puppeteer, his arms came up and, without Harden's volition, pushed his chest up from the block of smooth ceramic. Immediately he tried to resist, to counter what his body was compelled to do. His head lifted from the face-cradle.

Harden's anguish deepened. He had no control over his body. His left leg swung to the side of the slab to set his foot on the deck. Harden tried to reverse his struggle for control. He tried to let himself collapse, since trying to positively move had been futile, but his body stood up anyway. Initially hunched over, it stood unsteadily upright. Inside of his body but no longer in control, Harden grew absolutely frantic to no effect. He tried to make his body move, then he tried to let his body collapse, but his efforts were futile. His muscles didn't respond to him at all. His body responded only to the device that gripped his skull and spine.

Controlled remotely, his body walked erratically through a dimly lit corridor. One of the bird-reptiles walked past him, back the way he had come, but paid no attention to the naked human, as if Harden were an inanimate object beneath notice. His body walked farther, to a brightly lit vertical tube. The clear cylindrical cover slid aside, and his body stepped into the tube. The cylinder closed, and its small circular floor dropped away under him, much like his escape hatch had, back when the Aldebari seized his cruiser in their boarding assault.

The tube stopped within a dimly lit space with a low ceiling and opened. His body stepped from the tube and moved to a wall. His body turned and stopped. Harden could barely see a few other bipeds standing near him. They weren't human and they weren't reptilian. They did look vaguely mammalian and had dark hair, but he couldn't see any faces. The nearest was turned away, encumbered with a metallic neural control device, like a cowl or hood, very similar to the one that held Harden a prisoner within his own body. Then Harden's dry eyes closed, to his tremendous relief. Blessed wetness seeped from his closed eyelids, soothing his eyes.

Chapter 7: Perry Station Council

The message waiting on Steve's wrist communicator was a meeting request from David Lyman, the Chairman of the Perry Station Council. Steve accepted the appointment with a dab of his finger on the holographic communicator interface.

After helping settle Kathlyn and Stevie into their evening study routines, Steve checked the HoloNet. He let it run quietly in the background as he began preparing the family supper. Cooking with the new appliance that he purchased from Mary was too easy to enjoy. It took all the art out of cooking.

Then again, possibly the kids would prefer to eat food that wasn't as 'artful' as some of his recent creations had been.

There was a special documentary holocast on pre- Columbian religions in the Western Hemisphere of Earth. The holo focused on what was known of Quetzalcoatl, the plumed serpent. The presentation was well narrated, the history fascinating, and the contextual implications were provocative.

Despite the HoloNet story, Steve's thoughts wandered to the politics of Perry Station as he rose to clear away the evening meal's packaging into the recycler.

Since the appointment with the council came directly from David Lyman, it would probably be a more interesting meeting than just budgetary issues.

True, Security still hadn't uncovered the assassin that had made an attempt on his life months ago. But, other than conflicts between miners, the security situation in the Al Najid system had recently been fairly uneventful. Things had been far more quiet than Steve expected, once the discovery of modulinite ore had become widely known.

Everyone in-system was too busy making money to waste their time making trouble, even though prices on the futures market were falling. Time spent arguing or fighting still translated into lost money, so everyone with an investment focused on practical matters.

Steve was sure that the peace wouldn't last. There wasn't yet any shortage of available mining claims, despite the secretive moneyed interests who kept slipping credits to so- called independent operators just so they could stake more claims by proxy than the law would allow. Speculators were still buying everything the system could produce, so the conditions weren't yet ripe for the real trouble to break out.

Council Chairman David Lyman was adept in the arts of political maneuver. His talents included the science of persuasion, entailing both the ability to understand people and the ability to foresee consequences. David had been Perry's ambassador to Earth before the destruction of the planet. When Perry Station was built for the survivors, he had quickly cemented his position at the top of the Station's political food chain.

Steve still held a favorable impression of the man. He seemed principled, and his values meshed nicely with Steve's. How much of that congruence was honest and how much was artifice Steve could not know, but in practice it produced a good working relationship. Under Lyman's leadership the Station was expanding, the populace was satisfied and productive, and there was very little unrest.

The station used a representative system of government, which left the vast majority of citizens free to work their own businesses. Folks were convinced that what they paid in taxes would be used well.

A portion of their individual profits went toward the common wealth. Taxes seemed more like sharing than theft. And when there were momentous decisions to be made, and there was time, the Council could and did hold plebiscites so they could weight the preferences of their citizenry.

The new food appliance chimed, and Steve opened the insulated door. He checked the shepherd's pies to ensure they were fully thawed, then closed them back inside under the infrared setting needed to brown the potato crust. He was nearly finished preparing the fresh vegetables for their salad and called Kathlyn to set the table. She was vocal in her desire for little Stevie to grow up so he could take over the chore instead of her having to do it every day. Stevie was focused on making his drawn stars more symmetrical, moving the points that terminated the arms with his stylus. Steve smiled when he saw his son counting grid marks.

Steve then quietly watched his daughter set the table. He was thankful for the regularity of family life. When Kathlyn noticed him smiling at her she allowed the hint of her own smile to moderate her sisterly fury.

Not so long ago, Steve had believed that Kathlyn and her little brother had been among the casualties when his home planet, Perry, was destroyed. As it turned out, their mother, Steve's ex-wife Sandy, had taken their children off-planet to Oberon without telling him. Steve had been looking forward to visiting with the kids when their planet was attacked.

Steve and Sandy were separated at the time, but he didn't understand why she wouldn't return his calls. When he saw the planet break up, far below his fighter, he believed his family was lost.

Later, while he was in the HoloNet headlines, Sandy saw him interviewed by a news organization, and found out that he had survived. She had been quietly mourning him, and knew he must be grieving however well he hid it. So she risked disclosing her whereabouts and sent him an unsigned email letting him know that the kids were okay. He was overjoyed, but that disclosure eventually led to her discovery.

Pat, a contracted operative, discovered where Sandy and the kids were living by using the HoloNet's routing information embedded in Sandy's email. Sandy wouldn't respond to Pat's interview requests, so Pat went to find the house to ask for an interview in person. She didn't notice that she was being shadowed by Paul Harden's agents.

The agents knocked Pat unconscious and broke into Sandy's house. Sandy resisted and was killed. The agents abducted Pat and Steve's children and took Sandy's body before burning down the house to cover the evidence.

Harden's agents hoped to convince Steve to stop hounding

their employer. In a way, they were too successful. They intended that the threat to his children would stop Steve, but he had been on a mission with the *Jade Temple* and didn't even learn the children were missing until he discovered and rescued them from Harden's cruiser. Pat had been with them, but Sandy was never found. Steve believed she must have perished. He grieved for her, but at least he was able to embrace his children.

Steve now felt deep appreciation for even the most common of family routines. He had become sensitive to normalcy's fragility.

The evening passed. Before bed, Steve broke away from the apparently perpetual 'breaking news' holocast to read aloud to the kids. With Stevie warm in his lap and Kathlyn snuggled close beside, he read from an electronic children's book. Steve's eyes were drooping by the end of the chapter. His children dozed.

He shifted position to stand, and Stevie clung softly to him as Kathlyn slumped over into the warm hollow he arose from.

One at a time he carried them to their beds and tucked them into the sleep covers that would keep them from drifting if the artificial gravity system lost power. Kathlyn stirred sleepily and rose to get ready for bed. When she returned, Steve began the nightly ritual of wishing them sweet dreams. Ritual habits seemed to reassure Kathlyn, and helped her to sleep.

After their abduction by Paul Harden's agents, the children frequently woke from bad dreams. They seemed to be adjusting, however, and nightmares awakened them less often now.

But this night, in the dim light from the open door, Kathlyn looked into Steve's eyes and asked "Daddy, is momma dead?"

Steve didn't know how else he could rightly answer, and sorrowfully nodded his head to her. "I'm afraid she is, my love."

Kathlyn's expression fell from childlike hope. Her eyes welled with tears that glistened wetly in the light from the hallway. Steve bent to her, gently taking her into his embrace as she wept, and she held onto him with a child's open grief.

Steve felt his heart surge toward her. Though he was grateful to be there with Kathlyn to comfort her, there was nothing else he could think to do. He knew with certainty that Sandy would have laid down her life for her children. She never would have allowed them to be taken. Had she lived she would surely have made contact.

So he held Kathlyn, rocking her, softly patting her back in the rhythm of a beating heart as she wept: Thump-thump, thump-thump, just as Sandy and he had always done to ease and comfort her, ever since she was newly born.

His eyes were watery. "I miss her too, little one." he assured her. He felt the ache of compassion and his own grief, and he held his daughter close until she fell asleep. Very gently he laid her down in her bed and carefully tucked her in, gently kissing her brow. By some small miracle Stevie slept through it all, but that only meant Steve would have to endure his son's grief another night. He expected to endure grief many nights. Half asleep, he went to his empty bed and looked up into the darkness, listening to his children breathe.

Steve believed his wife when she explained that she could not bear the stress of living essentially alone, remote from everyone but the children while her husband the lawman traveled his rounds. Steve had seen no reasonable solution to their problem. He had to make a living, and his job left no time to look for other work.

Sandy never knew how long he would be gone. She worried over situations into which he might throw himself. She was alone most of the time, without a real social life. Social media over the HoloNet felt incomplete for her. Something was missing. Holodramas were unreal. There was little satisfaction without in-the-flesh social contact. Sandy was frustrated and unhappy. She recognized that her growing dissatisfaction wasn't good for her or her children, but she also couldn't see a way to make things right. Steve was a rural sheriff in that remote and lonely region, and there was nobody else to watch over the children.

Steve was constantly interacting with other people in his duties, but Sandy had just as constantly been isolated and alone, with only her children for company. She loved her children and her husband, but she was a social creature and wanted neighbors. She wanted friends. She wanted her career back. She loved Steve but she wanted him home with her, so she could at least talk with him.

It seemed like every time they had a shared moment they were interrupted by either another emergency call or by the children. Her sense of isolation was growing too great to bear. She began to feel desperate.

In the end Sandy made the only choice that she felt she could. She left him. It wasn't without regret. Steve had known something was wrong, but he didn't put it all together until she left her reasons behind, in a note. Those words came much too late. He hadn't realized how strongly she felt. There are consequences to choosing career over marriage.

This night he slept fitfully, but his wrist-comm atop the nightstand woke him on time. Steve rose groggily from bed to his shower. He gradually regained some semblance of coherence as he dressed, straightened his bed, then moved into the kitchen to warm the breakfast packets. He could hear Kathlyn and Stevie talking as they dressed for their day at the education center. He wondered again about his meeting with the Station Council.

Kathlyn arrived at the table sounding like her normal self, lifting a weight of concern from Steve's shoulders, but with a caution: Kathlyn was complex enough to seem one way, yet be another. She wasn't a deceptive child but, like her father, she seemed usually able to set her feelings aside in order to function.

On the positive side of the ledger, that ability spoke well for her practicality. The negative was a danger that she might excessively suppress her feelings.

He looked at his son. Stevie was more of an unknown quantity, as young as he was. Like Kathlyn, what he experienced now would be crucial.

Steve was worried about both of his children, and he wondered if he shouldn't also be worried about himself. When he was sheriff he had chosen his career over his marriage. He hadn't consciously reached that decision; it was just how things happened. He wondered of what else he wasn't aware. Because of his choices and career, he had made enemies who meant him harm. That endangered his family, and led to his wife's murder. He felt responsible.

There weren't any family counselors on the station, but just after Perry Station was first built there had been two Franciscan friars. He thought they might still have a chapel somewhere. He remembered the old priest he met in Old New York who suggested the rite of confession. That might work as counseling, at least for him. If he was psychologically fit then he could help his children better, but if he wasn't, then it might be that all the counseling in the galaxy couldn't help them. Children need their Dad at his best.

Steve noticed the time and irritably wondered what the Council wanted to discuss. He would rather use that time to attend to the wellness of his family.

He shook his head at the passing time. There was a day to get through.

Chapter 8: Negotiation

Council Chairman David Lyman contemplated the latest immigration figures and compared them with the number of outstanding applications. As he saw it, the station could either start to reduce the influx of new people, or begin planning yet another deck around the outermost bulkhead. To maintain efficient thermal equilibrium, all new decks had to start at the station poles on the axis, circulating the water supply between light side and dark side while the new bulkhead was built toward the station's equator. Two other members of the Council sat with him.

Lyman's administrative assistant, Margaret Lodge, sent him an alert that Steve was waiting outside the council chamber. His train of thought interrupted, Lyman turned to his colleagues, who nodded their assent. He used his wrist-com to remotely unlock the chamber door and admit the Council's special agent. He noticed that Steve was at last gaining a little weight. Having his children back made Steve much more relaxed and easy going.

"How have you been, Mr. Chairman?" Steve asked as he entered. He nodded to the Councilors. Lyman extended his hand and Steve took it in his own as the other council members resumed their seats.

"Busy, Steve, but that is a good thing. It keeps the day moving. I don't have enough time to realize how boring everything really is." the Councilman replied with an open smile.

"I'll take as much of that boredom as I can get, Councilor, after the past few years." Steve observed. The council present unanimously nodded in agreement.

In July of 3014, Earth Standard, the planet Perry was destroyed. A year later the core of Perry Station had been built by the three great powers for the survivors who had either been off-planet or were defenders in space.

The time since then had been inspiring, but quite harrowing. When Harden attacked again he destroyed the Aldebari Research Station that was studying and blockading the Al Najid/Trondheim anomaly. Had the *Jade Temple* failed to return when it did, Harden's cruiser would surely have attacked Perry

Station as well, and that would truly have been dire. The destruction of the Aldebari scientific outpost had been nearly total, but when finally defeated the wreck of the attacking cruiser yielded significant technical advances that had been shared with the Aldebari in appreciation for their stalwart aid. Fortunately, Paul Harden had to take time to recover his strength before he attacked for the third and last time. Once more this man, Steve Holbrook, with his squadron and the *Jade Temple* under the command of the Aldebari, Tibs, had stepped into the breach to defeat the madman.

"I can only imagine, Steve." Lyman said. "While you were in the thick of it all I could do was just stand by, hanging on by my fingernails. I felt like a helpless spectator to my own doom. And yet, you pulled our fat out of the fire again when you helped Tibs and the *Jade Temple* neutralize Harden's heavy cruiser."

"Nonsense, Councilman. *We* did it. We're a team out here: we have to be. And your role in the team is critical."

Lyman smiled slightly, pleased to be included, but he knew his role had been very minor, on the periphery of events. "Nonsense. But speaking of movers and shakers, I've received word that Tibs will be back next week. He's up to something again, but I don't know yet what it might be."

Steve brightened, hoping to see the Aldebar again. "I look forward to seeing him." The Council Chairman didn't respond the way Steve expected, but instead looked down at his comm unit. Steve tilted his head, curious. Something was up. Taking a different tack, he asked "Have we heard anything new on the alien?"

Councilman Lyman took his seat behind the desk while motioning for Steve to sit down across from him. When they had both settled in he responded. "The lab in Oberon has finished its first run of tests on the alien's tissue. The Earth labs are running about seven days behind. Oberon thinks the alien died between three and four thousand years ago. They agree with the initial assessments that the spearhead's shaft is mahogany, which suggests that the creature was in South or Central America on Earth when it was wounded. But why the alien came to Al Najid is still a mystery."

"So, there's some support for speculation that the alien may have been Quetzalcoatl." Steve suggested.

"We still lack independent corroboration from the other labs and conclusions from the academic community, but yes, I think so. Maybe we should be glad she never made it back to her home, wherever that might be. If she had made it back to her people they might have been upset, and then you and I might not be here today." the Councilman observed.

"Some myths attribute the invention of written language and agriculture to Quetzalcoatl. Its species might be benevolent." Steve surmised.

"Somebody tried to kill her, Steve. That wouldn't have been a casual event if she was believed to be a god. It suggests things weren't exactly peaceful." Steve had to concede the councilor's point, but wasn't moved to admit it aloud.

"I don't understand why the aliens didn't recover her corpse." Steve mused. "Surely she wasn't the only one of her kind. It takes a civilization to build a starship. Thousands of years is a long time for an explorer or scout to go missing. I know I would try to learn why my scout didn't come back, and it wouldn't have taken long for me to look really hard for her."

Lyman objected, "Aliens may not think the way we do. The other planets we've found haven't had alien civilizations, nor even any *un*civilized sentient aliens. Why would aliens even think Earth is something special? It may be that they didn't really know where their explorer went."

"Well..." Steve felt unsatisfied. "We probably can't predict how alien thought may differ from ours, but it seems to me that no matter how they think, practical considerations must surely apply. Any star-faring civilization that would send an explorer into the unknown would be interested in learning what the explorer found."

With a nod, Lyman conceded the merit of Steve's reasoning.

Steve continued "My guess is that they did look for her somewhere and decided, only after some effort, to write her off as missing. But that may tell us something, too. If they knew where she went and looked for her there, then they should have found and studied Earth. Yet they let us continue developing, without hostile intervention. And that suggests that they aren't a threat. Since the myth of Quetzalcoatl attributes the invention of writing to the god, they might well be benevolent."

The Councilor did not appear to be buying the optimism of Steve's conjecture. "They may simply have been preoccupied elsewhere, with other things they considered more important. Or, they may also have sent other explorers elsewhere, who did return. Knowing us, Steve, the fact that they didn't intervene tells me that either they didn't find us, or if they did, then they didn't study us very well. As violent as humanity has always been, had they found us they more likely would have tried to wipe us out, completely. I'd also point out that the alien's teeth don't look like the teeth of a peaceful creature." Lyman frowned slightly. Optimism, like pessimism, must give way to realism.

"But let's get down to business, Steve. We need you for another mission. It will not be convenient for you I'm afraid."

It was Steve's turn to frown. "I'm all ears, Councilor." Steve sat back in his chair. He tried to keep his face casual, but he was skeptical. If the Council needed him to go somewhere for more than a day, he was determined to fight it. A stable, regular life is what he felt his family needed. The well-being of his children was paramount. He knew Lyman wouldn't have brought him into the Council Chambers for a face-to-face if it was anything small. Steve felt his emotions rebel. His face flushed slightly and his eyes narrowed, as if for a fight. Councilor Lyman noticed the details.

Years of negotiation informed the Councilor's ability to read the emotional state of almost anyone with whom he spoke. He divined that Steve's concern probably stemmed from his devotion to his children. He turned to another council member, a woman. "Yvette?" he prompted with a nod, then resumed careful observation.

"The council would like for you to return to Earth to negotiate a deal for us, Mr. Holbrook." the councilwoman began. Steve's eyebrows rose a fraction and the muscles of his jaw hardened.

"An optimal near-term solution for Earth's overpopulation using our modulinium must be negotiated. We need to supply them with what they need in a way that minimizes any disruption or imbalance in the commodities market. An agreement must be reached with Antarctic Continental, the firm that inherited the contract when Paul Harden's Celine Interstellar failed."

Councilwoman Yvette hesitated at Steve's visible reaction and glanced over at the Chairman. Her eyes returned to Steve's chin, not quite meeting his eyes. She continued "The terms of the initial agreement are expected to expand both our market and Perry Station's available funds, while providing modulinium for Antarctic Continental's ten-year problem resolution plan.

"Antarctic Continental proposes to relocate a large portion of Earth's population, over time. They intend to construct a network of settlements in solar orbit. They want to use a variant of the 'Dyson's sphere' concept, a network of habitats and support installations in the circumstellar habitable zone. They believe the heat from Earth's sun can be made to balance the cold of space within their planned habitats."

The Councilwoman paused to be sure Steve was able to digest the concept before continuing. Steve appreciated her thoughtfulness.

"Antarctic Continental will need substantial quantities of our refined modulinium." she continued. "The agreement must supply them with enough to provide artificial gravity for the new installations, yet do so without upsetting the commodities market.

"Our ancillary objective is to avoid depressing the profits of Perry Station's miners and traders, as well as all the other people and companies here who depend on those miners for their livelihood.

"We must capitalize on this opportunity to generate revenue for Perry Station and our holdings. At the same time, we must be moderate. In other words, we will not do to Earth as Earth would do to us were our roles reversed."

Again Councilwoman Yvette paused for Steve, continuing when he again met her eyes.

"We don't want to force them to take the Al Najid system from us. We want to sell modulinium to them without exploiting their need unreasonably.

"Further, between us and Antarctic Continental, we must provide security. We don't want pirates seizing shipments and flooding the black market, since that would seriously compromise legitimate interstellar trade and either inflate or deflate prices that we need stable."

Relocating Earth's excessive population to solar orbit in a manner that would increase agricultural production in the solar system would be much simpler and more reliable than the overreaching plan that led Harden to destroy Perry.

Steve also understood why the council would prefer him as negotiator with Antarctic Continental. Martin Avery was the Chief Executive there. Avery was the industrialist who had provided Steve a recorded surveillance datacube that directly implicated Paul Harden as the man behind their planet's catastrophe. Avery's gambit had been a masterstroke that restored his own fortune and disclosed Paul Harden's plan.

But the bottom line for Steve in the whole mission was the prospect of separation from his children now, of all times. His family must come first.

"Did I hear you rightly, Councilwoman?" asked Steve. He allowed his face to grow stormy. His eyes hardened. "My children have lost their mother. She is apparently dead, and they don't understand that isn't somehow their fault. We just rescued them from an abduction, for God's sake. They are finally settling in to a vaguely normal childhood and you want me to just take off and leave them now and travel across the galaxy, just to set up a trade deal?" Steve shook his head at her. "Think again, Councilwoman." He turned his eyes to Lyman in disapproval.

The councilwoman flushed and looked down, then back toward Lyman, clearly holding her tongue. David reassured her with an apologetic glance before turning to meet Steve's eyes calmly.

Lyman remained composed, self-assured and friendly. His

face and manners were superbly compassionate. "Steve, you can of course take your son and daughter with you. They needn't miss any of their normal studies." Councilor Lyman soothed. Then he sweetened the deal. "The council would release your gunship to you for your trip."

Steve's eyebrows rose.

The gunboat had been built using schematics Steve recovered from the ship of Bobby Morrison's parents, who died in an attack on the Al Najid modulus patrol. They had been supporting an incursion that intended to clear the way for Harden's return. Steve had found young Bobby in an airlock on the disabled Corporate gunship.

From those schematics Chief Mackenzie had built a modified gunship that was intended for Steve, but the Chief went further and drew upon knowledge gleaned from advanced technology salvaged from the wreck of one of Harden's cruisers. It was a radical improvement in shield design that at the time was enjoyed by only one other ship, the *Jade Temple*. The ACM military determined that the technology had to be kept secret, and they imposed strict security measures that had kept the new gunboat under guard, hidden in her berth, and out of Steve's hands.

Something must have changed some minds in the Alliance. "The shields aren't secret any longer?" he asked.

David Lyman explained. "The alliance has built the shield enhancement vanes into one of their own units. It is in testing over in Cygnus system, and they want to start manufacturing more. So the level of secrecy has been lowered. We can release your gunship to you."

For Steve, the long-desired opportunity to at last take possession of his gunboat was a very enticing carrot, but if it wasn't held secret any longer it should be released whether he accepted the assignment or not. The gunship had been a dream in test flights.

Seeing Steve reflect on the offer, David shrewdly added "The children would probably like to see Pat again anyway, don't you think? I will ask her to assist you when you meet with Martin Avery."

Steve's eyes dilated slightly, his respiration increased, and his face was no longer angry. Lyman could almost see the thoughts bouncing around behind Steve's eyes, and silently congratulated himself that his guess had again struck true. Steve Holbrook had a romantic interest in Pat Williams, the contract investigator.

Steve kept his mouth closed. He did want to see Pat again. Bringing Kathlyn and Stevie along sounded almost like a much needed paid family vacation. There would be preparations that had to be made, but everything looked workable. Plus, he would finally have use of the gunship. Chief Mackenzie and the Perry Station shipyard built it for him as a prototype for the ACM Alliance, adapting schematics salvaged from the Morrison gunship.

"We'll need you to go over the proposed contract with Avery. To that end you should discuss the contract with our staff. You should already understand it when you sit down with him. When he makes Antarctic's counter-proposals, and we expect he will, just seal and send them by certified courier to our embassy in Old New York for evaluation.

"We don't think there will be much push-back. They haven't any other options, as far as we know. We've tried to put together a win-win package, but we should expect them to want some modification.

"Once you have Antarctic's agreement, you and your family can come back here to Perry Station." Lyman finished, gesturing vaguely around at the station's judicial center.

"Let me talk about it with the kids, see their reaction, and think about it overnight, David."

The Chairman was ready for the delay and assented without hesitation. "Of course, Steve. If you decide to not accept the assignment, maybe we can come up with some sort of alternative. A lawyer would be less likely to negotiate a swift resolution. Avery is familiar with you. He owes you a favor and he will surely listen to you more favorably than to anyone I can think of."

As Steve left the office David Lyman considered that Pat Williams would be a good match for Steve, but he wasn't sure that the timing of the match might not be premature. Steve still had personal issues from the death of his late wife. He needed to work through his grief.

~

That night Kathlyn was intrigued and excited about the prospect of seeing Earth, the home planet of humanity. She had been studying history at school, and Earth still conjured an almost mystical reverence in her.

But Stevie looked troubled. "You don't want to go, Stevie?" his father asked.

The boy frowned unhappily. "What if Momma comes home and we aren't here?" he asked. Kathlyn looked up at her Dad, her eyes large, and then at her brother but she was tactfully quiet.

"Kathy: Stevie and I have to have a man-to-man talk." Steve said solemnly. Kathlyn nodded unhappily.

Steve took his son's hand and they walked back into the kids' room and Steve closed the door. His son leaned against the bed, tears already beginning to form. He expected something bad, and he was at a loss trying to think of what he might have done wrong.

"Son, I don't think your momma will come home. I am sorry. I think she isn't alive anymore."

The boy struggled with his father's words, his face troubled and confused. He didn't want to hear it, but he didn't have another option. He was trapped by an event he couldn't escape. Then his face cleared, and he looked back up to his Dad.

"Did she go to heaven?" Stevie asked.

Steve was surprised and dismayed. His son hadn't burst into tears. He was such an innocent. He seemed even hopeful. Steve was trying to find the words to answer when his son spoke again.

"I thought I did something wrong and she didn't love me anymore." the boy continued. The thought brought tears to his eyes.

The boy had been blaming himself for his mother's disappearance. "No, son, your Mother loved you very much. You didn't do anything wrong, and even if you had she would still have loved you." Steve assured his son.

Stevie looked slightly relieved. "I'm going to miss her a lot, Daddy, but heaven will make her happy."

Steve embraced his son, attempting to comfort them both, and then he let go. Stevie still stood by the bed while Steve crouched to his level, one knee on the floor.

Steve was caught in a quandary. He had always wanted to believe in heaven but, having confronted death and dying too many times, heaven looked like a conjuring of kind but wishful thinking. He didn't want his son under any illusions, but he also didn't want to force the boy into more grief. He would much rather let the boy believe innocently that his mother was happy in heaven instead of floating frozen and lifeless, somewhere in orbit around Cygnus, which is where Steve believed she was.

He was at a loss what he should tell his son. He struggled to seize the moment, because he could feel it slipping away from him.

There is a point of self-reckoning when you counsel the bereaved. Steve had to face and answer the question of his own sincere belief, and he believed that he had to do so authentically, outside the comfort of formulaic religion. This was his own son. What he said now, or what he didn't say, would shape his son's world view into the future. He had to solve for a question he hadn't yet fully resolved for himself.

Is faith only a convenient shelter from harsh reality? Is faith misleadingly idealistic? Or is faith a kind of wisdom that has developed over centuries of trial and error?

Steve had seen too many people die. He knew that, no matter what he told the boy, eventually his son would realize how tenuous personal belief can be when confronted with the fragility of life and inevitable mortality.

Steve carefully observed his son. He was worried that the boy might be in shock. After a bit, sharing a few words with him, he decided little Stevie was okay, at least for now. He resolved to seek wise counsel in the matter as soon as possible.

There was a small community of Franciscans who had a small chapel on the station, but Steve's assignment to Earth brought him to think once more of the old priest he had met in Old New York, the historically preserved city on Earth. But the boy's next question dispelled that thought.

"I miss Momma. Will you take me to visit her in heaven, Daddy?"

For a moment Steve was again at a complete loss, but then his heart counseled him. For a parent, heaven is in the arms of your child.

"Come here, son." Steve said, and opened his arms to embrace him softly once more, then picked him up as he stood. Stevie rested his cheek on his dad's shoulder, feeling the warm cloth of his father's shirt. "We can't go to heaven, son, or we wouldn't be able to come back home. Your mother is gone, except in our hearts and in our memories."

"But I don't want her to be gone, daddy." He picked up his head from his father's shoulder, searching his father's eyes. "I want her to come back." Stevie pleaded, tears again beginning to form. They spilled down onto his soft cheeks.

"I know, son." Steve said, his voice cracking. His heart felt ready to burst. "You know she loved you. Listen, if she were here, do you know what she would want us to do?"

"What, daddy?"

"She would want us to be healthy and happy. She would want us to remember her. She would also want us to go on living and growing. She would want us to laugh and sing and to do all the things we need to do. And do you know what?"

"What?"

"She is within you right now, Steven. She is still here, in your heart, in the warmth of your love." Steve stopped and Stevie sat back on his father's arm. Steve placed his warm palm over Stevie's chest, feeling the flutter of the little boy's heart. When he looked at his son he saw Sandy's eyes, and she was there in the shape of his mouth. He looked deep into his son's eyes. "If you really need her you can whisper to her, right there, when no one else can hear. If you do, and if you listen closely, she might tell you whatever you need to know."

Stevie grew very quiet and still. Then, after a moment, he laid his cheek again to Steve's shoulder and said "I think I feel her in there. I think it feels like she is happy with me."

Steve was careful to not squeeze too hard as moisture slid silently from his eyes. "Me too, son." His voice was husky. "And I think I heard her answer."

Chapter 9: Transit to Al Najid

The *Jade Temple* passed through the Al Najid modulus from Cygnus system. Ahead, in the distance, were strewn the shattered tumbling stones that had once been the planet Perry. The stone field orbited the blue star in a long broad arc, brightly lit against the black of space. Nearby, four small patrol craft winked their running lights as they passed.

Master Kinkaid addressed the comm frequency opened for transmission. "Perry Station this is *Jade Temple*. We have cleared the modulus and are en route for resupply, do you copy?"

"Jade Temple this is Perry Station: Welcome back. We've been looking forward to your return. We have berth two open for you at the dock. Do you require a local pilot, or is there anything we can prepare as you make way?"

Tibs responded "Negative, Perry Station. We are glad to arrive, almost like coming home."

Kinkaid added "ETA for our arrival is three hours, Earth standard."

"Three hours affirmative, *Jade Temple*. The council will have a representative standing by to welcome you and handle any details. Transmit your requisitions and authorization when ready, we will be standing by."

Tibs nodded to Lu to authorize document transmission, then turned to his messaging terminal. He saw a note that Steve was already *en route* to Earth. Tibs felt slightly disappointed to have missed his friend. How long the *Temple* would be at the station really only depended on how long it took to resupply, but his crew could stand some time to get off the ship and relax aboard station on their personal time. There was no telling when they would again have the opportunity. He consulted briefly with his officers to set a reasonable window for shore leave.

Perry Station was thriving, and the needs and growing wealth of the miners had created a rather lively array of recreational attractions both legitimate and less savory. The Aldebari had a reputation as religious, but Tibs knew full well that his people were human and had tastes as varied as their personalities. Besides, his understanding of the Aldebari religion gave wide leeway to interpretation.

He gazed approvingly at the growing sphere of the station. A new deck was being built. There was a new hydroponics section in the last stages of construction, like a gigantic paddle near the docks that would always be tilted to catch the light of the local sun.

The shipyard teemed with activity, and light flickered from a welder on the great bulk of the heavy cruiser his Marines and crew had captured from Harden. Earth demanded the ship's return as stolen Corporate property, and a Corporate crew was scheduled to arrive within days to take the ship back to the mothball fleet, in Trondheim system.

Nearby, but separate from the station, a heavy manufacturing plant consumed asteroid ore provided by the miners. Rafts of compressed schist were held nearby, left over from ore processing.

Tibs gazed out on space and sighed for the broken planet. Perry had once been fertile and beautiful. Unbridled greed destroyed it all, leaving just that vast field of tumbling stone.

The Aldebari admiralty had negotiated an agreement with Perry Station for the *Jade Temple*'s mission to further explore the Al Najid system beyond previously surveyed system space. Tibs expected the Perry Station Council to want details.

The Council did not disappoint. No sooner had the bulk of his crew debarked for shore leave than Tibs received a meeting request from the delegation at the dock.

The Council's Representative was brief and polite, little more than a welcoming handshake with a statement of gratitude for past service and the Council's request for a meeting.

Perry Station had grown remarkably in the time he had been away. The docking bays were enclosed and their walls were insulated against the cold of space, but the noise was almost deafening. Tibs picked up his pace to get away from it.

Beyond the docks were machine shops and the offices of the shipwrights. Naval architects and engineers worked quietly and intensely, and their conversations were hushed. Tibs walked past those who didn't recognize him and casually greeted those he knew. Some appeared curious, but didn't challenge him. He knew where he was headed and seemed confident that it was right for him to be there.

He was stopped at the entrance to the research bay where the alien starcraft was being studied. A sentry turned Tibs away, telling him that Chief Mackenzie wasn't there.

Text messages to the chief remained unanswered. If Mackenzie was unavailable, then the next best recourse might be the Aldebari representatives on the science team studying the alien craft with the engineers, but that was still a long shot.

Bobby's suggested search path led Tibs to wonder what direction the alien ship faced when it was first discovered. It was possible that the alien came to Al Najid through the anomaly, even though the Modulus was more likely. Knowing the direction that the ship had been facing would tell him which of the two flight paths the *Jade Temple* should search.

Available public records describing the recovery of the alien clearly identified its original location, but they weren't clear about which direction the alien ship originally faced. Searching along the right axis would obviously save time.

Hours earlier Tibs had sent an inquiry to Steve's personal comm. Any response would take time, because messages can only travel at the speed of light and have to be repeated through intervening moduli. When Tibs' inquiry eventually reached Steve, he might not recall off-hand what direction the alien craft originally faced.

Since the *Jade Temple* needed several hours at minimum to re-provision, Tibs intended to use the time to pursue another possible line of inquiry for an answer. Chief Mackenzie recovered the alien spacecraft after its discovery.

If Mackenzie was unable to recall the facing, then a review of the mission logs might turn up a clue that could halve the *Jade Temple*'s potential search time.

So Chief Mackenzie wasn't at his shipyard office, nor was he at his quarters. He hadn't responded to his wrist-comm message. Tibs considered his next best bet was the tavern, the Cog and Sprocket. Besides, they made a good Martini.

There the Chief sat, his thick graying hair swept back unruly from his broad brow. He looked like he was presiding over the crowd from a seat just outside the tavern door, the same chair Steve always chose.

The tavern had been the first private business opened on the station, maybe two years earlier. Even so, the Cog and Sprocket seemed as if it had been there for ages. It already boasted a patina of profitable shabbiness. Currently it also boasted a chaotic crowd of patrons.

The Chief saw Tibs approach and he stood in greeting, waving him in as if Tibs might overshoot his landing. "Tibs! Good to see you!" he boomed. "Have a seat," he said, gesturing toward an empty chair at his table. "Rest here with me a moment." They sat down.

"What'll you have?" the chief asked. He looked over and between other customers seeking the eyes of a waiter. Though the hour was early, the tavern was already crowded with asteroid miners more than ready for their weekend.

"A martini would be good, Chief. I've been looking forward to one. But Mack, don't you ever check your wrist for messages?" Tibs asked, hands wide in friendly plea. "I've blown an hour looking for you, and you still haven't responded to my text. Your inbox is over capacity. I couldn't even leave a voice message, let alone a holo."

The Chief caught the eye of a waitress and raised a finger to beckon her. She approached the table with a smile and a nod of greeting to Tibs. Mackenzie ordered a martini for him.

The waitress looked to Tibs for his preferences. "Dry, please,

chilled and stirred, no ice. And if you have any, a green olive gar-
nish."

Tibs looked back to Mackenzie as she left. "Awfully crowded
here this afternoon, Chief." Tibs observed, his voice competing to
be heard over the din of the crowd. The chief was drinking an amber liquor from an old fashioned glass, presumably some breed of
whiskey.

A group of miners just inside the doorway suddenly cheered,
their voices rising in unison above the rest of the patrons, sounding almost like an ocean breaking on a rocky shore. The Chief
was nodding to his drink, waiting for the noisy tide to ebb, and
when it did he spoke loudly in anticipation of having to repeat
himself. Almost predictably everyone else in the place chose just
that moment to take a breath, and the Chief's voice boomed into
the sudden quiet: "If it isn't the media, it's one *brass*hole or another..." Startled by his own booming remark still ringing in the
quiet room Mack paused as the crowd digested his comment.
The room broke up with loud laughter from the patrons. Almost
universally they nodded knowingly.

The crowd turned back to their festivities and the Chief continued, more conspiratorially, "If it isn't the media it's one bureau-
crat or another wanting to exert his political muscle and get information he shouldn't have, doesn't need, and wouldn't understand anyway. The politics of saying 'no' and dealing with whatever fallout they can muster wastes my time on nothing. So I
don't even look at my inbox these days Tibs, sorry." He began to
scroll through his inbox to find Tibs' message.

"What was your message about?" he asked, still scrolling. He
would have to delete some messages before the server would
give him more.

Tibs explained the *Jade Temple's* mission, describing the idea
of attempting to trace the path of the alien and find out where it
had been going. Chief Mackenzie wasn't slow on the uptake.

"Tibs, I don't think there's a record of which way the alien was
headed when we found it. We couldn't see it to know. Had Steve
not bumped into it, the alien would still be adrift out there with us
none the wiser. But let me see if I can give you anything to go

on." The chief replied. Mackenzie closed his eyes and grew still, remembering the call from system dispatch and taking the recovery barge out to Steve's coordinates. The whole matter at the time was a mystery wrapped in skepticism. Had it been anyone but Steve reporting a collision with 'nothing' the report would probably have been ignored.

Mackenzie recalled that he had wondered whether Steve might have a bad oxy mix, or worse, brought alcohol along with him on the monotonous survey mission. Telemetrics showed Steve's oxy mix was fine. He sounded stone cold sober despite the incredulity everyone felt about what he reported. Steve's pulmonary and cardio readings were a little elevated, but that was understandable, given the circumstances.

By the time Mackenzie arrived on-scene with the recovery barge, Steve had laid out strobe buoys around the object's position but they were approximate, and more square than rectangular. Steve had recommended spraying it with something. The hydraulic fluid Mackenzie tried to use would not adhere to the stealth field. Instead the spray flowed around the energy field's edge to the other side, where it drifted into space.

"By the time we got it back into the hanger at base there was no way of knowing how much we might have moved it around, Tibs, I'm sorry."

His martini arrived, and Tibs sipped it in disappointment. At the taste of his drink he brightened. "Now *that,* Chief, is a really good martini. But tell me: in your examination of the alien spacecraft, do you think it is capable of passing through a raw anomaly? Isn't it more likely to have come through the modulus?"

The chief sat back and thought about it. "Tibs, I don't think we know enough to be sure. The fins seem too small to me to stand up to an anomaly transit. The shields emit too tightly to the hull. I don't think the terminal disks expose enough conductive area. The ratios just don't look right. That said, we don't yet fully understand the alien scout's main shield capacitors, even though the capacitors of the secondary array are very similar to our current tech. We don't know enough about the properties of the material the alien engineers used in the circuitry to know whether they might disintegrate under that load.

"The best I can offer is that it is more likely that the ship passed through the modulus than the anomaly."

Tibs nodded. He was of the same mind.

Chapter 10: Earth Approach

Kathlyn and Stevie played their evening game around the holoterminal in the darkened gunship cabin. The ship pressed ahead on an intercept course with the still-distant home planet. An hour earlier they had passed through the Aldebaran/Earth modulus to enter the solar system just beyond Saturn's orbit. Saturn, the planet, was on the far side of the sun, well beyond Earth.

The gunship was drawing close to a large number of starships. Steve suggested to the kids that they use the sensors to take a look at the ships.

The children were fascinated by Earth's majestic Second Fleet. The fleet was headed back the way the gunship had come, toward the Aldebaran modulus.

Stevie was especially impressed by the great battleship, *Trafalgar*. The boy kept exclaiming "Wow!" as he peered at it under high magnification. He was awestruck by the great vessel with its four massive rail guns in armored carousel housings arrayed radially around its bow. Steve spent several minutes talking with him about how rail guns work.

Seeing the Second Fleet as it passed toward Aldebaran was the most spectacular event of the trip so far.

Trying to explain what a modulus is and how one works had been time consuming, but it became interesting for them when they passed through one. The tremendous expanse of space, 'The Big Empty', with all its glorious stars was magnificent. But the sight of that battleship and its fleet left his daughter and son in awe.

The voyage from Perry Station had been relaxing on the whole. The gunship proved capable and well-made, and to Steve it seemed there was plenty of room, at least for a few days. His children weren't used to the confinement. It didn't take them long to grow weary of staring out at the seemingly immobile stars, glorious though they were when Steve dimmed the cabin's lighting. The children were marginally able to bear watching the sensor displays for obstacles, but that didn't keep them engaged for long.

Obstacles appeared very seldom anywhere near the gunship's flight path. There really wasn't much to look at in deep space, away from planets. The almost unchanging star fields, pretty though they were, became just a backdrop. So holovids, browsing the HoloNet, and virtual reality games they could play together provided all their entertainment when their daily studies were completed.

At least the VR games were interactive. Instead of passively watching a screenplay, players had agency within the virtual environments. They had to make decisions they would be virtually responsible for. They had to evaluate and compare risks versus rewards.

With so much time on their hands Steve felt compelled to use some of it to talk with his children about their mother. But first, Steve thought he should do some research himself on the Holonet about grief, and its impact. He discovered that he shouldn't assume too much based on what he or his children felt. Different people handle grief differently, and one way is really no better than another. There isn't a right or wrong way to grieve, although some thoughts and behaviors are more helpful and safe than others.

Almost everyone uses some blend of 'staying busy' and trying to control their emotions. Most also use a more intuitive behavior that focuses on exploring their feelings, considering their lost relationship, and talking about the meaning of life with others.

After his research he quietly watched his children while they played their virtual reality game. He considered that VR might be classified as 'busywork'. They seemed emotionally normal, given they were children. He worried that to interrupt them with a grown-up's talk about death would feel unnatural, however advisable it might seem in the abstract. But he could watch for an opportunity to converse with them, either together or separately, about the meaning of life, about what it is that people value and how those values are used to weigh our choices in life. If they displayed unusual behavior, or if they exhibited emotional outbursts, then they would have a conversation to draw them out and discover their thoughts and feelings. It wouldn't feel right to arbitrarily intrude on their play with what was, after all, his own worry. But at the same time he didn't want them to go spinning off into depression without his noticing, either.

Steve stirred himself and told his children it was time to bathe with cleansing gel and prepare for sleep. Once the gel dried it would be removed with a small soft vacuum brush without making a mess of the living compartment. Aboard small ships potable water is strictly for drinking and food preparation.

Other than Mercury, the inner planets were faint but visible and gradually growing bright. Increased magnification could now display details on the surface of Mars. As fast as the gunship was traveling, distances were still so great that their journey seemed at a standstill. Once it would have taken months to travel the distance between Earth and the local modulus. Now it took mere days, but even that seemed slow.

While he ordered a new course projection from the computer Steve pondered what he had learned about the alien. He had little more to go on than a matrix of mysteries that surrounded the mummified creature. He approached the subject as though he was trying to solve a crime. The clues were few but they led in many possible directions. He followed both mundane facts and intuitive guesswork to attempt to form a working hypothesis about how it came to be on earth between three and six millennia earlier. He tried to project where the dying alien might have been trying to go when it died, out in the middle of nowhere in Al Najid space.

It looked like a dinosaur. His HoloNet research showed that the prevailing theory held that dinosaurs died out on Earth when a comet or large asteroid struck the Earth some sixty-five million years ago.

Some paleontologists and geologists thought the extinction event that ended the age of dinosaurs had been caused by many smaller asteroids instead of one big one. The main competition to the 'sudden extinction theory' proposed a more gradual extinction, perhaps caused by erupting volcanoes and earthquakes.

A third faction thought a combination of these explained the extinction of dinosaurs. A major asteroid impact may have been so great that it was followed by ages of violent tectonic shifts and volcanic eruptions that changed the climate, which changed the ecology, and wiped out whatever dinosaurs survived the initial shock of the collision.

Steve was drawn to the hypothetical explanations of the end of the Cretaceous period much as he might have been drawn to a mystery holovid. Previously, when he learned as a boy about dinosaurs, it had seemed remote and abstract, not quite real. Now, with the alien mummy, it felt much more concrete.

He researched insatiably when he could. From a holo-recorded debate between theorists that he found linked in a Hol-oNet article, he learned that modern birds still alive on Earth were believed to be descendants from small dinosaurs that sur-vived whatever killed off most other dinosaur species. The pres-ence of feathers on the otherwise reptilian alien mummy sug-gested that there might be a connection.

Then there was the fact that, among the life forms found on the fourteen discovered habitable planets, those farthest from Earth along the network of moduli had the least diverse and least developed animal species, while those nearest Earth, and espe-cially Earth itself, had the greatest diversity and largest animal species. The consistency of the progression stood out to Steve as a significant pattern.

Steve's tentative personal hypotheses included one that ar-gued that the aliens might not really be alien. They were clearly carnivores, given their teeth. Maybe they had eaten their way across the galaxy from an origin on Earth itself, one planetary system at a time. That way Earth had the most time to recover. It was the only planet known to have had the time to evolve a fully sentient species. This would fit the mystery about which Tibs had voiced curiosity, that only Earth seemed to have produced unar-guably intelligent life. If Steve's conjecture was right, then he was glad the aliens were apparently migrating away, rather than to-ward humanity.

Yet the dinosaurs died out on Earth some sixty million years ago, at the end of the Cretaceous period. Human civilization was only about twelve or thirteen thousand years old, yet human technology appeared to be almost as advanced as what had been discovered of the alien scout ship. It seemed to Steve that, after sixty million years, a civilization traveling in space should be much more advanced beyond humanity than the alien appeared to be.

Steve was tempted to strike his pet dinosaur hypothesis from his very short list of reasonable explanations. There couldn't have been native dinosaurs that somehow achieved space travel without leaving some trace on Earth. And surely, after experiencing millions of years traveling among the stars, if the alien mummy was actually of an intelligent dinosaur species then her technology would be much more advanced than it appeared to be.

Steve sat quietly in the hum of the darkened cabin of his gunship and confronted his disappointment. It was a very interesting pet idea, and he found it difficult to quiet his thoughts. It wasn't easy to let go of what originally seemed such an attractive line of reasoning. It took willpower, but he narrowed his focus onto the current state of affairs.

The children were sleeping in their softnet berths behind his acceleration couch, and he knew he should be doing the same, but he felt full of nervous energy. For some reason his brain seemed to be churning out thoughts. If he tried to sleep he would just lay there, awake. Yet he knew he needed to get some rest.

He really liked his gunship, and was fond of thinking about it. It was a sweet machine. The gunship was easily twice the mass of his old light fighter, but it boasted a better thrust/mass ratio, not only in her main engines but in the maneuvering jets as well. The weaponry loadout easily doubled what he was used to. He had a pair of hardball cannon and four medium pulse lasers forward. The magazines boasted greatly improved capacity for his physical munitions. The stern of the gunship housed four linked Aldebari light fighter engines, each of which sported its own antimatter magnetic bottle, each containing eighty grams of antimatter. His gauges indicated he had plenty of hydrogen in reserve. Oxy and Nitrogen gases were as they should be and his atmo analyzer indicated that the cabin's CO_2 level was acceptable.

Steve was already traveling with all the speed he could safely use, even out here beyond the debris of the solar system's vast asteroid belt. By the time his autopilot could react to avoid a collision with an inert object within range of his sensors there would be precious little time to maneuver before the ship reached it. Granted, out here there generally were only a few dark masses of ice to worry about, and they were rare. Earth had emplaced beacons to warn pilots of all known navigation hazards, but even a small chunk of drifting ice or stone could seriously test a spacecraft's shields and armor if it was moving fast enough.

There was little danger of collision, but since he intended to sleep Steve slowed the gunship, set the autopilot, and enabled the auto-targeting cannon to try to destroy anything the ship couldn't avoid. He timed the boat's course and speed to hopefully allow himself a good eight hours of rest.

A text message arrived in his inbox from Tibs, the Aldebari commander of the *Jade Temple*. Steve learned then of the *Jade Temple*'s mission to try and find out where the alien had been going when it died. He was glad his friend had a new and interesting mission, but he felt regret at accepting this trade mission to Earth. Then he remembered that he wouldn't have been able to go with Tibs on this trip anyway, what with the children. Still, he missed his friend and would have loved to go discover and explore with Tibs and the *Jade Temple*.

Steve tried to recall for Tibs the direction that the alien ship had been pointed when he found it. Since it had been invisible, discovered only by accident, he hadn't even plotted its location until after he'd bumped it a few times. Steve replied to Tibs with an apology that he couldn't say what direction the alien had been headed. He added in a post script his thoughts about the alien. He laid out his argument against the tempting hypothesis that it might have been a dinosaur, suggesting that if they'd had spaceflight millions of years ago, then surely their technology should have been much more advanced than it was when the mummified alien died.

In the quiet hum of the darkened gunship, he heard the breathing of his sleeping children. He was so grateful to have them back after thinking they had been lost when Perry was destroyed.

Steve understood that he couldn't head off on an adventure just to gratify his curiosity anymore, not unless he took the kids along, and that would never do. Adventures are too dangerous to intentionally take children along.

By the time they were grown, with lives of their own, he would be ready to retire. Steve sighed. Although by rights he should be weary of adventure, and he should be glad for a reason to stay behind while others took all the risks, he missed finding himself in those unexpected situations that pushed him to the limits of his ability.

Adventure is best remembered, or read about. He consoled himself that living through an adventure was often uncomfortable. He already had more than his fair share of memories. Now it was time to let other people risk it all. People younger than he was. People without two wonderful children depending on them.

Steve knew he had to learn to be content with the comforts of the mundane, but part of him still didn't buy into it.

He compressed the files bearing the homework of his children and dispatched them along with his correspondence with Tibs. The data package would be transmitted through the moduli to Al Najid where it would be sorted and delivered to the school and to the *Jade Temple*. The kids' homework would be registered on Perry Station's academic server. Steve then readied and transmitted his planned course and estimated time of arrival to Earth. He submitted his scheduling request for customs and safety inspections from Old New York's port authority as required by Earth.

All ships that intend to land on Earth must pass through customs. If anyone entered the atmosphere from off-planet without processing through customs, they would be presumed to be a smuggler. Smugglers are hunted by licensed freelancers, eager to collect a corporate bounty. If there is anything corporate monopolies dislike, it is smuggling. A smuggler would receive no semblance of leniency.

Besides, Steve wanted to pick up Pat, his passenger for the next leg of the journey to Antarctica, and she lived somewhere in Old New York.

Pat had been Steve's security liaison during his first visit as Perry Station's representative to Earth. His mission had been to recruit skilled immigrants, hoping to build a suitable workforce for the new Station. She had been contracted to help Steve by Councilor Lyman, who had been a diplomat to Earth. Lyman knew that the operative political differences between Earth and Perry would be subtle, and much more dangerous than they appeared.

Steve, Pat, and the children would make a hopefully sedate atmospheric transit to Antarctica from Old New York. There were so many satellites and other objects orbiting earth that travel outside the stratosphere near Earth was perilous at any significant speed. Steve could have used a parabolic trajectory that would take him outside low orbit, but the navigational caution required would take almost as much time, be more dangerous and could end up costing more than simply traveling through the atmosphere.

While Steve waited for Old New York's La Guardia Spaceport to process and return their end of the landing and inspection authorizations, he composed an update on their schedule and sent it to Pat's inbox, letting her know when should be the best time for her to arrive for boarding.

Eventually the spaceport got back to him with a time and a berth number, and let him know that he had customs and safety inspections scheduled. Steve could finally leave his acceleration couch and go back to his sleeping net. He removed his shoes and tunic, closed his eyes, and tried to release his day. He focused on relaxing the muscles in his neck and shoulders. His lower back was relieved that he had lain down. He hadn't realized how tense he had been, and vaguely wondered what was causing the stress.

It wouldn't be the first time that Steve sensed a threat before there was any sign to explain his uneasy feeling, but there never seemed to be an apparent cause to explain why he felt that odd tension until something happened. It was inexplicable, but it had happened too many times to ignore. Something unusual was about to happen. This time, the sensation felt worse than any since the destruction of Perry.

He tried to relax and let everything go. Steve began to drowse at last in the darkened quiet, listening to his sleeping children breathe softly in the steady hum of the cabin. He fell asleep.

Like all pilots, Steve had neural augmentation implants that enabled him to remain in wireless communication with his ship. When the gunship changed direction and began to tumble he awoke, slightly confused. He looked over toward where the children slept but saw Kathlyn wasn't in her net. When realization broke through the residual webs of his sleep, he quickly opened his net, sat up in his trousers and headed for the ship's controls. Kathlyn was there, in the pilot's seat. She was in a quiet panic, attempting to return stability to the ship with an inexpert hand. She could look nowhere but where the flight attitude indicator was scrolling, showing how badly the ship was tumbling. She didn't see her father's approach behind her. He could see her expression in the plexiclear instrument panel and she looked as if she would, by fierce and unrelenting force of will, make the spacecraft obey. Steve was quietly amused and observed her efforts for a moment, hoping to allow her a chance to learn. There was nothing to run into out where they were, and the inertial dampener kept them from injury against the bulkheads.

As her panic grew, the odds of success diminished. She was beginning to tremble with effort as she tried to time the motion of the controls to counter the ship's tumble, and she kept overcompensating. If she hadn't had her hands on the controls Steve could have used his augmentation to stabilize the ship, but the manual controls automatically took priority over neural input. Taking action before she might spin into despair, he gently clasped her two little fists knotted around the controls with his warm and gentle hands. She gasped and looked up at him with fearful eyes.

"Watch." he whispered to her, motioning with his eyes back to the attitude indicator with his head. He guided her hands to gradually slow the tumble and bring the ship back under control. With the help of his augmentation he could work the foot controls that her legs weren't long enough to reach.

With her father so calm and reassuring, she lost most of her immediate fear and returned her eyes to the attitude indicator. She was fascinated, sensing with her hands some of what her father was doing and how he was doing it. It was like a ballroom dance might be imagined in her young dreams.

When the ship was again steady and back on course he looked into her eyes once more, tenderly. She sensed his gaze and looked up into his eyes with what might have been adoration. He felt his fatherly heart fall helpless before her, and he could do nothing but smile broadly back at her.

"So, little one, do you want to be a pilot?" Steve whispered.

She started to nod, then shifted to explain. "I- I woke up, Daddy," she confessed, "and I couldn't get back to sleep. And I thought about how we are alone together among the stars, and you seem so... so at home out here, and... I was curious... But then, when I touched this," she meant the control stick, and then she pointed toward the attitude indicator, "that thing went crazy and the stars started spinning." she quietly explained. She looked back up at him with large eyes.

It would be a long night if he tried to explain everything to her. "It's okay, my love. Go back to your net and try to sleep. I'll try to explain how things work when we get a chance. Maybe on the way home you can try again, but this time with me here next to you. Does that sound like a good idea?"

"Oh! Thank you, Daddy! I'm so sorry if I made trouble." she whispered. She hugged his neck with her slender arms, and smiled a secret smile at the stars as he hugged her back. She let go and rose from the acceleration couch, then padded back to lay down in her sleeping net.

Steve reset the autopilot with a quiet smile and then returned to his own net to finish his sleep.

~

When the children awoke, Steve was already in the tiny galley preparing their morning breakfast packets as quietly as he could manage. When he heard them moving and murmuring he started warming their food. He told the children as they entered that they had the day off from their studies for the approach to Earth but they needed to fold their nets to clear the living area for the day. Both brightened noticeably to hear that their studies would be put off for a bit.

Long trips are hard on bright children. There was so much for them to learn about Earth, yet there wasn't much yet to see or do except study and play games that entailed sitting still, and those could fill only so much time. The children were beyond ready to move around outside the confines of the gunship.

After they had eaten and cleared away the small galley table Steve called up a slowly spinning holographic image of the Earth at the comm station and began naming Earth's continents for them. He pointed out and pronounced the names of great cities that looked like sprawling splashes of light on the night- side. He pointed out and named the corresponding orbital cities, and told them of the vast fertile lands that produce the world's food. He showed them the green and orange stains in the oceans showed the aquacultural regions of the ocean. They learned of the orbital cities, where the wealthy and their servants lived, isolated from the mundane concerns of most of humanity.

Steve told the children that at one time the seas around the north pole had been covered in ice, and that the continents had been bigger and looked differently, back when the seas had been more shallow. He pointed out where, on the continent of Antarctica, their ultimate destination awaited, the home of Antarctic Continental. Then he pointed out Old New York City, where they would first stop to pick up Pat. Their interest quickened at that, and he could tell they looked forward to seeing her again.

The children had shared an ordeal with Pat, locked in the brig of Harden's flagship. They were separated for the first time from their mother. Kathlyn, Stevie and Pat had forged a bond in captivity. The affection the children showed for Pat deepened Steve's regard for her.

Little Stevie laughed and wondered why it was called "Old New" York, and Steve found the way he said it funny too. Pretty soon Kathlyn was laughing at them both. When they finished laughing at one another Stevie asked his Dad what "York" meant. Steve had no idea, but after barking 'York' back and forth at one another like seals they laughed some more.

A quiet alarm from his comm unit notified Steve that they were approaching their destination, and he returned his attention to the controls.

Fast, lightly armed cutters and other light military ships patrolled Earth's defensive perimeter. They intended to enforce tariff and import duties for the economic interests of Earth. They had already used low-power sensors to verify that Steve's gunship was exactly what it's transponder said it was. Smugglers and other criminals commonly tried to 'dupe' their identity by using stolen transponder signals.

The ships of Earth's Second fleet were now far out of sensor range, but a fast destroyer was nearby on patrol. It looked impressive under magnification. Her main weaponry was hidden but, as a reserve pilot for the ACM alliance, Steve knew its main armament would be long range torpedoes. The patrolling ship had visible laser turrets for secondary armament, designed for medium and close range fighting. The magnified image Steve examined showed she was bristling with kinetic and optical point defenses. A second superstructure aft probably housed a mine laying/mine sweeping mechanism.

Ahead of their gunship the magnificent sphere of humanity's home planet loomed, sentimentally magical and perfect beyond compare.

Steve would have to match the planet's orbital velocity, and then descend using antigravity at a rate timed to allow the planet's rotation to bring Old New York's La Guardia spaceport into range for a regulated landing.

Chapter 11: Sestrel, of the Skraa

Sestrel hadn't survived by ignoring details or lacking forethought.

The biolab notified him that his inoculation was ready. It was produced to respond to the bacteria and virus samples found in the blood of the newly discovered animal specimen. The females who attended the animal's memory recording had already been inoculated and, after a brief illness, they had recovered. The injection was deemed safe enough for Sestrel to use to gain immunity against the new diseases. He was the male, and must be protected.

Toxicology's biopsy had found nothing poisonous in the animal's flesh, which was a relief. Already the nutritionists were rationing the meat of the remaining livestock in the ship's pen. It was believed that there were practically no more meat bearing animals in the wilds of the star system's habitable planet. Nutritionists had already begun supplementing the food supply with complex vegetable proteins. Not only was the meat substitute they produced unappetizing, but it gave him gas.

Unless a new supply of livestock could be secured, the Skraa would have to subsist entirely on proteins from grain and vegetables, a repugnant thought. If the meat of this new animal was edible, and chemically it appeared to be, then the next nesting cycle should have him in full-throated song when the females secured their new food source.

Things had been looking grim until they read the new animal's memories.

Sestrel consulted a screen summarizing the fleet's population. Mature males were needed for fertilization, but there were few. Males are violently competitive, rather than cooperative. Males tend to kill one another. Sestrel killed other males whenever he could catch them. If he gave them a chance they would kill him. It was the nature of being male. There was no advantage to allowing inferior males to breed.

The males of his species competed with one another, and

they always had. Male teamwork was unnatural, almost unthink-able. Sestrel would not have lasted so long if males had been prone to team. Teamwork is what females do. Any male who even imagined working as member of a team with another male would have been killed in the attempt.

Females were a completely different story. Females would certainly use teamwork to rid themselves of him if he gave them cause. Sestrel was painstakingly conscientious to give his fe-males no cause to eliminate him. If they grew hungry that might change, so long as they had even a juvenile male to nurture to adulthood. It wouldn't have been the first time females coordi-nated to remove an idiotic male.

Sestrel was tolerably intelligent, and he excelled at decision-making. Decision-making was a necessity for an effective crew. Cooperation among females could too easily break down at the point of decision, when one teammate presumed to decide any-thing for the others. They could argue their way all around a problem, but when it came time to commit they turned to their male. Males and females were not equals. Males were outside the female political hierarchy expressly to make decisions.

Sestrel was esteemed as an intelligent and reasonably re-sponsible male by the team. He was respectful, and preferred to consult with appropriate specialists before deciding what course to take. When a situation demanded, he was able to make deci-sions timely, even when guesswork was all that was available to inform his choice. What is more, he had a beautiful and persua-sive voice.

This had been the way of male ascendancy since the earliest days of life aboard ship, and perhaps even before that. Males had always hunted one another. It kept the Skraa strong. So it had been, since the advent of history.

The songs of life, from the time before history began, were like distant, fabulous echoes, faint dreams short on detail and long on myth. After so long, the songs had inevitably changed with singing, like any tale that may be embellished for the sake of a syllable or tone. The scholars of memory records could trace those changes only so far. Even memories can change in the interval between the experience of an event and it's recording. Sacred songs may be unreliable histories, but they still formed what cultural memory was left of the time before the ships and cowls. The oldest songs were the source of dreams.

The way to power, if one were to believe the oldest refrains, had been the same since the days when Sestrel's race had first emerged from the first nest to seize the stars from the Makers, those who had given so much to the Skraa.

Males had always been few, yet if the Skraa were to take an abundant new source of food then the females would seek fertilization. Nothing could be allowed to withstand the reproductive demands of the blood. Once the food source was secured, it would be the first time in living memory that reproduction could be expressed to its full potential. The females could then nest naturally and securely on the planet surface. Their hatchlings could sort things out among themselves, as they always had, on the surface of a planet that to all appearances was covered with opportunity.

Sestrel had absolutely no desire to share this discovery, but it might be necessary to bring in other males to contribute to genetic diversity and express the ultimate potential for the Skraa. He thought deeper, reluctant to share. Even if the food beasts were technologically primitive, the memories of the captive animal suggested that there would be an intimidating number of intelligent livestock to subdue.

Sestrel decided that the other males should not be notified. Let them find their own way. If they were appropriately alert, then they would have his ship followed.

He then signaled the biotechs to begin manufacture of the vaccine. Universal inoculation of his females against the new viruses must be provided immediately. He added a note directing the team to also set up mass artificial fertilization. The singing of the females would not praise the male, but the egg.

Sestrel turned his attention to his summary livestock report. The memory record of the captured male animal was substantial but incomplete. Sestrel was not ready to slaughter it for its much desired meat just yet. He needed to know with certainty that it was edible, but he needed more information from it.

Language studies were only just under way, and the status report from Communications described the new language as 'challenging'. Possibly the challenge was due to an incomplete memory image. If so, then they would have to take another impression.

It was well documented that keeping a subject too long in a mental lock led to deterioration in the subject's ability to reason. If the animal was to be useful, he would have to be released from the mind lock soon.

Cowls had become almost scarce over time. The Skraa would need every one of them to imprint the young, once they hatched and reached adolescence.

Sestrel called up the recording of the animal's memory and browsed. The creature's home planet might actually be the Skraa homeworld. The most obscure myths, the oldest of his people's melodies, seemed to support that hypothesis. Yet the historical record in the main library assured the Skraa that after they had been taken to the sky, the homeworld had been sterilized by an unavoidable collision with a massive asteroid. It had been thought that the planet would be lifeless.

The technology of the animal's star ship was inferior. If it was a fair sample, then the animals' defenses should present negligible resistance.

It would be remarkable to discover the planet of origin. The fabled home nest, the first nest, from the time before the ships came and took the Skraa to the stars.

His stomach growled once again, a most unpleasant, disagreeable noise. The Skraa had hungered before. Surely they had sent scouts to locate new living planets. Why hadn't his predecessors thought to check the first nest?

Admittedly, Sestrel also hadn't thought to check the back trail, at least not until the new animal specimen was found and his memories were taken. The planets that the Skraa left behind so long ago had been picked clean of worthwhile prey. There was no reason to look back toward planets that had already been depleted.

But one of his researchers examined the old records. Among the histories she found that a few of Sestrel's predecessors had, in fact, checked their back trail. Every one of those efforts had ended in confirmation that the earlier systems were still not worth their return. True, sometimes the scouts sent back for surveys didn't return. The potential search area was simply too great to expend significant resources trying to find the lost, especially when all of the reports that did come back invariably confirmed the expected outcome. There were no signs of new food sources back the way they had come. It was always new living planets that offered bounty.

Unfortunately, this time, the way forward was not only hostile, but worse. The inhabitants in their path were inedible. The planetary systems they could reach had some edible wildlife, but not enough. The cost of hunting those planets would be too great, and the reward would be too meager.

But that was a concern of the past. Everything had changed, now that this new specimen had miraculously been found.

Sestrel's stomach rumbled.

Chapter 12: Martin Avery

Antarctic Continental's Chief Executive of Operations, Martin Avery, broke the red wax seal on a new bottle of Islay Reserve. The muscles of his forearm bunched as he pulled the stopper, carefully rocking the cork while keeping the bottle firm. It would be a sin to waste even a drop. He gazed fondly at the bronze figure atop the cork and saw it was one he didn't yet have in the set he had been collecting.

Martin swirled shaved ice to chill his thick crystal glass. When humidity condensed to cloud the crystal he dumped the ice and poured himself an inch of the precious liquid, then stoppered the bottle. Martin gave it a casual moment to rest before he swirled and sipped it, thinking, in the dark quiet of his carpeted living quarters.

Antarctic Continental was a leader in providing solutions for hostile environments. From the facility in Antarctica to undersea habitats to space station systems, their experience and know-how had built the business from a mining company into an enterprise with a constellation of revenue streams. One of those was the micrometeorite sealant gel used in all spacecraft. Another was the ubiquitous 'plasticlear' that all but replaced the use of glass in construction.

Martin Avery had been working on habitat solutions for living in Earth orbit for several years. Antarctic was one of the contracting companies who built Earth's orbital cities. It had been a shocking disappointment to him when the Corporate Board tasked Paul Harden and his company, Celine Interstellar, with finding a productive solution to Earth's overpopulation. Celine Interstellar was heavily invested in ship building and defense contracts.

Martin and his company had survived Paul Harden's early efforts to ruin Antarctic Continental and to kill Avery himself. He understood why he had been targeted. He alone, of Celine Interstellar's board of directors, had stood openly against Harden's 'cost effective' plan to obtain modulinium by destroying a living planet, even before he'd discovered that the settlers there hadn't been warned. Some costs are not objective. Some depend on values.

Martin had never wavered afterward in his determination to obtain justice. His resolve was bolstered by the desire for vengeance, but vengeance wasn't the driver.

Avery had been working for years to solve the problems posed to humans by hostile environments. He had never bought into Harden's plan to ship humanity into the unknown.

The Earth's need for modulinium was extreme, no doubt, and there was good reason to expedite its acquisition. But there were better ways to move Perry's modulinite ore into the oxygen-free vacuum of space where it could be refined than Harden had chosen. There were methods that didn't end in a planet's spectacular destruction. There were solutions Harden could have chosen that didn't entail the death of half a million people.

The food that Perry could have provided for Earth would have given them at least a few more years than they now had.

It would have been simple enough to fill deep Perry mines with nitrogen gas to eliminate any chance of oxygen contamination. Harden could then have used robotic systems to encase the ore in impermeable sealant. He could have used battery-powered electrical supplies to use the element's own antigravity potential to lift it from the mine shaft, through the atmosphere and into vacuum. Once in space, it would have been a simple matter to recover it for refinement and use. But oddly, for such an inventor as Harden had been, practical solutions weren't his long suit. Not to mention ethical solutions.

The man baffled Martin.

Avery sipped his whiskey and savored it before swallowing, and the taste forced him to show his good strong teeth. It was a fine, bold whiskey.

How could a mind capable of designing innovative technology fail to think through and responsibly solve the completely predictable problems that would attend mining a volatile ore from an oxygen-rich environment? True, he had thought of the problems, Avery admitted to himself, but he clearly hadn't compared the cost of his solution to the relative value of an obvious, but less dramatic method.

When Martin had confronted Harden that day in Old New York at the board of directors meeting, Avery's resistance identified him as an obstacle that Harden had to remove. Harden's company, Celine Interstellar, had quietly positioned itself for a take-over of Antarctic Continental. Despite his holdings, Martin hadn't been notified. That take-over was made effective on the same day that Martin's Old New York suite had been bombed. Then Avery's trusted chauffeur was suspiciously unavailable, killed as it turned out, and a taxi came for Martin. The taxi had a human driver rather than the usual robotic AI, and that driver had failed to follow Martin's instructions.

Martin had rolled out of the cab at a stoplight, and the driver had then chased him on foot, leaving the cab abandoned in the busy intersection. Martin had barely escaped, only to learn via a text message from his banker that he was being sought for arrest, on charges of embezzlement. His assets had been frozen where they weren't confiscated outright.

Martin Avery, the industrialist, had suddenly been forced to live by his wits. He had to go underground, figuratively and literally.

Fortunately, Martin hadn't been caught completely unprepared. He had kept a data cube with him, a surveillance recording of Paul Harden, recorded during the investor's meeting at which Harden had outlined his plan to acquire the modulinium in Perry's crust.

When Steve and Pat were recording an interview in Central Park, Avery had emerged briefly from hiding. Martin had approached Pat with his data cube. Pat was a professional he had worked with before, and she was then working with Steve Holbrook. Pat passed the data cube to Steve and he, with the help of the Aldebari, had used the recording to formally implicate Harden in the destruction of Perry in a manner that the Corporate Board could not ignore. That evidence, in turn, led to the restoration of Martin's interests in Antarctic Continental, freed his assets and cleared his name. Eventually, despite a vigorous defense in court fought by Celine Interstellar's lawyers, victory had given Avery control over some of Harden's assets in compensatory damages.

Those negotiations had also saddled Avery's company with Harden's old contract to productively solve Earth's overpopulation. Time was short. In less than nine years the population would inevitably exceed the Corporate Boards' ability to supply them with food unless something was done. There was really even less time than that, since the produce from planet Perry was no longer available. When the food supply ran short, there would be widespread starvation. That would lead to cascading problems with civil unrest, lawless violence, and destruction. The Corporate Board could keep the people preoccupied with various versions of virtual reality, but that would only last until the people grew hungry. If the food ran out they would rise up angrily, and one of the first things they destroyed would probably be the very infrastructure that distributed whatever food remained.

Harden had a wildly unlikely plan as his permanent solution. He would have had Earth invest vast resources into a fleet of colonization ships. He would send them off for unexplored star systems, never to return. He proposed to build new moduli with resources that nobody had, in order to open unexplored spatial anomalies. The chances were slim that unmodulated anomalies would lead to habitable worlds. As a 'solution', Harden's concept was already suspect. Yet somehow he had sold his plan to the Corporate Board, whether on the strength of his inventiveness, or the cleverness of his glib tongue. Most likely, the deal had clinched because some influential Board member had investments in Celine Interstellar, the company that would have made a killing on transport ship construction.

But it didn't make good sense, in Martin's view, to throw away money, resources and people with little to no hope of showing a return. There were other solutions, solutions that would keep Earth's investments in-system and working for the solar system's economy.

Martin saw that the overpopulation problem was not so much in *where* people were, but in how they might provide for themselves and their fellows, wherever they went. Human reproduction had been an evolutionary strength that was too successful. It became a weakness. He thought it would be better to turn that weakness into a strength again. If people were the problem, they should also be the solution.

Antarctic Continental's engineers were working on the design of agricultural habitats that would orbit the sun in space. Once supplied with the necessities, he had reason to believe that the habitats could become self-supporting. Several habitats working cooperatively should be able to provide for most of their own needs while producing surplus food for export to Earth.

Once a set of six agricultural habitats had been deployed, Martin planned to build a social, commercial and industrial platform as a hub between them. These would provide the inhabitants with most of the non-food supplies that the settlers would need, and a centralized common place to develop what should become their unique culture.

The habitats and the central platforms would all require modulinium, but instead of trying to transport a staggering number of people and resources into what might have turned out to be a long slow death in unexplored space, Avery wanted to build economically connected farming communities within the solar system. He didn't intend to invest precious resources into something that might never be seen again.

He would keep humanity's investment local. His plan would still move many people off the surface of Earth, but in a way that he hoped could feed both them and those they left behind on the planet, all while contributing to a greater solar economy.

Avery's team planned and calculated everything that they could imagine, from power needs and local communications to inter-habitat transportation systems, focusing especially on the maintenance of water and atmosphere, and on producing surplus food.

The current concern for the project was the mitigation of molds and bacteria. It was predictable that these might become scourges that would threaten isolated and atmospherically self-contained agricultural units.

Martin worried about everything that could go wrong and wished to provide for everything that might go right. The settlers' ability to interact with one another and enjoy a social life was a driving value. There should be a way for the inhabitants to cooperate, to build, and to evolve an eventually vast working culture.

If new planets were out there, beyond the anomalies, they would be no less useful than under Harden's plan, but the survival of the human species should not depend on unknowns wherever it can be helped.

An advertising campaign, intended to recruit settlers for the project, was ready to swing into action on the HoloNet once Martin gave the go-ahead. Industrial psychs and sociologists devised carefully crafted programs intended to market 'Life in the Sphere' as an adventure, where the real work of farming would be largely automated, but people were needed to monitor, service and operate the systems. If too few people were willing to volunteer, then they would be compelled by enticements. If that failed, then the Corporate government was prepared to use whatever means necessary to force compliance. There was too much at stake.

The essential detail that still obstructed his plan was the same problem that had plagued Harden's flight of fantasy. He needed far more modulinium than was available, let alone affordable, on the market. There was only one place to get it in adequate quantity.

Martin looked forward to meeting Steve Holbrook. This time he wouldn't look like some homeless vagrant. He would be in his native environment. Martin felt he owed the former sheriff some sort of consideration, but more importantly Holbrook was supposed to be bringing a solution to the last major obstacle to Avery's plan. If that solution was real, then what Steve was bringing would be crucial in Corporate efforts to alleviate the crisis of overpopulation, and perhaps even turn that liability into an asset.

One worry was whether the Perry Station Council could make enough modulinium affordably available. They knew Earth had to have it, and Perry was the only possible source. In a purely capitalistic universe such a monopoly meant that the price would be ruinously expensive.

Once he had assurance of an adequate supply of modulinium, Earth's manufacturing facilities in orbit could begin fabricating the habitats and the hubs. They would be made from parts produced by mostly automated orbital factories serviced by highly skilled operators. Orbital factories would build the hull frames from crushed and processed fragments from the asteroid belt, along with the mineral bulk of the soil. Once each hull was sealed, heated, and provided an atmosphere, the artificial soil could be finished with biological components that would otherwise die or go dormant in a cold vacuum. Starter biological packages were already being lifted from the planet to be mixed into previously sterile manufactured soil in precise, proven proportions. Fertility was expected to grow from those starter packages when the mixed soil was subjected to warmth, moisture, and a well-proportioned atmosphere. The soil would be held in place by artificial gravity, which required modulinium and frequency-regulated electrical current. Irrigation systems in space are simplified by the intelligent application of gravity.

Avery's prototype habitat was already in place in solar orbit. It was proving the concept in real time by supporting volunteer farmers and producing viable crops. The volunteers working at the prototype habitat understood the need and believed in the project. They offered feedback and made suggestions that were then evaluated by Antarctic Continental's engineers, accountants and psychologists for feasibility and cost- effectiveness.

Avery's team also had a wealth of experience to draw upon, born of humanity's history with the orbital cities. Indeed, had those cities been designed for utility rather than as pleasure domes and residential playgrounds for the elite and their servants, the problem of overpopulation could have been resolved long ago.

The first asteroid fragments gathered were already held in restraining nets in high Earth orbit, ready to supply raw materials. Delivery systems were ready to put components in place and to begin positioning new farming habitats as quickly as they could be built.

Once they were pressurized, the habitat plumbing would be used to fortify and recycle used water and organic waste into a solution to water and nourish the plants. After harvest, any stalks and roots left would be cycled through a conditioning process to resupply the hydroponics.

Ice reservoirs, called 'bergs', were ready and positioned. More bergs were already being towed from the asteroid belt. Between hydroponics and these artificial-soil hybrid systems, agriculture in solar orbit offered humanity a long-term solution.

Pure hydroponics won't work well for some crops. It would have been simpler to focus all food production on hydroponics, but adding soil as a hybrid medium offered greater variety.

Martin Avery smiled slightly at his whiskey. He was hopeful.

He ran a hand through his hair and looked out at the Antarctic landscape through a triple-insulated picture window that spanned his wall. There would still be problems but, as long as enough modulinium was available, it all looked workable.

There was only so much that could be usefully done to prepare and preposition. It was time to secure that modulinium. Martin hoped that his project might even liberate the masses from the HoloNet. In his eyes, overpopulation, automation and virtual reality had worked together to stifle mankind's potential for growth and advancement. Everything that could be automated, had been automated. There wasn't much of anything that he considered real for eighteen billion people to do. Much was gained, but much was also lost, when all basic needs were efficiently provided for.

People could survive without real effort. Without real problems to solve, fewer real solutions were developed. Virtual, preprogrammed puzzles were resolved by programmatic solutions. If a new problem should arise, Avery felt, human ingenuity might be found atrophied. Humanity might be caught short. Avery didn't imagine that starvation could be a good thing, but occasional hunger shouldn't be a bad thing, either, if it fostered ingenuity.

Martin found real accomplishment most gratifying. In modern times it was far too rare. Almost everyone was focused on living within holosensory reality. Human beings were valued most by the Corporations for their genetic variety, but genetic variety is a potential that can never find purpose in a hologram. The virtual must be programmed, completely thought out before it is even possible. That made holographic realities woefully limiting. Moving people out of the cocoons of holography and into shared physical reality, where unexpected problems often require inventive solutions, should resume humanity's development.

Progress might be meaningfully restarted in space. The people could rediscover, and maybe reinvent themselves. They might even start to question whether there might be a way to improve their lives.

But first there were contracts to negotiate. Martin set his empty glass down and reached for another handful of ice.

Chapter 13: Chosen Course

The *Jade Temple* released her magnetic moorings and backed carefully away from the loading dock at Perry Station. Once again at his holographic displays in the ship's central garden, Tibs watched the ship's status readouts with approval. All hands were aboard, provisions were loaded and stored, and the hydrogen and oxygen tanks were topped off. A few crates of munitions that the ship had been carrying in the hold had been safely stowed in a leased armory bay, just outside the Perry Station dockyard.

Tibs felt confidence in the search path Bobby suggested. It was unreasonable that the dying alien would have wasted time straying off course. It seemed very likely that the creature had been headed for an undiscovered modulus, somewhere in space outside the Al Najid system. So, as Bobby had reasoned, the *Jade Temple* should set course on a line from the Al Najid modulus through the site where the alien spacecraft had been found, and then travel straight beyond it. They should eventually find that other modulus.

Once the expected modulus was found and transited, then the alien's destination would probably be no longer predictable. Discovery of a new modulus, and what should be a habitable planet on its other side, would be a momentous find in itself. Possibly the undiscovered planet they should find there would hold a new clue or even an artifact.

Earth's overpopulation meant that each new habitable planet could help delay or possibly avert catastrophic consequences for humanity.

Tibs understood but disagreed with the more common Aldebari position that settling planets with the Earth's overflow would only spread overpopulation like a contagion. The Aldebari wanted to keep people from building more than isolated buildings on a planet. Planets should be wonderful places to visit, but nobody should live on one. Let the planets' flora and fauna evolve undisturbed. Humanity can live well enough off-planet, in space. There had nearly been an Aldebari civil war when the Academy began the ecological experiment on Matar IV, a planet where animal species were being carefully introduced to fill many available niches.

Tibs believed that if Earth had to offload excess population, then resettlement should be thought of as a practical option until a better constructive solution was found.

If the people of Earth ran out of food and water, they would grow desperate. Earth was an inextricable part of the galactic economy. There was no telling what might happen if Earth's economy collapsed. Unrest might disrupt the infrastructure that Earth needed to distribute what food could be made available, and violence, starvation and possibly the eventual loss of civilization could be the consequence.

The Aldebari favored living aboard their ships. Many never set foot on a planet. But the surplus population of Earth would probably not do well trying to emulate the Aldebari.

Most frontier planets considered themselves to be already at population capacity, unless the food they currently produced for Earth was going to be kept to feed new migrants.

Moving people to the new planet that Tibs expected to find would take a tremendous investment by Earth. They would have to invest in continuously supplying everything that the new planet would need until the migrants were self-supporting. Then, gradually, Earth could reap the profits. It wasn't a complete solution, but maybe it could be part of a solution. It would at least be something. Maybe the Aldebari couldn't help all of them, but the Aldebari could surely help some of them.

Having reached the axis of Bobby's 'cone of probability', the Jade Temple adjusted her direction and continued along the new course, making her best speed. It would still be days before they reached the edge of the system's explored region. There had never before been a reason to survey farther. There had been no practical need to prompt anyone to leave the productive inner orbits of the planetary system.

A reply in Tibs' inbox arrived. Steve was unable to give any assurance about the facing of the alien ship when it was found, but he mentioned an interesting thought in his last few para-graphs. What if the aliens were descended from Earth's dino-saurs? Thinking about it, the thought seemed reasonable based on the alien's physiology.

There had been a cataclysm at the end of the Cretaceous pe-riod that killed off almost all life on Earth sixty to seventy million years ago. Dinosaurs had flourished for more than a hundred million years before that. To compare, the ancestors of humans evolved to homo sapiens in only about six million years. Austra-lopithecus had walked the Earth four million years ago. The hun-dreds of millions of years that dinosaurs reigned afforded them plenty of time for there to have been an earlier intelligent spe-cies, a reptilian civilization. The sixty million years since that cat-aclysm that ended the Cretaceous was plenty of time for all traces to have eroded away.

But after suggesting it, Steve dismissed the provocative idea on the grounds that in the intervening sixty million years they should have become vastly more advanced than humanity. Man-kind had a mere ten thousand years of civilization.

After some thought, Tibs supposed a different opinion. Any civilization is unlikely to advance much farther than they have to, no matter how much time passes. If their current technology was adequate, what would drive them to advance? If technology al-ready supplied every perceived need, then there would be no driving reason to improve on it. Where there is no problem, no-body will seek a solution. Where there is pressing need, then people are inventive, but no one normally tries to fix what isn't broken. Why would reptiles be any different?

Invention can result from discovery and aspiration. New pos-sibilities can be revealed by an advance in science. Increased understanding may reveal that what didn't seem broken could be done better. But if technology already supplies every need, and nothing new is dreamed or discovered, then advancement might well be confined to efficiency.

Steve also pointed toward the trend that the farther away the planets were from Earth, the fewer kinds of large animals were found. Tibs had noticed that trend before. He felt that it was a reasonable inference that carnivorous aliens may have been hunting large animal species to extinction, one planet after another. The trend seemed to lend credibility to Steve's conjecture. Tibs chuckled at Steve's closing description of his hypothesis as 'food for thought'.

In the next unread message, Elder Kinkaid, one of the *Jade Temple*'s senior officers, calculated that they could extend the diameter of their search area by deploying a ring of scout ships about a day's travel beyond the orbit of the outermost planet of the Al Najid system. This was a valuable suggestion. At that point, the diameter of Bobby's 'cone of probability' would exceed the Jade Temple's unaided visual detection range.

A limitation of regular sensors, as regards finding a modulus, is that the physical characteristics of pure modulinium, together with the nature of an anomaly, would restrict the usefulness of active scanning. A modulated anomaly will absorb energy pulses rather than reflect them. This characteristic drastically reduces the range at which a new modulus can be detected.

All previously found moduli had been located visually. If magnification were used, the scope of the viewed area is reduced as magnification increases. The expanding diameter of the search area would eventually exceed the Jade Temple's ability to examine it all under magnification in one pass, unless the ship were to be slowed dramatically.

Kinkaid suggested operating under a practical working assumption, that what they were searching for should be an undiscovered modulus, because almost anything else would have moved since the alien expired.

If what the Jade Temple sought wasn't a modulus, then the more likely destination would be something in motion, and that would make it nearly impossible to find quickly, barring a godly stroke of luck. An anomaly, modulated or not, might be anywhere but it wouldn't appreciably move, anchored as it were to a shared location in two different star systems.

Kinkaid also pointed out that the outermost planet in the Al Najid system had been surveyed decades earlier. One of the names on the survey crew roster had been Paul Harden.

Clues were beginning to fit together.

Meanwhile, information broadcast from Perry Station about the alien mummy and its ship arrived on continuous feed. There were poorly understood systems found in the alien ship, systems that baffled the engineers. Recognized systems, such as weapons and shields, held great interest. The results of preliminary tests suggested that the circuitry would perform more efficiently than human equivalents. The shields and weaponry could handle greater loads with less resistance, but otherwise the tech did not seem much more advanced beyond what humanity had. The ability of the shields to render the starship invisible to sensors remained a mystery, and several other, apparently major systems remained unidentified. There appeared to be no ship's control interface. There seemed to be no way for the alien to steer or guide the scout ship, and it had all the engineers mystified. There were no signs of holographic or haptic controls, nothing.

The autopsy of the alien found no sign of integrated circuitry or implants in the alien corpse. Aldebari and some independent pilots, and to a lesser degree Legion and Corporate pilots used surgically implanted bioelectronics to help control combat spacecraft, but there appeared to be no similar interface grafted into the alien's nervous system.

Tibs looked away from his displays and waved his hand over them. The holographic imagery grew transparent, leaving him to appreciate his shipboard garden. As always the aerating rivulet of water that sounded like a natural brook helped clear his mind. Tibs sought clarity like a treasure.

Chapter 14: La Guardia

Old New York City looked amazing from the air, and as they drew closer and details resolved from the hazy blur of distance, the city view grew even more amazing. The roofs of buildings were vegetable gardens. The children had never seen so many ground vehicles as were visible on the streets, and when what had seemed dark smudges resolved into crowds and finally individual people, the kids were rapt.

Steve guided the gunship over La Guardia spaceport. Stevie and Kathlyn were engrossed in the gunship's sensor display, quietly arguing about what to look at next. There were more people in the streets and working on rooftops than they had ever seen at once, and that was only a small fraction of the city's population. When they wondered aloud at all the people, Steve told them that most people would be inside, above and below ground level.

When modulinium enabled the wealthy to use anti-gravity, the buildings rose higher in other urban areas, but not Old New York.

Old New York was a special case. As an historical preserve, the city sought to maintain its appearance as it had looked in photographs from the classical age. Instead of using the advantages of gravity control, when builders obtained better materials and techniques for sealing out groundwater the city grew deep. Subterranean networks of well-lighted and ventilated tunnels became commonplace, doubling and eventually tripling the city's paved streets and walkways without expanding the city limits or violating the ancient skyline. Old New York City was a preserve, but beneath the skyline it had grown into a modern labyrinth, an underworld of many levels that spread from the five boroughs out into and under the tributary suburbs.

The sea level had risen around the city centuries earlier. The ocean was held out of the city and spaceport by sea walls, massive bulwark systems pioneered in Denmark and Miami centuries earlier. The city invested heavily in seals and pumps to manage the seawater that inevitably found ways to infiltrate.

Freshwater aquifers in many regions had long been depleted. People could no longer simply drill a deep hole and expect it to fill with potable water. Even in rural areas, some remaining deep aquifers were so only because they had been fouled by early efforts to extract fossil fuels from below them.

The solution for coastal cities was to build nuclear, geothermal, molten thorium salt and solar power plants paired with distillation facilities. Energy production methods that generate heat as a byproduct came to be used to boil non- potable water into vapor. Cooling towers condensed that vapor into distilled water, which in turn was filtered through limestone and other filtration systems to make it tastier.

Desalinization creates other problems. In desalinization, evaporation leaves everything behind that had made the water salty or undrinkable. What is left is a salt-heavy slurry composed of nearly every element known to mankind. Fortunately, the technology to reclaim those minerals had advanced. Much of that was developed from advances pioneered in asteroid mining.

Inland cities required a complex set of solutions to solve their need for fresh water and those solutions were expensive. Reservoirs and industrial-scale atmospheric condensers could also be modestly supplemented by water produced as a byproduct of oxygen-hydrogen fuel cells.

Unfortunately, global average temperatures ranged higher than ever. Changed weather patterns rendered surface water reservoirs unreliable in many regions. Rain fell scarce where once it was plentiful. In other areas, notably the Sahara, there was now plenty of rain.

In dry regions, some inland cities were gradually abandoned as their aquifers were depleted. People and industries migrated to areas that had more affordable solutions to their water needs. There was a general migration to the seacoasts worldwide. As it turned out, migration to the coasts had an ultimately beneficial outcome. Not only is inland water needed for agriculture, but many inland cities had been built on the most fertile ground.

Old New York was imbued with a distinct ambiance, constructed, aged, and continuously reshaped by millions of unique inhabitants over the thousand years that humans dwelt there. It was far from the oldest of Earth's cities, but it was old enough to be ancient and it evoked a sense of brooding spiritual presence to anyone who contemplated history.

Steve's gunship had only struts to rest upon when planetside. He held his gunship centimeters above the star port's concrete apron, on its anti-gravitic fields. He had to be stern with his children to keep them buckled into their seats. There is nowhere a starship is more likely to suffer collision than in a spaceport.

An operator steering an ancient tractor, small-wheeled and heavy, pushed the gunship to couple with a gantry walkway. Once contact was made, and the gantry had secured the gunship's airlock with a grapple, Steve powered-down his antigravity fields, and systematically shut down the gunship.

It would take hours to process the gunship through Earth's distrustful trade and safety inspections. Pat would arrive at the spaceport toward the estimated end of that process to minimize her idle time.

The city beyond the plexiclear windows had been re- engineered beneath its exterior to be almost as self-contained and independent as it would be if it were in orbit, except that it was open to the sky.

Almost everything was done beneath the surface. The city's refuse was sorted, separated and recycled underground. Any organic matter was shredded for compost and moved to the surface for distribution to appropriate reclamation plants. There some was taken by gardeners for window planters and rooftop gardens, and the rest was traded to remote farms.

Deep cisterns caught rainwater and snowmelt to supplement the desalinized seawater that the city used and recycled. The atmosphere underground was dehumidified, warmed in winter and cooled in summer, and blown through shafts to the deepest inhabited level. From there, the air circulated back toward the surface, impelled by large slow fans as it cycled, back up toward the surface containing more and more of the carbon dioxide of the deep city's collective exhalation. As the air rose, level by level, some of it was channeled through artificially lit hydroponic gardens. More of the exhaust rose through grills hidden in surface parks and gardens. The remainder was pumped out through the sea wall to exfiltrate the city's ventilation system into large algae farms in the coastal waters around Manhattan. The carbon dioxide of millions of human beings nurtured agricultural and hydrocultural installations that were hidden from casual observation.

In New York's underground suburbs, deep in the borough of Brooklyn, Pat locked her apartment and walked her bags past the closest elevator, with its perpetual 'out-of-order' sign, toward a farther elevator that she knew was reliable. She had elected to carry her own luggage, rather than calling for an automated spaceport valet. The exercise would be no replacement for the exercise she would miss, but she considered the robotic valet an unnecessary expense. It would probably have balked at the contents of one of her bags, anyway.

Pat was an attractive, physically fit single woman who had assisted Steve when he first visited Earth. He had then come to New York to drum up popular support and recruit skilled workers for Perry Station. To Pat he seemed like an innocent, who didn't grasp that he had been made a celebrity for his squadron's defense of planet Perry and, more importantly, didn't realize how dangerous his status as a public figure could be for him.

She wore her clean brown hair cut fairly short. It was comfortable, low maintenance, and wouldn't get in her eyes. She was dressed for travel in comfortable but expensively styled shoes. She walked with the confident gait of a runner. She felt good.

She had a week's clothing in the larger of her bags. Behind an airtight, insulated seal in the other bag she had some hot freshly charbroiled and horribly expensive hamburgers with salted french fries. They were from the burger shop that Steve had obviously enjoyed on his last visit to Earth. Pat was feeling a little anxious, but she looked forward to seeing Steve and his kids.

Once her initial contract to help Steve had been fulfilled, she was troubled to discover that she missed him. She had scrupulously maintained a professional distance the whole time, yet she found herself feeling emotional about him. He was a bit older than she, and had seemed a quiet, sensitive man. He looked athletic. She found his face modestly attractive. He wasn't a pretty boy, but he was handsome enough.

Steve was encumbered with two children. Normally that would have given her pause, yet while she had been involuntarily confined with them by Paul Harden, she had quickly developed strong warm feelings for each of them.

Steve didn't seem to feel a need to prove himself with her, he was simply who he was. He wasn't an empty flirt, and he interacted with her as an equal.

She thought of him more often than was comfortable, and there was one thing remaining that she felt she needed to know: Why had he and his ex had separated?

Pat had no way to know whether he had been similarly affected. She had initially tried to dismiss it as an unnecessary and unwelcome entanglement. It would never do to be personally involved with a client. Yet when a second contract offer arrived in her inbox to locate and interview his ex-wife at Oberon, she seized the chance. She had felt alarmingly eager to meet and question Steve's ex-wife.

She hadn't noticed during the trip that she was being followed. The men who had tailed her had been skilled professionals. Thinking it over later, Pat realized that she had missed any signs that should have told her she was being followed. Her abduction might have been averted had she been more alert.

Paul Harden's security contractors had followed her to the low-income housing section of Oberon, the largest city in the Cygnus system. Steve's former wife, Sandy, had resettled there, alone with their two children. Pat had been preoccupied with too many questions. Why had it been the low-income part of town? If the separation had been formal, she should have had better quarters. Was she trying to hide, and if so why and from who?

When Pat arrived at Sandy's doorstep to make contact she was knocked unconscious by one of Harden's men. He appeared from nowhere behind her.

Pat had regained consciousness still recovering from a concussion. She found herself in the brig of Paul Harden's starship with two unknown children. Talking with them, she discovered they were Steve's children, Kathlyn and Stevie. She learned from them that she had been kept unconscious with drugs. She hadn't any idea how much time had elapsed.

The children were young and wanted to know where their mother was. Pat could tell them nothing, though she tried to comfort them.

The three developed a bond while in confinement together. The children had an unshakable faith that their mother and father would find and rescue them. Their faith went far toward reassuring her about Steve's character, though at the time, she thought the information would do her no good. It was just another of life's taunts. Pat was touched that slender Kathlyn was so fiercely protective of her when Paul Harden came with his men to interrogate her.

"Such brave children." Pat said under her breath. An overweight man also waiting for the elevator overheard, and looked oddly at her.

The elevator chimed and opened its door. Pat stepped in, and the overweight man followed. He wheezed slightly, and his breath smelled like algae, similar to an ornamental fish tank her father once had.

When she was an adolescent there was a month when she overfed the fish. The aquarium became choked with algae. Her father had tasked her with cleaning the tank. It had smelled very much like this man's breath. She tried to inhale less than she exhaled and, naturally, found she could not. The close confines of the elevator grew oppressive.

When they arrived at ground level Pat stepped from the elevator. The overweight man remained aboard, much to her relief. The entrance to the Manhattan Transit Authority's La Guardia Spaceport transit line was a short block away. On either side of the walkway, against the windowless walls and in doorway vestibules, unlicensed merchants bartered, watching for good deals to emerge, and especially for any pedestrian who looked employed.

Each barterer displayed only as much merchandise as he or

she could snatch back up quickly, in case a roving domestic security patrol came by. The merchants were hoping to trade cottage industry wares, whether vegetables or herbs from a surface window garden, jewelry and ornaments of polished, hand-beaten metal, colored glass and wire, sheets of handmade paper, or odd-looking devices built from reclaimed electronics. Most busy were the tailors and cobblers who specialized in reworking the generic, mass-produced shoes and clothing to actually fit their customers.

Dyes, beadwork and embroidery were an Old New York specialty that lent color to the crowds.

Pat stood out because she was wearing styled clothing, rather than generic. She carried matched luggage. The merchants thought she might be a rich tourist returning to High New York, the plush orbital city where the wealthy reside.

Some of the entrepreneurs sought to catch her attention with voices loud or soft, attempting draw her eye with invitation or even annoyance, just as long as they caught her eye. She was wise to their ways.

They hoped she would stop to take a look at their goods. Maybe she would see something of interest to buy, maybe she would see something artistic or quaint. Maybe she would let a few of those precious credits trickle down to them from what they dreamed was a heaven of wealth. Their world was the shadow economy. Credits have the greatest value to those who have none.

Goods in the barter-based economy circulated primarily by trading. Barter was common and normal. Credits were almost mythical. The upper class kept the money and exchanged it among themselves, sparing little with even the skilled or their servants. The unemployed masses of commoners made do, owning nearly nothing and trading nearly everything. Amid such paucity people treasured the most meager heirlooms. They prized what the wealthy considered worthless. Bargaining ferociously for possession of an ancient teakettle, or a faded, hand-sewn quilt was the essence of a good or bad day. Yet the people were just as happy and just as sad as people have always been.

It took millennia for civilization to learn that, if they weren't going to engage in genocide, then the most efficient, least expensive way to provide basic subsistence to the poor was to simply do so.

Everything beyond the basics could be classified as taxable luxuries. Luxury sparked ambition, and was the exclusive realm of the wealthy. The economic system was an unexpected hybrid of opposites, capitalism and its antithesis.

Pat tried to remain focused on the task at hand. The array of window sill vegetables, hand-made goods and salvage was diverse and interesting, but today wasn't a good time to go treasure hunting. She hurried past the merchants and past a small gathering of people waiting their turn at a Nibbles dispenser.

The dispenser doled out nutrition like a mechanical miser. Into the opened bags it poured a measure of rations after checking the receiver's identity. The ration dispensers were labeled 'Nibbles' in large, colorful letters. The rations were composed of a dry, rust-brown synthetic food compressed into nuggets. They were made primarily from genetically modified grains, seaweed, and legumes. It was impregnated with 'secret' seasoning, a crusty blend of freeze-dried sauce.

When moistened with hot water and stirred, the dry crusty nuggets would transform into something that resembled a meaty stew, though the "meat" was only textured vegetable protein. When ready it gave off a somewhat appetizing aroma.

Nibbles were the primary source of nutrition for most of the human race. The Corporate Board considered it a miracle of nutritional engineering. Nibbles weren't produced in variety, only in bulk. The Corporate government made much of their generosity in providing Nibbles to the general population without charge.

Variety was provided by the shadow market, the barter economy, where the unemployed, whose resourcefulness and good fortune made it possible, sold the produce of their rooftop and window gardens.

The Corporate Board knew quite well that real hunger would trigger violence. It had happened before. Social unrest had proven far costlier than simply giving out efficiently manufactured bulk food.

Pat arrived on schedule at the sliding door of the transit stop in time to catch the ground shuttle to La Guardia. She boarded the transport. It looked fairly new at first glance, but the synthetic carpeting was slightly discolored near the sliding doors and faded along the center between the seats and uprights. There were smears on the plexiclear windows where oily hair once rested. Three men in business attire were already aboard. They were lost in their wrist comms. They didn't seem to know one another and were seated separately. The nearest of them glanced up at her as she boarded, but after a moment's distracted gaze he looked back to his communicator.

The shuttle enjoyed the luxury of inertial dampening, unusual to find in a land vehicle on Earth. This perk was afforded to those traveling to the stars, the class of people who had a reason to use the shuttle to La Guardia. Inertial dampening made it easy to remain standing without holding onto a support bar when accelerating, decelerating, or rounding a curve.

After a brief ride she arrived at La Guardia Spaceport and the shuttle doors opened smoothly. She stepped out and strode into the terminal looking overhead for direction to her gate. There would be a security inspection line to negotiate, but because she would board a private vessel, security would be lax. She had plenty of time.

Chapter 15: Curiosity

Chief Engineer Mackenzie examined the articulated metal scales of the alien's cowl while he waited for his engineers to finish setting up their instruments on the alien ship.

By measuring the energy state at several points inside the ship when the shields were triggered, the engineers hoped to identify and map the specific circuitry involved in rendering the ship undetectable from outside the shield envelope.

Steve Holbrook discovered it while surveying a section of space near Perry, the broken planet, as part of preparations for opening the region to mining. To keep order, and to lease appropriate mineral rights to mining companies and free-lance miners, Perry Station had to have a catalog detailing the surveyed material content of dynamic volumes of debris-ridden space, within boundaries that matched the average relative motion of the material within those volumes in orbit. Rights to the mineral content of each sector offered for mining could then be reasonably leased, depending on the mass of the material in a cubic plot as it orbited Al Najid, the large local sun.

Fortunately, as it turned out, surveying space for mining plots required slow, patient measurement and mineral analysis. So it was that Steve had been moving slowly when his ship bumped into something large... and inexplicably invisible.

Mackenzie, after much convincing, had been dispatched from Perry Station to recover the object, whatever it was. It was all a mystery. Once they had it secured in an isolated hanger near the Engineering section at the station the Chief could not find a way to disrupt the shield that kept whatever it was invisible and inaccessible.

Then, early one morning when Mackenzie was about ready to give up and request assistance from Aldebari scientists, a maintenance contractor was cleaning the workbench to the hanger while whistling an old folk tune.

The shield vanished noiselessly, and the alien ship was in full view of holographic video and audio recorders. The janitor didn't see it, being turned the other way. He kept whistling his tune, and presently the shield popped active once more, hiding the alien ship again from view.

Mackenzie had been stunned. He ended up rewinding to play specific segments of the audio record to raise or lower the shields at will. Needless to say, he meant to gain a more complete understanding of how it worked.

As his engineers prepared for the energy-state tests, Mack was left with time to examine the odd metallic device that the alien had been wearing over its head and back when found. There wasn't an obvious reason why the alien would wear the cowl. It might be mere ornamentation, like jewelry, or it might be some kind of purposeful device. It certainly looked complex enough.

Mackenzie resisted an impulse to simply try putting it on. He turned it over to examine the underside. It was finely crafted. Metal disks were arrayed on the underside. Each disk appeared set upon a small set of tiny arms or levers that looked like they might be manipulated by micro servitors and what appeared to be... perhaps... tiny linear solenoids of some kind. The chief used a small metal rule to gently press one of the disks aside, to see beneath it. The disk was pliant enough in its reflexive supports to reveal what looked like insulated wiring. Electrical conductors, with a transparent amber tube, ran lengthwise under the disks. A probe with the steel rule showed that the amber tube was flexible.

Mackenzie turned the cowl over to examine the back. The weight of the cowl now rested on its disks upon the flat surface of Mackenzie's work desk. The cowl seemed to settle, almost as if it were relaxing. Mackenzie's brows knit together a moment, but his eyes studied what appeared to be three indented control surfaces among the broad scales. They, like the scales, were made of what might be brushed nickel. Mackenzie pressed three fingertips of his right hand onto his scalp above his forehead, just where those indentations would be if he had the cowl on his head. The position seemed natural to him, but he was human. Whether it would seem natural to an alien, only the forensic lab studying the mummified remains could really know.

He swung a holorecorder affixed to an articulated arm over

the alien metal cowl, and focused its aperture on the three depressions, increasing magnification. The image that appeared over the holographic display plate revealed more detail. The indentations could now be seen to bear fine oval seams. There were etched and inlaid pictographic symbols on each, suggestive of meaning. Mackenzie had no idea what the meaning might be. The pictographs were slightly raised. He supposed they could be identified by touch as well as position. The one that would be leftmost, were he wearing the cowl, looked slightly more worn than those of the center and rightmost surface. The raised inlay that might be writing looked like gold. It was slightly worn, as gold would be. The oval seams suggested that the indentation could be depressed, like a button. It seemed reasonable that the leftmost showed slight signs of wear because it was more often used by the wearer. But for what was it used? The other two buttons looked relatively unused.

Mackenzie was deep in thought. The alien ship had no recognizable control system. Modern human spaceflight and military technology incorporated bio-electronic implants to facilitate neurally-enhanced ship and weapons control. Human spacecraft used a throttle and a control stick or yoke. Small military spacecraft also made use of foot pedal controls to increase a pilot's ability to maneuver. The alien ship had none of that. Chief Mackenzie supposed that this cowl might be an integral part of a variation of a neurally-controlled guidance system.

Or it might not. It didn't seem like a good idea to experiment casually with an alien device that might interact with and possibly affect his central nervous system, but he felt a powerful pull of curiosity.

His assistant sent him text that the instrumentation was in place aboard the alien ship, and the team was ready to measure changes in the electrical circuitry during the activation and deactivation of the alien ship's shields. The chief had a great deal of curiosity to satisfy there, too, but he would be able to examine and analyze the test results when the department finished the run. For now, the cowl had his attention. He responded with approval to begin the test, and smoothed back his hair with his hand. He lifted the cowl to settle it on his head, and waited to learn what might happen.

Chapter 16: First Blood

The Skraa huntresses that Sestrel sent ahead of his main force were filled with intensity and focus. Their ships already coasted silently toward the prey. Hidden, they approached two pair of unsuspecting ships that slowly patrolled the vicinity of the modulus.

The alien ships were undetectable behind their fully powered shields. Only the needles of their sensor probes were extended through their forward shields. The probes were possible to notice. If detected, the needle-like sensors might give their positions away, but the quarry was unlikely to realize what they were even if they were detected. They should appear as unremarkable as slow micrometeorites.

The information the slim probes provided was gained passively. Passivity limited the sensor capabilities, but they sensed what the huntresses needed to know. It required almost all the energy output from their ship's power plants to maintain the shields that rendered them invisible. Only life support and passive sensors would be afforded. Active sensors would betray the presence of the hunting ships.

The hunting group had selected their individual targets and set their courses and speed before raising shields for the approach. Until stealth was dropped, there would be no way to maneuver. Maneuvering thrusters would reveal them prematurely. The idea was to disallow the prey any chance of survival.

The modulus had not noticeably moved since the Skraa left this system several millennia earlier. True, a local planet that should have been habitable nearby had been reduced to debris, but the focus now was on the hunt.

The male had advised them before they left that, although the planet's remnants bore valuable resources, the primary mission was to invest all available assets in securing the home planet of this new species as a source of nutrition.

The passive sensors of their probes continued to reveal the positions of their targets. The unsuspecting prey were surely piloting combat-capable spacecraft. They were an obstacle that would attempt deny access to a plentiful source of nourishment, and the Skraa were hungry.

The targets would predictably try to oppose them, and that could not be allowed. The survival of the species might hinge upon the success of this one hunt. Catastrophe need strike only once, but success must always prevail. The prey would not be allowed a fighting chance, whether their technology turned out to be strong or feeble.

Each huntress coasted toward her prey. Each pilot was confident that her ship had not been detected, but each also felt building tension. The quarry hadn't altered direction or speed. Unless the targets changed course or speed the first huntress would acquire the proximity she needed ahead of schedule. The error was negligible. She would discharge the sum of her shield's energy into her target. Once the target's shields were disrupted by hers, she would fire all the energy in her main weapon's capacitors in a single burst.

In the past, against other species, this tactic of surprise coupled with overpowering force was invariably successful. There was no reason to think it would not be equally successful now. There was the nagging problem of depleted shields involved in the tactic, but shield regeneration was quick and the risk was considered acceptable. The technique required only discipline, patience and timing.

One variable that the Skraa could neither predict nor control was the behavior of the oblivious prey. Though unsuspecting, they might alter course at any time and move to a position that would require the huntresses to maneuver. If that became necessary, then the huntresses would continue coasting until out of sensor range, and then try again. Patience is key.

Already the ships' tactical systems calculated that one of the targets would enter range before the others. That target was designated number one. Once the huntress emerged from stealth the ambush would be sprung and there could be no recovery. The second ship would be very close by, and its pilot would probably still be unprepared. Even if that prey had phenomenal instincts and reflexes it should not have time to react effectively before the second huntress attacked.

The spacecraft of the other two prey could be more of a problem. It would be several seconds after the first huntress revealed herself before they could be reached. The revealed huntresses would be defenseless until their shields recharged. The huntresses targeting the third and fourth ships had given themselves a bit more speed to try and narrow the interval between attacks, but it was already evident that there would be a gap. The remaining two quarry would have some warning before the second pair of huntresses revealed their presence and attacked.

There was an obvious fifth target present, nearer to the modulus. It was an automated communications relay and would have to be disabled as soon as possible.

Since a spatial anomaly prevents direct communication to the planetary system beyond, each modulus is served by specialized drones that shuttle back and forth through the modulus. These automated drones record in-system communications while broadcasting what had been recorded from the far side. When transmission is complete the drone returns back through the modulus to broadcast what had been recorded and to receive new communications for rebroadcast. The operation is orchestrated to permit no lapse. The comm relays operate around the clock.

The huntresses were well aware of the practical need for such communication systems, but there was no way for them to know whether the drones were unarmed. They only knew they had to eliminate the communications system before secrecy was compromised. It couldn't be helped that the consequent loss of communications would itself cause alarm and confusion, but the animals could not be allowed more information than was unavoidable.

While the huntresses in their hidden ships silently approached their primary targets, another communications drone came through the modulus. The drone that had been present disappeared through the modulus. Since their ships were still con-

cealed, the timing of the sequence was optimal. The newly arrived drone should now be recording and broadcasting on station
longer than it would take to eliminate it. Once successful, they
could stand-by in hiding, alert for the other communications
drone to return, or for any other ship that emerged from the modulus. Once the first engagement was concluded, then until the
main force was ready to transit into the next system, theirs
should be easy duty.

The first huntress reached optimal range and used a mental
command through her cowl to discharge the energy of her
shields into her target. In her intensity she vocalized a hawk- like
call. Her cowl interpreted her imperative intent as literal, and
broadcast her war-cry on an open radio channel.

The electrical energy held in her shield array arced out into
the minimal status shields of her target, overcoming them immediately. Her ship hung stark and alien before her prey in the light
of Al Najid, the giant blue star. She then released all the power in
her main capacitor array, and a lance of white hot energy seared
from her ship's primary weapon. The stream of energy bored almost instantly through the photo-ablative enamel of her prey.
The ablative properties of the enamel normally made it expand
into a protective cloud. That cloud should have slowed the pulse,
but her weapon's powerful beam burned straight through. Strong
metal armor beneath, intended to turn aside any kinetic projectile, was exposed to the ferocity of the beam and collapsed molten, despite the spattering metal and gases that would have oc-
cluded the coherent beam of any mere laser. The pilot was incin-
erated before he even realized what was happening.

The three other human pilots heard the hawk-like cry of the
first Skraa huntress and began to realize that they were under attack. They saw the first alien, but before they could pivot to the
counterattack a second huntress revealed her ship. The output
from her shields battered down the defenses of the second unprepared human's ship. Another too-bright lance of light seared
from her main weapon, and her target was vaporized before the
escape pod had time to deploy.

Both of the remaining humans released hydrogen into their

anti-matter drives to accelerate, to buy time and room to maneuver, but a third hunter ship suddenly appeared, as if out of nowhere, ahead of the third pilot as she unloaded the energy of
her shields toward his. He was already in motion, under the violent thrust of annihilated hydrogen molecules. The huntress'
shields were spent. She was unprotected from an unavoidably
catastrophic collision. Neither pilot survived when his antimatter
containment system was breached. Nearby ships and wreckage
shuddered in the expanding plasma of the explosion.

The fourth human pilot was accelerating to gain position, or to
escape if he could. The huntress who had him targeted reduced
the feed of power to her shields to maneuver, and when she did,
her ship became visible, very close to port, on his left. Time
seemed to slow as he saw her, a reptile wearing a cowl, looking
coldly back at him. Her ship was turning to acquire him as target
and to fire. His attacker looked... bejeweled. Despite his mounting
fear, part of his mind thought she was ... beautiful. Another part of
his mind was startled by the incongruity of that beauty, but
immediately he thought of the mummified alien he had seen on
the HoloNet. The dull scales of that long dead creature did not do
justice to the vivid coloration of a live one. This lizard-bird was
very much alive, her black eyes glittering back into his own. Then
he was past her and maneuvering to try and throw off the aim of
the three aliens. Already one of them had fired her powerful beam
weapon, but her shot was premature and missed. He diverted the
power of his weapons to bolster his aft shields. He keyed his
radio to try and warn Perry Station. The station had to be warned.
Then he felt his ship falter as it was struck.

Chapter 17: Breach

A lone lifepod streaked into an automated holding pattern near the Perry Station docks. The rescue launch was immediately dispatched to recover the pilot and the stored digital flight records from his pod. Station Command was still unaware of what had transpired at the modulus, other than a brief register on sensors of what must have been heavy weapons fire and that odd transmission of what sounded like the cry of a bird-of-prey. The situation was certainly enough to raise the alert. Command awaited more information.

The recovered pilot was uninjured. He immediately warned the recovery team that the attackers were aliens, which was met with skepticism, but the recovery team kept the record intact. The surviving pilot was shaking with intensity. He reported making visual contact in the brief battle. The recent context of the mummified alien, and an undeniably alien spacecraft in a secure bay helped to persuade them that his urgent warning might be credible. The survivor was hustled straight toward the command center at Station core for a full debriefing. The pilot continued talking to the rescue team as they moved.

The lieutenant leading the recovery team knew the communications specialist in the ACM Command center personally. Through her, he sent a briefly worded summary directly to the Officer of the Watch, cutting through protocols.

That summary was encrypted and sent by wireless text. It was received, decrypted, and immediately forwarded to the secure comm station of the Officer of the Watch, Commander Gerald Cortes of the ACM Alliance in Al Najid system. Cortes had been keeping an eye on the recovery team leader, and read the message immediately. Cortes slowed himself, and read it again from the beginning. Cortes ordered the station's sensors to make a single active scan of the area near the modulus. He then ordered a silent alert upgrade aboard station, and requested Flight Control to ready the duty flight and call up a stand-by flight of light and medium fighters. The flight crews began arming the ships of the third watch.

Cortes wasn't ready to alarm the civilians, but comm lists

were in place to bypass a general alarm and notify select on-duty and stand-by station defense teams and the station's law-enforcement personnel.

There was no point in trying to dispatch a message to ACM Headquarters in Oberon, Cygnus System, because the modulus communications relay was unavailable.

Cortes directed a warrant officer to initiate the procedures required to bring Perry Station's active and automated defenses online, but stopped short of full activation. He took a deep breath and sent word to his superior, who was off duty and probably asleep. He sent a notice marked urgent to the station's council. Cortes had his communications officer compose a briefing on the situation to fill in the blanks for the council when they did respond.

Cortes held little hope that the Council would respond quickly. They were civilian. If they were asleep or distracted, as he expected, then they might be quite a while getting back to him.

Once he had brought his preparations as far as he felt was safe he paused. If the pilot was right and the intruders were alien, they might not know the Station was there. He didn't want to give away the Station's location to a hostile force.

There was a risk that the pilot was mistaken: in normal times the situation would have been incredible. Yet even if he was mistaken in identifying the threat as aliens, three pilots were missing. Cortes would rather risk his reputation than let the Station take a hit on his watch.

Active sensors emitted a single pulse into the region of space near the modulus. It would take some time for any reflected signals to return. Time elapsed.

"Positive contact, sir, near the Modulus" his sensor lead reported. "Pulse return indicates at least one capital class vessel approaching the modulus. It wouldn't be the *Jade Temple,* because the Aldebari are out beyond Al Najid V. I also see some scatter. That might be from the small bank of asteroids near the modulus. Or they might be small craft, escorting the capital ship, sir." reported the specialist. "If we cycled a few scans we could get a course and speed, sir" he suggested.

"Negative that last, Specialist. I'd rather be wrong than give us away to an unknown but apparently hostile capital ship. This station isn't ready to handle a hostile of that class."

Going silent was his best option, but his duty extended to all the miners out in the system.

"Communications, broadcast one signal to the miners on the emergency frequency. Make it brief to minimize the chance that hostiles will calculate our position. We have to warn the miners out there to lay low. We don't know what we are facing, but the contact is reported hostile and the miners need to avoid attracting their attention."

The communications specialist had been around miners at the Cog and Sprocket and she knew some of their culture. She broadcast a single word on the Al Najid emergency channel: "Stone", and then began powering down her systems to reduce or eliminate possible emissions. The station would have to rely on passive sensors only.

Everyone on the command deck knew that first active pulse would have been noticed by whatever was out there. If the station went totally signals quiet, then if the hostiles were alien it might take them quite a while to locate the Station in the tremendous volume of interplanetary space.

Whatever local noise the inhabitants might make on the station was irrelevant, since sound waves cannot pass through vacuum. But if they actively broadcast electronic signals or activated sensors then the Station's location would become as obvious as a flame in the dark.

The communications officer was thinking whether there was anything they had overlooked. Everything seemed reasonably handled... except... "Sir. We should ensure there isn't anyone welding in the shipyard. Those arcs make quite a racket on some frequencies."

The question for Cortes whether to inform the civilians was out of his hands until the Station Council weighed in, but he could get the shipyard to comply. He looked at his watch and then made a call to Chief Engineer Mackenzie.

"Morning, Mack. Sorry to disturb you but we have a situation and I need your help." Cortes said onto his wrist comm.

"Early of you, Commander. How can I help you?" returned the Chief's voice over wireless.

"We need to maintain complete radio silence for a while. I need to make sure your people in the shipyard aren't using their welders until we can give you an 'all clear'. Can you do that for us?" Cortes added for emphasis.

There was a slight pause. "Of course we'll comply here at the yards, Commander. But if you need radio silence why are you using a wireless comm unit?" asked the Chief.

Cortes blushed within view of his watch team. The officers pretended to not notice and the enlisted remained studiously quiet and serious at their tasks. Cortes immediately ceased wireless transmission.

While the wireless signal of a comm unit has limited range, there was certainly merit to the Chief's point. It would be a mistake to assume anything about alien capabilities.

~

"One! Perry Station has just broadcast a message on the emergency frequency."

"What was the message, Comms?" Tibs responded.

"Perry Station sent one word. 'Stone', sir, just 'Stone'. Then the signal went silent, as if the transmitter had been powered off altogether."

Tibs raised his eyebrows. "Stone?" He asked the air, puzzling. They probably meant 'Be one with the stone', a colloquialism peculiar to the mining community. It was derived from a defensive measure used by asteroid miners and mining installations. When a threat approached that was considered too powerful to beat, miners among the asteroids will power down to the minimum needed for life support. They become almost undetectable, presenting an energy profile to any seeking sensors that is mostly indistinguishable, at least at range, from a lifeless rock in the asteroid field. For Perry Station to broadcast that one command, and then go silent, meant the station felt threatened by something that over- matched them.

Tibs keyed a channel to the bridge. "Helm, come about. Set course back to Perry Station."

"Coming about, One. Affirmative. Setting course to Perry Station."

"Make it fast, Helm. Who has the deck?" "Master Kinkaid has the deck, sir."

"Tibs out." He keyed Kinkaid's channel. "Kinkaid: Perry Station is in trouble. I don't know what it might be. They've gone silent, as if they were attempting to avoid detection. The puzzle is that anyone who might attack them should already know exactly where the station is. It doesn't make any sense to me for them to go silent."

"I heard it too, Tibs." Kinkaid responded. " Be advised: the signal from the Modulus comm relay has also stopped transmitting."

Tibs ran a hand through his scalp. The only reason he could imagine for a large installation to attempt stealth as a countermeasure is if there were a threat that didn't already know the station's location. Since everyone in Al Najid space would know very well where Perry Station was, then either they had lost their collective minds, or there was a threat that might not be from human space, which seemed absurd.

Perhaps Paul Harden, the man who destroyed the planet Perry, might somehow have returned in force. Yet Harden, and whatever forces might remain to him, would certainly know where to find Perry Station.

The most likely answer was that somehow someone in control of the Station's command communications had gone completely nuts. It had happened before, elsewhere.

Maybe the mummified alien brought an unrecognized contagion aboard? Perhaps a virus that affects the mind?

Whatever it was, the Station was in distress. If it was a mad-man then he should hear all about it shortly, but the consequences of madness in space could be catastrophic. Everyone must rely on one another.

Whatever the problem might be, it could not be ignored, even it meant a delay in his mission. That was an unwritten law for the explorers of space. There could be no exception outside of active combat when it came to a distress call in deep space. That rule had never been abused by any spacer, even during the Aldebaran enclave's secession war.

"Let's get the *Temple* back there and get to the bottom of this. Go signals quiet, but make best speed. Passive sensors only. Stay alert and make ready for action."

"Understood, One. I hope they're alright." Kinkaid replied. "So do we all, my friend. Tibs out."

Kinkaid clicked his comm twice in acknowledgment. The ship's alarms sounded an alert and all duty personnel calmly moved into their positions and began running through their lists of procedures to verify their function's state of readiness. Second watch personnel reported to damage control.

The three active flights for the watch boarded their fighters, ready to launch. Each flight was of four spacecraft. Two flights were three light and one medium fighter. The third flight was composed of three mediums and a heavy. Second watch suited up to stand by in the ready room.

Third watch was allowed to continue their sleep uninterrupted. Third would be awakened and sent to ready status if second watch went to launch.

Chapter 18: Release

The technician managing the ship's sensors advised Sestrel of the powerful sensor pulse. The signal had surely revealed their presence to someone. They were unable to determine where the signal source originated because there had been only the one pulse. The sensor produced multiple echoes reflected from their escorting hunters and from a few asteroids near the modulus. The single pulse had been followed by a differently broadcast signal. The second signal provided them a general direction, but not enough to obtain a location.

"Were we able to translate the communication?" he asked.

The technician was apologetic. What had been broadcast was not in the incomplete lexicon that had been built from the memory of the specimen. The language of the animals had proven quite difficult to interpret, in no small part because there was so little in the way of song involved. The language wasn't tonal and it wasn't elegant. Instead it was brutish and barbaric.

Sestrel made a decision. "No matter." he said, dismissing the issue. It was irrelevant to his plans. He had hoped to get farther into the systems that these animals had settled before he was discovered, but as long as the animals were kept from alerting other systems beyond the modulus, local awareness was only a minor concern.

Sestrel was irritated that the huntresses he assigned to secure this modulus had botched the mission so badly that they suffered a casualty and allowed an animal to escape. They needed to learn patience and planning. They should have coordinated better. They should have better calculated their approach so that each arrived at her target simultaneously with the rest. That would have secured the objective without loss.

He passed judgment. "The three huntresses who lost our sister and allowed their prey to escape will remain in this system until they have hunted the animal down and either captured or killed it. We will temporarily leave four more huntresses here at the modulus, in case the three prove themselves *inadequate* to their mission. They must either succeed or die." Sestrel sounded ferocious as he delivered his verdict.

"Meanwhile, we will proceed with the primary mission. Launch two hunting flights through the modulus to secure the communications relay at the next modulus. They should not divert from their mission for any distraction. Charts have been uploaded, but they are old. Once enough time has passed for the huntresses to have interdicted the next communications relay and secured the modulus, then we will make transit. The immediate mission is to prevent the transmission of any warning beyond the next modulus, whatever that takes."

It could not be helped if the advance of the Skraa would be marked by a loss of communications at each intervening modulus. That risk was acceptable, even desirable. If the prey became confused and disorganized by fear of the unknown, all the better. If they took it as warning and used the time to better prepare their defenses... well, it couldn't be helped. The outcome would be the same. Any casualties would be made up when the home planet was secured.

Sestrel's senior female gave voice to her doubts in disbelieving tones. "We will leave prey behind us for your brothers?"

Sestrel gazed knowingly upon her. He had not shared all that he had learned from the captive specimen. He swelled his song into the elegance of oratory. "Our objective is not only their homeworld." His volume diminished momentarily into a quiet, anticipatory tone. "It is also our own." Then his voice increased in volume to the threshold of oratory. "The first nest of the Skraa. Let the others have the scraps we leave behind." Sestrel invoked the opening refrain of the magnificent song of Awakening. "We shall strike for the heart, as is our way. I shall hold the heart in my fist, and will consume it before my brothers. They will know awe."

Several of the technicians rustled their crest feathers quietly. All knew and adored the oldest of songs, the song that told of the first nest. Misty with dreams, that song soared with melodies they had heard since they were hatchlings. The song described the conquest of the fallen gods, and how through them the Skraa found the stars. Yet now their male suggested it wasn't all just a myth. Instead, he suggested that the Awakening was an historical account. They looked at one another in surprise.

He could have been doubted and overruled. Sestrel had not been the only one to experience the new animal's memory. His senior females could disagree.

Yet his pronouncement was not contradicted by the elder sisters. It was very strange to imagine, and the majesty of his song was exhilarating. There was an undercurrent of excitement, almost erotic, the way his voice modulated, using tones that only males could voice. No, it was certainly erotic.

"Let my brothers have these sparse planetary systems. They shall know true envy when they learn what we have seized. We will bypass these lesser systems and strike first at the heart of our prey. We will have no need to defend supply lines. We shall have the home planet, its nourishment and its resources. Once we are there we will need all the power we can bring to bear. We *must* not dissipate our strength. We *will* need to focus our strikes unerringly.

Sestrel fell back for a moment from the epic tones and scale of formal oratory. "We know already that these animals are resourceful. They are extremely numerous. That will be good for our bellies and for our young, but it will also make the animals challenging to hunt, once they recognize their peril. We will not dissipate our strength garrisoning secondary systems that can offer only meager rewards."

His voice again waxed with resonance. "Instead, we will seize our ancestral home from them, and we shall make of it our nest once more. We will feast there for as long as we wish to hunt, until our young have grown to take our places, and their hatchlings *theirs,* after them."

Sestrel's tones escalated his song with masculine timbre, evoking primal emotions in his female audience. His volume increased as he spread his arms and his feathered crest swelled. "We will live engorged, and will raise many young. No more will our eggs lie broken and wet in the nest. No more shall our hatchlings hunger. Sisters," Sestrel used an unusually personal inflection, "we will find our *home*." Sestrel's feathered crest slowly smoothed as his song rested into silence. The females were breathing heavily, rapt, their eyes dilated.

The other males would learn, sooner or later, that he had taken his whole force with him. They would wonder what he was doing. One or more would surely task a scout to find where his force had gone. They would then find the new species, eventually, and report back. The other males would follow of necessity, out of hunger, but they would probably not immediately realize the significance and value of his objective until they captured their own specimens and read their memories.

Their dismay would be great when they learned what he had done. Only then would they realize the scope of his victory, that what he left for them was so much lesser. Their envy would sour their meat. Sestrel felt joyous anticipation.

The pheromones of his aroused females triggered an innate need in him to... to hunt, and to eat. He wanted hot blood. The despicable vegetable protein cakes would not satisfy his carnivorous desire. They were not satisfying to bite into, to feel the heated gush of blood. Vegetables did not surrender, struggling in futility in the crush of his jaws. Desire was fierce in him to finally taste the flesh of the new animal in the livestock pen, to crack its bones and slice through its gristle with his teeth.

Sestrel paused, considering the temptation. The creature's memories were unreliable to the point of uselessness anyway. Sestrel had denied his own appetite too long for the sake of the greater good, and there was no need for the animal. He stalked like he was hunting toward the pens, his feathered crest rising and falling with each step.

But the further from the aroused females he strode, the less he was ruled by his chemistry and the more his reasoning regained sway.

The new animal's memory had probably become useless because it's mind had been captive too long, trapped in a body it could no longer control. It might recover, were its mind released. If it regained control of its body, its mind might heal and provide useful information again.

Sestrel descended to the deck dedicated to maintaining the livestock. The pens were empty. Feed hoses dangled unused over the metal latticework flooring that allowed animal waste to be flushed into the recycling system. Sestrel stalked to where the new animal stood motionless under the cowl. Its eyes were closed. He stopped in front of the filthy animal, appraising its sorry condition.

So. Creatures of this type had, in the absence of any natural apex predator, risen to infest the original nestworld. Sestrel marveled at the providence. It was almost as if the fallen gods had reached out from the dim past to engineer even the future. This specimen had shown up exactly when most needed.

Sestrel paused. The fallen gods were long gone. This opportunity belonged neither to the past, nor to the fallen gods. This moment belonged to him, Sestrel of the Skraa.

He had diverted his forces from where they were garrisoning a depleted planetary system on this gamble. The Skraa were almost out of natural food. The artificial food substitute that the biotechs came up with was... intolerable. The whole ship smelled of flatulence.

Sestrel looked at the dirty, pitiful creature. This animal's memory record had revealed a planet that was literally crawling with meat. And it wasn't just any planet. It was the original nestworld of the Skraa. He was convinced of it. His exobiologists assured him that, according to the tissue samples they had taken, these creatures were edible.

The resourcefulness of nature is profound. Life is tenacious. This opportunity meant destiny.

Sestrel used his cowl to summon the livestock handler. She arrived quickly and obsequiously, and Sestrel indicated with scorn the soiled condition of her charge. The animal was an embarrassment. It was foul with its own excrement.

Sestrel commanded the keeper to remove its cowl. He wanted it to recover. He admonished her sternly for failing to keep the animal clean.

The keeper obediently gripped the cowl that draped the animal's head and upper back and pressed a recessed spot on the crest. The cowl promptly released control of its muscles and mind and the animal collapsed limply to the deck. The articulated metal cowl was still gripped in the keeper's hand. The dirty animal made a tangle of limbs on the deck. It began screeching horrible, incoherent noises that made Sestrel and the keeper wince. Sestrel covered his sensitive ears in pain.

The keeper put the cowl away and returned quickly to spray the beast with a cleansing disinfectant solution. It immediately put its paws over its eyes and its wailing ascended in scale and volume, making the keeper duck her head in pain as she worked. The threat of her male could not be ignored, and she continued cleansing the beast, cringing from the noise as she did.

Sestrel could take no more of the animal's cacophony and walked away to the lift tube, disgusted by the pathetic creature. He had been wrong to think of the animal as a bull. It was only accidentally a male of its species, an accident of gender rather than an embodiment of virility. It didn't respond to an opportunity to grow aggressive, as a proper male should. And its loud cries hurt the ear. Perhaps captivity had damaged it irreparably and it should just be eaten. Maybe it would prove resilient and recover, but it seemed unlikely.

Paul Harden was incapable of anything because of intolerable agony in his back and legs. His body had been standing for days, maybe weeks. When the cowl relinquished control of him his body's excruciating pain crushed him, and he collapsed utterly. The pain was so great that at first he was unable to move. He feared that moving at all would hurt even worse. He could do no better than scream, and even that hurt.

When he collapsed, the sudden change in position triggered an agony of spasms in his legs and his back and abdomen that inevitably forced him to thrash about loudly on the floor despite his fear of moving. His movements indeed triggered more pain, just as he feared, and to pile onto his despair he was wracked with more spasms. His face was taut in anguished rictus. He could not help but scream.

At first it was a high whine, high and almost quiet as his dia-
phragm constricted his lungs. His voice increased in vehemence
and he poured out his agony to the extremity of his breath. The
sensation of transcendental pain escalated well beyond coping.
Behind his shut eyes his visual cortex interpreted his distress
into a bright strobe of light that turned red as it faded to darkness, then refreshed blindingly white with the next strobe.

Mental reality, memories built since childhood, even self- interest burned away like spider webs in a firestorm. Their eradica-
tion obliterated his education, his cerebral objectives and his vain
desires. In moments that seemed to span eternity, physical pain
reinforced and emphatically underscored his awareness, but that
awareness was only of pain. Harden's universe, for now, was all
encompassing, and it was absolutely excruciating. If he could
have abandoned his life he would have rid himself of it then, just
to end the pain.

His mind hit his limit. He lapsed unconscious.

Chapter 19: Gone South

Pat negotiated security and entered the small noncommercial terminal at La Guardia spaceport. Kathlyn and Stevie ran toward her excitedly. With a dawning smile she saw them coming. She set down her bags and crouched with her arms open to receive them. It was as if they transformed from young students into happy children again, and the effect wasn't lost on Steve. Seeing it he realized that his influence on them was incomplete without their mother. His children looked happy. He was glad of that, but he also felt a small pang of envy when he realized Pat offered them something that he did not.

He put away his self-doubt and approached Pat with a welcoming smile. He opened his arms to her.

For a moment a solemn expression flashed across her face. Then she released the children from her hug and stood smiling to meet him. After that slight hesitation she slipped into his embrace and returned his hug, then looked up into his face. She had never been so close to him. He was warm. He was clean, and he smelled good.

Kathlyn watched them with the same rapt focus she displayed when reading her young-adult romances.

Stevie watched Pat and his father intently as well, but with a less enthused sentiment. He felt expectant, but also somewhat alarmed. He clung to a hope that his mother would return. The boy's face began to cloud when he saw how deeply his father focused on the woman. He didn't understand what he felt, but there was something about the way the adults seemed so intense together that didn't feel right.

Steve looked down into Pat's eyes and found bright magic there, but something drew his eyes to his son. The boy looked troubled, and Steve thought he sensed his son's disapproval. Pat's eyes followed Steve's to his son, and she let go.

Steve considered what he thought he would feel in his son's place. He certainly didn't want his son to think he was betraying his mother. Rather than follow his impulse to kiss Pat, he reluctantly released her. It was still too early. Stevie hadn't had enough time to realize and accept that his mother was gone. Steve looked to Pat, concern on his face. He hoped she understood.

Pat certainly had noticed that the anticipated outcome of that first warm embrace had diverted unnaturally. When she saw Stevie she immediately understood. Intuition isn't mystical. Intuition is sensitivity. She and Steve exchanged a quick glance of understanding, and stepped back to resume the cultural rites of a friendly reunion as they boarded the gunship.

Attraction remained strong between them, so powerful that it might have registered on sensors, but they clung instead to informal social rituals. Kathlyn hummed happily as she helped orient Pat to life aboard the gunship while her father gained clearance to depart La Guardia.

As they waited, Pat opened her insulated bag and introduced the children to charbroiled hamburgers. On his previous visit to Earth she had seen Steve eat a burger and it was plain that they were a favorite of his.

For his part, Steve had not realized how hungry he'd grown. The real problem with a good hamburger is how quickly it can be devoured.

Soon little Stevie was in the copilot's acceleration couch, devouring a burger and watching his dad prepare the ship for flight. Apparently any misgivings he felt earlier about his Dad and Pat had been forgotten.

Clearance arrived from the control tower, and after a few moments of gradually feeding more current through the frequency regulator the gunship lifted smoothly on the strength of her gravitic fields. When he reached his designated departure altitude there was a delay. Steve had to wait for a commercial transport to clear from their flight path. It wasn't long before he was allowed to accelerate south using the gunship's maneuvering thrusters.

Making the transit to Antarctica within the planet's atmosphere would come at a cost. Pushing through the air requires considerably more thrust than moving through vacuum. The ship's primary engines weren't intended for atmospheric use, and were not rated for the trip. Only his secondaries, his maneuvering thrusters, could be used safely within Earth's atmosphere.

The hull of the gunship was moderately aerodynamic. The bow tended to pull slightly to port, due to an asymmetrical drag profile. The ship used no airfoils, and had no stabilizer to help compensate for the ship's tendency to drift to port. Anti-gravity provided lift for the ship. Steve's maneuvering thrusters could make the ship move in any direction he desired, but the air through which he traveled was also moving. So his direction had to be recalculated as the wind speed and direction changed. Fortunately, he had a computer to handle the bulk of that.

The sound of turbulence caused by the ship pushing through the atmosphere was hardly noticeable, muffled by the gunship's thick armor and insulation. The turbulence was reduced as the small ship gained altitude. Life support systems and cooling for the electronics were nearly silent. The rhythm of his son's breathing was too regular for him to be awake.

On course and traveling at their designated altitude there wasn't much to do beyond checking sensors for other flying craft and occasionally correcting direction when the winds shifted. Before long they passed the coast of the mainland and eventually the narrow island of Florida that stretched south from the beach resort of Clermont. Then the deeps of the Gulf of Mexico were far below them, south of the sunlit Floridian shallows and the civil engineering marvel that was the island of Deep Miami. The glistening horizon was wide. A distant weather system to the West displayed tall thunderheads backlit by the descending sun in a salmon-colored sky. Beneath those clouds, the sea was dark with rain and dusk, flickering with occasional lightning. The storm was away and below them. It posed no threat at their altitude.

Steve heard Kathlyn complaining quietly behind him in the living quarters, and he heard his son stir. Kathlyn's complaint had something to do with the HoloNet. She wasn't normally a child to complain, so his curiosity was mildly piqued. Pat was with her, so he assumed that whatever the problem might be, it would be worked out.

They were high in the stratosphere. The air was thin enough to allow the minimally aerodynamic gunship a respectable speed compliant with their flight plan. Steve looked over toward his son strapped into the copilot's couch. He looked like he was about to fall asleep once more.

The girls were agitated over something. They were on the HoloNet, judging by overheard phrases and ambient sounds. Kathlyn's tone was full of complaint, but her words were indistinct. Pat's voice murmured assurance in response. It sounded like she was concentrating on whatever the problem might be.

Steve speculated about what might be going on, but he couldn't leave the flight deck to learn what the issue might be. Before long Pat approached closely behind him to inform him in a whisper. She was attempting to not disturb Stevie, who was sleeping in the copilot's couch.

Her soft breath tickled the back of Steve's neck. The scent of her breath and the warm smell of her skin were delightful, and he felt a pleasant sexual tension that he hadn't enjoyed in what seemed like ages.

"The HoloNet has lost the feed from Perry Station." she whispered. "We were wondering about the latest on the alien. A reporter was just describing the most recent revelation from the alien autopsy, saying the medical examiner was puzzled by hollows inside the long throat of the creature. The reporter was mid-sentence when the feed cut out. I tried to refresh the feed, but only got a message that the service is currently unavailable.'" she said quietly.

"Was there an error number given? Steve asked.

"There was a number, yes." Pat concentrated a moment. "404. The error number was 404."

"My recollection is that a 404 error is an addressing issue. It may have been caused by any number of things" Steve replied, continuing "...almost none of them local. It isn't likely we can solve it beyond trying to refresh the feed. If you can reach other HoloNet addresses, then it isn't anything on our end."

Despite his assurance, Steve was troubled and it felt urgent. Something he couldn't identify resonated with that sense of foreboding he had recently been feeling.

But this outage was surely just a technical glitch. "It should clear up shortly." he said reassuringly. Then, in a tone harsher than he intended, said "Kathlyn may just have to be patient. Technology has limitations." There was no reaction from Pat. He glanced back and saw she had already returned to Kathlyn, and he felt relief that she hadn't heard his too-harsh reaction.

Shoulder to shoulder she and Kathlyn were browsing the HoloNet. Pat glanced up to see him looking. Steve turned back to his controls.

After a bit he heard them laughing together about something. His daughter's laughter was like music.

Tension eased from his shoulders. He hadn't realized it, but he had been bracing himself for something. Conflict, he thought. Knots of ill-defined worry had bothered him since leaving Perry Station.

Steve looked over at his copilot. His son still slept.

Chapter 20: Comm Relay

One of the less publicized reasons that skilled labor commands hazardous duty pay in space, particularly aboard a communications service craft, is that usually only the pilot and copilot are afforded the expensive emergency life pod systems. Pods would preserve and carry them to the nearest safe haven in the event of lost hull integrity or critical systems failure. Maintenance personnel making transit in the hold are not similarly provided for. There is a lifeboat for them if they have time to board it, but in space that kind of time is too often unavailable.

Just such a repair crew was dispatched from Oberon to repair whatever had disrupted communications with Al Najid system.

There was no sign of a communications relay drone on the Cygnus side of the modulus, so the crew transited the modulus to Al Najid system in their civilian support craft.

They emerged into a killing zone of hostile fire from not only multiple small combatant spacecraft but also the point defenses of an immense alien capital ship. Five of the seven people aboard died immediately. The pilot, and the foreman next to him in the copilot's couch were automatically ejected in two life pods almost before they realized they were in trouble.

Earlier the Skraa huntresses had seen first-hand how rapidly escape pods accelerate. They knew the general direction the first escape pod had taken. With forethought, one of the huntresses was in position to chase the pods if another manned ship came through the modulus.

Although a spacecraft equipped with inertia dampening relieves the pilot of most of the stresses of rapid acceleration, the modulation of inertia doesn't remove the requirement of an object at rest to accelerate gradually. Life pods are small and extremely quick. As a result, the huntress attempting to follow was only able to see where the life pods were headed for a few minutes. Soon she lost contact altogether. Nevertheless, life pods aren't designed to evade or deceive anyone trying to follow. The course of the two pods gave their pursuer an exact heading.

Two other hunting ships followed the first while the main force of the Skraa made transit into Cygnus space. These were the other two huntresses of the flight that had lost one of their number. They had been ordered to compensate for their failure to properly coordinate the initial attack.

That failure allowed prey to escape. Sestrel consequently assigned them to locate and neutralize the animal that survived the initial engagement at the Al Najid modulus. Prey that was allowed to survive an attack by the Skraa might have learned too much from the experience, and that was impermissible.

The shamed huntresses knew their mission, and they knew there would be no allowance for failure, regardless of odds. The only reinforcements they would be permitted was a second flight of four hunter ships that Sestrel would leave temporarily to guard the modulus. Those four could be called upon for reinforcements.

Perry Station was hidden only by its distance from the modulus. It orbited the star fairly close to the bulk of the planetary debris. It had been built at a safe distance from the tumbling stone.

The first pursuing huntress studied the structure of Perry Station and divined that she would need reinforcements. The size and potential of the station excited her. Such an installation should provide a significant supply of food for however long the animals there could be kept alive.

She brought her ship to a stop to await the others, and began to report her findings to them. The situation would require in-depth planning. As any competent female knows, thinking is best done together, whatever idiocy overly competitive males might spout.

Communications personnel aboard the *Jade Temple* were puzzled by what they heard on a little-used comm frequency. It wasn't anything they could have expected to hear. It sounded like a bird warbling a complicated song over an open comm set. A second, much more brief birdsong responded to the first, and then the frequency went silent.

Chapter 21: Oberon

Oberon is the largest city in the Cygnus system. It hosts the headquarters of the ACM alliance. Its spaceport was home to the ACM Defense Force. The resources of three planetary systems on the frontier (Al Najid, Cygnus and Mazzaroth) were pooled to form an alliance, not only military but economic. Together they managed to procure and maintain a frigate of Earth manufacture, the *Brandenburg*, to supplement resident squadrons of interplanetary spacecraft. Fighters, gunships, and striker attack craft formed the bulk of the space borne defenses that shepherded commercial transport and trade. The *Brandenburg* was the largest ship in the alliance.

The frigate was the de facto flagship of the Alliance. She was fitted with a robust command and control suite, strong sensor suite, and advanced electronic warfare capabilities. She bore a potent missile loadout, and her point-defense armament was more robust than standard for her class. The *Brandenburg* was state-of-the-art, purchased new from a Corporate shipyard orbiting Paradiso in Dante system a year earlier, shortly after the presence of modulinite in the Al Najid system was revealed to Alliance command by the Perry Station council. The ACM realized then that they could afford the acquisition.

When communications with Al Najid were disrupted, Oberon had dispatched a repair crew aboard an unarmed maintenance spacecraft. In a matter of hours, they had arrived at the modulinium ring of the Cygnus/Al Najid modulus. The crew had found no sign of trouble on the Cygnus side other than that there wasn't a communications relay drone present. Trying to locate the missing relay, the maintenance crew made transit to the Al Najid side of the modulus. They did not return, even to report. The status of crew and vessel remained unknown.

ACM Command in Oberon realized they had a situation. There were too many unusual events happening to sit back and hope they were coincidental. ACM Command was determined to not be caught off guard again.

Command ordered the active wing of the system defense squadron to fly cover for the frigate *Brandenburg* to investigate.

Active duty planetside defenses were placed on alert. Reserve units were notified to report to base for activation. Support crews for the second defensive wing commenced fueling and arming the star craft in their charge.

The people of Oberon were growing alarmed. Something unusual was taking place. When communications were cut with Al Najid, many had been actively engaged by the news about the mummified alien and its starship. When the news feed was cut, local news and HoloNet feeds from Earth grew congested with speculation.

The *Brandenburg* cast off from her berth's magnetic moorings at Oberon's orbital terminus for what might be her first live action. Her missile and torpedo tubes were cleared of seals, and protective plasticlear munition sheathes were removed and stowed. Calibration tests cycled methodically. Systems ship wide were running comprehensive self-checks and the crew checked status on shipboard comms.

Commanding the *Brandenburg* was Captain Elaine Hall, ACM Navy. She had worked her way up through the ranks despite several instances of biased judgment against her. She had earned an advanced education, held prestigious certifications, and more than earned her command of the flagship of the Alliance. Her crew was proud of their captain.

Interplanetary light and medium fighters formed up as the combat escort for the *Brandenburg* while she made way. A flight of heavy ordnance tactical strikers equipped with standoff missiles launched from Oberon Spaceport for rendezvous with the frigate and her escorts.

Losing communications with Perry Station was bad enough. When the farther relay at the Cygnus/Arcturus modulus went offline as well, Oberon's communications with Earth, the Legion, and the Aldebari were severed. There had been no systemic alert, nor any sign of impending malfunction.

Military staff at Oberon, not prone to speculation, felt like some impending doom was upon them. They had lost communications with the rest of human space. No longer was there a way to call for assistance from any of the three major powers if it was needed. The comm link had already been cut with Perry Station, one of the farthest habitations from Earth, and now there was no response earthward either. Only communications through the Mazzaroth relay seemed functional, but the Mazzaroth planetary system had no more military assets than a single interplanetary defense squadron.

ACM command demanded information from the patrol that had been at the Arcturus modulus regulating commercial traffic. The flight did not respond. The commanding officer for Cygnus system at Oberon was at a loss whether to redirect the *Brandenburg* and her escorts toward the new problem at Arcturus modulus, or to stick to the original course toward Al Najid. Reasoning that the progression was from Al Najid and toward Earth and under the assumption that Arcturus would mobilize, ACM Command decided to continue the *Brandenburg*'s mission toward Al Najid.

Whatever was happening, it began there.

Chapter 22: Antarctica

Knutzen Peak is in the Ellsworth Mountains of Antarctica's Sentinel range. It was home base for the mining and manufacturing operations of Martin Avery's company.

Antarctic Continental was one of the Earth's largest terrestrial mining and manufacturing concerns. The corporation had its beginnings in the Antarctic mountain range shortly after an international treaty expired that had prohibited exploitation of the continent.

The installation didn't look like much from the air, just some bright lights in mountainous terrain shining out on a landscape of ice and stone. It looked terribly cold down there.

A traffic controller on the frequency specified in Steve's instructions provided him bearing, altitude and speed for his approach. Steve was careful to keep his ship where traffic control expected him to be. The industrial facility's loading docks were carved into the stone in the side of a mountain.

Inside the brightly lit loading dock were six numbered ship bays, three to a side. Two were occupied by freighters. Large wheeled robotic machines were moving freight into the ships over raised ramps through their open bay doors. Few people could be seen. When the travelers stepped out of the ship the reason why there weren't people outside was immediately apparent. Despite the bulwark of hewn mountain stone, the opening through which they had just flown allowed the Antarctic night air into the dock interior. It wasn't windy so much as it was unbelievably cold.

Steve, Pat and the two children weren't completely unprepared. They had been warned to dress warmly, but what they had thought was 'warmly' wasn't.

Someone wearing a thick hooded coat with face mask and thick gloves... man or woman Steve couldn't tell... waved them toward a well-lit door nearby. They needed no further prompting to move quickly from one nearly ineffectual infrared heat pole to the next on their way to the promise of warmth that the light from that heavy door suggested.

142

Beyond the insulated door was a warmer vestibule that opened into an echoing room with concrete walls and a wet floor. The ceiling and walls were white with sprayed insulation that also coated structural beams and electrical conduits. A round brass grate drained the floor beneath a wooden bench between two rows of tall lockers. The room's drafty warmth was a needed relief for the newcomers, still shivering from the bitter cold of the docks. They were shown to a set of lockers for their inadequate but still bulky outerwear. It was a brief introduction to the cold of Antarctica.

Through another door was a warmer room that didn't echo. To one side, through an open archway, workers could be seen around tables. They were eating informally. Faint aromas from the kitchen smelled delicious and inviting.

Then none other than Martin Avery himself entered through the dining hall doorway to welcome them. He was escorted by his attractive personal assistant. Martin introduced her as Amanda.

Avery first approached Pat with open arms for a welcoming hug. They had worked together before, and apparently had a friendly history. "I apologize for the cold reception out there." he said to Pat. He turned to explain to Steve "We had a system malfunction in the atmo barrier we normally use."

Pat received Martin's brief hug and reciprocated his kisses to both her cheeks. Steve felt unsure whether he would be expected to similarly brush cheeks with Martin. Pat turned to Steve and the kids to introduce them.

"Martin, may I introduce Lieutenant Steve Holbrook, ACM Alliance, from Perry Station. He's the man I was with when last we met in Central Park. Steve, this is Martin Avery, of Antarctic Continental. It was he who gave us the evidence against Paul Harden."

Avery's smile looked genuine and his handshake was firm. "Thank you, Steve, for literally everything." Martin looked Steve in the eye. "Your actions saved this company for me. It's been my life's work." He spread his arms wide to gesture toward the installation around them.

Martin turned and urged them toward the dining hall. "I realize saving my company wasn't why you did what you did, Steve," he continued, "but the consequences for me are real." He turned his torso to face Steve as they walked. "I'm glad to finally meet and thank you, face to face." Steve noticed his son looking up at him as they walked, and saw himself magnified in his son's eyes. He felt gratitude to the man for saying these things, but he knew he had only played a minor role in some great events.

Steve stopped at the entrance. "It wasn't just me, Mr. Avery, it..."

"Nonsense... and call me Marty." Avery interrupted. "Events shape what's possible, Steve. It's individuals who make events good or bad. Even armies are made of individual soldiers. I owe you a big one, and that's the fact."

Avery paused mid-stride to gaze at Steve for a moment, then he nodded and turned to the children. He crouched down to speak on the level with them. He moved and acted like he was thirty instead of maybe fifty or so. "I count your Daddy as a good friend. I think you'll have fun here, and," he glanced up at Steve then back to them, "you'll be safe. We have many young people your age living here, the sons and daughters of our workers. I'm sure you won't be lonely unless you want to be." He smiled.

His eyes were alive when he stood and looked again to Steve. He stood taller than he had seemed that cold wet day in Central Park. Avery had then been a wanted man, a fugitive on the run. "You must be tired from your long trip. Are you hungry at all?" He waited just a moment, and hearing no reply he turned toward the buffet.

The fragrance of the food was stronger here, and it was savory. "Well, I'm hungry!" he declared, and stepped through the door. The man possessed a powerful aura of presence.

Avery's employees were clearly not subsisting on 'Nibbles'. Here people that were dressed in spotless linens manually served piping hot food from heated serving trays. They happily served up real mashed potatoes with a beef gravy made from the juices of massive roasts. Perfectly roasted beef, seasoned with crushed cloves of garlic, sea salt, and fresh black pepper was generously offered. The next stations featured fresh navy beans seasoned with smoked ham; a dish of flaky white sea fish served with a rich pale sauce; pasta with meat sauce, and more. Steve couldn't resist a tender slab of the roast, slightly rare, and mashed potatoes under some garlic-savored gravy. He added a side of crisp green salad and spent time deciding which dressing to use.

Steve commented with a broad smile to one of the servers carving the roast "You just don't find this kind of food in space." and the man in the puffy white hat smiled his reply, keeping his eyes on his work after a friendly glance up into Steve's eyes.

The kids had no idea what anything was except the salad. Stevie chose the spaghetti with meat sauce because it looked funny.

Once they were seated Martin mischievously whispered to the boy that the pasta was worms, but Stevie didn't have any idea what a worm might be. To Martin's consternation he just nodded and ate it right up. Avery was disappointed that his tease fell so flat under the boy's indomitable innocence.

Pat and Kathlyn each had a helping of the baked cod under Hollandaise with a green salad. Steve noticed Pat had chosen a different dressing than he.

"Evening, Marty. New family?" asked a man in work clothes who sat down next to Pat.

"Evening, Billings. No, this is Steve Holbrook and his family, and Pat Williams, a private contractor out of New York City. I've worked with her before." Martin turned to Steve and Pat. "Steve, Pat, this is Mike Billings, one of our engineers and a friend. He's on the prototyping design team." He turned back to Mike Billings as he finished chewing and then swallowed his bite. "So how did our polarization solution work out?" He turned back to Pat and Steve and explained "Billings is working on a way to polarize the dome of the habitat prototype. We want it to emulate twilight but show a blue sky during the day."

Steve asked "Habitat prototype?"

Billings replied to his boss "The occlusion was still too abrupt, in my opinion, but it's closer to the ideal than it was, Marty."

Martin then nodded back to Steve. He continued to explain the project for his guests. "We're putting the final touches on what I think should eventually solve our overpopulation problem for the foreseeable future, if we can contract for a sufficient supply of modulinium.

"I want to build agricultural and industrial habitats in solar orbit. I've scheduled a tour of our facility for tomorrow. I'll show you where we're at in the project and we can talk about what we're planning to do. In fact, if you aren't ready to sleep after we eat, we can swing by my place and talk more about the plans. I'll show you some concept art, and we can check out a scale model of the most basic version."

He turned back to Mike Billings. "'Progress' is good, Mike. 'Perfect' takes longer. We need our people to be able to live there, long term, without going nuts. Every little bit we can build that helps them feel at home will be for the best."

Chapter 23: The Brandenburg

The frigate *Brandenburg* was approaching the Cygnus/Al Najid modulus. Three flights of four fighters and the detachment of Strikers boosted her escort to sixteen combat spacecraft. All of the frigate's stations were manned and her weapons were ready when a huge star ship of unknown design emerged though the modulus before them into Cygnus space. Smaller unknown star craft swarmed around it.

It wasn't immediately clear whether the alien was hostile, although it was assumed that it had caused the failure of trans modular communications. The subsequent failure of the comm relay at the Cygnus/Arcturus modulus was presumably related. Coincidence was considered unlikely.

Captain Elaine Hall of the *Brandenburg* confronted a quandary. Before an irrevocable act was committed by someone under her command, she needed more information. She diverted quickly from an obviously untenable collision course, and her escorts followed suit. She commanded her communications section to attempt contact protocols. This entailed a slight delay. A closer reading of once-hypothetical regulations was needed, and never-used first contact protocols had to be located for broadcast. On the upside, the aliens did not open fire. The ACM flotilla had changed course to get out of the way.

~

Aboard his great ship Sestrel wasn't interested in minor distractions. He thought it quite sensible of the animals to flee from his course. If he engaged in unnecessary combat it would be counterproductive, a diversion from his mission. He was focused on transiting the distance to the homeworld. Neither was he interested in stopping to chat with the animals along the way, just because they were bleating at him on comms.

His advance force had secured the next modulus and his whole focus was on reaching that way-point. Then his huntresses would secure the one beyond that. For a moment Sestrel considered taking a few of the animals, to begin to restock his ship's depleted supply of food. He decided to forego the pleasure of fresh meat for the present. Hunting might delay the more promising reward of taking the homeworld of these animals for his own. Even a minor diversion would delay him, possibly enough so that one of his brothers might steal the prized objective while he was entangled in a hunting expedition. He didn't know whether the others might be close.

He had been alarmed when his huntresses failed yet again to eliminate all their targets at the second modulus. Was it possible that he had underestimated the animals? After a moment's hesitation he decided it was unlikely. His huntresses had fallen out of practice during the long harvest of the animals from the former nesting planet.

~

The aliens failed to respond to any of Captain Hall's attempts to open communications. The aliens didn't respond to hails from Oberon either. Instead, the massive ship and its smaller escorts, apparently fighters, powered past without making any aggressive move beyond eliminating the modulus patrol and the communications relay to secure their way forward. The aliens were steady on course for the Arcturus modulus, and they were moving fast.

After the patrol of four human fighters and the pair of comm relays at the Oberon/Arcturus modulus were lost, ACM Command had no assets remaining in a position to get ahead of the main alien force in time to warn Arcturus or anyone beyond.

Command directed Captain Hall to make transit to Perry Station to check Al Najid's status as the next best course of action. It would be futile for the *Brandenburg*'s small flotilla to engage an alien warship nearly as massive as one of the orbital cities of Earth, a starship greater than any that humanity had ever built.

The lifepod of a survivor from the lost patrol at Arcturus modulus entered orbit around the planet Oberon. The pilot inside was wounded and unconscious. While a search and rescue shuttle departed the spaceport for recovery, the combat log was downloaded remotely. What the technician saw of it led him to flag down the watch officer for immediate review. That officer requested and received approval to re-transmit under an alert flag to the *Brandenburg*, which was nearing the Al Najid modulus.

The alert flag brought it immediately to Captain Hall's attention. It was a priority alert so she elected to scan it for content before she made transit, and the *Brandenburg* and her escorts slowed. The whole message was a two-dimensional digital video capturing events immediately prior to the recording fighter's last moments. Across the bottom were green readings showing normal systems powered and operational. In the field of view, at first, there was only a clear star field. Nothing showed on sensors. Then a milky white oval appeared which quickly shifted in translucence until its shields became transparent. It revealed a small, lean star ship of unknown manufacture. Then the ship seemed to radiate energy, almost like lightning toward the ship that recorded the log. The recording ship lost shields, shown when a green system status light turned red. Then a brilliant shaft of light erupted from the unidentified star ship and the recording ended, presumably because the survivor's pod deployed.

Captain Hall opened comms to her escorts to share and discuss the recording. She needed to prepare her pilots for an otherwise completely unknown threat. She was unhappy about the lack of more intel, but she had to share what she did have. The imagery caught by the combat log was all she had to give them, and it was important that they have something to go on before making transit.

The only thing she knew her people had in their favor was the training they achieved together. She had to rely on that training and on their teamwork. Training and teamwork will carry you through where nothing else can.

"I want you ready." she told her pilots. "I hate that we know next to nothing about what we are facing. But if you see a dull milky oval appear like that, where there was nothing before, don't be caught off guard. Watch for it. Don't be surprised. Don't hesitate or you'll give them the first shot.

"Going in, I want your forward shields strong.

"When we get farther in," she continued after a brief moment, "you'll need to balance your shields. But initially I expect them to be right in front of us, even if we can't detect them.

"We will not fire blindly in hope of hitting them. We cannot afford to waste our limited munitions or divert energy from our shields until we have any targets acquired. Stay alert, and cover each other. We don't know if there are hostiles there but let's not take chances. Call your targets by alpha as designated by the target acquisition system so we can focus our fire on any opportunity. Maintain comm discipline on the other side." Her pilots were silent. They knew all this by heart. "We're attempting to fit an unknown situation into standard procedure, but standard procedure is what we have to work with. Standard procedure and your teamwork will do wonders if we execute perfectly, as I know you can do." she finished, at a loss what to say further.

"Any Questions?" she asked

"Rally point, Captain?" someone asked without identifying themselves. She looked at her comm scanner. It had been Matthews.

"Right, Matthews. Good question. We are going in to check on Perry Station. If any of us has to pod, the Station's where we'll go, so if we get into a furball and things get out of control, or if anything else separates us, then we will rendezvous at Perry Station. Every one of you, be careful: I want to see you on the other side of this mess.

"*Brandenburg*, out."

The escorts went through first, followed by the *Brandenburg*. The first flight of four light fighters immediately turned away from one another at nearly right angles to cover all 360° in quadrant flanks and began balancing their shields. The second flight of medium fighters immediately angled away radially at 45°, and the third transit, composed of two flights, the four tactical strike craft and the four heavy fighters, pressed ahead far enough for the following frigate to make way. There was no sign of hostiles until four eggs of light appeared to one side, near one of the light fighters. The pale eggs clarified until one of them unloaded its shield into the fighter, beating down its shield. Then the unknown ship fired a searing beam of energy into the small ship. The pilot had just called his target "Bravo!" and fired both lasers and cannon.

Unfortunately, the pilot had targeted one of the hostiles that hadn't unloaded its shields. His shots were absorbed and his fighter shuddered askew under ferocious fire, scattering fragments of his armor before the power supply to the magnetic antimatter containment system lost power. When the magnetic bottle lost integrity antimatter touched a molecule and the light fighter evaporated in a spectacular explosion. The pod hadn't a chance to deploy. The pilot was lost.

The remaining escorts pivoted to acquire Alpha, the alien fighter that expended its shield to kill their teammate.

Alpha was attempting to evade fire while it accelerated away from their combined fire.

The three other hostiles did not discharge their shields. They engaged the humans with energy weapons more powerful than anything the ACM pilots had faced in a fighter-class vessel.

One clean shot nearly dropped the fully charged shields of a light fighter. A second hit dropped her shields completely and burned away photo-ablative enamel to penetrate the armor, leaving a hollow crater under an expanding hemisphere of vaporized metal. The human pilot rolled her fighter to present her most armored side to the enemy. She hit her antimatter annihilation drive, attempting to open up the range. She had to avoid fire until her shields could regenerate, so she focused on a pursuit of Alpha, the fleeing alien.

Cannon rounds fired from the human fighters were slowed to a stop by the alien shields, actually adding to the effective armor of their targets until the alien starship changed direction or speed. Rapid-fire pulse lasers used by the human light fighters were simply inadequate. They hardly affected the enemy shields. Heavier boats could power heavier weapons, and those were accordingly more effective, but even they lacked the punch the pilots needed.

The *Brandenburg* called "Bravo, targeting Bravo" and

151

launched six Badger II short range anti-ship missiles toward the farthest undamaged enemy fighter. The missile battery crew bested their record and was able to get a second half-dozen loaded before the first salvo struck.

When Bravo's shields slowed the first missiles, they were already inside the kinetic shield envelope. Each missile's artificial intelligence sensed the sudden deceleration and triggered the warhead.

Badger II warheads use a shaped charge to focus the energy of the detonation in the direction of travel. The directed explosion then propelled a fifty kilo payload forward.

The first six Badgers unloaded fifty kilograms of small nickel-iron spheres each, punched into a cone pattern by the explosion of the warhead's shaped charge. Armor integrity visibly withered on the impacted side. The armored hull seeming to melt and erode, even though the shields were still largely intact. The second salvo of Badgers performed similarly, penetrating the shield and unloading their shot into the armor. The enemy craft crumpled and went inert, lifeless. The hostiles did not appear to have lifepods.

Captain Hall ordered the activation of two torpedoes from the Brandenburg's forward tubes for target Alpha, the fleeing alien that killed her pilot but was caught with shields down. It seemed likely that the target's shields would have regenerated. The first torpedo should at least strip away its armor and the second should make the kill, but Elaine worried that the target might vanish into stealth and lose the torpedoes unless she launched immediately.

Torpedoes are relatively slow compared to short range missiles like the Badger II, but they are still faster than any ship design known and they have great endurance. Even at stand- off range they will catch up to their target and run it down, so long as they can maintain sensor contact.

Two torpedoes acquired Alpha as target and were launched from the forward tubes on Elaine's command.

The two remaining aliens, Charlie and Delta, were now engaged by ten fighters plus the secondary weapons of the Strikers. They were beyond effective range of the *Brandenburg*'s point defenses. Friendly combatants were too near to the aliens for the Strikers or the frigate to launch missiles. The aliens' powerful offensive weapons and stubborn shielding made it difficult even at those odds to predict how the battle would ultimately go.

Doggedly, the humans wore down the enemy shields and eroded their armor until finally Delta broke apart.

A communications band broadcast came from the alien designated Charlie. It sounded, to a few pilots who had immigrated from Earth, very much like the song of a lark.

An alert chimed from the ordnance officer's console. The torpedoes had lost contact with Alpha and were beginning a search pattern. Alpha had entered stealth. More worrisome, the pilot who had given chase was dangerously near them.

It was Matthews.

"Matthews! Get out of there!" she commed urgently to her pilot, but it was too late. A distant milky oval appeared behind her before unloading its shields into Matthews' fighter.

Both torpedoes re-acquired their target and homed in for the kill. Alpha inexplicably failed to fire its main armament.

Matthews was laying fire from every weapon she had into the alien ship. She didn't 'turtle up' to regenerate her shields. When the torpedoes detonated, one after the other, Matthews' fighter was within range of the twin blasts.

"Charlotte!" Elaine cried out in naked distress. She turned to her helmswoman. "Get us out there as fast as you can." she snapped. The captain turned to her second, eyes fierce, and ordered sharply "Ready a recovery team."

The captain stared at her display, seeking a sign of life. Matthews might have survived. Her ship had been caught by the explosions that ripped apart the alien craft. Her pod might have jammed. She might still live. She *must*. There was no signal from the fighter, and no life pod deployed.

Captain Elaine Hall tasted blood, and looked down at her hand. She had bitten through the skin on the side of her index finger.

Matthews was the pilot's married name. Her maiden name was Charlotte Hall, the captain's daughter.

"She is moving again, Captain." sensors reported.

Chapter 24: The Furies

The three Skraa remaining in Al Najid system braved the defensive fire of the station to destroy the communication and sensor arrays that Perry Station relied upon. Then, once they were moving out of the station's shield envelope they routed almost all power to their shields and disappeared. The fire from the station defenses had been fierce, but once the alien ships were concealed, the defensive batteries became useless against them.

The three then used short range communications to confer as their ships hung invisibly just off Perry Station's docks. They faced death from the male if they tried to rejoin the main force without accomplishing their assigned mission. Yet the prospects for mission success looked improbable. There were clearly more animals in that large spherical habitat than the three could hope to handle. Their reinforcements had been lost. Alternatives appeared scarce.

Despite the probability of failure, and despite the shared sentiment that their punishment had been unreasonably severe, the three reached a consensus that, since there was no way back, the way remaining was forward. None of the three Skraa had a store of food, so they could not remain concealed forever or head off into the unknown. One of them would bear eggs in the near future, and the other two were of bearing age. Assuming at least one of the hatchlings turned out to be male, and he could be kept alive long enough to use the cowl, the intimidating situation did bear at least a slight chance for success in the long term. They had to successfully board the station.

The cowl would imprint the minds of the hatchlings with the knowledge that would make them fully Skraa. They couldn't be imprinted until their nervous systems had sufficiently matured, and their bodies had grown to adolescence. The cowls would give the young the knowledge required to fabricate everything that would be needed to build a new ship, and it would bestow upon them the legacy that their ancestors had seized so long ago.

The prey within the station showed promise as nourishment, if only the huntresses could manage to board the station and stay alive.

The habitat of the animals was imposingly large. Three Skraa were too few to even consider a frontal assault.

But if they withdrew beyond the effective range of the defenses, they could make a cloaked run to the outer surface of the spherical station and set down. The curvature of the spherical hull should give them a spot, somewhere, that was out of direct line of fire. The Skraa studied the geometry of the station's weapon emplacements and identified where it should be safe enough to put down. Once on the station's surface, the ships should be safe from the fire of point defenses. Then, somehow, the huntresses would have to gain entrance without compromising the integrity of the atmosphere within.

They would need the animals alive if they wanted to have food for their hatchlings.

The three Skraa reduced power to their concealing shields in order to increase power to the engines. The diversion of power from shields revealed their ships, but they were beyond the effective range of the animals' crippled sensors.

In relative safety, the huntresses spun their ships to line up on the selected landing site on the station's hull. The hull was a sphere, so the closer they went to the surface before they revealed themselves, the fewer defensive emplacements could fire on them. The three ships accelerated to a modest speed toward the target and then coasted. They diverted all power save a trickle to the capacitors that stored energy for armament and other essential systems. The ships vanished as they coasted unseen, signals silent toward the station. Once they approached closely enough they would reduce shields and decelerate to set down. The intended site for contact was at a spot on the spherical surface farthest from the visible defensive emplacements. If they didn't reveal their ships until just before contact, their ships should be out of immediate danger.

As their ships slid closer, each huntress strapped a utility harness to her torso. She looped one end around her tail and adjusted it to be snug at her shoulders. The harnesses fastened comfortably across the broad pale scales of their chests. Each checked her portable power supply on the harness for her weapon. She checked the condition of the respirator on her pressure suit before putting it on, donning the helmet and sealing the neck. A cord connected her weapon to its power source near the bulky personal shield on her back. Then it was just a matter of waiting as their ships silently slipped unseen to the station, exactly on the intended course.

Chapter 25: Boarding

Kyle, against his doctor's recommendation and despite Lian's objections, resumed lawful command of station security after being welcomed back to duty by his de facto second Gabriella.

Before he was wounded, Gabriella had primarily worked dispatch and managed the clerical staff at the security office. While Kyle was recovering in the hospital and Steve was gone to Earth the big job had become her responsibility: she had performed admirably as acting chief of Perry Station security.

Kyle had ten officers on the force. The interplanetary command charged with the security of Al Najid space was operated by the ACM, aided by a detachment of Legion fighters based at Al Najid V. Kyle also had a small cutter patrolling the fragments of Perry and supervising mining activities in the asteroid belt. When the external communications array and main sensors had been destroyed, the docks, shipyard and the naval engineering section had been evacuated. The docks were thought to be the weakest point in the station's defenses.

Beneath the envelope of Perry Station's primary shields, the open docking area was unprotected from space except for a weak atmosphere retention shield, which was easily penetrated by ships wanting to dock. If a hostile force intended to board, that was the most likely place it would happen.

At the same time, Kyle didn't want to deploy his people out on the dock because it was too open and vulnerable. If a hostile spacecraft fired on the inner bulkhead, it might disrupt power to the atmospheric retention field and expose the whole dock to the vacuum and cold of space.

So Kyle deployed his officers to defend the doors that gave access to the inner station from the dock. If atmospheric pressure in the loading dock was lost, those doors would seal against vacuum almost instantly. If the station was boarded, that was where he expected to confront whatever threat appeared.

Coming back through the corridor were dock workers and a few people that Chief Mackenzie had driven from the engineering section. One of Kyle's security officers loudly repeated instructions to seek shelter in the core area of the station.

Kyle made a mental note to have his people check to ensure the chief engineer also made his way safely down toward the core of the station.

Once his officers were positioned to defend from cover they could only wait, watching the monitors expectantly. The monitors showed only the deserted docking area.

"Kyle," Gabriella reported over her comm, "we have a breach in section seven, external hatch 24. That's a maintenance hatchway to the outer hull. Section seven is the new residential block. No... verifying... Update: they just activated an airlock in the water supply maintenance station."

"It wasn't maintenance?"

"Maintenance sent us the alert, Kyle. They had a water pressure drop there at the same time. I'd say it wasn't their doing."

So the aliens hadn't tried a frontal assault. Kyle didn't feel surprised. Nothing is ever easy. "Thank you, Gabriella." he replied. "Jon," Kyle said to one of his two sergeants, "take your group and secure the entrances to section seven, but don't go in until we can get more of us there to provide you with support." There were two corridors that accessed section seven. Jon would have to divide his unit until he could be reinforced.

"Gabriella," he commed, "have our reserves head down there to reinforce Jon. You stay there at comms to coordinate. I'll leave a couple of officers here to secure the civilians and head over there myself with the rest of our people."

~

When the Skraa in their ships reappeared to stop just short of the surface and set down on the station, the huntresses saw no immediate point of entry into the station's interior. They could either seek an airlock elsewhere, or they could force entry directly through the lightly armored bulkhead.

The problem with seeking an airlock was that it would have to be done crawling across the surface. To move the ships at all would bring them into the arc-of-fire of one of the several auto-mated weapon emplacements defending the station.

The problem with forcing entry was that any breach they made would decompress the section of the station they entered. The animals' habitat would surely reseal farther bulkheads in-side, and that meant the huntresses would still be sealed out, even if they were inside the bulkhead.

Only full entry would be acceptable, and that meant they had to locate an airlock. The huntresses set their ships down on the station's exterior and disembarked onto the airless surface of the station. They intended to begin searching in a spiral outward, gradually expanding the area examined.

Once outside on the station's starkly lit surface, they signaled their ships with a command to engage shields to maximum. This would conceal the ships from sensor detection, even at visual range. Then they moved together in their pressure suits to seek an airlock.

There was only micro-gravity to influence their movement out-side the hull of the station, as large as it was. The artificial gravity generated in the decks deeper in the station was of limited range, and would hardly affect them on the outer surface.

Gravitic coil assemblies intended for use in multilevel archi-tectures are paired with a discrete modulinium disk which will counter the gravity conducted by the coil above it, feeding the ef-fective force's gravitons back into their home dimension. This renders gravitic coil assemblies mono-directional. Humans con-struct space-borne habitations to have the equivalent of Earth gravity at the floor, but the influence of artificial gravity is reduced markedly at the standard height of a ceiling. This practice came to be called 'light-headed' architecture. It was popular with maintenance, because it made the crawlspaces between decks nearly weightless and reduced the energy expense of plumbing.

To move quickly, the Skraa did not tether themselves to the station, but instead tethered to one another. They moved prone, grasping handholds and propelling themselves along to the next handhold they could find, gliding carefully along the surface of the station. They tried to always remain within arm's reach of the surface. They maneuvered across and around the various obstacles and protrusions. There weren't many real handholds, but there were many superficial surfaces to use.

When one of them slipped, the other two grabbed hold of whatever they could and used the tether to pull the incautious member back to the surface, where they started moving again. It took constant attention and focus to avoid drifting away from the sphere. The exertion was exhausting.

They finally found a round maintenance hatch, but it was locked. There were no lights, switches or other electronic or mechanical tell-tales they expected to find at the entrance to a pressurized chamber. Most likely it would open to an unpressurized passage, which in turn should lead to an airlock.

A huntress unlimbered her weapon, a long rod with an unadorned handle and a polished disk of crystal on the other end. She extended the crystal end beyond the perimeter of her personal shield and a small raised light turned from yellow to orange, indicating that the crystal was beyond the shield and safe to fire. She fired a focused beam at the locked latch. After a few tense moments when it appeared the hatch might fuse shut rather than melt away, the lock melted away. Inadvertently she also penetrated a thin section of the adjacent bulkhead, exposing and rupturing a pressurized water duct.

The leak was detected as a drop in pressure and was noted immediately by maintenance technicians. Pressure valves regulating and routing the flow of water automatically shut down the leak, and transmitted an alert code to both maintenance and security.

For the Skraa, the experience was more startling. The exposure of liquid water to the frigid vacuum of space caused it to immediately vaporize. The vapor froze into a fog of ice crystals. That burst of ice crystals expanded from the leak explosively, and pushed the nearest huntress from the bulkhead and into space, coating her in frost. The tethers to the other Skraa snapped taut, but the two huntresses grimly held onto their handholds and kept their ice coated sister from drifting off into space.

Soon, all three were through the hatch. There was an airlock in the shaft beyond.

Chapter 26: Avery's Solution

Martin Avery's residence at his company's facility in Antarctica was tasteful but, considering his wealth, almost utilitarian in design and decor.

Martin was a bachelor and an engineer. His unobtrusive staff kept everything immaculate. Amanda, Avery's personal assistant, reported that the visitors' luggage had been put in their quarters for them, and asked if there would be anything more for her that evening. Martin replied that she had the evening off, and thanked her.

The children were ready to watch a new, well-received Hollywood holo in a comfortable adjoining room that was furnished with large, deeply cushioned chairs. Avery inserted the data cube and initiated play. As they watched the opening scene they ate something new to them that Martin called 'popcorn'.

The main room was paneled in dark natural wood, dominated by a draped picture window that looked out onto the mountain. Steve drew close to the window and sheltered his view from the reflected lights of the room, cupping his hands around his eyes close to the plasticlear pane to see the cold world beyond. Antarctica was dark, out beyond the bright lights shining from the facility, but the sky showed a hint of pale rose near the horizon. The stars overhead were brilliant. Faint green curtains of an aurora danced beneath the stars. The window was made from three panes of gas-insulated plexiclear, according to a tiny decal stuck to a corner of the window.

The room was carpeted in rich green. There were leather-bound paper books on shelves lining two walls. Steve had the impression from his earlier visit to Earth that paper books were forbidden. He didn't recognize the titles or authors, but the books looked very old.

Martin indicated that they should sit where they liked and moved to a cabinet stocked with cut crystal decanters. "May I offer you some refreshment? I think I have a little something here you might like, Steve."

Steve was immediately interested. He was a Gleneagles man,

but whatever whiskey Avery might have at hand was undoubtedly a cut above that. "A whiskey?" he ventured.

Martin nodded with a small smile as he looked down and bus-
ied himself. "If I recall, Pat, you are a devotee of wines. Do I remember rightly? I have a European Chablis chilled."

The thought appealed to her. "When I can afford it, yes. Your
memory is undiminished, Marty. Thank you." she replied. The
compliment pleased Avery.

A small couch was upholstered in rich fabric, matched at the
flanks by comfortable, well-made chairs. The three matching
pieces enveloped on three sides the centerpiece of the tableau.
In a display case of dark polished wood, behind leaded crystal
panes and lit brightly by lights overhead, was a meticulously detailed scale model. The case had to be as old as the books.
Within it was a model of the design Martin had in mind. It was a
plexiclear sphere. Within the sphere was a disk of what appeared to be cropland. What looked like low buildings of different
sizes were strewn irregularly along two diametric axes, like a
crossroad.

"It will rotate on its axis once in twenty-four hours, giving resi-
dents a day and night cycle that correlate with the natural human
circadian cycle. It was the disruption of their circadian sleep cycle that led to the rebellion at Aldebaran III." Avery pronounced.

Steve winced to think what Tibs might say to that. "I think the
Aldebari have a different recollection." he pointed out.

"Oh, quite different I am sure. Confronted with a characteristic
of natural evolution in themselves, just like every other cult,
they've manufactured an ideological cause to remember as their
motivation."

Steve's countenance hardened visibly. Again Pat interceded
to avert a political confrontation. It would not serve the negotiations for these men to argue politics.

"Martin, your vision is much larger than I imagined. I was
thinking each habitat would house a single family." she observed.

"We will probably also offer single family versions eventually, but making them community-scale is more practical in several important ways. Paramount among those is how rapidly we can move populations off earth and into food production. More far reaching, it is for the sake of children" he added, looking at Steve. "Children must mature socially as well as physically if they are to survive in community as adults. They have to be able to gain their social skills first-hand, rather than virtually. If the other kids can only be reached across a vacuum, opportunities for socialization will be limited.

"Second, if family units are isolated they will less easily form communities. Together they will develop mutual awareness of practical interdependence. The inhabitants will need a real sense of social and political responsibility." Martin responded.

"Political responsibility? You mean you want them to adopt democracy? I was under the impression that Corporates believe that democracy is an error." Steve questioned.

"'Corporates' are individuals too, Steve. We frequently have opinions that differ. Stop me if I'm wrong, but I think the official corporate argument you're talking about holds that since half the population is necessarily of less than average intelligence, democracy entrusts big decisions to those least prepared to make them. And in the classical age, to some measure anyway, that was partly proven true. People were persuaded to give up the responsibility for their votes. The problem with doing otherwise, though, is more long term." Martin leveled his gaze at Steve.

Pat edged forward, intrigued. "How otherwise?" she asked.

"Consider the alternatives." Avery led.

Martin finished his conjurations at the bar and brought a heavy crystal glass bearing three fingers neat of his favorite whiskey to Steve. In his other hand he bore a delicate crystal tulip of Chablis to Pat.

"Thank you" each said. Pat swirled her wine and gently inhaled its aroma. Martin watched as she nodded her appreciation, then went back for his own drink, identical to Steve's.

"Ein prosit der Gemutlichkeit!" he gave toast, and the three glasses were raised. 'A salute to fellowship!', in German.

"Prosit' responded Steve, while Pat raised her glass and sipped through her smile. The Chablis was cool, and offered promise with scents reminiscent of fruit and fragrant wood.

Steve's whiskey was smoky but clean like Gleneagles, and held a ghost of peat. "Oh my, but that is tasty." he remarked, swirling his glass. Martin smiled benignly. "A single malt" he ventured. "What is it, Martin?"

"Cooney. Irish. Single malt."

As Steve looked quizzically at his glass, Avery looked down at his carpet and began to pace. "You know, Steve, revelation of Harden's excesses at Perry triggered more consequences than you probably realize. His so-called 'solution', as well as the means he used trying to obtain your modulinite was a product of isolated thinking. The same kind of thinking that results when decision-makers, however bright, are socially isolated from the less educated, less powerful people they govern.

"Had Harden's ideas been discussed more openly, then together we would surely have reached a different conclusion. There is no way his plan could have done what it must. He apparently had no realistic sense of how many people he would have to move, how many ships he would have to build and supply, or how long it would take.

"He had nowhere to send them anyway. Just because you pick an anomaly and have enough modulinium to build a modulus doesn't mean there would be a habitable planet on the other side. And even if he *could* build enough ships to move that many people, he wouldn't have enough food to stock those ships while also feeding the rest of the people who stay on Earth. He was going to build a disaster. Harden was clearly not an engineer. I cannot imagine how he came up with the tech he patented. The 'solution' he was pursuing, and the means he used to try and accomplish his mission tell me he simply wasn't thoughtful enough to develop the technology with which he is credited." Martin looked at Pat thoughtfully and sipped his whiskey.

"So," he continued after clearing his throat, "when the Corporate Board recognized that they had been complicit to Harden's crimes, they began to rethink a few of their cognitive biases and to question the romanticism of Harden's vision. And I think that willingness to rethink speaks well for them.

"We would have more time if the Aldebari and Legion would agree to our colonizing Aldebaran again. The Aldebari resist planetary colonization. Each of their planets would buy us another ten years, easily. The Legion doesn't want us to solidify our control over that strategic star system. We could relocate settlers there while we build a lasting solution. And the Corporate Board didn't press the issue I think because they don't want to lose control of so many people as they would by settling those planets, just like they lost control of your ACM alliance.

"I've presented, and by the way had approved, a less romantic, more flexible system but it will require limited self- governance for the settlers of our solar orbit residence system. It is roughly based upon the principles of a Republic. The winning argument I made was that the people in these habitats will be much too widely dispersed for an overly centralized government to manage, whether Corporate or otherwise. Centralization just isn't feasible in the long term for such a widely distributed solution. Our communications technology notwithstanding, the logistics dictate the outcome.

"We have all these people, but they are wasted, other than professionals like Pat here, and sole-proprietorships and small businesses like our less well-paid service industries. Earth needs to grow a new class of people to buffer and moderate between the elites and the unemployed. Working people, small businesses with an active interest in arriving at the best economic outcomes with the means to earn their way to active prosperity. To do that, they should have a say in politics. We need a political and economic buffer between the increasingly isolated elites, along with those who work for them like myself and my crew, and the unemployed masses who are spending their lives in virtual reality.

"How the new class carries out the general directives of the elite will vary. Otherwise, the Corporate Board will try to dictate how each runs their business. They would do okay at first, but they will not do well trying to micro manage as many entities as we end up with. We would inevitably face troubles like we saw at the end of the Classical age, when the people rebelled against all the governments that had run out of good options.

"Centralized governance works here on the surface only because almost everything, including agribusiness, is automated and our communications are so good. That overly centralized control will not, I predict, work well for a distributed population that will ultimately form a sphere with a circumference the equivalent of the Earth's solar orbit.

"As for your point, that *representative* democracy means rule by the least fit, I disagree. We must take into account the fact that representatives will tend to have above-average intelligence. It takes intelligence to achieve and maintain such a position."

"Faulting democracy isn't my position at all." Steve objected. "If my recollection of history is right, the *representative* political design failed toward the end of the classical age because those who vie for power tended to value the control of that power more than whatever good they could do with it. It became less about what they could do and more about who they were. But isn't this 'solar republic' you intend risky?" Steve asked.

"Probably riskier than engineering the habitats, frankly." Martin admitted. "And that," he pointed toward the model, "is a difficult feat."

"Why build a scale model, Martin? Er, Marty?" asked Pat, trying to divert the conversation back to the matter at hand.

"If you're more comfortable calling me by my formal name that's fine, Pat.' Avery responded. He looked distantly toward the carpet at his feet and raised his eyebrows as he reflected on her question. Almost since the advent of holographic displays it had been considered wasteful to actually build a physical model to scale.

"I guess I get something of value out of touching my work, Pat. That's the 'why' of it, I think." he said, looking fondly at his model. He turned back to Pat. "More than once I've thought of a solution while physically holding or exploring a model by touch." He turned back to his model, waving a meaty hand. "Holography is fine, as far as it goes. It's superb for putting you virtually within an image, but there is something about simply touching a thing that just seems to work better for me."

The soft tone of a chime pulsed quietly from the direction of the wet bar. "Excuse me a moment: That signal tells me that someone thinks something is too important for me to miss." Martin rose from his chair next to Pat on the couch with Steve and strode to the bar to read his priority message. He had a communications station there, and he was frowning at it. After a moment he returned to share his news with them. "We've now lost contact with Arcturus." he explained, resuming his seat and retrieving his glass from a small side table.

Whatever the cause, it was coming closer.

Chapter 27: Section Seven

Jon Morgan sent two of his officers around to the farther end of the corridor that led to section seven. He positioned the other two officers nearby his own position where they would have a corner for cover. Then Jon approached cautiously but alone, stepping quietly to the small hallway that led to the airlock's pressure door.

Someone had entered the station through section seven's external utility hatch, and then used the airlock. This all happened shortly after the Station lost long range comms and sensors to weapons fire, so a connection was assumed.

At the corner of the hall Jon turned to look back toward his men. At that moment one of the Skraa stepped from the hallway and struck him in the lower back with the handle end of her weapon. As he crumpled in pain she fell back to get some range before firing her weapon into him.

The blow staggered Jon with pain from his kidney, but he turned quickly to bring his sidearm to bear. It was a rapid-fire, short range fletchette pistol.

Jon's mind registered surprise when he saw, not the human he expected to see, but a feathery humanoid with a lizard's face on a long neck. It wore a flexible harness fitted with some kind of pack on its back. Behind it whipped a long tail that compensated for her quick movements. Her eyes glittered as cold as space. The lizard adroitly reversed and extended what Jon took to be a weapon toward him. He squeezed his trigger and his sidearm ripped off at least ten fletchettes at her, nearly point blank. The short range, high-velocity/low mass razors should have ripped the creature to bloody shreds. Had he extended his arm further his weapon would have been inside her shield envelope, and his fletchettes would have torn her apart.

The fletchettes were slowed and deflected by her shield, but Jon caught the full effect of her shot directly into his chest and he dropped onto his back, dead.

When Jon went down his officers at both ends of the hallway

opened fire on the lizard with their pulse rifles. Her portable energy shield easily handled the laser fire. Then the other two Skraa stepped out into the hallway and together they cut the four remaining humans down.

The Skraa didn't have time to take any provisions. They had to secure a concealed and defensible position to set up a base of operations. They retrieved their pressure suits from the airlock and hurriedly packed them tightly into their elongated helmets. One decided a direction, and they moved cautiously but quickly deeper into the station.

~

Kyle was not prepared for what he found in the corridor leading to section seven. Five of his people lay dead in their own blood. He motioned the officers with him to take cover and then moved ahead cautiously, checking the fallen with fading hope as he went. One of his new officers went back around the corner, trying to be quiet, but he was sick.

There was no sign of whoever killed them. He found a scattering of fletchettes near Jon's body, some stuck point-first in walls and others stuck in both floor and ceiling. A few were lying flat on the floor in the middle of the corridor. Jon was good with a fletchette pistol. He had qualified with it specifically, and the metrics on the interactive range were challenging. He was unlikely to have missed his target so badly.

Kyle hung his head in self-doubt. Jon had family. The others... he barely even knew them. They were new, fresh immigrants from Earth's law enforcement community.

He queried the empty air: "If not us, then who?"

Kyle yearned to talk with his old wing mate, but Steve wasn't there. Steve would have known the way forward, but Steve was on Earth. It was up to Kyle now, to keep the people safe. He had a notion of how Steve must have felt when their world died under them, and everything was destroyed that they were trying to protect.

Kyle had been the deputy, the wing-man, always following

Steve's lead, keeping him safe. He cared, sure, but Steve had borne it all on his shoulders. Now Kyle shouldered the duty, and it was heavy.

Kyle commed Gabriella to send their *new* new forensics specialist for a deep analysis. He had an inkling that Jon hadn't missed his target at all. Instead, his fletchettes had been deflected by a personal shield. That would account for the even pattern of deflection, and especially for the darts lying flat on the floor. Fire a burst of those deadly little razor blades and they stick into everything. These few had to have struck the shield dead-on, but they were stopped by something that didn't bend or distort them. Something like a permeable anti- kinetic shield envelope.

It wasn't the first time Kyle wished the Council had been more generous with the budget. His people should have shields too.

"So, Steve. What do I do *now*?" he asked the air in front of him. He had at least one unknown hostile, probably multiple, wearing personal shields and armed with some kind of powerful energy weapon. The perpetrator was loose on his station. *Two* hostiles, counting the assassin who tried to kill Steve but still hadn't been found.

Maybe the assassin somehow managed to leave the station. Kyle thought about it and shook his head. With the measures Gabriella set in place Kyle believed it was more likely that the assassin was still on the Station somewhere.

Kyle motioned his officers to come forward with a wave and pointed silently toward the corner of the short hallway to the airlock as he started forward. Whoever killed his people might have left a clue inside but he wanted his people safe. He didn't believe he would find anyone or anything in there, but it wasn't something to skip. And if the intruder entered through an airlock there had to be a ship outside.

Chapter 28: Dante System

When communications from Arcturus system ceased, the Corporate Board of Earth finally began to stir itself. The sequence of losing contact with Al Najid, then Cygnus, and now Arcturus suggested that something was very wrong, and whatever it was, it approached too quickly to ignore.

The Corporate Board wasn't yet alarmed enough to call up the reserves, or to dispatch crews, or to ready the greater part of the fleet. Naval ships are expensive to build and more expensive to actively operate.

The bulk of the Corporate fleet had been left dispersed, moored in out of the way regions of Earth-controlled space when it became evident that neither the Legion nor the Aldebari were particularly interested in attacking Earth.

The Corporate Board was alarmed enough to order a small naval squadron to investigate Arcturus and report back. Elements of Second Fleet assembled around the heavy cruiser *Ivanhoe*, freshly arrived in Aldebaran system alongside the battleship *Trafalgar*. The new squadron was designated a task force.

The greater concern was that intersystem shipping had been disrupted by whatever was severing the transmodular communications relays. More than a quarter of Earth's food was imported from the frontier. As those systems went silent, the flow of their goods was disrupted. Earth did have modest stockpiles, but eighteen billion people use a tremendous amount of food. Stockpiles would be depleted in short order if this situation continued.

Dante System has two moduli, one to Arcturus and one to the Aldebaran System. The Aldebaran system was the threshold of the rest of human space, including the systems controlled by the Aldebari and those held by the Legion.

The habitable planet in Dante system was Paradiso, the largest city of which boasted the same name. It was anything but paradise. Paradiso was heavily populated by the officially unemployed, many of whom constantly sought 'alternative' means of income. Nominally ruled by the Corporate Board of Earth, it in fact was run by underworld strongmen.

To be sure, Paradiso engaged in legitimate commerce, including light manufacturing. But culturally, the city of Paradiso was synonymous with criminality. It was where pirates went to sell their takings.

Shaky, nebulous deals had been made over the years between the criminal empires of Paradiso and the ruling interests of corporate Earth.

Aldebaran, the system neighboring Dante on the way to Earth, was a strategic point of control. The planetary systems controlled by the Aldebari and those controlled by the Legion connected there, through two of Aldebaran's wealth of five moduli. Earth maintained a quarter of its fleet there to assure control, even though the system was claimed by the Aldebari.

The habitable planet in the Aldebaran system had once been subjected to intensive kinetic bombardment. At the time it was populated by the people now known as the Aldebari. They were a scientific community of settlers from Earth attempting to improve the ability of humanity to efficiently live on other worlds. When control of Earth's government was engineered by a consortium of the dominant corporations, part of their plan was to defund the 'wasteful' scientific settlement. The scientists began to resist. With regret they judged that too many significant policy decisions by the Corporate Board were contrary to the interests and objectives of humanity.

The mission at Aldebaran was, at the time, intended to solve the problem of overpopulation by improving humanity's ability to realistically settle in artificial habitats constructed in space, as well as on other worlds.

Not only did the Corporate Board decide that the mission of the scientists on Aldebaran III was wasteful, but they also outlawed printed texts, even textbooks and references, and even in museums.

What was imprinted on paper couldn't be easily changed, whereas digital text can be altered world-wide wherever electronic texts connect to the HoloNet. The Corporate Board began to purposefully change the definitions of key words, gradually altering entire languages to better suit corporate interests. They rewrote formerly standard representations of history. Digital alteration of the meanings of words and, in some cases, the words themselves that classical authors had originally written changed the meaning of their writings. All books in digital format changed, at first slightly, and then more radically.

The Aldebaran enclave noticed all of this early. They rebelled in protest, and began to openly warn anyone they could reach about what was going on. Sadly, though few on Earth believed it was happening, the Corporations would not tolerate such discontent.

The Corporates contracted with a large mercenary company, now known as the Legion, to either bring the scientists back to Earth or remove them as a problem. To the mercenaries, elimination appeared simpler, cheaper and more efficient than capture and transport.

The Corporate Board provided the mercenaries with most of the military starships they had in order to get the job done. The scientists on Aldebaran convinced a small naval squadron and several transport captains that were stationed there to join in with the Aldebari insurrection. The Legion didn't bother to engage the Aldebaran squadron directly, but instead moved asteroids out of natural orbit and used them to bombard the settlement on Aldebaran.

Before it was over the Aldebari on the planet were nearly exterminated. Grieving, the surviving scientists were forced to conclude that building homes at the bottom of a planetary gravity well is indefensible. An enemy can easily move asteroids to make them fall planetside.

The survivors resolved to live in deep space, leaving planet-based lifestyles behind them, and became known as the Aldebar. The systems they came to control each had a habitable planet, but the Aldebari only studied and visited those planets. They would not permit anyone to settle on their systems' planets.

The Legion believed they had fulfilled the letter of their contract, and they expected fulfillment of the terms. Earth rejected the demand, saying the job wasn't finished. The Legion rebelled and declared itself independent. They seized three planetary systems to establish their state, defended by a navy larger than Earth could then field. The Corporates launched an intensive ship building program to defend Earth.

Now, in the Aldebaran system, seven ships were detached from the Corporate Second Fleet to form a distinct squadron. The heavy cruiser *Ivanhoe* carried the flag of the task force. She was accompanied by two destroyers, the *Jordan Graham* and *Donnybrook*. These destroyers were primarily torpedo platforms, but their point defenses were considered formidable. Two missile frigates, the *San Antonio* and the *Galway* carried fast intermediate range missiles, and were well-endowed with point defenses. The remaining two, the *Braunschweig* and the *Barroso* were corvettes.

Corvettes are considered 'boats' by some civilian critics, rather than ships. Corvettes form an essential and integral element of modern navies. They have maneuverability and the appropriate weaponry to effectively engage interplanetary fighter craft that could otherwise enter a ship's shield envelope and overwhelm the point defenses of a capital ship. These workhorses bridge the gap in displacement between frigates and fighters.

The flag officer aboard the heavy cruiser was Admiral Deepraj Singh. Captain of the *Ivanhoe* was Bernard 'Bernie' Tucker. Captain Tucker ordered deployment of his fighter cover, and the first flight of four light fighters launched from the bay in the side of the *Ivanhoe*. The second flight of the ship's compliment, four medium fighters, were moved into position automatically in the hanger and their technical crews prepared them for launch.

This small task force approached the Dante-Aldebaran modulus. Their mission was to investigate Dante system and return to report.

Moduli are large, but in space there is no room for error. Commanders of naval and civilian vessels larger than a fighter prefer to traverse moduli single-file. The *Barroso* took point. *Braun-*

schweig was close behind, with the foreknowledge that if *Barroso* came under fire on the far side and needed to maneuver she would break to starboard, to the right. This assurance allowed *Braunschweig* to move through without fear of collision, so long as she did not also swerve to starboard. The frigates and destroyers queued for the transit next, with the *Ivanhoe* set to transit last.

Without active comm relays, unless a ship returned from the far side there would be no communications through the modulus. Each ship would have to enter Dante system blind, uninformed of what the transit of the modulus would reveal in the Dante planetary system.

The *Barroso* raised shields. Upon entering Dante system her sensors immediately sounded collision warnings and she veered to starboard and started taking fire. *Barroso's* intelligence officer reported to the command deck that none of the fighters contesting their passage could be identified.

There was no indication of surprise. As if they had been awaiting the *Barroso*, eight unidentified fighter craft immediately targeted her and fired. They fired coherent beams of energy more powerful than would be expected from any known fighter spacecraft. The strength of the alien weaponry was the equivalent of the main armament of a much heavier ship, and together their fire was more powerful than the corvette's shields could fully absorb. Torrents of energy seared through her shields intermittently and cratered her armor in heavy strikes.

Molten metal spattered glowing from each hit in expanding hemispheres. The angry orange and red glow of molten metal faded as it spattered and radiated, cooled by the utter cold of interplanetary space.

Well beyond the skirmish an immense capital ship of unknown type approached rapidly within a cloud of more of the fighters. Sensors showed it approached the modulus rapidly.

The *Braunschweig* came through and recognized her peril. She veered to port and began to fire on the eight fighters, attempting to coordinate with the already heavily damaged *Barroso*. At first *Braunschweig* was clear of hostile fire, but as the cloud of fighters that had been surrounding the capital ship came within range she, too, began struggling to maintain shield integrity under an intense and growing barrage of coherent energy.

Barroso's return fire came from thirty pulse lasers firing staccato. Each pulse laser seemed weak compared to the power of the alien weapons, but there were thirty of them. The shields of the alien fighters were stronger than the humans had anticipated. After focused effort, one of the alien's shields was overcome and the fighter broke apart. The gunners of the *Barroso* remained grim.

The *Galway* and then the *San Antonio* started their transits as soon as *Braunschweig's* fantail slipped through the placid blue surface of the modulus' aperture and vanished. These missile frigates, on entry, saw seven hostile fighters focused on the battered *Barroso*. The approaching swarm of the main force was beginning to engage *Braunschweig* and would soon further envelop *Barroso*. Both captains recognized that the *Barroso's* defenses were overwhelmed, even though her armament and defenses were designed exactly for the fight she was in. *Braunschweig* would most likely fare no better.

The missile frigates *Galway* and *San Antonio's* point defenses opened fire to assist the corvettes against the nearest fighters while their Badger and Scimitar missiles acquired, locked, and launched toward individual fighters in the swarm that advanced ahead of the hostile capital ship.

The two destroyers of the task group were next in queue. *Donnybrook* entered Dante system first, followed by the *Jordan Graham*. Upon arrival *Donnybrook* saw the predicament and immediately ascended relative to the galactic plane, and began rolling.

To be sure, the destroyer could have fired both port and starboard at the same time without rolling. Torpedoes fired away would just as surely have reached the intended target... eventually. However, it would take those torpedoes more time to reach the target by such a roundabout route than it would take to simply spin the ship and alternate batteries as they came to bear.

While the opposing fighters were engaged with the corvettes and frigates, *Donnybrook* needed to get her torpedoes on target and disable or maybe, with a hefty dose of luck, take the capital ship out of play altogether.

Long-range sensors readily acquired the enemy capital ship, and *Donnybrook* launched four torpedoes from her port tubes. Rolling, she brought her starboard tubes to bear as her port side crew reloaded. Her ballistic defenses hammered rounds of nickel-iron slugs at the outermost fighters swarming the corvettes despite the potential for friendly fire damage. *Donnybrook's* coherent energy point defenses would be ineffective at that range.

Jordan Graham cleared the modulus, saw the battle and began to roll as well, launching as she acquired her target and descended. The *Graham's* torpedoes gained target lock and arced gracefully toward the alien capital ship.

The heavy cruiser, *Ivanhoe*, with her deployed fighters entered Dante system last. As the engines at her fantail cleared the modulus her second flight of fighters launched.

Chapter 29: Animal

Paul Harden opened his eyes. The light was dim. The bird-lizard that always seemed to be around was thankfully somewhere else.

The air temperature was neutral. The atmosphere was wetly humid and smelled of metal. The muscles of his back and legs were stiff, but they no longer paralyzed him with pain. He rolled to his side and stood. He noticed he had lost quite a bit of body fat.

He had been laying on the deck, an expanse of wet metal grating made of something like black steel. It was the flooring of what he assumed was a livestock pen, where he and those other creatures had been held. The others weren't there any longer. He and the other creatures, whatever they were, had been penned like livestock by his captors, like animals kept for food. The others were gone. He had to escape.

Escape is a tall order for a captive aboard a hostile ship in space.

First he had to get out of the livestock pen. Doing that looked like it would be a serious challenge. At least, for now, he seemed to be unobserved.

The only exit visible in the twilight was a vertical tube made of something like plexiclear with a lift mechanism he didn't quite understand, but possibly it used modulinium coils to manipulate gravity. Where that tube might lead was a question, except he knew it was part of the route his body had taken from that first room, the one that was like a medical laboratory. The room where his memories were ripped from him, using that metallic cowl. It had been a mental form of rape. His rage overcame his fear, and gave him energy, but he had no time to relish his anger.

There wasn't a doorway or any openings in the walls that he could see in the poorly lit darkness. He would have to check more closely, maybe by touching the smooth walls. There had to be another way in and out other than that elevator tube. The door must be machined to close tolerances, making it invisible from a distance.

He took stock of his physical condition as he stepped toward the wall. His muscles were stiff, but otherwise he felt more fit than he had since his youth. Apparently whatever it was they had fed him was good nutrition. That still didn't account for his improved muscle tone, but he inferred that the device that had controlled his body so completely had somehow also exercised it, probably in ways he would never have voluntarily endured. During his captivity his body had shed fat. Perhaps there had been electronic stimulation of his muscles by the cowl. Whatever, it had improved his physical condition... perhaps it had been a measure intended to increase the amount and quality of meat he carried. Harden shuddered involuntarily at the thought.

He had to escape the pen. He was the last person in the room. All the other humanoids he had glimpsed were gone. Wherever they had gone, he would probably be next.

Harden felt growing despair that threatened to overwhelm him. He had no idea how he would escape the alien ship altogether, other than by dying. He caught himself, determined to take things one step at a time. He would drown in hopelessness if he thought too much about his predicament. It helped when he remembered how hopeless his situation was when the Aldebari took his ship, yet he escaped that situation against the odds. Maybe something would turn up if he just kept going.

He peered up to the ceiling, to where the nearest feeding tube dangled. There was an opening there through which his body might fit. The tubing was flexible, and it seemed fairly tough. Harden gave it a tentative tug. It might bear his weight. But if he tried to climb it, the tube might be torn from whatever held it. That would leave him still trapped in the pen with clear evidence that he was awake and mobile. If he couldn't escape by climbing the tube and they discovered he was awake, then they might subject him to the cowl again.

Just the thought of the cowl triggered an immediate, searing anger in him, but beneath his anger he was terrified.

He needed to hurry. For once he listened to his feelings, rather than presuming his mind knew better. At any moment the aliens might return. When they came he very much wanted to be gone. Harden crept apprehensively to the wall and began feeling his way along it, seeking a seam.

Chapter 30: Authenticity

"So, what did you hope to gain in there?" Pat asked Steve in a whisper as they carried the sleeping children to Steve and the kids' room.

Kathlyn was as light as a feather embraced in her father's arms, such a light and comfortable burden Steve felt that he could hold her forever. Pat's question posed a puzzle. "What do you mean?" he whispered back to her.

They arrived at the room and entered. The lights came on automatically. Three narrow beds were fitted into the smallish room, already made up with clean linens and blankets. The cases holding their clothing sat at the foot of the beds. Both children flopped limply as the adults dressed them for sleep, and soon, grumbling sleepily, they rose and obeyed Steve's command to clean their teeth. In the morning everyone would have an opportunity to truly enjoy the luxury of a planetside bath or shower instead of cleansing gel and a vacuum.

When the oral hygiene appliances were humming in the small lavatory, Steve turned again to Pat and asked again what she had meant.

She shook her head in dismay. He didn't already know what troubled her. "You are supposed to negotiate a deal on behalf of Perry Station, not change Martin's views on politics and history." she began. "Martin's political opinions and grasp of history will not be changed by an evening's conversation, Steve, even if he already thought he had been misinformed, which he doesn't."

"Alright, Pat." Steve lifted his hands as if in surrender. He had suspected that was the problem, but hadn't been sure. Since childhood, like most people, he had grown accustomed to relying on his preconscious self, the part of a person that notices minute details, the part that infers causes and consequences. It was the part of him that yielded his motivations. It was the guidance of his core values. But he also knew that the spontaneous inner self isn't fully reliable. It needs supporting brain work. That is why he had a brain, he thought.

Human nature is seldom ideal. Steve's father taught him that virtue is a man's real vocation. Decisions have consequences, and some of those will be unexpected. Since that has always been the case, Steve sought meaningful reasons for what he did. Since we have to live with consequences, we might as well live with ones that we choose. Granted, reasoning too often comes after the fact, but Steve also tried to consider outcomes when he could.

"I see your point, Pat. But at the same time," he objected, "consider the significance of authenticity. It's a safe bet that Martin is practiced in reading people. I will need his credulity if I am to be effective. He won't believe me very long unless I stand for something. If I agree with him in all things he may tend to presume what my position is, and so may not give voice to real differences. Or, he might just think I'm a pushover, and that would lead to problems when it comes time to actually negotiate."

"I just hope you bet rightly, Steve." she replied.

"Our differences should be in the open between us, and we must find priorities that we share, if our agreements are to endure. I have to have palpable character to merit real negotiation. Should he have cause to disbelieve me, or if I give him cause to think I'll say or do or pretend whatever is convenient for the sake of an advantage, then I'd betray my own purpose in the long run."

Pat looked for a long moment at him with clear eyes. His eyes were glorious. It did sound a little like he might be rationalizing. Yet he hadn't been thoughtlessly contesting Avery's take on history and politics. He had thought it through, and factored personal honesty. Maybe there was more to Steve than just a handsome face.

She didn't know why he and Sandy had separated, but he looked tired. The moment didn't feel quite right for pressing him about it, even though this penchant for authenticity might be relevant.

"Okay, Steve, it sounds like a stretch, but maybe I can buy into that. But I think that what you're talking about can lead people into unnecessary and dangerous polarity. If you entrench in your position, and he fortifies into his, then instead of negotiation, or even conversation, you will trap yourselves in division. Rather than having a chance at a good deal, you may end up with only confrontation. We might come away empty- handed or worse." she warned.

Steve nodded thoughtfully to her as the children finished cleaning their teeth, turned off their appliances, and returned. Stevie and Kathlyn climbed into their beds, and the adults tucked them in.

Steve told them he would be right back, kissed Stevie and Kathlyn's brow, and urged them to sleep. They didn't look like they would have any trouble with that, as their eyes were already struggling to stay open. As they drowsed more deeply he explained to them that he and Pat had a few things to talk over. Pat then wished them a good night and gave each a light kiss on the cheek while smoothing their coverlets. As she did, Kathlyn reached up to give her a hug, pulling her slightly off balance. Pat had to support herself on an arm while the girl hugged her neck, giggling. Then Steve and Pat stepped into the hall and closed the door.

Pat felt she could wait no longer. "Steve, I need to know something." She looked up into his eyes, searching. He was tired, but he wasn't that tired, and she could only keep her heart on hold for so long before things would begin to stray.

"What is it, Pat?" he asked, his tired eyes gentle, but concerned.

"I wouldn't pry, except that I've begun to care more than is comfortable, without knowing: why did you and Sandy separate?" she asked him, half afraid that her hope would blow up in her face, yet struggling to keep that hope from overwhelming her.

His eyes fell from hers as he remembered his wife, standing there at the door as he left for work, her eyes filled with what she wouldn't say except in the note he came home to. Steve turned half away and said "I only know what she told me, Pat. There's more that I think I've figured out, but that's just my guesswork."

"Tell me what you know, and what you think, Steve. You may

have guessed that I care for you and for your children, but I want to know what my heart is getting me into." she confessed.

Steve nodded once looking down to Pat's left. He looked up into her eyes. "Sandy needed a social life. She gave up her career to be with me, out in the Perry countryside, far from town after I left the service of the ACM military. My new job kept me away most of the week, so it was almost like she had thrown away her career for nothing. We didn't even really have our weekends to ourselves. I was always on-call, and every time we got some time together we were with the children. We had hardly any quality time alone together.

"At first it was okay. We were in love, and that filled in all the blanks for us. Then the kids came along and we were totally focused on them. But somewhere along the way, our love drew quietly into the background and I took it for granted. My job took me away more and more often as people came to rely on me.

"And I assumed she was okay, even though we talked less and less, until our relationship joined with our love in the background, just part of the scenery, something taken for granted.

"But she wasn't okay. I wasn't there for her, to pick up on that. She needed social contact, and she wasn't getting it. She needed her career, and the people her career brought to her, in social contact.

"She gradually grew discontented. Her discontent grew until I think I became just another part of the scenery for her, too. Then all she had was her discontent, and the children she loved, who loved and needed her constantly. They didn't fade into the background for her, they were ever-present beacons of light for her. And I think she saw in herself that she wasn't everything she should be for them, because of her deep discontent."

Pat thought she saw a sheen of wetness on his cheeks.

"So she left with them. And I found myself alone with her note, in which she tried to tell me what went wrong without pointing blame or defending what she did. And I thought it might blow over, and maybe she would come back, so I maintained the home fires and left the light on for her. But she never came back.

And then she wouldn't return my calls. I didn't realize it then but she had moved to Oberon with the kids to try and restart her career there.

"And then I thought they died when the planet, Perry, was destroyed." He explained, turned half away, his eyes distant.

Steve turned to Pat to continue, but before he managed to resume she reached a perfect finger to his lips, placed her hands gently upon his shoulders and stretched up to kiss him with firm but tender lips.

Chapter 31: Inferno

Captain Bernie Tucker of the *Ivanhoe* moved past his initial astonishment at the ferocious attack. His executive officer was reading off the summary of the *Barroso's* current damage and casualty report. On his command screen he studied the approaching capital ship. Sensors relayed what could be detected. The alien fighters engaged with the cruiser's fighter cover and the corvettes and frigates. Both destroyers had already launched multiple torpedo salvos as they rolled over their tubes.

He thought the fight would be a fair match but for the overwhelming number of alien fighters. Dante Command reported that the fighters of their system defense force would arrive within an hour. The promise of reinforcement was appreciated, but practically it was little more than an empty gesture. The battle would be decided well before the fighters could arrive.

The effectiveness of the weaponry and the shield resilience of the enemy fighters reported by the *Barroso* was alarming. If the alien fighter craft were so powerful, how effective would their capital ship prove to be? Captain Tucker ordered 90% of power allotted to *Ivanhoe's* forward shields. He would have to rely on the rest of the task force to cover his flanks as *Ivanhoe* bored ahead to engage the great alien ship directly.

With the *Ivanhoe* in-system, Admiral Singh was once more in direct command of the task force. The situation looked dire, but initially it appeared manageable. A heavy cruiser is formidable, and with two destroyers and other escorts he expected to have the upper hand in the engagement.

The admiral knew the first order of business must be to get word of the alien incursion back through the modulus to the rest of the fleet, and to Earth. The *Barroso* had already suffered heavy damage. She might soon be lost altogether if she wasn't withdrawn. He needed her firepower, but she had already lost many of her weapon mounts and her defensive capabilities had been seriously eroded. Duty required him to order the corvette to withdraw to Aldebaran system to report the action immediately.

The admiral wrestled with another concern. Humanity had

never before found living sentient aliens. There had been no doubt about the existence of other intelligent species in the universe among reasoning people ever since the first modulus had been found, just outside of Saturn's orbit.

The military had long ago been saddled with a regulation that determined what must be done when aliens were encountered. The protocol was to attempt communication with the aliens.

To comply with the requirements of the untested 'first contact' protocol, the Corporate military had long ago prepared a binary message package for its ships to transmit on contact with aliens. The message packet would attempt to bridge the gap between languages using binary code. Binary code was presumed to be understandable by any space-faring race. The binary code then progressed to present rudimentary English. The message packet itself intended to establish peaceful and profitable relations.

In the current context of a desperate battle, such a message of peace seemed absurd. Nevertheless, there was no reasonable way for a career officer to get around the regulation.

Admiral Singh transmitted the prepared binary package as required. As expected there was no immediate reaction. His task force was locked in combat with these unknown and clearly hostile aliens, but he had complied with regulations. He could hope the message package would distract and confuse the foe for a moment, but now he was free to fight.

"Captain Tucker," the admiral advised, "I have transmitted the diplomacy package as required. Order *Barroso* back through the modulus to report the engagement to Second Fleet. If we alert them, the rest of the fleet may get here fast enough to help us. Now the *Ivanhoe* and the destroyers must take out or at least cripple that capital ship. The frigates will cover our flanks. The *Braunschweig* and our fighters are to help them keep the fighters off our backs."

"Aye aye, admiral." Bernie Tucker responded. He doubted the *Braunschweig* was up to her mission, but the *Barroso* was effectively neutralized anyway. Tucker nodded to his communications ensign. The ensign relayed the admiral's orders to the rest of the task force.

Gunnery advised them that the first salvo of torpedoes was about to reach the target. Both officers turned intently to their displays.

Torpedoes are intended to be relatively slow, long-range weapons. Guided by a reasonably sophisticated artificial intelligence and an array of sensors, torpedoes attempt to close with their target slowly enough to get through the shields, the way a fighter might. Shields deflect and absorb coherent energy like lasers, and will stop fast projectiles.

As the captain and admiral watched their displays, beams of energy lanced out from the alien ship's point defenses and eliminated the first salvo of torpedoes. It was the expected outcome, and why so many torpedoes had been fired.

Since their own point defenses could reliably eliminate such slow projectiles, any competent enemy would most probably do so as well. But the second and more likely use for torpedo fire is to incrementally overload the target's shields with energy.

Energy is neither created nor destroyed. A spaceship's energy shield works by absorbing destructive energy. Shields accept and absorb the energy, converting it into a form that can be managed. The energy is 'managed' by converted it into an electrical charge, which is added to the shield's capacitor array. If the charge exceeds tolerance, then the capacitors can fail catastrophically. Even a well-shielded ship can be disabled or destroyed by overloaded capacitors. It just takes time and ordnance.

The alien ship returned fire at the closer of the two destroyers, the *Donnybrook*. A brilliant shaft of blue light instantly connected to the destroyer. In a moment the shields of the destroyer grew visibly translucent, and then nearly opaque as the shields struggled to manage the searing intensity of the beam. The shields collapsed, overcome. The shaft of energy burned, ate through her armor and hull, and in short order emerged to blast through the far side. The expanding, super- heated metal of the destroyer's armor plating could not endure the irregular stresses of the heat and came apart, spinning off into space. The *Donnybrook* exploded.

Without more pause than a quick refocus, the intense blue beam next struck the *Jordan Graham*. The *Graham's* shields almost immediately turned milky white, and then failed completely. The beam burned through the hull amidships, cutting through the ship and scattering her metal. The *Jordan Graham's* crew had slightly more warning and a few lifepods successfully ejected. Not one lifepod was seen separating from the wreck of the *Donnybrook*.

Captain Tucker was shocked, to say the least. The loss of two modern destroyers in under a minute was unthinkable. Without question, the *Ivanhoe* was over matched, and should attempt to withdraw. "Admiral..." he began.

Admiral Singh was thinking furiously. The strength of the destroyer shields was known, and the time elapsed before shield failure enabled calculation of the power of that alien weapon. That was vital information to get to the fleet, but he didn't see how he could get it to them. *Barroso* had just passed back through the modulus to give warning, moments before the alien demonstrated his weapon.

Warning the fleet about what had looked like a manageable fight when the Barroso left might mislead the fleet into overconfidence. Singh decided he had to send another of his too few ships back through the modulus with an update. Neither the frigates nor the corvette could withstand a direct hit from that alien weapon.

The admiral gave his orders. "*Braunschweig* is to withdraw through the modulus and transmit the metrics we've gathered on that weapon they're using."

"The rest of us have to buy the fleet some time. *Ivanhoe*, *Galway*, and *San Antonio* will focus all our fire on the alien's forward hard point. Try and take out that beam weapon. It's firing from outside their shields, so it is vulnerable. Whatever that weapon is, I don't think the fleet will fare any better than we have unless we can knock it out. If we can disable that weapon we might have a chance. Then if we can't take it out, we have to try and give *Braunschweig* time to clear the modulus and transmit everything we've learned.

Captain Tucker bowed his head for the slightest moment. The end was fast approaching, but the Navy had been his life and he was determined to hold course for as long as the flag required. He saluted his admiral and ordered the signalman to relay the orders to the corvette and the frigates, then ordered the *Ivanhoe's* crew to target the alien's forward weapons mount and open fire. The main forward battery opened up with rotary autocannon firing a ferocious stream of fifty millimeter nickel- iron slugs and the Ivanhoe veered to port to bring her aft weapons into play. The third flight of fighters launched and the hanger crews prepared to receive the first flight to rearm.

"Incoming lifepods from the *Graham*, captain."

"Redirect the survivors to Paradiso, ensign. We are not a safe haven." Captain Tucker replied grimly. "How many pods?"

"We're taking fire!" warned someone through gritted teeth.

Before the ensign could answer his captain the lights in the command center dimmed unexpectedly. The air recyclers quietened as if they would stop. Captain Tucker looked to his display and saw it flicker as it tried to recover. The shield capacitors had overloaded. He reacted. Bernie Tucker's palm hit the red emergency button to eject the crew's battle-station lifepods as his universe went blindingly white.

Chapter 32: Quiet Station

On approach to Perry Station, the crew of the Aldebari cruiser *Jade Temple* could see why communications from the station had not resumed. The comm tower supporting the antennae, receiver dishes, photo sensors and emitters, and primary energy sensor arrays of the station had been wrecked by weapons fire.

The station's docks were well lighted as they would normally be, but there were no workers visible. The heavy autoloader machines were stationary. They looked like they had been abandoned hastily, doors open.

The *Jade Temple* was in contact with an alliance officer near the modulus, Captain Hall of the ACM frigate *Brandenburg*. Captain Hall shared with them her information. The ACM wasn't formally allied to the Aldebari but, along with Steve Holbrook, Tibs was a bit of a hero to the people of the Alliance because of all that had happened after the destruction of Perry. Captain Elaine Hall provided as much information about the aliens as she had.

If aliens boarded Perry Station, it would explain why the docks were deserted. Everyone would be evacuated to a more defensible location.

Tibs turned to his communications team. "Broadcast an update on what we have learned for the sake of the miners out there and for the Legion base on Al Najid V". Ask the Legion to dispatch a fast craft to Legion space to report events. Tell them we will send word to our people.

Tibs then spoke into his wrist comm. "Lieutenant Matsuo, please come to the bridge." He turned to Master Lu who had overheard Tibs' message to the Legion. He was already speaking into his wrist comm to have the hanger deck prepare a fast courier boat to depart as soon as possible to inform the Admiralty, the military arm of the Academy of the Aldebar.

The station could neither receive a request nor give clearance for the cruiser to dock.

The more Tibs looked, the more the empty, abandoned appearance of the station alarmed him. Usually the dock was bustling with activity, but now there were no dockhands visible. There were two small cargo ships moored on the ways, but those also seemed deserted.

Lieutenant Matsuo arrived promptly, as he always did. Tibs had asked the Lieutenant to come in person instead of simply using internal comms. He wanted to get a sense of how Ishi really felt about the mission he was being handed.

Tibs shared his concerns about the status of Perry Station. "Ishi, I want you to take one of your squads and board the station at the docks. I don't know whether it will be safe or perilous in there. The docks look deserted. Information has been shared with us by a Captain Hall, whose ACM force successfully cleared the modulus of hostiles. She suggests that there may be aliens on the station."

The lieutenant enjoyed working with his commander. Together they had led the boarding action that captured Paul Harden's flagship. Though Harden escaped, and casualties among Tibs' pilots had been high, the marine lieutenant's performance and tactical leadership had been flawless. Matsuo's quick thinking saved the lives of Steve Holbrook's two abducted children and another captive civilian.

Tibs continued "Conduct your reconnaissance cautiously. Make contact and report back. I need to find out what's going on in there. Fill me in just as soon as you safely can. Do you have the layout of the station on your wrist comm?"

"We're a step ahead of you, One." the lieutenant responded.

'One' is an honorific used aboard Aldebari vessels for a respected commander or captain.

"My squad is already suiting up." Matsuo continued. "The maintenance techs should finish preparation of the assault shuttle in just a few minutes." Lt. Matsuo continued.

"Intelligence has already loaded the most current layout of the station onto our comm units." Matsuo assured him.

"Very good. Everything else I would say you already know.

We should be welcome, and our boarding action should be forgiven us under the circumstances. Just do everything that you reasonably can to avoid casualties." Tibs concluded.

"Aye, aye, One."

The Aldebari maintain specialized professional infantry called marines aboard their larger ships, including the *Jade Temple*. Marines guard critical points aboard Aldebari vessels, such as engineering and airlocks. They are also trained to assault and seize hostile starships by boarding them, a tradition dating back to their conflict with the Legion, when they had to fight without the benefit of armed vessels.

Now, of course, the Aldebari could field a quite competent navy built to their own specifications, using their own engineers and shipyards. But originally, in the early days following the loss of their scientific facility and its enclave in the Aldebaran system, the only real military ships they could muster they had seized by close assault.

By luring enemy warships into assault range and then capturing them, volunteers who eventually came to be known as the Aldebari Marines seized several of the Legion ships that had been hunting them. They didn't often win in the early days of their conflict, and they never won easily, but as they grew experienced and improved their tactics they fought on more equal footing with the Legion.

An Aldebari assault shuttle is low, wide and boxy, with a single armored turret forward. Photo-ablative enamel covers plate armor that is the equivalent of the armor found on a medium fighter. The stern houses two chemical engines for propulsion. Military grade antigrav and inertia dampening improve the shuttle's agility.

Six marines followed the shuttle pilot and Lt. Matsuo up the ramp into a broad armored hatch between the engines, angling into the shuttle. The Marines were clad in pressurized body armor, their heads encased in sensor-laden helmets. Once aboard they buckled themselves into their seats across from each other. If needed, the seats would seal and eject as lifepods, just like the

195

commander's and pilot's couches.

Down the center of the shuttle interior two Aldebari 'Crawler' exoskeletons were folded, ready for deployment. It could be safely assumed that Perry Station wouldn't be actively defending against assault, so it wasn't expected that the crawlers would be used in this landing.

With everyone in position and secured, the pilot sealed the shuttle hatch. He fed power to the antigravity fields and the assault shuttle rose from the hanger deck. He increased thrust and the shuttle slipped through the atmospheric shield of the *Jade Temple's* hanger bay to begin their descent to the deserted Perry Station docks.

Chapter 33: Genevieve

Genevieve Trent surreptitiously adjusted his hip padding. The disguise was proving problematic in confined quarters. What looked like the bulk of Perry Station's population had been evacuated into the central education facility where they would crowd until the intruders were captured or killed. The area was packed with grumbling civilians.

Genevieve's target, Steve Holbrook, had left the station on a mission and was out of reach. He had taken his children with him. There would be no foreseeable opportunities to exploit until Holbrook returned, but his absence might be made into an opening in itself.

The assassin had been tempted to move on, but the thought was dismissed almost as soon as he recognized it. He had accepted the contract and the money was in dark escrow. His professional obligation was known through the shadowy organization that held the money. He might be able to start a new life on one of the frontier planets but, face it, he was addicted to his job.

Genevieve pretended to study the infantile animated imagery on the wall of the preschool education center while he contemplated his situation.

Station security was conducting a sweep of the station. They were attempting to locate the intruders. Progress seemed glacial. Current conditions were unacceptable.

His stress level was elevated. He was unable to gain enough privacy to fully relax. It had been one thing to maintain Genevieve for a few hours at a stretch, but wholly another to maintain her persona around the clock. He was afraid he might talk in his sleep, so he remained awake.

The food brought in from the cafeteria was tasteless and unsatisfying. The whole situation was undesirable.

Plagued with the uneasy, overhung feeling that comes of early stage sleep deprivation, Genevieve made the decision to escape his overcrowded confinement. He needed room to breathe, let alone maneuver. He knew what his escape route would be, and he had everything he needed to get away.

He didn't believe the hysterical rumors that the invaders were aliens. Civilians make things absurdly dramatic, and then convince themselves their fantasy is true.

He would find whoever was actually out there. If there were too many, then he would stay out of their way. If there were few, or they were incompetent, then he would make them pay for inconveniencing him.

Almost the whole station was built with ceilings that seemed like they were made for his purposes. A lattice of extruded supports was suspended from the sub-flooring of the deck above. Thin white sheets of resin compound were lain flat between the flanges of the suspended lattice. Better, in order for workers to maintain the artificial gravity coils for the deck above and the coil shields for the deck below, the ceilings concealed catwalks, making it easy to move unseen almost anywhere in the station.

True, there were areas where the maintenance catwalks were secured by alarms, such as over the administrative offices. He had to be alert for surveillance sensors, but those were hardly more than inconveniences once he found them.

There was only one place in the crowded education center where Genevieve could go to reach and move aside one of the ceiling tiles unobserved. He delicately made his way to the restroom and locked the door behind him.

He climbed onto the platform of the lavatory sink and stretched to lift and slip aside an off-white resin sheet. As expected, the catwalk was well out of reach. He withdrew a slender knotted cord from a soft cloth bag he kept under an imitation breast. From the bag he also pulled a small weight fixed with an eyelet. An expert cinch and deft toss later he had one end of the cord anchored around the catwalk above him.

He hoisted himself hand over hand up the knotted cord as lithe as a gymnast.

He turned cautiously to reach down and carefully slide the panel back into place. He paused then, for a moment, to think through his steps. He walked his way meticulously through his memory, trying to recall any evidence he might have left behind. If it was there, he needed to remember it now, before it was too late to go back and recover his tracks.

To be sure, the locked lavatory door would annoy someone eventually, but they would think the locked door was merely someone's carelessness.

He concluded that he had brought nothing to the education center that he had not carried out. He hadn't engaged in conversation, so Genevieve's sudden absence should raise no alarm. He could probably even resume the role of Genevieve later, if her persona was expedient.

Satisfied with his escape, the assassin removed his disguise and hid his prosthetics and costume. Then, like a ghost, he faded into the depths of the station along the catwalks toward a supply cache. Once again he was himself, a hunter of the most dangerous animal.

Chapter 34: Escape

Conquest is not a sport. There is no question of fairness to it, only ruthless advantage. The animals did not have the technology at Sestrel's command. He did not withhold the full power of his weaponry. Their efforts to disable his primary weapon were futile, and their sentiments while opposing him were irrelevant.

Unfortunately, it had taken more time to dispatch the largest of their ships than he liked, and the two small ships remaining were now on his flanks. He was unable to maneuver as quickly as they, and if he used his inertia dampening to turn on either of them he would expose his stern to the other.

The exhaust of a starship's main thrusters must vent outside the envelope of the shields. That makes them a weakness to be exploited. The two small ships had clearly decided that the better way to disable or destroy his ship would be to get behind him. His secondary defensive armament was powerful and accurate, but did not have the range needed to stop the frigates or the few remaining fighters with them.

He had a different, and vastly more important use for his fighters, so he recalled them, back to the ship. Losses had been light, but he could afford to waste no more of them.

If one or both of the animals' ships did manage to acquire and target his engines, then he would retract the thrust nozzles into the shield and rely on his aft defenses to destroy their missiles. Yet those two nipping at his heels were annoying.

The time for subtlety was past. Two other of the animals' ships had withdrawn damaged through the modulus. They would surely transmit information to the rest of their forces, whatever and wherever those might be. Sestrel was not alarmed, but what he needed now was speed, not a distraction. He directed the helm to power through the next modulus. No more wasted time waiting for stealthy fighters to seize moduli or neutralize transmodular communications.

For the moment then, there was time to attend to a detail that mildly bothered him. When the animals attacked him they transmitted a cumbersome message packet using binary code. It was clear almost from the start that the bulk of it was a language primer, but Sestrel hadn't the slightest interest in learning how to grunt with beasts. He had a translation system already down in the livestock pens, however unwilling it might be, Sestrel intended to use it. By reasserting the cowl and retaking control of the animal he could link his captive's linguistic understanding to the ship's computers. Then from the computer he would gain a better translation much more simply and elegantly.

When the apologetic animal handler responded to his directions a few moments later, Sestrel's mild irritation grew incendiary. The captive animal was no longer in the pen. The animal could not immediately be found. Yes, security had been alerted and were searching the ship. No, the animal could not have used the elevator tube to escape. It would have been noticed and caught. And no, the animal was not in the feeder mezzanine above the pen.

Sestrel was enraged, but he would not leave the bridge as yet. The females nearby faded back unobtrusively, as far from his seething wrath as they could get without leaving. They could still perform their functions using their cowls as consoles.

~

After what seemed like hours of seeking and testing, in every way he could think of, Paul Harden finally located a wall panel narrower than those beside it. In every other way it looked in the dim light identical to the others. Yet it wasn't completely firm when pressed. It moved slightly under pressure. When he pushed upon one edge and immediately released, the panel popped ajar on a hinge. There was a vestibule behind the panel. Had he closed the panel behind him, he would have been in complete darkness. With the panel left open there was a little light, enough to show the rectangular outline of a hatch with a recessed handle in the floor.

Harden couldn't see well enough to detect what might be on the ceiling, but he quickly bent to feel the outline of the floor hatch. It opened on a dark rectangular shaft. It couldn't be a ventilation shaft since the hatch had been closed. Warm air rose from it, smelling musty and old. It was very dark and he couldn't see anything down there. The only light was dim, filtering in from behind his back.

Reaching down with his hands he found a rung on one side of the shaft. Holding the rung with his right hand he felt around deeper for another, the skin of his left hand hissing against the smooth metal side of the shaft. There was a second rung. He sat back up and set a foot on the second rung. At the edge of the hatch Harden hesitated.

A noise from the room he left alerted him. Something was moving around in there. Harden felt a lurch of fear surge within his chest.

Quickly, but careful to be silent, Harden pulled the open panel to the room shut behind him. In total darkness he worried whether to remain still or descend into the shaft. Whatever was down there, descent would at least be choosing to avoid recapture. He hesitated in fear that he might make too much noise.

Through the wall panel he heard a plaintive call, like bird, which he interpreted to mean that his escape had been discovered.

Paul's heart hammered in his ears as he fit himself into the narrow opening of the shaft. His hip brushed the side. He felt for a third rung with his other foot. He was careful to avoid bumping the side of the metal shaft as it might make noise, but the shaft was awfully narrow. He found the third rung and moved down, feeling for further rungs with his naked feet. The rungs felt gritty, chill and a little oily. At any moment one of the lizards might open the panel and catch him. He closed the hatch above and tried to descend as quickly and quietly as he was able. His feet were missing the rungs, like they hadn't been designed for someone as tall as he. Deeper, the shaft gradually lost the influence of artificial gravity. He stopped trying to use his feet and propelled himself downward more easily. His breath sounded unnaturally loud in the confined space and the pumping of his elevated pulse was loud in his ears.

As he descended further he felt the influence of gravity return and he caught a gritty rung under his bare foot. It stopped his progress, but dim lighting appeared from two translucent tubes that ran parallel along the shaft on either side. Apparently touching the rungs there activated the illumination.

All signs suggested that the lizards hadn't used this access in a very long time. He continued his descent. He must have passed a deck because the artificial gravity faded once more. Without a significant influence of gravity, the rungs were only handholds to use to propel himself. It felt unnatural to move down the shaft feet first, but there wasn't room or time to reorient his facing. He wasn't going to slow himself any more than he had to. He was desperate to get away.

After a few more meters of descent in the weightless shaft, he came to a small vestibule where the sensation of weight returned. He paused, listening, but heard no noise beyond that of his tightly controlled breathing. He decided it was too soon to exit the shaft.

Harden cautiously resumed his descent while revisiting his decision to not take the first exit. It didn't seem an effective way to evade pursuit if he took the first branch he came to. His ears sought any sound or sign that an alien might be near the opening, but thankfully all sounds were his own. The air seemed less stale. Perhaps he was only getting used to it.

After a few more meters he bypassed another small vestibule where his weight returned. He continued further along the ship. Weightless, he lost his sense of up and down. It was disorienting, but the side of the shaft at the rungs gradually became the floor and soon he was crawling backwards. When he released the rungs to crawl, the lighting dimmed into darkness.

Unexpectedly his bare foot touched a cold smooth wall with another hatch inset into it. He was at another vestibule but this time the panel he would need to open was behind his back, above him. He gathered his legs under him as he waited, listening. There was a rhythmic mechanical humming. It did not sound close by. He pressed up with his back and felt the panel give way, again on a hinge. He turned to keep the hinge at his back and slowly pressed the panel open with his head. Bluish light flooded the vestibule as he scanned the room beyond with his eyes. The way looked clear. He cautiously stood. The room was filled with rows of identical round-edged hexagonal boxes or containers. They were perhaps two meters across and a little over a meter in height. He stood fully and looked over them to where they stretched into the distance of a great curved room. The deck, and the objects on it, formed concave ranks along the inside wall of a cylinder, possibly the hull of the ship but the radius of the cylindrical deck seemed too small. When he climbed from the vestibule and stood up the ceiling was almost close enough for him to reach. Pale blue light filled the curved room. The mechanical humming was louder, but Harden couldn't see where it was coming from. Over his head a latticed ceiling curved like the deck, crosshatched into hexagons slightly larger than the containers here beneath them.

A thought stopped him. He bent to look closely at the deck adjacent to the nearest container. There was a suggestion of light coming from it. His knee cracked loudly in the humming quiet of the room as he bent, and Harden froze, waiting for any stir of alarm. But no, he was apparently alone.

He spotted a slight regular gap between the nearest container and the deck. He knelt again. Peering through the gap, he could make out what looked like the edge of another hexagonal container on a deck below.

Harden peered up toward the deck above him. He could see what appeared to be three clasps holding another container in place above him. The bottom of each container above him displayed identical machinery.

The boxes had to be significant, to be so orderly and so many. He found no way to open one.

There was a different mechanical noise from somewhere on the deck and he ducked behind the containers. After a moment the different clatter stopped, and he cautiously peered out over the top. He couldn't see what had made the noise. He grew more curious and began moving stealthily among the boxes, looking for the source of the whirring sound. He was hunched low enough on bent legs to be able to duck quickly out of sight. The curvature of the deck led him to keep a close eye beyond the curved ceiling to the farthest containers visible. It wasn't long before he spotted a tall mechanism moving among the containers. It moved a mechanical arm. Harden stopped to observe. It was placing something into an open container.

The container's lid was open in two halves, like a clam shell. Harden carefully moved closer to see. The device was placing balls, small elongated spheres into the interior. The balls were ovoid and pale. He approached close enough to pluck one out of the container. It was soft and warm, but heavy, like it was filled with a liquid or gelatin. He set the oblong ball back into the container. If he had to escape, he would need both hands free. Were these some sort of anti-personnel munition? Harden's stomach rumbled, reminding him of his hunger. If these were eggs, he wanted one. If they were something else, something that would harm him, he didn't want any.

The room's lighting made everything appear blue. The mechanical arm deployed a tube at the end of the mechanical arm. The ovoid balls appeared uniform in size and emerged from the tube with a dull pneumatic pop and dropped them one at a time into the container.

Presently the mechanism folded its arm and retracted into the ceiling. The container closed the clam shell lid with a snap. The container then moved mechanically into the ranks with the rest, identical with those Harden had hid among. As it was moved it made the other noise that had alarmed him. A panel opened in the bulkhead and an empty container emerged. Its lid opened and the depositor arm swung back into play. Harden resolved to return when he had found somewhere to base himself, hopefully with something to carry an ovoid ball he wanted to examine in detail.

The room grew completely silent, other than a quiet unvarying hum that was so constant and mechanical that he would forget about it until he listened closely again. Harden examined the room. At intervals cubes that weren't as tall as the hexagonal containers, so they were hidden from casual view. They were identical to the vestibule where he had emerged. Each had a panel on top that responded to the pressure of his hand to pop ajar. He assumed they opened onto maintenance shafts similar to the one from which he had come.

It seemed odd that the maintenance shaft had lain unused for a very long time. The thought rose up from his preconscious that these aliens weren't actually the builders of this ship. He felt the design of that maintenance shaft, its narrowness, the spacing of the rungs, and even the lighting wasn't really suited to what he surmised of the aliens' physiology.

Harden's objective was to find a place to hide. Then he could explore. He might seek nourishment back in the animal pen if he was careful. He dreaded seeing the pens again. He was reluctant, for fear of capture.

Chapter 35: Twilight

Martin Avery, Steve and Pat were on the tour that Martin had offered them the night before. Stevie and Kathlyn were visiting the facility's school. There they were being questioned by the local children about life on Perry, the Station and their trip to Earth.

Steve stood near a worktable with Pat in a large, metal sheathed room while Martin spoke. On the worktable was a sample of the composite plexiclear material that was to be used for the habitat domes. It was held clamped in a hydraulic fixture. Mike Billings, whom they had met briefly the day before, was intently measuring the light from a laser he was using to test whether a polarization solution he had mixed would appropriately moderate the equivalent of sunlight in vacuum.

"The dome has to be polarized to mediate the sun's radiation. Otherwise the unfiltered light of the sun would kill not just the plants, but anyone trying to live there.

"Our artificial soil will be a meter and a half deep everywhere. Nutrient-rich water will circulate to bathe the roots from within the artificial soil. The inhabitants and their crops will have a twelve-hour day followed by a twelve-hour night due to that rotation." Martin Avery paused for questions.

Martin nodded to acknowledge that no questions had been raised. "Solar cells, on what we're calling the night side of the habitat, will supplement a small nuclear generator. We'll cool that generator with water. The water will circulate throughout the habitat, using pumps and valves, the same way it works at Perry Station. I believe we can keep it quite comfortable. I'll admit we are still working out exactly how far away from the sun these must orbit and how much light to filter out to ensure they don't get too warm or cold, to be frank. The temperature of the water cycling through the hydroponic infrastructure will have to be carefully controlled. We don't want to cook the plants before they can be harvested, after all." he smiled.

Pat had a question. "Why are you investing so heavily in soil-based agriculture when you will have hydroponics to grow food?"

"This actually is a type of hydroponic system, Pat." Avery replied. "Our method, feeding and watering plants from within the soil itself, has proven to be one of the most productive, and allows greater variety of crops. Productivity will be a primary consideration. Our soil-based hydrocultural design will also give people somewhere to walk. I dream of the day when folks become creative with the potential of their new homes."

Steve considered the limitations of farming in space. The hydroponics at Perry Station were woefully deficient in some kinds of produce. "If you have seed stock ready for planting, Martin, I'd really like a packet of vegetable seeds to take back to Perry Station when we go." he said.

"Assuming these habitats work the way you hope, do you think you'll be able to build enough of them and settle people in time to harvest crops and avoid a famine, Martin?" Pat asked.

"I don't know, Pat. But it is more than a hope, and I believe it's our best shot." Avery admitted, looking at his hands. Then he looked back up at her. "If we miss our target, some will still be better than none."

Martin turned to Steve "Yes, Steve, we have seeds from the planetary repository in Scandinavia and another seed bank in the eastern Baltic."

He looked again to Pat. "We have an early prototype in testing, just inside Earth's solar orbit. We still have to perfect the solar light polarization. I'm not quite content with the orbital distance yet, either."

"Don't forget mold." Mike added.

"Yes, we have to solve for mold. Analysis of the air filtration system still shows too many spores. It is a problem. Mold propagation can get out of hand quickly in these habitats." Avery admitted.

"It's part of my vision that the ACM, the Legion, and the Aldebari can be convinced to join in parallel deployment of these habitats around their stars." Martin continued. "But we have to finish testing and perfecting our prototype before we can convince anyone that it is the best solution to overpopulation without constricting human genetic potential. Fortunately, much of the design work was already done by other people in history."

Steve thought, then weighed in "I think it will be an easy sell to the Aldebari, but the advantages may appeal to the Legion as well."

Pat added "We should have started something like this in the Classical age, before the first great famine. They already had most of the technology they would have needed."

"They thought about it, but remember that they didn't have artificial gravity or energy shielding way back then. Modulinite hadn't been discovered, and they probably would have shied away from nuclear power. The early technology was frightening to them. They couldn't really have used this design, but a centrifugal solution, like a wheel rotating on a twenty-four-hour cycle might have worked for them." Avery responded.

Martin looked toward Steve. "We need to take care of that contract, Steve. When can we start taking delivery of the modulinium?"

"We could start shipping product almost as soon as we know Earth has removed the minefield around the anomaly at Trondheim" Steve replied.

Avery stopped in his tracks. "Trondheim?"
Steve was about to explain when Martin's wrist comm emitted a warbling alarm.
"This is something flagged as urgent. Excuse me a moment." Martin walked a short distance away from Pat and Steve.

Martin's back was to them as he tried to listen closely to his wrist comm. Pat remarked quietly to Steve that she didn't see how there was very much to negotiate. Then Martin stood upright too quickly, like he had been shocked. His voice rose in pitch, like he was either excited or afraid.

"Martin, what happened?" asked Pat, concerned.
Avery tapped his wrist comm and waved them back in toward the main facility door. "Come on, you're going to want to hear this."

Chapter 36: Matsuo

Lt. Ishi Matsuo turned to watch the pilot as he brought the assault shuttle closer to the well-lit but deserted station dock. The marines behind him reported one by one their readiness to deploy. Matsuo's readouts showed that everyone's suit and helmet had a good seal and their vital signs read green.

Scanning from side to side there was no visible movement on the dock. Matsuo had a good field of view from the copilot's seat and he scanned for motion on the dock, focusing on each point of cover from the nearest to the farthest. The shuttle's sensors should pick up any detectable target and highlight any threat, but there is nothing like the human eye to notice details that might get past the sensor's detection parameters. The eye responds almost instantly to motion. Although the sensors would detect and display targets simultaneously on the monitors, it would take precious time to orient his attention to whatever the sensors might pick up. On the other hand, the sensors were scanning in all directions at once. They weren't limited by directional facing.

The assault shuttle entered the environmental shield that held the dock's atmosphere from the cold vacuum of surrounding space, and the deck itself grew close. The pilot chose a spot shielded on two sides by crates and equipment, and he spun the ship to give the turret an advantageous field of fire. The shuttle's landing gear touched the deck and absorbed the weight of the assault shuttle on articulated struts. The thrusters began powering down. The hatch ready light changed color from yellow to green and with a hiss the hatch opened. The pilot reported their arrival to the *Jade Temple* as the marines hit their buckles and stood to a crouch under the low ceiling of the shuttle. In pairs they deployed into a defensive arc, taking cover where it could be found. There was no discernible reaction. The dock was as deserted as it had seemed.

Their arrival had not gone unnoticed, however. The deck was monitored by motion detectors. Station security was alerted. A quick view of the monitor showed the insignia on the shuttle was Aldebari. It was possible but unlikely that the shuttle was displaying a false insignia, but pirates or criminals would be much more likely to use ACM alliance markings than Aldebar. Gabriella in the security command center immediately transmitted notification to Kyle, the station's security chief. Kyle notified the council by comm as he and another officer headed for the dock. Councilman Lyman responded and asked him to welcome the marines and see whether they might lend a hand with the situation.

Kyle had lost five officers to unknown intruders, possibly aliens, in the Section Seven incident. He didn't have enough people now. He hoped, but wouldn't assume, that the Aldebari would pitch in.

Kyle still had difficulty with the idea that hostile aliens had actually infiltrated his station. With human criminals he would know what to expect. He could have put together a sure plan to neutralize the threat. Aliens presented too many unknowns, both behaviorally and in terms of technology. There was no telling what an alien's motivations and objectives might be. He was sure that they outclassed his people in equipment. There were too many wildcards in play.

When Kyle showed up at the docks without a helmet accompanied by only one other security officer, Matsuo put his men at ease. He stood from behind a shipping container, and unsealed his helmet's visor. Removing the helmet to greet Kyle would have filled a hand and he wanted both hands free. He and Kyle had met several times, before and after the assault on Paul Harden's cruiser and occasionally later, when the *Jade Temple* had visited the station.

The lieutenant updated the *Jade Temple*. Tibs himself answered with a compliment. He asked Ishi to give his personal regards to Kyle. What happened on the station was foremost on the mind of the One.

Kyle and Matsuo met on the open dock and shook gloved hands amid the marines. Without preface Kyle started briefing Ishi about the situation and the events leading to it.

The lieutenant assured Kyle that his marines and the *Jade Temple* would do what they could to aid Perry Station.

Kyle's plan was to extend the sweep of the station outward from its core, where the civilians had been gathered in the defensible education center. Then, as the sweeps extended farther, the civilians could be allowed to return to their homes and more normal daily routines.

Kyle wanted to check on Chief Mackenzie in engineering before anything else. The engineering section was next to the shipyard. Mack hadn't evacuated as he had been asked. He also hadn't been responsive to recent comms.

Lieutenant Matsuo turned to his marines. He directed them to coordinate with the rest of security while he and Kyle checked on Mack in engineering. His lance corporal recommended that two marines accompany them.

Ishi agreed. Kyle gave the marines the frequency and passcode to one of station security's comm link channels, and each of them checked their comm unit designation with Gabriella.

The alien spacecraft Steve and Mack had recovered was secured in Engineering's section of the shipyard. It hung sleek and silvery in the lighting of the pressurized dock.

There was no response from the door to Engineering, so Kyle had Gabriella unlatch the section's door remotely. It was quiet inside and fully lit. A large window looked out onto the shipyard and the alien ship. On either side of the room were large digital drafting pads, scattered styli, writing instruments and portable consoles, all powered off. On the walls were blank monitors. Another door stood partly open at the back and Kyle and Ishi headed into the Chief's office.

Chief Mackenzie was sitting upright in the office chair next to his workbench. On his head and neck was an articulated metal cowl. His eyes were closed. Matsuo saw his chest rise as the engineer breathed. He did not appear to be in distress, but he was also unresponsive to their entry into his office. On his workbench was an open console pad and keyboard, powered on. Its screen was covered in text, some of it formulaic.

"Mack?" Kyle asked aloud.

Chief Mackenzie lifted his hand without opening his eyes, clearly concentrating, and he raised his index finger toward them, gesturing to wait a moment. After a few seconds he opened his eyes and turned to his keyboard, typing furiously. Then he stopped and turned back to them. His hand reached up to depress an indentation on the crown of the cowl. The cowl's scales had been slightly parted, and now they seemed to relax closed. A moment more and he lifted the cowl from his head and neck with both hands, to lay it almost tenderly on the workbench next to the keyboard.

"What a marvelous device." he proclaimed.

"Is this why you didn't evacuate as directed, Chief, or respond to our attempts to contact you?" Kyle asked.

Chief Mackenzie nodded in the affirmative, and the laugh lines around his eyes crinkled. "This cowl is amazing. I need to study it more, but I shouldn't have tried it alone."

"Chief, the station has been boarded by hostiles, and I think it is a small group of these aliens of yours." Kyle lectured. The chief's smile changed to solemn concentration.

"They killed five of my people, Chief.' Kyle continued. You did-n't respond to us, so we didn't know if you might be dead or hurt. Why didn't you respond over comms?"

"I didn't know, Kyle. When I want to get work done I shut everything off that might distract me. You know how it is." The chief was visibly alarmed by the news of casualties.

Kyle considered the chief's point. Meetings often did seem endless and without practical use. But that doesn't mean a person can shut out the rest of the universe.

"You said you have information about the aliens?" Lt. Matsuo asked, more interested in the Chief's discovery than in making the man comply with the needs of security.

Mackenzie nodded to the lieutenant. "But I was mostly fo-cused on their technology." he said, gesturing toward the limp metal cowl.

Kyle realized browbeating was pointless. But Mackenzie needed to stay alert for threats to the station the same way as he was alert for workplace safety issues. He intended to have a se-rious talk with Mack when there was time.

Kyle's wrist comm lit up with an alert. "Go ahead, Gabby." he responded.

Gabriella sounded breathless. "Kyle we've got imagery of the aliens on our internal sensors. Someone found them, and they're fighting!" she reported.

"Where?"

"Near Mary's shop, but in the ceiling mezzanine. No! They've just crashed through the ceiling and are in the hall now."

"We're on our way, Gabriella. Keep talking. I won't be able to watch it on my comm while we're running."

Kyle motioned to Mackenzie to stay put and waved for the Marines to join with him as he hurried toward the outer office and the hallway beyond, away from the docks. "Gabby, can you tell who we have fighting them?"

"I can't make an ID, Kyle, but he's awfully fast on his feet." There was a slight pause. Kyle heard her inhale sharply. "Wow! This guy is good."

~

The assassin knew there was a security monitor close-by, but if he stayed low and to the inside of the catwalk, it shouldn't catch sight of him. He was focused on avoiding the sensor when he rounded the corner of a partition and nearly bumped into what looked like a big snake in the dim twilight above the ceiling. It scared the hell out of him.

It looked like a snake when he first saw its head and eyes atop the long, sinuous neck. When it saw him, feathers on its head stood up, as in alarm. The creature was as big as a man, and displayed fast reactions.

Out of the corner of his eye the assassin saw the bright red speck of the powered security monitor. He was now onscreen, if anyone was watching. A detached part of him felt amused that observation by security seemed suddenly desirable.

There were at least two other aliens behind the first. The closest one was trying to bring some sort of long weapon to bear, but it was close enough for him to reach out and deflect the tube, which he assumed was dangerous.

He couldn't get away, so he prepared to fight. He wanted to keep the fight on the catwalk. That would put the first lizard in the way of the others and prevent them from surrounding him. The first lizard tried to bite the hand he used to deflect the weapon and he snatched his hand back just as her jaws snapped closed. He did not at all like the sound of the lizard's teeth as they clenched. They sounded like the shearing snap of sharp scissors.

As he pulled his left hand back to avoid the teeth, he released his grip on the weapon. The lizard had been pulling back on it, and was already off balance. When he released the weapon the alien lost her balance on the catwalk and fell onto the false ceiling close below, which in turn collapsed beneath her weight. As the lizard broke through the ceiling she grabbed hold of the assassin's arm, the one he was propped upon. Her sharp claws extended as she gripped, penetrating the skin of the assassin's forearm.

The assassin's punctured arm was pulled and his chest struck painfully on the catwalk. He was pulled down to fall heavily onto the lizard below.

The lizard released her grip and tried to scramble out from under the animal's fall.

The assassin tucked into a roll, trying to dissipate the impact and gain some room to move. As he rolled his foot struck the alien hard. Her weapon slid pin wheeling across the smooth hallway floor. The assassin felt blood soaking the skin of his forearm. He glanced up as he finished his roll and saw the second lizard pointing another tubular weapon at him. He had little room to work.

He reached behind his neck and pulled a flat throwing knife from a thin sheath. His bunched shoulder made his roll skew slightly to the side. He pushed up from his roll and leveraged his left arm to get his feet under him, then raised his bloodied hand for a throw. He whipped the knife expertly toward center mass of the second alien.

Practice pays. His knife flipped once and struck true, just

where the alien's long neck met her breast. The surprised alien reacted with a leap, writhing, tail lashing. Her scrabbling hands clutched at the knife handle. The lizard fell onto her side, halfway off the catwalk, then sagged off and fell to the floor, her tail whipping. Her legs thrust out and kicked with large wicked-looking claws, as if trying to disembowel the air.

At the edge of his vision the assassin saw a shadowy form in motion. The first lizard launched herself at him from across the hall.

The assassin's right hand was already extended from the follow-through of his throw. He hooked his bloody forearm around the creature's long, sinewy neck as she came and he stepped slightly aside. He felt the muscles of the creature's neck under her scales. The feathers threatened his purchase. But with a twist of his hips he used the alien's own momentum to slam her face-first into the wall. She collapsed, at least stunned. There wasn't time to take her out altogether yet. There was another one behind him. He turned to face the third alien.

The big bird-lizard had dropped to the floor like a cat, the claws of her feet clicking on the smooth flooring. The creature was well out of reach. She brought her weapon up smoothly and fired, striking the assassin in the chest, opening a large hole that immediately spattered a gush of dark blood. The assassin fell backward and struck the floor wetly.

For a moment the assassin saw the light of the ceiling. His eyes dispassionately studied the dappled texture of a ceiling tile: it was speckled with crimson. He felt like he was floating. There was no sensation of pain, but his hands tingled, almost like they were on fire. He died lifting his hands to look at them.

~

"Our man is down, Kyle, but he got at least one of them, maybe two. I saw three in there." Gabriella commed.

Kyle, still running, struggled to get enough breath to reply. "Still no idea ..." he managed, "who he was?" His hospital time had left him much weaker than he had expected.

"Negative, Kyle. But something about his face seemed familiar."

Kyle was breathing heavily. Matsuo, next to him, ran like he was a machine, puffing lightly in time with a regular cadence to his running steps. Kyle felt like he was wasting too much energy with all his gear flopping as he ran.

Then Gabriella gasped into her comm and exclaimed "Oh my God! Kyle, one of the aliens is taking the man's leg off. It has some kind of tool, like a surgical laser."

Kyle's legs were burning with exertion, and he was developing a painful stitch in his side. His calves protested against every footstep but he pressed himself, trying to keep up with the marines.

"Kyle, two of the aliens survived." Gabriella sounded like she felt sick. "One of them... One of them looks hurt. The other is carrying that man's leg. They are running further down the hall. I don't have sensors there to track them."

Kyle didn't have the breath to respond. He hadn't run this much in a very long time. He avoided thoughts about his hospitalization, like that would be an excuse. He felt scornful of his weakness, but another part of him was desperate to just stop and lie down. He stubbornly didn't accept any excuse. He was able to move only because he didn't let himself stop, but it was a close thing. At any moment his legs might go out from under him.

They ran through the little piazza and passed Mary's store. They entered the scene in the hallway. One alien was collapsed unmoving on bloody broken ceiling tiles. Diagonally across the hall was the human who had fought them. He was dead, laying on his back. His black, form fitting clothes were badly ripped, and he had suffered deep lacerations to his right leg and his arms. He was missing his left leg. There was a seeping hole in his chest. The floor was pooled with crimson blood that was beginning to darken unevenly.

Kyle bent over, trying to catch his breath, trying to keep from collapsing. He pointed down the hall and breathlessly asked the Lieutenant "Follow... the blood trail?" he gasped. "Watch... for... ambush."

Matsuo nodded to him and flashed a hand signal to his marines. Matsuo followed them while updating the *Jade Temple* on his wrist communicator as they trotted farther into the hallway following a trail of blood drops.

Kyle silently thanked the lieutenant. Then he turned to the dead man.

The dead man's face looked familiar. After a few moments of not quite remembering Kyle called up the open case files on his wrist comm and tabbed through the faces. Soon he found the one he sought. It was a copy of a standard issue ID for "Jack Graham", a former employee, a fraud who used a stolen identity to get close. He nearly killed Steve Holbrook. Kyle straightened John Doe's head just a bit and superimposed the ID's hologram onto it, making a positive identification. He'd still have to verify officially by DNA tags, but he was personally sure.

Almost too quietly to be heard, Kyle asked the dead man "Who *were* you, bud?"

He raised his wrist to capture the scene in imagery and to contact Gabriella. He scanned the scene again with his eyes. He was trying to notice and memorize every detail. "Gabriella," he commed, "the man who died fighting them was Jack Graham, the assassin we've been trying to catch. I'm certain. The bone structure of his face is a match, and the skills he displayed are a good fit.

"The scientists will want to examine this dead alien. Would you contact them for me and arrange an escort?"

"You got it, boss." Gabriella responded. "Should I leave the Graham case open for you, or should I just close it, Kyle?"

"Case is closed if I have anything to say about it. I can just attach the DNA tag when it arrives from the lab. Kyle, out... and thank you Gabby: you're stellar."

As Kyle stood, he turned back toward the plaza in front of Mary's store. His breathing was nearly normal again. Something was out of place. There, on the floor, was something that looked like it might be a weapon.

Chapter 37: Aldebaran

Corvette *Barroso* was heavily damaged when she cleared the Dante modulus back into the Aldebaran system. Her armor was scored with still-molten scars. Plates of seared metal hung loose, some still glowing with residual heat. Her hull was compromised and from several places a fog of frozen atmosphere streamed into the vacuum. The corvette had difficulty maintaining course as her asymmetrical leaks acted like random thrusters. Intermittently the *Barroso* had to apply maneuvering thrusters to keep from tumbling. Her surviving crew worked hard to tend the wounded, restore hull integrity and atmospheric shields.

Barroso's communications suite was still intact, however. Her captain's initial alert to the fleet was broadcast unencrypted over a voice channel, after which she transmitted encrypted recordings of the battle up to the time she had left Dante system.

The *Barroso* was so far from where the fleet orbited Aldebaran III that transmission of the report would require almost forty minutes to be received.

Within minutes of *Barroso*'s initial transmission *Braunschweig* also returned through the modulus heavily damaged. She broadcast an encrypted report detailing the loss of the heavy cruiser *Ivanhoe* and destroyers *Jordan Graham* and *Donnybrook*. Status of the frigates and the *Ivanhoe's* fighters was unknown.

The *Braunschweig* proceeded to transmit the updated metrics gathered by the task force, just as Admiral Singh had ordered. Her captain added verbal affirmation that the required first-contact protocol had been broadcast.

Then the monstrous alien ship came through the modulus, followed closely by the lone surviving frigate, the *Galway*. The frigate blossomed with lifepods and then exploded. The *Galway*'s pods attempted to home in on the *Braunschweig,* but were redirected to the Aldebari station over Aldebaran due to the precarious status of the corvette.

Coherent beam weaponry uses optical amplification of electromagnetic radiation. The power of this type of weapon is a function of the energy source, the medium through which it is focused and the precision of amplification. The effective range in vacuum is as far as linear coherence can be maintained, largely a consequence of machining during manufacture and the quality of subsequent maintenance. When the range grows so great that coherence is lost, amplification becomes inadequate and electromagnetic radiation is diffused. Energy shields negate coherent amplification and prematurely diffuse the energy of the beam, which in human ships is absorbed by the shield capacitor array.

When a beam pulse does manage to penetrate and hit a spacecraft's armor, as happens when a ship's shields have been overcome or weakened, the pulse' coherent radiation causes rapid heating and evaporation of whatever surface is struck. When a surface is struck by a coherent beam of sufficient power, that surface will rapidly become superheated, causing sudden expansion. This sudden expansion produces explosive evaporation, which generates shock waves in a solid. Connected solid material may further communicate these shock waves.

The alien ship's identified offensive armament was in its bow. When it wasn't being fired, the weapon retracted, protected beneath the envelope of the ship's energy shield and, it was assumed, beneath the armor. To fire, the weapon's lens mount was extended through the energy shield envelope. The lens mount was also heavily armored, but the lens itself was completely vulnerable during the firing sequence.

That weapon was now extended through the alien shields. Extremely powerful coherent energy was unleashed and struck the armored stern of the already damaged *Braunschweig*.

The armor of *Braunschweig* disintegrated where the beam struck. Power from her engines was severed, and her inertial dampening failed. Fortunately for the surviving crew, the engine compartment's antimatter containment system had a good backup power supply that maintained magnetic field integrity. Power loss was not immediately catastrophic. The backup battery afforded the crew time to decide whether to jettison the antimatter core or use their lifepods to abandon ship.

The *Braunschweig* began to tumble from a secondary explosion that vented through the breached hull. Her captain grimly launched the crew in their lifepods. The antimatter core maintained by battery was an inevitable self-destruct mechanism. He abandoned ship himself, once he knew his surviving crew was away.

The *Barroso* was farther away. Her captain cut power to the engines, shields and running lights. He ordered his executive officer to cease active sensor emissions and communications.

The corvette's partially restored shields were utterly inadequate as a defense against the power of that alien weapon. The captain of the *Barroso* hoped that by cutting all power his vessel might appear lifeless, and so avoid the alien's attention as she drifted. Without engines, the ship could rely only on batteries to keep life support functional and antimatter contained. Power from emergency lighting was rerouted by a Petty Officer and an E-2 to preserve the charge of the chemical battery, they hoped indefinitely.

Weightless in the red darkness of the ship's interior, without active sensors, no one could tell what the alien was doing. Each moment that passed seemed to stretch interminably as the Captain and his crew awaited destruction, effectively blind.

The crew was comprised of men and women from all over the world. They were of many faiths, though most claimed no religion. Waiting silent in the red darkness, nobody can see who prays.

The alien ship powered past the *Barroso*, deeper into Aldebaran system. It ignored the tumbling, leaking corvette.

Twenty-eight minutes later, the *Barroso's* initial unencrypted voice message was received by Second Fleet. It was also recorded by an alert Corporate news service ship that had been monitoring the system. The news service had hoped for a news story about what was happening to cut communications through the modulus. The *Barroso's* report that a hostile alien ship had engaged and defeated a Corporate task force in Dante System was irresistible. The original unencrypted warning was relayed immediately to Earth. The news service was a minor player in the Earth news market. The company capitalized on the scoop rather than seeking and awaiting clearance from the Corporate government.

That news story set off wildly speculative commentary among competing news agencies, some of it cautionary, some of it inflammatory. The recording surprised Corporate censors. It was suppressed by the Corporate government too late. Since the news was now common knowledge, the Corporate Board took the opportunity to declare martial law, announce a curfew, and impose food rationing.

Many of the people on Earth who learned of the alien conflict reacted with panic, especially after hearing emotion-driven speculation enflamed by sensationalists. Some were radicals who spent their time online seeking converts and, whether they were believed or ridiculed, they embroidered the narrative with oracular and self-serving end-of-days pronouncements.

Those people who weren't either asleep or too engrossed in their online games to notice began to swarm out in search of supplies. Many tried to hoard whatever food they could obtain. Home grown vegetables became scarce in the barter market. Some Nibbles kiosk dispensaries ran out of supply, and when they did multitudes of regular, law-abiding citizens became unthinking mobs. Fear became anger that was finally expressed in destruction. Food kiosks were damaged. Supply vehicles were besieged when they were found, and were overturned and looted.

In the Aldebaran system, the *Barroso's* report of a hostile alien vessel spurred the fleet toward readiness. Naval intelligence analysts were only just beginning to decode the rest of the report and absorb its import.

Fleet leadership had no ready contingency plan for the situation, but initially a generic tactical deployment would be the default. The fleet sounded general quarters and began to power up.

Although the *Barroso* had been badly damaged, the analysts of the fleet initially believed that, if the alien ship was alone, then it should find a heavy cruiser with two destroyers and sundry smaller ships at least challenging. Even in the worst case, in which the task force was compelled to withdraw, the alien should arrive also heavily damaged.

Then the *Braunschweig's* report was received and the fleet was shocked to learn that the task force' main elements had been lost altogether while the alien ship reportedly remained untouched.

The reports from the corvettes delivered a tremendous amount of information that had to be organized and understood under pressure. The idea of an unprovoked alien attack was difficult to accept. Naval intelligence analysts were anguished that they could not learn what was already happening near the modulus until long after it had already occurred.

Despite the losses in Dante system, the fleet was still much more powerful than the reconnaissance task force had been. They were simply out of position to render any assistance to the surviving corvette.

The flagship *Trafalgar* was a state-of-the-art battleship armed with the latest kinetic strike weaponry. Her railguns were so powerful that they could magnetically accelerate massive slugs of nickel-iron alloy to a significant fraction of the speed of light. In space, their munitions could travel forever, or until they hit something, but they needed a targeting solution to know where to fire.

Trafalgar's principal escort was comprised of three cruisers. The *Ivanhoe* had been a fourth of their number. The other escorts were comprised of a squadron of destroyers along with sundry smaller ships, frigates and corvettes. The battleship and cruisers could deploy their own fighter cover, and they were prepared to do so.

Some junior officers argued whether the alien threat had been overstated, but most remained quiet and focused on doing their jobs.

Experienced captains examined the decoded report analyses closely and prepared for the worst. The data could not establish that the alien ship was alone, only that no others had been detected. The alien may have used only the one weapon to take apart the task force because that was the only weapon it needed, outside of the point defenses that neutralized the destroyers' torpedoes. The alien may have not bothered to use maneuver to seek advantage over the task force because it hadn't needed more advantage. All arguments attempting to minimize the threat assessment fell quiet when reminded that a single alien ship destroyed a task force that should have been able to hold Dante system.

The senior captains had all known both Admiral Singh and Bernie Tucker. They dismissed any suggestion of flawed tactics.

The flag, command of the fleet, was held by Admiral Ezra Crow aboard the *Trafalgar*. The alien's motives were a complete mystery. Known motivations make an enemy more predictable. These aliens were attacking for no apparent reason. They were complete strangers to humanity. Ideological issues could not be the cause. There was no economic competition to fuel antipathy. Humanity hadn't trespassed and had no history with them whatsoever. That meant the aliens weren't defending their territory. Motivations of vengeance were most unlikely.

Near Aldebaran III, the *Trafalgar* was preparing to leave orbit, still spinning up power for shields and her rail launchers. Sailors on leave, down on the beaches of the beautiful but unpopulated planet, were being recovered by Navy shuttles.

The alien was still quite remote. The Aldebaran-Dante modulus is between the orbits of the Aldebaran V and VI. The fleet had been in orbit around Aldebaran III.

The alien would have to skirt the star of Aldebaran to reach the modulus leading to Earth. Since the course and speed of the alien was unknown, Admiral Crow ordered the destroyers to set course around one side of the star to acquire the target's location and bearing for the rest of the fleet. The rest of the fleet would set up to defend the modulus that led to Earth's solar system.

The destroyer squadron was under way and accelerating. They were fast and nimble ships. They began to gather speed toward the star, and beyond it, toward the Dante modulus. Their sensors ranged active to acquire the target for the fleet, and for their long range torpedoes.

Two of the three cruisers, the frigates, and the corvettes were ready to move as well, shields powering up, but they remained with the *Trafalgar*. The third cruiser, the *Macao*, was still recovering sailors from shore leave on Aldebaran III.

Admiral Crow directed his communications officer to establish communications with the Aldebari and the Legion through their respective moduli comm relays. The moduli to their domains were near and messages should be relatively quick, assuming they were responsive. If they had forces at the ready, they might even factor in the coming battle.

Admiral Crow hoped his fleet would be adequate to the task without their help, but the metrics received from the *Braunschweig* were troubling.

The admiral dispatched a further request to the Corporate Board, outlining his intention to appeal to the other powers to join with Earth in common cause. He requested the Council's authority, just in case he had to negotiate an understanding. The Aldebari and Legion were human, but they weren't allies.

Chapter 38: Corporate

Steve turned to Pat from the monitor, his face a picture of concern. "Aliens?" Pat didn't know any more than he did, and she shrugged with open hands out.

"The first comm relay failure was at Al Najid." Avery pointed out. "The sequence suggests that is where they came from. And it looks like they are headed here, to Earth. Were your people doing something with them out there?"

"No, unless they picked up the broadcast detailing the autopsy of the alien mummy we found, but if that was it, we had no idea they might be out there listening." Steve could only guess, feeling futile.

Several alarmed Continental employees raised their voices in the communications center, trying to be heard.

Steve wondered aloud "Do you suppose the alien scout transmitted an alert when we opened it?" After a moment he shook his head, "I can't imagine where they could have been hiding in Al Najid system. To receive an alert, they would have to be in-system. We've been exploring and surveying for years out there, and we never found a sign of them before we found the mummy."

"Maybe Harden." Pat suggested. "He vanished, but he had to go somewhere. The ACM couldn't find him. They never found aliens either, and apparently they were there somewhere. Maybe Harden stumbled across them while trying to escape. Maybe he did something that ticked them off."

"That sounds like something he would do. But where could he have found them?" Steve objected. "Could they have been just hanging out there idly in deep space? That doesn't sound likely to me."

Martin Avery saw little benefit to conjectures based upon insufficient data. There would be predictable and serious consequences to an alien incursion. The hostilities at Aldebaran had cut vital shipping lanes. Those were trade routes that Earth needed.

Avery spoke his mind aloud "Wherever they came from, and for whatever reason, they've cut off about a quarter of our food supplies." The room went silent.

"The system we've set in place to feed Earth's billions is too complex." The whole room was listening. "We have to feed all of the people, all over the globe. It's too complex. Without the supply of grain from the Legion worlds we can't make enough Nibbles, and that's what our systems are built to distribute. We don't have a substitute ready to distribute, not even in an emergency." He moved to the terminal and input his credentials.

Everyone in the room was quiet, listening to his fingers on the keys. Leadership makes others prone to follow, but followers aren't supposed to stop thinking for themselves.

Pat estimated the consequences. "It will be like the end of the classic age. People will begin to destroy everything that we've built, once they get hungry."

"Fear might do that first." Steve warned.

Martin found the information he sought on the corporate Holo-Net. "We have maybe a month of grain stockpiled worldwide. I'll have to check with the nutritionists, but maybe the Corporate Board can halve the grain per unit. That would buy us some time." He used the terminal at his fingertips to check news bulletins, and then nodded, closing his eyes. "We already have reports of idiots destroying some food kiosks. There was a run on the supply by hoarders." His eyes opened and he turned to Steve. "They'll probably start hijacking the supply transports next. Drivers will probably have to activate defenses, and if their machines open fire things will escalate."

Avery shook his head as he turned away. "We should have begun our habitat project a century ago, but sentiments on the Corporate Board were still too strong against giving anyone anything more than they thought was necessary."

In the still silent room, Steve asked "What changed, Marty?"

Avery considered the tangential question for hardly more than a moment. It was no less impractical to go into history than to describe the obvious, but even if it wasn't working toward a solution it was at least a change of subject. There was little that could be done anyway.

Avery stopped pacing and looked at Steve. "There was this guy named Damon Zeus. No relation to the laser optics manufacturer."

Martin interrupted himself to turn to his personal assistant. "Amanda would you be so kind as to see if a Board member is free to take my call? Thank you." Avery turned back to Pat. "You know the story of Zeus, don't you Pat?"

Pat turned to Steve "Super rich," she told him. "Heavily invested in agriculture, pharmaceuticals, and genetics among other things. His most famous quote incited a riot among the bereaved during a pox epidemic when he said: 'The pharmaceutical business is about profits, not cures.'"

Amanda indicated she was on hold, so Martin took up the story. "Believe it or not, that was the guy who came up with the numbers that proved costs outweigh benefits when you employ too many people to make stuff too few can afford.

"Damon's numbers showed that the members of the Corporate Board would save serious money if they simply housed, fed, and clothed the unemployed and redefined that condition as the new normal. The practical conclusion was that mass production and automation coupled with overpopulation made Zeus' findings necessary.

"We needed, and still need, a continuous supply of brainpower. The only way to get more brainpower is with more population. Increase the population, and you increase the number of top-end brains. But increasing the number of top brains means supporting a greater population. Reduce the population and new good brains become more scarce."

Steve guessed "Somebody tried artificial genetic modification?" Martin and Pat nodded.

Martin added "Maybe I am only being paranoid, but for the

sake of the resilience of our species, at least in the face of an uncertain future, I hope genetic engineering never does solve that."

Steve agreed. "If we standardize our genetics, the universe might come up with an unpleasant surprise."

Avery nodded to him. "Evolution developed our DNA over millions of years of trial and error. After a process like that, human genetics aren't anything to casually tinker with.

"So our corporations have historically held almost all of the world's wealth, at least since the height of the classic age" Martin continued. "The way capital cycles in Earth's economy, almost all the money worth talking about just flows back and forth between relatively few entities.

"In the old days a larger portion of the wealth took a roundabout route as it flowed, cycling all the way down through the population, partly through redistribution to the poorest people by the public government, but mostly through the instrument of private employment.

"Then automation drastically reduced the need for employees. The population continued to grow. The employed became an ever-shrinking portion of the population. Yet the only way most people could eat was to buy food from a producer or distributor. The unemployed had nothing to buy anything, and small businesses that depended on consumers who had nothing began to fail. Starving people began to do desperate things. Destructive, expensive things."

"Handing out more and more money to the increasing number of unemployed proved unsustainable. So Zeus suggested that the most efficient non-destructive approach would be to directly distribute generic necessities.

"That gave relief to the populace. Instead of handing out money to individuals, small businesses received subsidies to produce and distribute generic goods, including food. The corporations knew everything they needed to know about those small businesses. Local proprietors could regulate distribution."

"Nibbles." Steve offered.

Avery nodded to him. "One problem with what Zeus proposed

was that people would make trouble if they were idle. If their waking hours weren't occupied, they would invent real- life dramas just to entertain themselves. For better or worse, entertainment had answers for us. Much of industrial psych eventually backed them up. Virtual Reality could supply all the drama, competition and virtual chic people wanted.

"So the Corporate Board found themselves in a situation where they could market themselves as the saviors of humanity, with a benevolent worldwide social welfare program that incidentally saved us a boatload of money."

"And every non-luxury product became generic, bland, functional and inexpensive." Steve contributed.

"You've got it, Steve. Generic. It was the end of planned obsolescence. We didn't want to give away something that would break and make us give it away twice. People had needs and the products we supplied were again functional and durable. We moved from a wasteful consumer model to an efficient producer model. People used what we made simply because there wasn't much of anything else to use, unless they made it themselves or had credits... and frankly, one result has been some amazing art and home-made products. Not everyone is a good fit for Virtual Reality. Most small businesses became sole proprietorships that operate within a mixed barter environment where credits are very scarce. Credits are so scarce for most people that even low wage employees are widely envied.

"Big business colluded to supply the essentials, in exchange for very real advantages and subsidies. The Corporate Board takes a small portion of every luxury transaction. It's part of the cost of doing business. Then, instead of destructively competing, most corporations merged. Almost all the money now flows between and within conglomerates. Relatively little is paid to employees. Personnel costs for recruitment and retention are almost nil. Employees are invited to open positions on the basis of personnel data derived from what they do in virtual reality."

Martin turned back to check with Amanda, who shook her head. She was on hold, judging by the generic light music come from her comm unit as she tabbed the audio.

Martin continued "As I was saying, we constantly need a supply of truly intelligent people. To find the right minds for us, corporate media implemented some highly technical solutions.

"There were plenty of problems that came up as we tried to change, but we had to change or die. We adapted. Business evolved. There was considerable resistance against some of the changes we had to implement. We had to come up with a business model that would work for what we were trying to do. Even generic goods aren't free, after all.

"Employment had historically been the big carrot and stick of social control. We had to replace it. Virtual reality and online games gave us a cost effective substitute when employment opportunities became too rare. Virtual reality provides potentially unlimited virtual luxury, for next to no outlay, but to engage people the games have to meter virtual rewards. So that virtual success was marketed as an achievement. Oddly enough, most unemployed people ate it up. They bought into it. The media made it possible for us to pretty much toss away the stick and eat our own carrot.

"The kicker was that we could data mine everything individuals were doing in their virtual reality. Using those metrics, we could positively identify candidates who merited advanced training, no matter where they were, no matter   what they looked like, no matter *what* they thought they wanted. It was a win-win solution.

"Bottom line is that we *are* taking care of the people, and we're doing it efficiently. It works, just as long as they don't run out of food, shelter, clothing and especially entertainment."

Amanda flagged Martin down from his oratory and he excused himself to make his call. Steve looked at Pat, who looked back at him curiously.

Steve spoke quietly to her "In that case what is the point of making money? It sounds meaningless."

"It isn't meaningless, Steve." Pat told him. "Money circulates as it's used, from here to Perry Station. The Corporate Board controls that flow. The measure of money's value isn't ever at a standstill. Right now, it is feeding humanity and working to build a sphere of habitats in solar orbit, habitats that can someday feed and shelter our species, however populous we grow. Right now that money is out there in Aldebaran system trying to defend humanity."

Martin turned to Steve from his call and said "I am pretty sure that when we get enough people out there on the habitats, things will balance out, Steve. It will expand the middle class."

Chapter 39: Objective

Sestrel considered a digital chart of the planetary system on-screen. One of the technicians found it in a search of the ship's computer archives. The animals would surely defend this system. If they had a grasp of strategy, and he believed they did, defense here had to be an imperative for the animals. Five moduli connected to other systems. Their trade routes would converge here. They would see it as a choke point for the Skraa. It would be well defended here if they were at all prepared against him.

He had enough experience with these animals to know that their instincts were pretty good. They were space faring. Planet-bound species are much simpler food sources.

The animals used what technology they had rather well, but their spacecraft were weak. Sestrel wasn't particularly interested in destroying their ships and wouldn't go out of his way to do so. Destroying them was a waste of food, but eventually it would have to be done. It would be so much simpler if they were rendered unable to even reach orbit on their own.

Sestrel's stomach rumbled, unhappy with the synthetic proteins he had to live on. It didn't taste like meat; it didn't have the right texture. And it gave him gas.

Sestrel considered: Just before one of their ships was destroyed, the animals would leave that ship behind and launch into space in small, unarmed capsules. That might work out conveniently for the Skraa.

His objective was the same planet where the Skraa had originated, the first nest. He wished to avoid killing the animals any more than necessary for the sake of his hatchlings and the future.

Thinking about them led him to think of the captured specimen hiding somewhere aboard his ship because of an inept handler. She wasn't around any longer to make another mistake, to be sure, but he still had the problem of an animal roaming loose, and that was a problem that had to be corrected. It wasn't as if the animal had anywhere to go, but

Sestrel couldn't allow livestock to wander about getting into things.

Sestrel summoned a team of huntresses. He briefed them on the problem, how it began, why he had removed the cowl, and where the animal had been when it disappeared. He directed them to discover how it got out of the pen, to find the animal, and to impose on it once more the control function of the cowl. Then they were to bring it back to the livestock pen and notify him.

He told the team he wanted the animal alive to translate. Four competent huntresses should have little trouble. They must track and recover it immediately.

That matter handled, Sestrel returned to the chart to consider his objective and what he expected to happen on the way to achieving it. They would fight, of that he was sure.

He had endured losses among his huntresses when they sortied in their fighter craft, but the weaponry of the animals had failed to even strain his shields. He considered keeping the females aboard. When he came under fire he need only ensure that his exhaust and weapons were retracted within the shield envelope. He wouldn't be able to maneuver when he did that, but once his course was clear of the local star he could keep moving on inertia alone and get through the last modulus. That would probably make his transit of the system more effective and efficient, except in the matter of capturing any surviving livestock to supplement his diet.

There wasn't time to let his females hunt down meat, he decided. The timetable was already set. The nest had to be secured. Until they made orbit at the nest world, his huntresses would remain aboard.

Chapter 40: Nest

The huntress was alarmed when her companion began to falter. She could not bring herself to abandon her friend to the animals pursuing them, but she was slowing them down, in obvious pain. Her face and neck were swollen and she held her head at an unnatural tilt. Even more urgent, her abdomen periodically convulsed in spasms. It was time to nest, and all other considerations were as nothing beside that.

She didn't want to drop the heavy load of meat she carried. It had marked their trail with blood, but they were both famished. The meat she had cut from the animal had finally stopped bleeding, giving them a chance to lose the pursuers and find shelter, a place to hide. A place to nest.

Their pressure suits, cowls and helmets were safely stowed, hidden in a small pipe-filled compartment in the station's outermost bulkhead. If necessary she would still have a way to escape the station if she had to, but if they lived, there would be no way to take the hatchlings with her, once they hatched. At least she would have a cowl to imprint them, once they were grown. Then they could use the cowl for themselves to learn how to construct their own ships.

The two Skraa bypassed one intersection and turned into the next, seeking a place to rest.

Ahead of them at the end of the hall was a wide set of doors with inset viewports. These were the first double-doors they had encountered on the station. The expansive interior beyond the doors was brightly lit. The room contained elevated green disks beneath a bright translucent ceiling.

The doors opened easily when she pushed upon them. The atmosphere was ideally warm and humid. Against a bulkhead to one side of the vast room was machinery, a system of pumps and pipes and large drums, all painted a uniform blue. The pipes leading to and from the blue machinery led under the disks which could now be seen to contain a large number of leafy plants. The artificial gravity was much reduced as they drew closer to the gurgling disk of plants. An elevated walkway with guardrails stretched over the plants to the center, where there was a circular hollow.

The plants on the outer edge of the green disk were mature, while those toward the center were just sprouts.

Moving closer, they could see that each plant was growing within a separate container suspended at the upper edge from arms radiating from the central area. The bottom of each planter was bathed in a few centimeters of water swirling in the bottom of the disk, a nutrient reservoir.

There was an open space beneath the bottom of the shallow reservoir, unlit between supporting beams. There wasn't much headroom for an adult, but there was enough room to crawl. The two Skraa moved into its close and welcome darkness beneath the gurgling waters in the reservoir overhead. There was ready water access nearby, toward the central clearing. It may not have been an ideal nesting site, but a better one seemed unlikely in the station's hostile environment.

Chapter 41: Change of Course

The trail of blood led Lt. Matsuo's team no further. No matter how far they ranged along the hallways no more blood could be found. There was no sign that the aliens had managed to get back into the ceiling catwalks, but that was no guarantee. The aliens left no discernible trail on the polished station flooring, and they had moved too fast for the marines to catch sight of them.

When Lt. Matsuo reported in with the facts, Kyle recalled the squad. The security chief used a stylus to mark the end of the blood trail on security's digital floor plan, and mused over it, trying to divine where the aliens had gone. It was close to hydroponics but nearly as close to the docks and engineering.

Kyle was worried. He hoped he could find something on Gabriella's monitors. He couldn't field enough officers to maintain normal operations around the clock in the station as it was, let alone hunt down the aliens. Neither duty could be abandoned, but he just didn't have enough people. He didn't feel he could draft the ACM pilots. They had to maintain their patrols at the modulus and along the debris fields where the miners were back at work. Otherwise there would be even more trouble, guaranteed. If pirates and smugglers took advantage of the alien distraction to steal modulinite his failure as security chief would be serious, but there were lives at stake if he didn't neutralize the aliens.

"Gabriella: Set up a protocol for responding to emergency comm signals, then circulate it for civilians to use it if they see the aliens. Also, get a technician to install video surveillance and motion detectors in hydroponics. There's too much traffic at the docks for that, but assign someone to watch the dock access points."

"On it, Kyle." she replied. Kyle once more thanked his lucky stars that he had Gabriella.

Kyle went to the Security Office to review the holos that had been recorded on security sensors. He was seeking a weakness to exploit. He sat watching and listening to the aliens' fight with the assassin. With their shields active, the aliens could still see, and they sang to one another, therefore they could hear. So visible light and audible sound weren't blocked by their personal shields. Maybe he could use those facts. Further, none of the aliens wore a respirator, so the shields were permeable to air. After more thought, Kyle commed Mackenzie with an idea.

Tibs and his protégé Bobby had by then spent hours with Mackenzie and the alien cowl. They received word from the *Jade Temple* that the ship was ready to recall the crew to go find where the alien ship had come from, so Tibs and Bobby took their leave of the Chief.

Communications with Oberon through the Cygnus-Al Najid modulus had been restored. News was alarming from there and beyond, as far away as Dante system. There was no word from beyond the Dante system. There were no communications from Earth, or from Legion space, or from the Aldebari.

A brainstorming session with Chief Mackenzie and Counselor Lyman of the Perry Station council had produced a plan for the *Jade Temple* to deploy sensor buoys, starting where the alien capital ship had first registered on the station's sensors. Then the *Jade Temple* would place more sensor buoys on a line extending out through that point from the Al Najid/Cygnus modulus. If they followed that line far enough, then the *Jade Temple* should discover where the aliens came from. The sensor buoys were to provide early warning if more aliens approached.

To put a ship that was the size of the alien's into space would require a tremendous industrial base. That ship also shouldn't be imagined to be the only one out there.

Everyone, with the exception of Chief Mackenzie, felt sure that Earth's fleet wouldn't have much trouble stopping the alien, but the ACM alliance didn't have a fleet of warships to protect Perry Station if another one came.

Chief Mackenzie worried that the alien technology was too advanced to assume anything. His engineers had their hands full trying to just understand the alien ship in the station's secure R&D dock.

Mack felt he needed someone to assist him. His investigation of the cowl device seemed promising. He sent a request for Tibs to assign someone suitable to stay and help him. His fellow engineers were studying the mummified alien's scout ship. There was a vast store of information in the cowl, more than he had time to examine, let alone understand.

When Tibs received Mackenzie's request, he understood the chief's sense of urgency and immediately thought of Bobby. He would have liked to help Mackenzie himself. Duty required that he remain aboard the *Jade Temple,* so he asked Bobby if he would stay behind to help the Chief.

Bobby recognized that the unofficial nature of his role aboard the *Jade Temple* made him particularly expendable when it came to naval operations. He felt he would rather stay aboard the ship, but agreed to remain with Chief Mackenzie until the *Jade Temple* returned.

Councilor Lyman contacted Tibs with a different request. He pointed out that Commander Cortes and the ACM staff weren't available to fill out security's ranks. With intelligent aliens loose somewhere aboard the station, the command staff had to focus on keeping the local ACM Command Center secure around the clock.

Lyman submitted a request that a squad of Lt. Matsuo's Marines should be assigned temporary duty to help Kyle's security officers aboard the station. Tibs considered the request, and then asked Ishi Matsuo for his input. The lieutenant weighed in favor of the councilor's request: Perry Station was for now their forward base of operations and should be secured. Station security needed a hand doing that. Tibs acceded to the Council's request and advised Master Kinkaid and Elder Lu that the *Jade Temple*'s Marine platoon would be understrength for the *Temple*'s mission.

Life aboard Perry station was slowly returning to something approaching normal. The sense of emergency that had everyone on edge was fading. What was unknown nevertheless seemed more familiar. The aliens were mortal. There had been no further sign of them.

People were still jumpy, to be sure. They didn't walk around alone, but they were also no longer sequestered in the education center. Packing nearly a thousand people together in the station's school had been stressful. Life has to go on. Business demands action. People had time-sensitive contracts and other obligations to fulfill. Even if clients and consumers on Earth were cut off from the rest of human space, the citizens of Perry Station had to continue functioning. As sections of the station were searched and found clear, they were sealed off from areas that hadn't been searched and reopened to civilians.

An autopsy and medical analysis of the alien that the assassin had slain showed no identifiable threat of any new diseases. It was as if the bacteria and viruses present in the alien were a subset of those to which humans already had exposure.

Kyle worked the Aldebari marines into Security's duty roster and Gabriella coordinated their billeting. Matsuo's squad didn't at all mind having access to the 'Cog and Sprocket' tavern during their off hours.

Bobby cleared his few personal belongings from his locker aboard the *Jade Temple* and moved them into a vacant residential unit on the station near Chief Mackenzie's quarters.

Station Security posted patrols throughout the most heavily populated areas of the station. The marines would conduct reconnaissance on the aliens, thought to be in hydroponics. Maintenance crews were instructed to keep to patrolled areas, but workers returned to the docks and maintenance and to other essential duties, except in the hydroponics section. The two exit doors to hydroponics were locked remotely. Kyle was convinced the aliens were in there, but considering that they probably wore portable shields he wanted to avoid putting people in harm's way before he had Mackenzie's solution ready. The station would just have to live with only half the fresh vegetables and greens in the interim.

The *Jade Temple* chimed digital bells and blinked her running lights. Her access gangway was withdrawn and the polarity was reversed on the mooring arms to release the magnetic cleats fore and aft from the Perry Station pier. The mooring arms retracted and the cruiser edged out into open space using her maneuvering thrusters. Once the crew confirmed they were free of the structure, Tibs gave the order, and Master Kinkaid metered out hydrogen gas to the antimatter annihilation chambers of the main engines. The *Jade Temple* picked up speed quickly.

To starboard there spread a vast sunlit crescent of broken stone and dust that not long ago had been the agricultural third planet of Al Najid system, Perry. To port was the star of the system, Al Najid. Some call the star Bellatrix.

Tibs set course toward the nearest point on a line projected from the center of the modulus through the position where the alien ship had registered on Perry Station's sensors. There, the *Jade Temple* corrected course to back trace the projected route of the alien toward its origin on the assumption that it had kept an undeviating course prior to contact.

The *Jade Temple* deployed the first sensor buoy. It would send a periodic update to Perry Station staff in the station's ACM command center whether or not any ship was detected. If it stopped transmitting the pulse on time, then that would also be significant. The buoys would also serve to amplify and relay any communications signals to or from the *Jade Temple*.

Tibs wasn't altogether happy about leaving Bobby and Lt. Matsuo at Perry Station, but Kyle was right. Perry Station was where those marines were most needed, and they deserved the best field commander available. As for Bobby, it would be unconscionable to argue with Mackenzie about the importance of investigating the alien cowl device.

Bobby finished stowing his kit at the small apartment next to Chief Mackenzie's quarters, and then headed to engineering, near the dock.

Chapter 42: Virtual Worlds

The Corporate Government shut down the public news feed from Aldebaran, and broadcasters were left with little more than speculation. There was plenty of controversy for them to gnaw on. Some of the inferences were pretty wild, but Steve and Pat were ready to reunite with Kathlyn and Stevie for the evening and felt no need to listen to the corporate imagination.

Antarctic Continental housed perhaps a hundred employees and their families at the Knutzen Peak installation. Most were engaged in mining, others worked on Martin's habitat project, and the rest were either facility support personnel or administrative staff. Their children weren't distinguished by what their parents did for a living, but by their performance in their virtual reality worlds.

Stevie was seated with a group of children, male and female of various ages, who were playing 'Flames of Stalingrad'.

Kathlyn was with another group of children engrossed in a holoworld where, judging from the observational display, they found ways to acquire fashionable clothing and ornamentation for their avatars and a wide variety of exotic pets. Their virtual occupations seemed to revolve around a more social experience, wherein a wide array of occupations were represented, from marketing and sales to investigations, the role Kathlyn had chosen.

There were other groups of children playing other holoworlds.

There was no real need for the children to be grouped the way they were. With networked applications the players could have been physically far apart, yet the children tended to sort themselves where they could.

Steve and Pat walked together about the room, watching the children interact. On supervisory monitors they watched what appeared to be the users of powerful magic working their way through some sort of underground labyrinth, solving puzzles and defending themselves from predators. Apparently those predators were either being operated by another group of children somewhere, or possibly the opponents were controlled by a terribly sophisticated artificial intelligence.

Another group of children was preoccupied with a virtual world that had been devastated by some kind of cataclysm, and the players were salvaging 'lost' technology, searching a once- urban wasteland for means to not just survive, but to thrive.

Each holographic virtual world simulation was beautifully rendered with magnificent craftsmanship and believable detail. Each taught the children that little of value is accomplished alone, and everything is easier when done with others. In theory it was a cost effective means of nurturing social interdependence and responsibility while teaching the negative consequences of 'lone wolf' behaviors.

Steve found it disturbing to see positive independent thought and action suppressed along with the negative. 'Lone wolf' behavior triggered harsh consequences in the virtual environment. In worlds where the primary challenges were operated by artificial intelligence, solitary behaviors triggered an escalation in the number and difficulty of artificially intelligent opponents. The opponents overwhelmed the individualist. The environments were programmed to ensure that a player could not be successful alone.

The consequences of solo play negatively affected the experience of other players sharing that virtual environment. The cause of increased difficulty was made obvious, and it compelled team players to apply peer pressure on the soloist to reform and join.

After a brief moment, while the children set down their controllers, removed their interfaces and seemed to reorient to reality, Steve and Pat were rewarded for their patience with hugs from Stevie and Kathlyn.

"Did you have fun today?" Steve asked both of them, and both nodded and began to answer with rapid fire accounts of their day. Then both stopped and looked at one another, then looked back and started talking, again at the same time.

"Kathlyn what did you do?" Pat asked, solving the conflict. Stevie looked unhappy that his sister was called on first, but held his peace.

"It was really interesting!" Kathlyn responded with enthusiasm. "Somebody broke into a museum and stole an artifact. We had to figure out who it was. Then we had to chase them in the lower city." Kathlyn explained. She had clearly enjoyed her day.

"Did you get them?" Steve asked.

Pat wondered "An artifact? What kind of artifact, Kathlyn?" "No, we didn't, Daddy, but we can try again tomorrow, if we'll be here." Kathlyn looked hopefully at her dad. He smiled at her, thinking it likely they would still be there.

Kathlyn turned to Pat. "It was the golden crown of Montezuma."

Pat hesitated, then wondered under breath "I didn't know Montezuma even had a crown. What did you do, Stevie?" Pat asked the boy.

Stevie perked up. "I scored a head-shot on a lieutenant!" "A head-shot on a Lieutenant?" Steve mused with interest.

"Yeah! We had to rescue prisoners from a prison camp. I was all lined up on a guy who was peeking out of a guard tower when I saw another target running in an alley, straight toward me. I took out the guard but hardly even aimed when I dropped my sights and squeezed the trigger on the lieutenant. She moved right into my shot!"

Steve grinned widely at his son's excitement while shaking his head slowly. He opened his arms and Stevie swept in for his hug. Steve picked him up. "That sounds like a great shot, son." he said.

"You think that's okay, do you?" Pat asked him, surprising Steve. He stopped in his mental tracks, only slightly confused.

Steve furrowed his brow toward her. Was she concerned about what the simulation taught?

No adequate response came to Steve's mind. What he wanted was to celebrate his son's accomplishment and to encourage him. What troubled Steve was that there were apparently some points where his and Pat's cultures just didn't match.

If Pat's point was that Stevie shouldn't be encouraged to kill, then there wouldn't be much room to maneuver. That would be understandable, but the virtual death of an artificial entity, within a digital world created for that virtual death, should only be an incidental event.

Steve decided there could be no 'winning' at the end of such a conversation. Or argument. Whether Pat's sentiment was born of her culture, or if it was a more personal philosophy, the one thing that was clear was that Steve and Pat were still a long way from knowing one another. His observation suggested that his sentiments for her might have less to do with who she was, and more to do with who he hoped she might be.

The physical attraction was certainly real, but apparently the rest might be due to some sort of myth about her that he had built from his own hopes. Such a myth, if that's what it was, would be unlikely to endure the passage of time.

There was much about this woman he really liked. She was certainly in command of her point of view, she was independent and she had a strong character. There was a tantalizing amount of possibility there that he desired to explore. But just the same, he needed to rein himself in a bit, maybe see how things developed.

Steve just hugged his son a little tighter. That hug seemed all Stevie needed, and he hugged his father's neck and shoulder even closer.

Despite what his brain advised, Steve had emotional trouble letting the matter go. Things he could have said rose up from his depths, like bubbles into his operational consciousness, one-by-one. He judged and dismissed each as pointless, precipitous or irrelevant. He was obsessing, and it had to stop. He finally settled on responding with "I believe it is important for Stevie to train his reactions and eye-hand coordination."

Pat flashed him a stormy look and he realized he should have just let it go... but just letting things go was, to his mind, part of what had led his marriage into failure.

It might be best to focus the conversation on his and Pat's relationship. Yet if he did that he might be getting ahead of himself. He didn't really know how she felt about him. She hadn't said much... other than giving him her kiss.

At that point he stopped. That kiss had been wonderful.

The four arrived at the cafeteria for supper. The room was alive with conversation about the threat of aliens.

Martin was there at a table, sitting across from Mike Billings. Avery looked up from his plate and his eyebrow arched. Pat and Steve stood more closely than they had, but he also thought he sensed trouble in paradise. They would make a good couple, but he hoped that there wouldn't be a negative impact on negotiations. He needed that modulinium.

Martin took another bite, wondering about the ultimate impact of the alien incursion on the habitat project. Whatever happened, if humanity survived then the project would still be needed.

The aliens had already affected humanity. Their interdiction of interstellar traffic disrupted the flow of food from the stars. Hungry, humanity might turn in on itself violently. Fear of starvation could become as destructive as starvation itself.

Martin motioned Steve over before swallowing. He turned his eyes back to the food on his plate, with his fork poised thoughtfully among the fingers of his hand.

The facility in Antarctica was well stocked with provisions and other necessary supplies, but unrest along his supply routes might threaten or cut off the facility in the future. He considered having his food manager reduce the variety of entrees offered each day. He decided to float the idea at a scheduled meeting later that week, if the situation continued to deteriorate.

Steve and Pat arrived with the kids and trays laden with plates and drinks. "Any news, Martin? You look troubled." asked Steve.

Avery finished chewing his bite and swallowed. Perhaps what he had interpreted as 'trouble in Paradise' was due to the worry everyone seemed to be feeling. "Only that the Corporate Board has shut down the public newsfeed from Aldebaran." he replied. He looked down at his plate and dabbled with his fork to round up another bite. "I still have a privileged newsfeed, but censorship is a signal. It tells me the elite cadre is worried. The last I saw; the fleet was forming up to make a stand near the modulus on the Aldebaran side. I was thinking after we eat, maybe we would go up to my quarters again and I'll log in. We can see what the senior management feed is reporting, if you like."

"Are things so bad that they don't want people to panic?" Pat asked.

"The Corporate Board has imposed rationing and martial law. There's already a rush on food supplies out there. Some Nibbles kiosks have already run out. People are confronted with a problem they have no solution for, so they do what they think they can do. Right now that's grab all the food and hide. We've tried everything to make people think like team players, but the public isn't reacting like a team so far."

"Had the people thought ahead, they could have stored their own supplies." Mike Billings added to Steve "Nibbles are freeze-dried. It has a long shelf life. Unfortunately, people haven't had to think ahead. The Corporations have taken care of just about everything for them, for their whole lives up to now. They just play their games and ignore whatever isn't easy."

"Well, Mike," Martin objected, "if we were engineering the distribution system, wouldn't we think pretty hard to avoid an inevitable problem like inadequate supply? We would have built a first-in, first out store of reserves into the product flow. There isn't a single engineer on the Corporate Board. No doctors. Nobody in construction, or at least not on the practicing side of construction. They're all either legal or accounting, focused on efficiency instead of risks. They should have thought things through, or hired people like you and me to do it for them."

"Law and economics are complex systems in their own right, Martin." Mike argued. "They should have known they would eventually need a backup system. Risk management is vital in systems analysis. It should have been a priority."

"You and I know there is a big gulf between theory and practice. The evidence makes the case that they didn't think things through well enough." Martin observed.

After an exasperated silence he added "But this is the situation we have to work with. It won't solve the problem to figure out who is to blame, not unless we can go back in time with a big hammer."

Avery turned back to Steve and Pat. "Anyway, come on up this evening if you like. We'll find out what's happening out there, and I want to hear about your idea of delivering your product through Trondheim system, of all places. We can find a good holo for the kids, maybe."

Steve looked at Pat, who gave a slight nod. Then he looked to Kathlyn and Stevie "You guys want to watch a holo tonight?"

Stevie and Kathlyn looked at one another. Then Kathlyn looked back to her Dad and nodded, wondering whether she would get her choice, or if Stevie would get his. "That would be okay, but Daddy we want to know what the aliens are doing too."

Steve and Pat looked at one another like they had shared a realization. Each of them was careful to not presume on the other, but in doing so they hadn't given due consideration to Stevie and Kathlyn.

Children have points of view. They are more than just the roles they are expected to fill. They know when something is going on and shouldn't be left to guess. Steve resolved to talk with them about what was happening, to hear their questions and share their worries. Pat reached across the table linen and touched his hand. Her eyes were seriously beautiful.

Martin looked up toward the ceiling with a good humored hum. "Hm-m-m." He looked down at Kathlyn with a smile. "Matter of fact it seems to me there was a new release yesterday, starring Kelly Strange."

Kathlyn perked up avidly. Kelly Strange was a media sensation, especially among adolescent girls.

Stevie rolled his eyes, and Martin grinned at him. "It's an adventure cube, Stevie. I'm pretty sure you'll like it."

Stevie looked dubious.

Martin noticed it, and asked "What is it, Stevie? Don't you like holovids?"

The boy looked at the floor between them and began swing-ing one foot. Steve thought he seemed to have a pretty good sense of balance.

With everyone waiting for him to reply Stevie said "Holovids don't have room for me to do anything. If I don't want the girl to go down to the basement because the bad guy is down there, and I can't do anything; then she goes down anyway, even though I know what she is walking into. I don't really like feeling that I can't make a difference when things go wrong."

Martin nodded his understanding. "I like to be able to make a difference too."

Media entertainment had grown into a science, refined by consumer information gathered from online behavior. The inter-ests of everyone browsing Earth's HoloNet, whether through their comms or using residential computers, was meticulously tracked and analyzed. Since almost everyone interacted over the HoloNet, the data that the corporations held about HoloNet par-ticipants was staggeringly complete. Entertainment companies made full use of the information.

Steve wanted to finish the contract negotiations in a hurry and get the kids back to Perry Station. Events ongoing in Aldebaran system would be critically important to his family. Open hostilities might trap him on Earth. He didn't want to take his children into a war zone, and he didn't want a war coming to him. He responded "We'll be up with the kids after supper, Martin, thank you. The way back to Al Najid space looks pretty dicey just now."

Martin nodded at him, eyes serious. He looked at Pat, who nodded her agreement and then looked at Steve thoughtfully.

Chapter 43: The Cowl

"You'll notice that the cowl weighs less than we might expect, just looking at it" Chief Mackenzie said to Bobby. "I'm not convinced that it's metal, despite the appearance. I haven't tested the material yet.

"Notice the three control surfaces here at the top. If you look at the depressions around them, especially under magnification, you'll see that the leftmost button, viewing from back to front, shows greater wear at the edges around the depression. Call it a button. The button on the right shows the least wear. Each button has three possible states. Between them you can set different modes. I only explored two setting combinations before I concluded that I needed help for this."

Chief Mackenzie was looking at the cowl explaining what he had already learned. He looked up from it, and saw Bobby closely focused and attentive.

"The cowl exterior is limp when you just hold it in your hand, like this. It's made of linked scales of a metallic substance that I think may be a ceramic. The scales are held together by simple metal rings. The part that covers your head uses a thin flexible insulation to house what has to be a computer that controls the ambulatory terminals for the neurosensors, these metal disks on the underside. I say 'ambulatory' because they actively reposition themselves on the scalp to make the right connections. I think they work using the body's natural neural bio-electrical fields.

If we turn the assembly over, you can see many small smooth metal disks. I believe those are the neural sensors and transmitters. If we lift one aside and examine the circuitry and structure beneath, we see it looks superbly engineered.

"So the front is this roundish end, ahead of the three control buttons." Mackenzie advised. "The back is of course the pointy end. You put the front onto your forehead the rest will fit itself to your skull. The back lays down to conform to the medulla and down the back of your neck." Mackenzie stepped back from the cowl. "Give it a try. Don't be alarmed when the sensors begin to move." Mackenzie warned.

"How does it move?" Bobby asked.

"I don't know much yet about the mechanism, but the sensors do move around and adjust. It isn't easy to describe. Just try it and see, okay Bobby?" Mackenzie asked.

Bobby gave the chief a wry sidelong glance and then picked up the cowl. He was curious, but apprehensive. It was limp and flexible in his hands. He held the rounded front of the cowl and lifted it onto his head. The cowl wrapped and draped, and it felt cool to his scalp. For a moment he wondered whether his hair might be a problem. Then he felt the sensors, the polished metal disks, begin to adjust position around his cranium. His nervousness grew elevated, but he held himself still, determined to complete the exercise.

"Let me know when they've stopped moving, Bobby" the Chief directed.

When Bobby nodded in response the cowl didn't shake or wobble. It was like it had become part of his head. The cowl was light, but not weightless. It felt like it was fixed to his scalp. It didn't shift at all. Bobby's brow creased and he shook his head experimentally to see whether it might wobble or slip, but it didn't.

"The sensors have stopped moving, Chief." Bobby said.
"Okay, I'm going to press the first button. Report your experience aloud, Bobby, for the record." Mack pressed the flat button inside the rightmost depression on the cowl and pressed a key on his keyboard.

Bobby had no idea what to expect. He saw what vaguely looked like an organized array of symbols superimposed across his field of vision. They were translucent glyphs that might signify underlying information, like a table of contents. The glyphs looked like pictographs, like Chinese or ancient Egyptian. But if the characters were intended to be intelligible images, they were stylized and, to him, indecipherable. Still, three he sensed were in reference the three control buttons on the cowl. If he assumed that's what they were, then what was described in the tributary boxes beneath each might represent the contents of the cowl's functions.

Bobby paused in his thinking, wondering what led him to be-lieve those particular glyphs corresponded to buttons at all? There was something peculiar happening, but he felt increasingly sure that is what those pictographs intended.

He began to verbally describe what he was seeing, and hesi-tatingly reported his impression of what the images might repre-sent. His voice trailed off into silence as his mind raced.

As he focused his attention on the images, the three glyphs that appeared to be associated with the three buttons somehow began to make more sense to him. They represented the numer-als 1, 2, and 3. He started to report the change, but then his voice trailed off again.

"What is it? What's happening Bobby?" Mackenzie asked.

Bobby was thinking excitedly. The glyphs were beginning to make sense. "Chief I think this thing is learning from what I think, and it's associating the glyphs with meanings in my own memory. The pictographs for what I supposed were descriptive of button categories organize what can be accessed by different button combinations. The pictographs have obtained association in my mind with the numerals one, two and three. And now I am gaining understanding of what their subtending pictographs mean!"

Chapter 44: Admiral Ezra Crow

According to the preliminary and remote debriefing reports of those who survived the previous encounters, the alien defenses hadn't yet been penetrated, let alone degraded by any of the Navy's weapons.

Admiral Crow felt that the *Trafalgar*'s heavy railguns should be more successful. Even if the alien shields were so strong that they could stop or deflect the projectiles, the energy that the railguns delivered should eventually overload the aliens' shield capacitors. Assuming they used shield capacitors.

Energy absorbed is energy retained. Too much energy delivered to any shield exceeds its capacity. It could, and occasionally did cause catastrophic overload.

Word arrived from the Legion that their fleet would respond, but they would take more time to reach Aldebaran system than the Admiral believed he had before contact led to engagement. Still, it was reassuring to know that the Legion recognized the safety of Earth wasn't all that was at stake.

The Admiral recognized that the Legion's willingness to try had little to do with sentiment. Their economy was heavily invested in supplying grain to Earth. It was in their best interests to help defend their threatened customer. They undoubtedly also recognized the possible threat to their own people.

How the Aldebari would respond was an entirely different question. Their treatment at the hands of both the Corporates and the Legion, in the past, turned what should have been a sure thing into a question. Would the Aldebari engage with him against the aliens, even if they were in position?

Aldebari installations were wholly space borne and dispersed. They didn't aggregate anywhere after the brutal lessons they learned on Aldebaran III, and they especially didn't congregate at the bottom of any planet's gravity well. Living space-borne meant that their culture was more adaptable to the threat of a single ship, no matter how powerful it might be. Their economy was more self-contained, less dependent on Earth's wealth.

Still, Admiral Crow reasoned, they were human and would

care that humanity's ancestral home was threatened. What they chose to do would be a reflection of their true character.

The first reply to the Admiral's plea for assistance from the Aldebari came from a member of the Celestial Brotherhood, radical fundamentalists of the Aldebari religion. The Brotherhood was a relatively small sect of religious extremists. They were the faction most likely to tell the Corporates that Earth was on its own. Admiral Crow was therefore unsurprised when the Aldebari captain's text pointed out that a single alien ship should present little threat to Earth, a planet of eighteen billion people. The Celestial concluded there was no need for the Admiral's hyperbolic panic. The Celestial assured the Admiral that a Brotherhood research vessel would be on station in time to monitor and record events for study. The Celestial then had the gall to thank the Admiral for advance notice of, as he described it, 'the Corporate event'. The Admiral's color deepened while reading the Celestial's reply.

A second Aldebari message arrived, this time from the Admiralty, the military arm of the Academy, the dominant faction of the Aldebar. The Academy, and by alliance the Elders of Draco, assured Admiral Crow that they would respond. They reported that it would take time to reach Aldebaran system, but would make best speed to assist. The Admiral was heartened to read that their fleet was only hours out from the modulus. The message went on, but the Admiral gained hope. Only hours? He began to re-evaluate his options for the coming engagement.

An attached addendum to the message bore news that the *Jade Temple,* a ship of the Admiralty, was engaged in a mission in Al Najid system to discover where the alien mummy came from. That information would have to be considered later.

Just now there was a battle to be won.

The Legion and the Aldebari weren't allies of Earth, but they were humans. They were smart enough to realize that their fates were tied to that of Earth. The Admiral found it encouraging that whatever the outcome, the other two great powers would do what they could to help his fleet in the defense of Earth.

It was still possible that the aliens might unexpectedly divert to a different modulus. Admiral Crow felt certain that they somehow knew exactly where they were going, and that their objective was Earth.

The admiral checked his readouts. It should not be long now before the destroyers had a contact reading on the alien's course and position.

If the Aldebari were that close and *en route*, then even though the metrics provided by the lost task force indicated that Second fleet might be beaten by the technology they faced, there would still be a chance they could keep the aliens from reaching Earth.

Admiral Crow then allowed himself to simmer over the Celestial Brother's callous point regarding the limited threat of a single alien ship. If the Alien managed to win the encounter with the *Trafalgar*, supported as she was by the massed firepower of a modern fleet, then the threat to Earth was inestimable. Not only had that one ship already cut Earth's supply lines, but Earth would be effectively helpless if the *Trafalgar* failed, at least until the rest of the ships Earth held in reserve could be mobilized. The alien could pick Earth's planetary defenses and infrastructure apart from orbit. It could destroy Earth's orbital cities with impunity. If the support infrastructure on Earth was rendered inoperable the people would begin to starve. Starving people grow violent. Earth's civilians planetside might destroy themselves earlier than the alien could.

To the best of Admiral Crow's knowledge, communications and navigation on Earth relied heavily on satellites. Satellites would be easy targets for a hostile ship unopposed in orbit.

No matter what, the alien had to be stopped before reaching Earth. It had to be stopped here, in Aldebaran system.

The alien's aggression baffled him. What could they possibly hope to gain by attacking, unprovoked? A human enemy could hope to conquer Earth, to take as his or her own the greatest prize of all, but what could an alien hope to gain without even attempting a peaceful approach?

Then the Admiral grasped a terrible intuition of the aliens' motivation.

Like almost everyone else, he had watched the autopsy of mummified alien remains over the HoloNet. He remembered the unease he felt when he saw the teeth in its jaws, clearly carnivorous, and not in the least herbivorous. Admiral Crow felt growing horror as he realized that somehow he already knew what the aliens wanted. He hoped his insight was wrong, but he knew he was right. It was more than a flash of irrational paranoia that informed him that the aliens were *hungry*. Having thought of it he could not ignore his dread. If they were driven by *hunger* there could be no negotiation, even if they decided to communicate. They wouldn't be bought off, not unless humanity could find a way to feed them.

"Mark, I need a secure comm channel directly with the Corporate Board. No intermediary, and no text messaging that might be overlooked, leaked, or misinterpreted. I need it fast. It won't be long before we engage." Admiral Crow paused, then turned to his aide to explain "I think I know what they want, Mark, and I don't want any leaks."

His aide went to work to secure a communications channel with the Corporate Board, the people at the very top who held control of the entire Earth. When he made connection, the subsequent conversation passed in bursts with long waits for replies as the communications signals traveled all the way to Earth and back. But the corporate board was actively interested in what the Admiral had to say.

"Admiral, I have an aide to Board member, Amrita Patil, on a secure channel awaiting your message. The board member is standing by."

Admiral Crow addressed the board member. His words were only for the Board, but when his transmission arrived at Earth the aide would be excluded from the loop. "Member of the Board Amrita Patil, my assessment is that we have a chance to stop the aliens here at the Aldebaran modulus, but we may be overcome. The Corporate Board should prepare for the worst. Recommend you relocate to your prepared sites on and under the planet's surface. The orbital cities will be vulnerable if Second fleet fails our mission. We do not intend to fail." The Admiral then went on to inform the board member of the responses received from the Legion and Aldebari Admiralty.

A few minutes later a female spokesperson representing the board member responded. "The board understands your predicament, Admiral. I am instructed to reply that the board will take your recommendation to relocate under advisement. Quote: 'We have confidence that you can pull a victory out of this. Even if the alien gets through, we aren't all convinced that they are a serious threat. Some of us consider the Celestial Brotherhood's remark may have merit. The alien is only one ship. Has there been any response to our first contact protocol?' end quote."

"No response has been received to the protocol, Ma'am. I suspect they aren't interested in negotiating." The Admiral weighed his next words. "We have reports from pilots who made visual contact, and these aliens are like that mummy that was found out in Al Najid space. We saw the teeth on the specimen at Perry Station. They are carnivorous. Vegetables and grains wouldn't work well for them. I think they are hungry. I think they want us for food." Admiral Crow advised.

"I don't want to underestimate the threat." he continued. "Second Fleet will do everything we can to keep Earth safe. It is my hope that our railguns will give them a serious surprise. At the very least, we will try to hold them here long enough for the Aldebari fleet to reinforce us, unless you object to their assistance. We will transmit a running account of events here over this channel. Second Fleet, signing off." the Admiral concluded.

Board member Patil had voiced no problem with accepting help. The Corporate Board was anything but stupid. Admiral Crow composed and sent messages of gratitude to the Legion and to the Aldebari, stating that the *Trafalgar* and her fleet would make a stand here at the Aldebaran/Earth modulus. They would try to engage the alien long enough for the other fleets to arrive.

The *Trafalgar*'s main armament was comprised of four powerful railguns. Each could throw a potent payload that, in the vacuum of space, had a potentially unlimited range. The projectiles they could throw were composed of a heavy hardened steel core, tipped with tungsten alloy, and clad in aluminum. The heat

generated by the electricity and friction of the shot would vaporize the aluminum cladding into a superheated ionized plasma,
reducing the net friction of the projectile on the rails. The electromotive weapon could produce a continuous firing cycle of under
ten seconds per shot because of the rotary design that allowed
spent rails to be replaced as other shots were fired.

A direct hit from one of these projectiles could penetrate the
shields and destroy the armor of any human ship, assuming it hit
dead-on and wasn't deflected. Shots that penetrated the target's
shield envelope but were deflected by sloping armor would still
deliver a tremendous kinetic impact.

When they designed the *Trafalgar,* the naval architects of
Corporate Earth held no illusions about the fighting capabilities of
the Aldebari and Legion. All three powers had access to essentially the same technology. The *Trafalgar* was built with a heavily
armored hull intended to present as few flat surfaces as possible.
On every aspect the ship used sloped armor. A successful kinetic strike that was able to penetrate the battleship's shield envelope should be sufficiently deflected to minimize the transfer of
energy, assuming the captain of the battleship was able to present his ship's best defensive profile.

The design's 'best' combat profile was focused on delivering
and deflecting kinetic projectiles. Railguns were the most effective type of anti-ship ordnance in humanity's arsenal, and that
was what governed the battleship's design.

When viewed abaft the beam (from the side), a *Trafalgar*-
class battleship looks like a four-bladed Morningstar, where the
head of the mace is the bow. The handle of the mace is where
the crew has quarters. Small craft could be launched there as
well, in the stern, just ahead of the great engines.

The hold is amidships, between the crew quarters aft and the
railguns forward. The hold houses the ship's stores, her ordnance, the main anti-matter bottle for the engines, and four long
magazines for the guns' replacement rails and munitions.

The tremendous energy involved in flinging heavy projectiles
using electromotive force causes erosion in the rails. The rail
magazines are used to replace expended rails. Eroded rails can

later be refurbished in storage.

The battleship was also fitted with the weaponry and point defenses of a cruiser, but the requirements of the main armament dominate the battleship's design.

The angle of *Trafalgar's* armor would not much matter to the aliens' high-energy coherent beam. If a coherent energy weapon was so powerful that it could penetrate the shield envelope, the angle of the armor would be irrelevant. The question then was only how well the armor could resist

The alien didn't even use ballistics or missiles, or hadn't yet. The thought occurred to Admiral Crow that a ship dedicated to beam weaponry had a greatly reduced dependency on supply lines. Logistics were essentially removed from the equation.

There was no need to stockpile and move ammunition, which in turn reduced opportunities for an enemy to interdict supplies. They would need only food and water, and more rarely supplies of antimatter, but that could be gathered in the magnetosphere of any proper gas giant planet.

Humanity had never before encountered beam weaponry as powerful as that of the alien ship. According to the numbers received from the task force lost in Dante system, there was so much focused power in the beam that shield envelopes failed much too quickly, before they could even absorb enough power to put a load on the capacitors. Electrical conductors could only divert so much power so quickly. Beyond a shield system's capacity to absorb power, the alien beam had seared as if unopposed, superheating its way to eat through the armor and spatter the interior with molten metal, even before full penetration. Thermal expansion destroys hull integrity and splits nearby seams as a secondary effect.

But the *Trafalgar* was able to generate shields that were much more powerful than those of smaller ships. Her armor was much heavier, and more robust in composition.

Admiral Crow believed in his ship and crew. His railguns had unlimited range, while the enemy's energy weapons did not. All he needed was the location, speed and bearing of the alien. If the target held course and speed, then the targeting solution for his guns would become calculable, factoring for planetary and stellar gravitational influences. One well-placed salvo of his four railguns should destroy or disable any ship in space. Ezra Crow would not be so conceited as to count on that.

The destroyer squadron's sensors finally acquired the enemy and transmitted the alien's course and speed. The destroyers launched their first salvo of torpedoes. They were still too far away for the data they sent to be received by the fleet in real-time, but when it did arrive the data was enough for the *Trafalgar*'s targeting computers to calculate a firing solution.

To minimize incidents of friendly fire, the solution for each salvo from the four railguns would be transmitted to the squadron. The destroyers should receive the information in time to ensure they were out of the way.

The alien vessel was holding course directly for the Earth modulus, as if contemptuous of Corporate weaponry. Assuming the alien craft maintained course, the Admiral was confident that at least the first four solid projectiles should hit the target, even at extreme range. If the aliens survived the first salvo they would surely begin to maneuver, reducing predictability. That meant that he could only count on one salvo until the range was reduced enough to render the enemy's evasive tactics futile. In case the aliens failed to react quickly, he decided the *Trafalgar* would fire a second salvo as well.

The projectiles should be extremely difficult for the target to detect before impact. They carried no energy signature beyond residual heat, and had hardly any profile facing for sensors to detect. They would have an infrared signature but it would be much reduced at range. The needles would be moving just as fast as they had when they left the railgun's muzzle, about three kilometers per second. Even if the aliens detected the needles coming at them they shouldn't have time to react.

The downside to the railgun system is that the rail conductors are eroded by each discharge of the equivalent of lightning. The technical solution to rail degradation is what gave the Trafalgar class battleship its distinctive 'Morningstar' profile. The conductive rails were mounted within an armored housing on a carousel that could continuously replace eroded conductors with fresh rails from stores maintained in the ship's hold. The carousel housings could pivot to acquire targets, but design limitations slowed rail replacement unless the railguns were aligned with the keel axis, directly in the battleship's line of travel.

Admiral Crow ordered that a salvo should be fired as soon as the next solution for all four railguns was calculated. A moment after the order was relayed, all four weapons discharged the electricity that had been stored in their capacitors into their rails. A conductive armature in each weapon was compelled forward by electromotive force. The aluminum sheathing of the accelerating projectiles formed a plasma around each of the four hardened steel needles tipped with tungsten alloy. When the aluminum cladding was expended, each of them looked much like a polished needle, two meters in length and ten centimeters thick. They were launched into vacuum exactly toward a point calculated to coincide with the hostile alien ship now speeding for the Aldebaran/Earth modulus.

As the railguns launched their needles into the projected path of the alien ship, the *Trafalgar* transmitted trajectory projections to the destroyer squadron to reduce the chance of casualties by friendly fire.

Chapter 45: Hunted

Paul Harden was convinced that the starship was not built by the lizards. Had it been otherwise, he would have been caught the first time he slept.

When the four huntresses first caught sight of him, he had been searching for food, for water, and for some kind of weapon. By pure luck he evaded and lost their pursuit using the narrow maintenance shafts. The four huntresses couldn't use the shafts except with great difficulty. Their tails and the skeletal structure of their hips and legs made the shafts too narrow for their feet to use the rungs. They avoided using the shafts.

Apparently the lizards were more interesting in capturing him alive than in killing him because they didn't shoot him when they had a chance.

Harden needed something long, something like a spear, so he could stab them while he stayed out of reach. If a lizard could be lured into a shaft and he had a spear, then he could kill it, he felt sure.

He had even been able to get some sleep in the weightless section of the shaft he was using. Fortunately, he had managed to eat, to drink water, and to relieve himself at the livestock pen, but then the lizards nearly caught him.

They were actively hunting him. They knew where he had to go to find nutrition and water. Now he was hungry again, and his throat and mouth were parched. He knew they would try to catch him the next time he left the shaft for nourishment there.

At the top of the rungs he opened the shaft hatch just enough to peer cautiously into the room where he had first escaped. They were there, but weren't looking in the right direction. They had left the wall panel open but their attention had drifted. One of them sniffed the air and started to turn. Harden silently let the hatch close again, thinking. He didn't know where he was going to find anything to drink or eat. He would have to bathe soon. All his effort to sneak and hide would be wasted if they could already smell him.

Harden hadn't yet found anything to use as a weapon. As attractive as the idea was, he could think of no practical way to kill one of the lizards without some kind of weapon. He didn't have claws, and he didn't have a mouth full of knives.

As he started back down the rungs of the shaft, he knew he needed to find a weapon, and he needed to find it before hunger and thirst weakened him. While he was at it, he wanted a way to cut meat from one of them, once it was dead. A way to cook it would ... Harden almost chuckled at himself aloud. *Why not wish for a butler while I'm at it?* Harden thought.

He didn't know whether lizard meat was edible, but his desire to find out was growing serious. The emptiness in his belly was enhanced by fear and anger.

Those might be eggs dropping into the big containers on the deck below. The containers looked like they were intended as a means of transport or deployment. But that suggested that they might be weapons or ordnance of some kind. If they were eggs, why would they package so many together? Eggs didn't make sense. Besides, if they were eggs they should have brittle shells instead of those flexible, tough exteriors.

But they might be eggs. Or, if they were weapons of some kind, he might use them for his own purposes. When he handled the one he had examined, it had been warm and leathery. When he rocked it, it gurgled like it was filled with a thick fluid. If the gelatin they contained was an explosive, then they might be safe enough to open. Explosives would probably need a detonator to be dangerous.

But if the jelly balls contained a biological or chemical agent, then if he opened one it would probably mean his death.

They had to be eggs.

Harden had yet to explore two vestibules that he found branching off from the shaft he used as his base of operations.

They probably opened onto areas of the ship that he hadn't seen. He had no idea what he might find beyond either of them, or whether they actually led anywhere. The lizards who had been waiting to capture him should still be at the livestock pen, but there were many others. He needed to be careful.

Harden stopped at the unexplored next exit from the shaft with caution. He hoped that he wouldn't be caught as soon as he opened the hatchway there.

Again, the clasp that held the door was almost soundless to disengage and was easy to open. There wasn't light inside. Whatever was there was hidden in darkness. Harden stood still, listening intently at the opening for a few moments trying to hear any sound from beyond.

He gently opened the door onto complete darkness. He stood still there, listening. Though he waited for his eyes to adjust, he could still see nothing whatsoever. He felt conflicted about exploring further. Maybe if he came back there would be some light. Perhaps a step beyond the doorway would trigger a motion detector and an alarm would sound. There might be sleeping aliens there that could awaken. His ears detected no sound of breathing but his own.

The darkness was warm and utterly still. He again had the impression that the lizards had not been in the area in a very long time, as unlikely as that should be, aboard a starship. Yet Harden had found places where the aliens never went, or so it seemed.

He stepped from the doorway into what, judging from the sound of his breath, might be a hallway. He didn't want to run into anything. He carefully extended his hand and waved it cautiously ahead. The motion of his hand triggered the area's illumination.

Light flickered into being from the ceiling, revealing a short narrow hallway leading to a central area. On the floor just ahead was a crumpled bundle of what looked like fabric, possibly dark clothing. Harden wanted the fabric to fashion some kind of sack, to carry what he needed while leaving his hands free.

Within the clothing he could see what must be bones. The bones were thick, more thick than comparable human bones would be. The skull, too, was different from a human skull. It was obvious that these weren't from a lizard. The teeth weren't those of a carnivore, but of an herbivore, with bicuspids and molars.

The bones did not look like they would be from one of those bipedal creatures he recalled standing helplessly with him, back when he was first held captive. Those aliens had been as tall as he. These thick bones suggested to him that the remains were of someone short, but wide-bodied.

When Harden tried to examine the fabric, he found that the dark fabric disintegrated into shreds and gritty dust between his fingers. So much for the sack idea. The cloth must have been extremely old. Harden stood up again and looked around the room, wondering who this had been, and what might have happened here.

There were three obvious exits from the room. One he had just emerged from. Another, to the right, looked like a door secured by a wheel latch. The wheel latch had been jammed from the inside by a metal bar that was wedged through the circular latch handle. The bar was inserted to prevent the wheel from turning.

The metal bar might make a weapon. It wasn't sharp, but it might be effective as a bludgeon... if there was room, if he could swing it.

Harden stepped to the hatch and lifted the polished metal bar, sliding it just a few centimeters out of place. Then he let it slide back. He winced when it made a solid, ringing sound in the silence. It had slid all the way to solid contact. He estimated it was too heavy to swing. A swing would put him off balance. Harden thought harder, and his eyes narrowed with determination. His ability to focus had always been his pride.

The bar was quite heavy. It was of dense metal. If caught in a narrow place, as seemed likely, he could use it to deliver a punch that should be unstoppable, and without throwing him off balance. He could visualize it. He could see himself thrusting the end of the bar into the forehead of that big lizard that raped his mind. Harden focused on the image and in his mind he practiced that thrust.

Ferocity left his face. He returned to examine the room. The

bulkhead straight ahead didn't offer any sort of exit. It was occupied by a low console and a seat. Arrayed on the wall above it
were dark rectangular sheets of glossy material, three rows of
five, possibly unpowered viewing screens.

Facing the console was a short but wide-backed seat secured
to the deck. The back and the seat were scooped, joined too
closely to have been designed for the tail of a lizard.

The console itself was built lower to the deck than it should
have been for a human, or for a lizard for that matter. The flat
plane of its angled, metallic face was covered in neatly etched
lettering that Harden found indecipherable. The characters of the
language looked like they might be stylized pictures. It didn't look
like any language he had ever seen, but there were spaces between groups of the characters and a horizontal line beneath the
rows of glyphs. Harden assumed that these conventions signified
distinct words or ideas. The machined engravings looked right-
justified, so Harden intuitively surmised that the language would
read from right to left.

There didn't appear to be a switch anywhere to connect the
console's power.

Harden looked again at the door secured by the metal bar.
The barred door was large enough to be accessible to the lizards. Harden didn't see how that would stop them from getting in
if they wished. They had energy weaponry, so surely they had lasers able to slice through the door if they wished to.

There was no way to readily tell whether there was atmosphere or vacuum on the other side of the door, but his sense of
direction suggested he should be deep within the ship. There
shouldn't be vacuum this deep inside the ship. Yet if that was so,
then why had the builders installed a pressure seal on that door?

Harden turned to check the third exit. A brief corridor led to
rungs leading up to an overhead hatch. Harden walked to it,
climbed, and with some difficulty pushed the overhead hatch
open to look up into a dark cylindrical shaft. The light from the
opened hatch showed that the rungs continued higher into the
darkness.

Harden felt tired. His hunger and thirst had already affected his endurance. Peering up into the unexplored shaft, he hesitated, weighing his needs. He wasn't sure whether to rest, see whether those ovoid things in the container room were eggs, or press ahead.

Then rang a deafening sound like a bell, and the whole ship lurched violently to one side, threatening his grip on the rungs. The shaft above him echoed, loud and metallic as the hatch swung shut. Harden could imagine only that the ship would react so violently if it had been struck by something. Something powerful or massive. It might mean the ship was under attack by someone, or even been rammed.

Harden had no idea where the ship may have traveled after his capture, but he suspected that his purloined memories had given these meat eaters ideas about Earth. If so, Harden wondered whether, perhaps, his people had struck a blow in self-defense. Then he considered that if humanity won he would probably die without anyone knowing he was there.

He decided he had better find someplace where he could hold on, to ride out whatever was happening. He descended and made his way toward the seat at the console.

Chapter 46: Morrison's Log

After meeting with Kyle, Chief Mackenzie arrived at Perry Station's Engineering section to begin his workday. The noise of his entry woke Bobby Morrison, who lifted his groggy head from his arms on the desk. He was still wearing the alien cowl.

Bobby's eyes gradually gained focus. He reached up to depress a control button and removed the cowl. He placed it limp upon his workstation desk. Mackenzie stood with arms crossed and a tilt to his head. "Bobby, you should go get some sleep." the Chief recommended. Bobby nodded with some reluctance, then turned to his screen to finish a log entry before powering down his system.

The chief looked out the plasticlear window onto the alien scout ship resting in the secured atmospheric dock. Something seemed different about it. Behind him he heard Bobby rise from his chair, and he turned back to the young man. "Find anything interesting, Bobby?" he asked.

Bobby realized that he hadn't yet shared what he had learned. "The middle button, second level. The first category provides the controls for the scout ship. I powered her up from here."

Mackenzie was at a loss for words, but felt excitement leap in his heart. "That is how the scout ship moved, I take it. Anything else?"

Bobby nodded. "The third button apparently has a file transfer function, but it doesn't seem to have any way to attach a storage device, like a data cube or anything we would expect. When I fell asleep I was trying to learn how it's meant to be used. I did find a large file there. I was hoping to see what was in it, but I didn't find a way to copy it to our holographic systems."

There was no sign of physical damage to the ship or to the atmospheric dock, so Mackenzie knew Bobby had at least tried to be careful, but the young man needed to keep his curiosity under tight rein. "We need to be careful with this device, Bobby. We don't know what it can do. I need to ask you to not use it again without my being here, just in case you find yourself in trouble with it."

Mackenzie saw an unspoken thought flicker in Bobby's eyes, but the young man just nodded his head and agreed wearily. "Of course, you are right, Chief. Now I think I need to go get that sleep."

Chief Mackenzie smiled and clapped the young man's shoulder. "Of course you do, lad. Go get some rest. I shouldn't have left you alone last night. We want to understand this tech, but we want to stay safe while we do. Tibs would have my head if anything happened to you, you know." Mackenzie smiled.

Bobby nodded and headed for the door. In quiet then the Chief gazed longingly at the cowl on Bobby's desk. A large file?

Mackenzie realized Bobby hadn't left. He looked over his shoulder at him. The young man had noticed the chief looking at the cowl and he met the Chief's eyes. "You too, Chief." Bobby said meaningfully. "We want to be sure and keep you safe too."

The chief looked down at his hands like they had been caught in the cookie jar. He needed to keep his own curiosity in check as well.

His team had been studying the scout ship for the past year. They were puzzled by the lack of manual control systems. Now Bobby found a virtual control system for the ship in the cowl. A control system similar to, but possibly advanced beyond, the famed neural implant systems developed by Aldebari scientists.

Mackenzie tuned a flat simulative holographic monitor to the reports incoming from Aldebaran system. He could keep tabs on goings-on there while he worked. Then he accessed Bobby's project log on engineering's primary server to examine his findings.

Earth's second fleet was making a stand of the engagement in Aldebaran. Mackenzie was worried at the news. A heavy cruiser with destroyers and frigates had been lost in Dante system, unable to penetrate the shields of the alien. The Chief evaluated that second fleet's chances were slim, though Mackenzie had high regard for the railguns of the battleship's main armament.

Turning to the log of Bobby's cowl research, Mackenzie's attention gradually became absorbed in his reading.

Chapter 47: Trafalgar

The projectiles thrown by the *Trafalgar*'s four great railguns were deflected when they struck anywhere but within the central third of the alien ship's shield. Those that struck off- center struck only glancing blows, and even those that struck dead-on hit the hull with only a fraction of the force they arrived with. While the enemy's shield strength was disheartening, their shields were still having to absorb a tremendous amount of energy. Admiral Crow was certain it would not be long before the shields were overloaded, and then the envelope should either collapse alto- gether, or the capacitors should overload.

Yet when the alien's shields did begin to turn translucent, the alien revealed another technology that the *Trafalgar* did not have. One of the fast missile frigates, the *Canberra*, was trans- mitting visuals of the alien ship for analysis. The imagery showed only superficial damage to the target's interlocking armor, but when the shields began to overcharge and cloud the ship ex- tended some kind of conductive rod into the shield envelope. The rod appeared to drain excess charge from them. This reve- lation was a jaw-dropping turn of events. The admiral was begin- ning to feel despair.

Second Fleet received the signals from many Aldebari tran- sponders near the Spica modulus, and communications were es- tablished. The Aldebari fleet had made transit into Aldebaran system and was racing to join with Second Fleet. Admiral Crow ordered transmission of data encryption keys and comm link in- tegration. He also directed Naval Intelligence to coordinate a cur- rent situation report with their counterparts.

The alien ship maintained speed, barreling in toward the Earth modulus, but ever since the *Trafalgar*'s needles began to strike the hull it had been veering randomly to reduce predictability. Admiral Crow was determined to keep his battleship between the alien and the modulus. If he was unable to destroy the damn thing, then he would deny passage by getting in the way.

It would not be long before the alien drew close enough for its defensive maneuvers to be pointless. The railgun needles would be too fast for them to dodge. At about the same time, the Admiral knew the *Trafalgar* would come within effective range of their powerful energy beam.

The damage that the railguns inflicted on the alien ship was light. The alien ship had some kind of interlocking armor that absorbed and spread the shock of each strike. As ferocious as the electromotive projectiles were, the rounds that actually penetrated the shield were slowed to where they caused little more than dents. A few defensive emplacements were demolished, but the alien's point defenses were still numerous and they still eliminated every torpedo the destroyers launched. Anti-ship missiles were apparently ineffectual. The energy they communicated to the alien shields was quickly drained off, and the interlocking armor seemed impervious.

Admiral Crow didn't understand how the aliens managed to avoid internal overload even when they drained excessive energy from their shields. One of his analysts searching Milnet for ideas came across an intelligence report on the debrief of a survivor of the recent debacle at Trondheim system. According to the report, the Aldebari cruiser *Jade Temple* had somehow used an excess energy build-up in her shield capacitors to supplement the power supply for her main forward armament.

On reflection the Admiral decided that might work. The principle seemed clear enough to the Admiral to forward the concept to the *Trafalgar*'s chief engineer, Mike Hawkins, for evaluation.

With the range closing, more and more of the needles fired by the *Trafalgar* hit the 'sweet spot' in the alien shields where they weren't fully deflected.

The balance of the human fleet could do little more than hang back, enveloping the alien beyond the range of its main weapon. They were focused on keeping the alien fighters inside the alien ship's launch bay. Had the fighters been able to fly unopposed they would surely have penetrated the Trafalgar's shields and whittled the battleship down.

The alien's main weapon emerged from the armored hull and pushed through the shield envelope to fire.

The bow of the *Trafalgar* was superbly well armored, especially the great blades that housed the railguns with their reloading carousels. The ship had been designed to successfully engage a similarly armed ship.

The alien commander chose to disable the railguns first. Those were the only weapons that had been able to penetrate his shields.

An awful torrent of energy was transmitted immediately across intervening space from the lens of the main alien weapon. The strike was only marginally reduced by the *Trafalgar's* shields. The raw power carried by the beam was too great for the shields to adequately draw into their capacitors. When that overwhelming beam struck the armor that was intended to protect the rail gun and carousel, the armor superheated. It began to vaporize where the beam struck. It liquefied nearby metal. That vaporized metal expanded explosively, spattering liquid metal radiantly in all directions. The alien didn't have to completely destroy all the armor to disable the railgun because splashing molten metal effectively closed the railgun's muzzle.

The alien flicked the focus of its weapon without pause to the second of the *Trafalgar's* four railguns.

~

Sestrel felt immense satisfaction disabling the animals' only effective weapons, one after another. Once more his technology over-matched what the creatures could field. He intended to pick that ship apart piece by piece, to slice it up like a slab of meat. It was gratifying to toy with an animal that presumed to defy him.

The small ships harrying his flank were irritating but irrelevant, now that he finally had this target in range. He would not rise to their taunting attacks. His engines were safely tucked into the shield envelope, where the animals couldn't touch them.

Once he was through the modulus, he would inevitably have to dispatch the animals' smaller ships in order to proceed with his plans for the homeworld. True, there would be some danger when he did, because he would have to be able to maneuver to catch them, but catch them he would.

It hardly mattered at all that the ship ahead blocked direct passage through the modulus. It would take only a minor course adjustment to get around the obstacle. It didn't matter to the modulus which direction he entered. He could make transit from the other side if need be.

The only real issue was that to maneuver quickly, to change direction, he would have to extend the engines through the shields, exposing a vulnerability. Maneuvering thrusters would work eventually, but their low thrust/mass ratio was not optimal.

~

The admiral was basically out of options. The alien ship was reducing his forward armor to misshapen slag. It wouldn't be long before he had to tell the forward crew to abandon their posts and pod out.

His communicator chimed. It was Hawkins, in   engineering. The admiral responded "Any ideas, Chief?"

"Sir, the alien will have to maneuver to get around us, and that will expose his main thrusters." Mike Hawkins began.

"But the timing of that effort will be critical. I don't have a way to predict when he'll make the move, Chief."

"Affirmative sir, but we can play the hand we've been dealt. And we have a card left that we may be able to use. We can force his timing and make him predictable."

The Admiral perked up, slightly suspicious. "I'm listening. Go ahead and lay it out, Mike."

"Our main magnetic bottle of antimatter is amidships in the hold. It has a battery backup for the power supply that will give it roughly fifteen minutes before it blows. That fifteen-minute window starts when the main power is cut." the Chief offered.

"Right. So, what card do you see there? You aren't suggesting..." the Admiral prompted.

"No sir, or not quite. But the naval architects built a safety measure into this ship that I previously thought was a waste. It turns out they may have been prescient.

"In case someday we weren't able to restore power to the

main antimatter containment system in time, the Trafalgar's stern here can separate from the hold amidships. The rail gun carousel in the bow would be lost with it, but the carousel looks like a write-off to me."

The Admiral grasped what Hawkins was suggesting. It was another shot at the bastard when he thought he had none. "Got it, Chief: Next beer is on me." Ezra Crow smiled a thin smile. "The accountants will scream bloody murder."

Hawkins chuckled "Always finding the silver lining, sir." "A hard earned talent, Chief. Hard earned. Carry on."

The Admiral switched his comm to address the crew forward and commanded them to either evacuate aft or pod to safety.

~

Sestrel saw the large ship ahead blossom with escape pods and felt satisfaction. His enemy knew he had won. The animals continued to grunt at one another over their communications band.

"Target is accelerating." reported one of his technicians.

"Continue fire." Sestrel commanded serenely.

They were going to make a run for it. "As they turn, target other areas of their ship."

The animals' lesser ships were repositioning. They, too, knew their cause was lost. Sestrel was glad he had preserved his huntresses. They hadn't been needed in this fight as it turned out. He had nearly had them launch when his ship was being battered by the projectiles of the animals' largest ship. He had still been too far to return effective fire. Had he lost another female it would have been a terrible waste. The hatchlings would need all of them, once they reached the homeworld.

"Target has continued to accelerate. They are not diverting from their course. I think they mean to collide with us."

Startled, Sestrel looked at the sensor viewscreen just in time to see a nimbus of gasses blast radially from the animals' starship. The massive bow and central hold of the starship separated from the stern that housed their engines. The rest of the ship was heading directly for Sestrel's vessel like a thrown hammer while their stern veered off under powerful thrust.

"Evade!" he commanded the helm in the imperative tone of command. Helm almost immediately fired maneuvering thrusters to turn the ship while not adding forward motion. The great alien ship was agonizingly slow to turn. While the ship came about, the main thrusters were extended so they could ignite and push the vessel out of the huge projectile's way.

Sestrel belatedly understood why the small ships had been moving as they had. It wasn't to cover the escape of the large ship at all, but instead to bring his now-exposed engines into their effective arcs of fire.

"Fire at will!" He commanded in futility. Even if they cut the threat to pieces it would not save him. Only getting out of its way would guarantee survival. He hoped, however, that his weapon's fire might cause an explosion in the projectile to divert it. Such an explosion might alter the projectile's course in exactly the wrong direction, but it felt better to fire than to not. The massive bow of the battleship would not be slowed by his shields. It wasn't moving fast enough to cause resistance until it struck his hull. If his ship did not get out of the way in time, the collision would be titanic. Such a collision might be enough to destroy his ship and everyone aboard.

Exposure of his main engines was an immediate necessity. It was not at a time he would have chosen; it was at a moment convenient to the animals.

"Withdraw main thrusters into the protection of the shield as soon as you know we will be out of the way. The animals are going to try to disable our main engines." Sestrel commanded with dismay.

There was no time for his huntresses to launch a sortie in his defense. That would be a foolishly futile gesture. He wasn't going to waste them without an achievable objective. If his main engines were taken out by the animals that were launching their missiles at his stern, then it would be better to reach orbit of the home world using his maneuvering thrusters than it would be to waste his females.

His main engines roared to life to provide the thrust demanded of them. Fast incoming missiles were many. The aft point defense weapons were already firing, and their fire was withering, but some missiles might get through.

"Evasion is successful. Withdrawing engine nozzles into the shield envelope." Hope filled Sestrel at these words, only to evaporate as two of the animals' missiles struck explosively into an exposed nozzle. The ship twisted violently under him.

"Engines withdrawn into the envelope. One engine remains operational. Damage control has been detailed to assess and limit damage."

"Minimize any exposure of our maneuvering thrusters, but get us back on course."

"All animal vessels are fleeing at what must be their maximum rate of acceleration."

They should have continued their attack. Something wasn't right. Sestrel's feathered crest began to rise in alarm. He sensed dangerous implications but before he could otherwise react, the misshapen forward hull they had just evaded detonated with unbelievable force.

The batteries in the Trafalgar's hold that were meant to maintain magnetic containment of the antimatter had faded. Unconstrained by electromagnetic fields, antimatter touched matter. The contact of matter with its opposite annihilated both, triggering reactions in the rest of the antimatter particles with whatever they were pushed to contact.

The explosion shattered the separated battleship's forward hull and armor in an expanding sphere of violently radiant energy and debris. The hull and armor disintegrated into massive chunks of shrapnel that hurtled from the explosion.

Despite its great mass, and the influence of its inertial dampening, the Skraa vessel was shouldered aside as if by a giant. Shields flickered and died. Power to the bridge was interrupted

and for a moment, inertia regained full effect. Any Skraa not secured into their stations were thrown about, causing injuries.
Sestrel struck forcefully against a bulkhead. A section of the hull
was sprung beneath the linked armor and atmospheric integrity
was compromised, spewing atmosphere.

But the ship endured, a marvel of engineering. Power was restored to the bridge. The shields came back up until they were
as strong as they ever were, and before the ships of the animals
could come about and open fire. Damage control responded
promptly to seal the sprung hull leaking atmosphere.

Sestrel waited for the computer system to finish its self-check
and recovery process, then checked the status of the eggs. No
damage. He breathed more easily, but his side hurt.

Another herd of the animals' ships was approaching from behind, to supplement those still harassing him from the first herd.
Two of the new ships were as large as the one whose aft section
was now retreating.

His ship was reduced to intermittent use of maneuvering
thrusters. He did not want to expose his remaining main engine
because it would most likely be too slow to retract beneath the
shield envelope. That left no chance to regain effective range on
the retreating aft section of the large ship he had defeated.

Sestrel was weary of the meaningless noises of the animals
that filled his communications bands. He wished the animal he
wanted to use as a translator was in custody, where it belonged.

Chapter 48: Far Modulus

The calm blue disk of a modulus shone ahead of the *Jade Temple*. It was the farthest modulus humanity had ever found. Tibs sent a message to Perry Station to advise them of the location. He courtesy-copied the Aldebari Admiralty.

The news feed from a Corporate HoloNet news reporter, in Aldebaran system, was hours old but the situation did not look good. Tibs was glad that his people were attempting to assist Earth's Second Fleet, but they were still out of range. The likelihood of hitting the *Trafalgar* with their rail-guns instead of the alien was too great. The strength of the alien's shields alone was intimidating enough. If its weapons were similarly powerful, Tibs feared that the *Trafalgar* was doomed no matter how valiantly it fought.

Once the *Jade Temple* transited the modulus the news would be cut off altogether. Tibs knew that what he was hearing had taken time to reach him. Had he thought of a brilliant solution, any message he might send couldn't reach anyone in time to help. Yet he couldn't stop listening to the reporter describe, blow-by-blow, everything that was witnessed at the battle.

Over shipboard comms the astrogation section announced an alert: "Transiting Modulus in ten, nine, eight..." and Tibs sighed. He looked forward to seeing what was beyond the modulus, but he was also apprehensive, and not just about events in Aldebaran system.

As soon as the *Jade Temple* passed through the modulus the ship might attract the attention of other hostile alien ships, possibly just like the one at Aldebaran that was single-handedly beating a modern battle fleet into scrap. If the aliens had one of those, they probably had more. And yet wouldn't more of them have accompanied that invader if they were able?

Modulus transition was marked by flickering screens and a momentary lapse in consciousness almost too brief to notice. All outside communications channels were suddenly silent. Tibs watched his viewscreen as it clarified, and for a moment he thought something had gone wrong. In fact, he was only seeing, for the first time, what the universe would look like without stars.

A distant white speck was the only sign that his sensors were working. He tried to stroke his screen, as if the white speck might be some object he could wipe away before he remembered it was a holographic projection that his hand would pass through. What he was seeing, and what it meant hadn't yet registered.

"Transition complete." astrogation advised the crew. Then the astrogator addressed Tibs with his honorific, "One, my initial guess is that we are at the galaxy's edge. Maximum magnification displays recognizable galactic referents. And... the view astern confirms my guess."

The position of galaxies is the constant that enables astrogation. Transiting a modulus greatly alters the apparent relative position of stars within the Milky Way. Were space faring ships reliant on only local stars to know their location, they would be lost after modulus transit. The faint galaxies, on the other hand, were so far away that movement inside the Milky Way left their positions nearly unchanged.

Tibs quickly verified that the view astern was filled with the jewels of his galaxy, as well as the local system's as-yet- unidentified star. Then he calmly focused once more on the white speck, this time greatly magnified.

It was actually two objects. One of them looked like a small ship of Earth design and the other was alien. Tibs immediately suspected the Earth ship was Harden's escape vessel. The other one... looked like it might have been disabled in combat.

"Master Kinkaid." he spoke into his wrist comm.

"One?" responded his Executive Officer.

"Have my heavy fighter prepared and select a wing mate for me. I see something I wish to investigate." Tibs ordered.

"As you say, One." Kinkaid acknowledged.

Tibs rose from where he had been seated in the central atrium of the cruiser and went to a small hidden cubical nearby. This was where he slept, and where he kept what he possessed.

From a stand secured to a shelf, above his sleeping net, he removed an unadorned wooden scabbard and the blade it held. The tine of the blade was covered by a matching hardwood hilt. The sword was his only family heirloom. It was given to him by his father who had it from his grandfather. It had been in Tibs' family for as long as anyone could remember. It was his custom to take it with him when he piloted his fighter.

Personal arms were commonly lasers or ballistic weapons like the fletchette pistol. Swords were so archaic that security scans usually didn't recognize his blade as a weapon. More often than not, when he carried it in public, people assumed it was just a polished wooden stick carried by a very eccentric man.

Using this blade, Tibs had sliced open Paul Harden's hand, disarming him aboard his cruiser. Harden's men had captured Tibs earlier, but assumed the weapon was only a crutch.

His flight suit and helmet were in the locker near the ship's ready room, a short distance from the launching bay.

Tibs' fighter was ready in its hanger at the back of the fighter bay in the *Jade Temple*. Tibs walked inspection around the outside of his fighter with a meticulous eye. There were no signs of fluid or dust, nothing loose, all external connections were secure. He boarded his ship via its airlock next to the engines after checking the airlock's tethers and cleats. All was in order and shipshape.

He walked through the spotless cabin to the cockpit. Everything was secure and well-ordered. Nothing was missing. He buckled himself into his acceleration couch and paused, listening for a moment to silence before starting his preflight process. He initiated his power system.

Chapter 49: Memory

Seated in Chief Mackenzie's office, Bobby picked up the metallic cowl. His hand felt the jointed scales slip and softly click as he lifted it onto his head. He depressed the third button, the one on the left, when he felt the cool sensor disks stop in position on his scalp and neck.

The cowl influenced the visual cortex of his brain to superimpose a translucent representation of a directory structure over his field of view. There was something represented in that directory. Attempting to understand what it was only gained him an awareness that it was digital and "large". The cowl failed to resolve a further interpretation. Bobby surmised that it was a record of something outside his language and understanding because the cowl couldn't find a way to correlate it for him.

Bobby had arranged his time to open the file with the Chief present. Mackenzie sat nearby, ostensibly as an observer, while he worked on a small device for Kyle. They had a research safety agreement in place that specified if Bobby appeared to be in distress while viewing the file's contents, Mack would shut down the cowl and let Bobby recover.

Bobby mentally commanded the cowl to open the file. He didn't know what a challenge it would be for the cowl, but as capable as the device was, the file was far advanced beyond simple holography. There are differences between what an alien might sense, such as the ability to see in the infrared spectrum, and what a human can sense. Those differences had to translate into what Bobby's brain was able to interpret.

Mackenzie had a holorecorder running to capture what Bobby said and how he appeared during the session. There were moments when Bobby would report aloud, albeit haltingly, what he experienced, but there were long periods when the young man seemed too engrossed to comment.

To pass the time during the long silent intervals, once he had finished assembling Kyle's devices, the chief played a game of three dimensional chess against himself on a holodisplay, having the hologram turn opposite sides after each move.

For Bobby the experience was fascinating. He grew so engrossed that for long intervals he forgot to report aloud for the
verbal record.

He supposed the memory recording must have been left by
the alien mummy before it died several thousand years earlier.
The language of the... he heard a name the aliens called themselves that began with a musically sibilant sound and ended with
a warbled exhalation. It was musical, like a birdsong. Bobby did-
n't understand the sung language, but he gained a sense of
meaning from his impressions of the alien's understanding communicated by the cowl. The alien felt honor about her assignment. She was charged with scouting a place for which she felt
reverence and... a sense of myth, a history.

Bobby wanted to know more of the history, where the alien
came from and how they got to where they were. Unfortunately,
the female alien wasn't thinking of those. She did associate her
assignment with a... religious (?) anthem or hymn toward which
she felt great reverence.

Then the memory record detailed her launch from a great ship
in orbit around a planet. The planet was orbiting a blue giant star,
so the planet may have been Perry and the star Al Najid.

She was hungry, as if it had been too long since her last meal.
Bobby verbally noted an impression that her hunger was related
to her scouting mission.

As the memory progressed, Bobby noticed that the memory
stream the cowl uploaded into his mind improved and clarified as
it worked. When he closed his eyes he could see the imagery
clearly. Mackenzie remained silent and the office was quiet,
which helped Bobby hear the sounds the alien heard in the
memory record. He drew deeply into the memory, and it came to
dominate his five senses.

The scout successfully passed through an anomaly. Bobby
grew frustrated by the detail of journeying through another system, possibly Trondheim system. From there the scout transited
through what appeared to have been Aldebaran system and finally into Earth's solar system. He sensed that the alien was
growing very hungry. She ate a ration of some kind of paste from

a package. She found it most unsatisfying, but she knew it would nourish her.

When she approached Earth she seemed confused over the Caribbean Sea near the coast of the Yucatan, like she was expecting something that she didn't find. She ran an array of remote scans from orbit on several small groups of humans in the peninsula, a pod of whales offshore, and herds of animals in northern South America but again she didn't find whatever she was looking for. There was a particular part of a ritual song that she seemed to revere, and she kept recalling it to mind as she searched.

The alien reached an unsatisfied decision and set the ship down in a clearing within a dense tropical forest, near the equatorial western coast of South America. The clearing was part of an oval, thatch-roofed village surrounded by small planted fields. The people of the village clearly relied on agriculture, supplemented by hunting and fishing. The village was built around a central communal fire. There was no paving, only bare dirt between the dwellings.

The people of the village stared up toward the descending ship and then fled, plainly terrified as it descended from the sky. They ran into the surrounding forest. They were obviously not aware that the alien could see the heat of their bodies where they hid in the brush. The alien thought of them as animals and hoped they were edible. Bobby could feel how hungry and impatient she was growing. She ran some tests on the atmosphere and then opened the ship's hatch to descend to the ground.

The alien was awash in pleasure at the scent of the air, there in the tropical forest. Bobby felt her reverent emotions, like she wanted to embrace the planet she stood upon. It was like a sense of homecoming, a gratitude, and with celebratory emotion she lifted a tube-like device and used it to kill one of the more daring, curious villagers who was lurking across the clearing, at the edge of the vegetation. The other humans were obviously awe-struck by this feat. The tube-like device was an energy weapon of some kind.

The huntress walked casually across the clearing and began

to dissect her fresh kill with an incredibly compact cutting laser, like a small scalpel. She sampled the meat, which intellectually Bobby found revolting though she clearly relished the consistency and flavor. She didn't like the fat, finding it greasy, but the person she killed had been lean. She particularly liked the way the still-hot heart felt when she bit into it. She seemed to find the flavor especially satisfying, and she derived physical pleasure from the way it resisted the shearing of her teeth while pressing around her gums.

Bobby's distaste urged the memory record to skip ahead, just as he had for some of the monotonous trip to Earth.

He slowed the memory again later to find the villagers bringing gifts to the alien. Most of the gifts were gold and seashell ornaments, in which the alien took little interest.

There was an old man who would approach her obsequiously with the offerings while the rest of the survivors stayed prostrate, far in the background. Bobby surmised he was a priest, or maybe a chieftain.
The alien had grown curious about the humans, although she still thought of them as animals. When the old priest offered her some seasoned, flame-charred meat she enjoyed it so much that she was inspired to try imprinting the old man with knowledge, using the cowl. The villagers again looked awe- struck as she arranged the silvery scales of the cowl on his head and down his back. The alien pressed a combination of buttons on the cowl that Bobby tried to remember, then opened his eyes to make a note of the sequence. When his focus returned to the memory the man was standing under the cowl, rigidly upright, and visibly trembling.

Later, when the old priest had recovered from the cowl's imprint, he began to carve the symbols he had learned into a plank of wood. Bobby saw him speaking with the villagers while gesturing at what he was doing, and Bobby inferred that he was attempting to make them understand that ideas were associated with the carved images. When the alien looked at the priest's carvings Bobby looked as well, and he recognized a few of them from his study of the cowl.

By this time, Bobby had grown familiar with some of the notable villagers. There was a truly beautiful young woman he felt very attracted to, graceful in her every motion and gesture. She was almost always escorted by a youthful hunter whose adoration of her was plain as day. He seemed very proud to be her companion when he wasn't away hunting, and he always returned to share with her the best of his hunt. Bobby very much liked looking at her and was horrified when the alien chose her for a meal.

The villagers had developed spiritual sentiments about the alien. The young hunter's face looked both anguished and enraged when he returned to find his beloved dead. The alien- god unthinkingly opened the dead woman's chest with her cutting laser in front of the man to take her heart. The hunter's rage overruled his common sense.

As the alien raised up the heart to consume it, there was a powerful impact in her side. It radiated intense pain. The alien whipped her head on her long neck down to her side and bit powerfully at what caused her such pain, and her jaws snapped the mahogany haft of the hunter's atlatl dart. The pain was overpowering, and the alien dropped the woman's heart. She unlimbered her energy weapon from the harness, glaring at the hunter. The villagers pulled back from him in fear.

He stood there in a throwing stance, and his face looked deadly with anger. He was preparing a second stone-bladed dart to throw when she shot him, dropping him instantly with a shot to the chest that threw his body backward, a corpse.

The alien looked down at her side where the blood flowed from a swelling, angry wound. The pain was severe, and worsened sharply when she touched the broken shaft. She could not gain enough purchase on the hard wood even using her claws to remove the barbed head. She raised her jaws to the sky and screamed a shrill war cry

She knew she needed to bind her wound to staunch the flow of blood. She had to somehow reach medical help. The huntress staggered to her ship and ascended inside. There was a hidden cabinet to one side of the cabin that she opened by pressing and then releasing it.

There were no bandages to bind the wound. Instead she had chemical sutures. She still couldn't remove the barbed obsidian from her side. The alien held the wound tightly despite the horrible pain as she attempted to slow the bleeding. With her other hand she donned the cowl. Through the cowl she closed the hatch and the scout ship lifted swiftly from the planet surface. She not only needed to get medical help, she needed to report the results of her mission. She might not make it. Once she was in orbit over the planet she set course for the modulus to Aldebaran. Then she initiated the upload of her memory.

The memory replay stopped. After a few moments Bobby removed the cowl and sat back dazed, scratching his scalp where it itched. It left his hair standing in disarray. He rubbed his eyes while he tried to digest what he had seen. He could still feel a ghostly sensation, as of a tail extending from his lower spine.

Mackenzie raised his eyebrows at him. He had waited many hours.

Bobby was silently collecting his thoughts before recounting to Mackenzie the highlights of his experience. What must have happened after the alien uploaded the memory recording? She had to get to her people for medical treatment, and to report. She came Al Najid expecting to find her people.

Bobby's eyes turned to focus on Chief Mackenzie. "I see now where I went wrong in my hypothesis when I attempted to predict for Tibs where the alien might have been going."

"Oh?" asked the Chief.

Bobby nodded. "She wasn't going anywhere else. She thought her fleet would be here, in Al Najid system. They had run out of food on Perry, the planet. My guess is that the aliens who sent her out to scout found another source of food while she was gone. She may well have searched around for them here, before she died."

Mackenzie absorbed that information, then returned his gaze to the young man. "This is extraordinary. I should debrief you for the record, Bobby. Let's start at the beginning."

Chapter 50: Point of View

When Paul Harden sat down before the console the darkened screens above it lit with imagery. Apparently the on- off switch was linked to the seat.

Most of the views onscreen were of places aboard the ship that he hadn't seen before. The shafts that had given him access to the ship had also channeled his exploration.

Most screens were either empty of movement or populated with aliens, going about unexplained but apparently mundane tasks.

Other scenes were more intriguing. One in particular showed aliens in a corridor entering and leaving doors arrayed to either side. The creatures looked tired and drawn when they emerged.

With a clang, the ship suffered another sharp jolt to the side, reminding Harden of why he sat down. He gripped the sides of the seat to stabilize himself. There was no external viewscreen, but one of the images was crowded with alien fighters and scout ships. Beyond them, a regularly shaped dark rectangle may have been an open launch bay.

A launch bay and hanger aboard Harden's old cruiser had extended deeply into the ship like that. A similar design here would account for the placement of an airlock through the hatch to his right, wedged shut by the heavy metal bar. Harden looked at the hatchway thoughtfully. He wondered whether he could pilot one of the alien ships.

The ship seemed to be no longer engaged in active combat. No more impacts knocked the ship around. He took a chance and released his grip on the seat. He paused, listening, ready to grab hold again. After a few moments he decided there was no need to delay further. He stood and walked to the airlock hatch. If he was right, and it seemed likely that he was, then the airlock was a safety measure against the possibility of the launching bay losing atmospheric integrity in battle. Unless the ship had been more severely damaged than he thought, there should be atmospheric pressure on the other side, which meant he could safely open it.

Harden extracted the metal bar from the hatch wheel handle. It took a moment to figure out what to do with it, because it was heavy and there wasn't anywhere nearby to put it. He didn't want it rolling loose on the deck if combat resumed, so he stood it leaning into a corner, next to the hatch. The floor was smooth and hard, and he realized it would ring like a bell if it slipped and fell. He decided to lay it down, out of the way next to the bulkhead. Then he grasped the hatchway's rotary handle and, with more effort than he expected, turned the wheel. Metal battens all around the door pivoted slowly aside, creaking as the wheel turned, until the cams cleared the edge of the hatch.

The hatch would open inward, toward him. Vacuum on the far side would have held it closed. The hatch seal, like a gasket, was stuck to the jamb along the edge nearest the robust hinges. When he tried to open the hatch it resisted. He saw the gasket seal stretch. Harden retrieved the heavy metal bar from the floor. He opened the hatch as far as he could by pulling and wedged the end of the bar into the gap. Using that leverage, he tried to pry the door open. He had to exert all of his strength, but finally the seal began to release, and the pressure door opened fully on hinges that could have used some lubrication.

The compact pressure chamber beyond the hatchway was full of containers made from what looked and felt like plastic. To get through it, to try and see what was beyond the farther hatch, he would have to move some of the containers into the room behind him.

He lifted the topmost box. It didn't feel very heavy and, though Harden was curious about the contents, he set the container down in the room outside to get the next.

Suddenly the ship rocked aside with a great crushing noise, and Harden was thrown sprawling. The airlock hatch swung heavily to shut, but was stopped by a fallen container. The ship lost power for a moment, and Harden lost his footing. He spun weightless across the room unable to see. Utter darkness swarmed him, but he knew there would be a bulkhead somewhere and he was afraid of striking it. Harden panicked as he struck the bulkhead clumsily. He was sure that it was the end of his life. It was all over now, and he was hurt. He couldn't tell how bad it was in the darkness. Then the lights flickered back to illuminate the room and airlock, and Harden fell in a painful tangle onto the deck with the return of gravity.

The hatch had slammed violently on a fallen container, and it had cracked open. Some of the contents, a thick folded fabric, spilled out. Harden picked up a bundle and unfolded it. It was a pressure suit made for one of the aliens. In vacuum it would insulate and maintain pressure for one of the lizards.

Harden had been naked since he had been stripped when first captured, and it had made him feel very vulnerable. He sat on a carton and tried to squeeze his feet and legs into the flexible pressure suit. He could get the fabric over his legs, but the material wouldn't stretch enough to get the suit up over his shoulders. He was slightly bothered by an empty tail section dangling behind him, but he felt less vulnerable than he had when naked wearing something that could pass for trousers. Thinking about it, he decided the tail of the garment might be useful if he wanted to gather more things than he could hold, such as lizard eggs. He let the arms hang empty at his sides.

The more he thought about it and the hungrier he grew, the more convinced he felt that the ovoid balls in the room of containers were eggs. Eggs would mean nourishment.

Food was a pressing priority, but there were now loose containers in his safe room and more containers in the airlock. Two were still blocking the door. He didn't want to leave the door open while he ran off to get what hoped was an egg. Open, his safe room could be compromised while he was gone.

He also wanted to see whether there was a way off the ship on the other side of the airlock. He also felt intense curiosity about what might be in the rest of the containers in the airlock.

Harden stood back up to think and decide. He was irritated that he was half naked, dressed in makeshift trousers adapted from an alien pressure suit that wouldn't fit over his shoulders. The empty tail of the pressure suit hanging limp was unsightly. Harden resolved to move enough containers into the room from the airlock to let him reach the far door and check what was on the other side.

It felt like the pressure suit was slipping down to expose his backside while he worked. He knotted the two empty arms of the suit over his right shoulder. His makeshift strap now held the legs of the environmental suit in position.

Once he reached the far hatch he paused, listening. He could hear nothing through the door. The second hatch was built to open inward again. When he tried opening it, the seal thankfully wasn't stuck, suggesting that the outer airlock hatch had been more frequently opened. The airlock was used as storage space. The wheel turned freely and the cams turned quietly.

Harden cautiously opened the hatch just enough to see a crack of light, then enough to see beyond. The area beyond was brightly lit. There was a faint hissing, and a steady ringing noise, like the sound of pressurized gas moving through a pipe. From somewhere reasonably distant came intermittent metallic clanks. He cautiously opened the hatch further to see that indeed it was a large hanger. It was filled with alien spacecraft, probably fighter craft. They blocked his view from seeing what might be farther away, but he saw enough of the alien vessels to think there might be a way to escape that way, assuming he could get control of one of the small ships and could figure out the controls.

Chapter 51: Planning

When the alien ship passed through the modulus into the solar system the Aldebari fleet was in hot pursuit. They launched all of their marine assault craft as they gave chase. The alien had been damaged and slowed by the Trafalgar's last desperate ploy. The assault shuttles should be able to catch it. The blue disk of the modulus should shield them from detection until they, too, made transit.

The intent was to board the alien ship in force through the aliens' launch bay. The marines would seek to neutralize or degrade it from the inside. This tactic could even secure its advanced technology for humanity.

The defeat of the Trafalgar and Earth's second fleet amply demonstrated, to both the Aldebar and the Legion, that extraordinary effort, extraordinary cooperation would be required. Even the most advanced human technology was inadequate against the aliens. All they had was one another.

Seeing parallels to the dark days of their early fight against the Legion, the Aldebari were convinced that boarding the alien ship in force offered their best chance at victory.

In the eyes of the Legion, the Aldebari plan was better than anything they had come up with. They had learned the hard way to never underestimate Aldebari Marines.

A serious and predictable problem for the assault would be the alien's point defenses. The only counter would be for the fighters to take out or at least preoccupy those defenses. The combined forces would use their nimble fighter spacecraft to get inside the shields and attack, distracting fire away from the assault shuttles. Once the Marines were aboard, the fighters could withdraw to await the outcome.

Once the Aldebari boarded the alien ship, a second obstacle would have to be overcome: reports out of Perry Station warned them that the aliens would use personal shields in tactical   infantry combat. The aliens on Perry Station had effectively used personal shields in tactical combat to defeat a numerically superior security force.

Personal shields were new technology for humanity. Only recently had shield generation and capacitors been made so light and compact that they could be easily carried and used by an individual soldier in combat. Unfortunately, the new miniaturized capacitors and modulinium-powered inertia coils were rare and extremely expensive. Neither the marines nor the Legion had them. Personal shields were almost unobtainable for anyone except Earth's elite.

The Legion fleet was racing to coordinate with the ships of the Aldebari and the remnants of the Second Fleet. Fortunately, the alien ship had been slowed. This gave the Legion and Aldebari a little more time to coordinate. Their transponders had to recognize one another for their targeting systems to automatically avoid friendly-fire casualties.

Historical antipathy between the Aldebari and Legion would be set aside until the crisis had past. Unresolved differences would not be allowed to compromise the defense of the home planet. The Aldebari did not allow the prospect that they might come out of the fight at a disadvantage to weaken their resolve.

The Aldebari requested that the Legion fighters should launch and rendezvous to help cover the boarding action. The Legion commander approved. The Legion then opened layers of their secure systems to the Aldebari in common cause, a convincing display of cooperation.

The plan was in motion.

Aldebari assault shuttles are quite maneuverable, but they aren't fast. Aldebari fighters caught up, swept around them, and transited the modulus to Sol system in pursuit of the alien ship. Legion fighters were coming up fast when the shuttles transited the modulus. Fast frigates and Corvettes began to funnel through the modulus in support.

~

Near the Earth/Aldebaran modulus, a small, relatively motionless Galactic News spacecraft waited quietly, intending to be unobtrusive. The reporting team aboard were feeding imagery and sensor data via communications laser to Earth.

The Alien ship made transition into the solar system, and shortly the remnants of Second Fleet followed, dogging the great vessel. Their harassment was mostly ineffectual, but they did keep the alien from using its remaining main engine. A cloud of Aldebari fighters emerged, followed by the bulkier assault shuttles. Legion fighters were mixed in with them, passing the shuttles to join with the agile Aldebari.

The Galactic News ship's communications laser transmitted the imagery and reported using binary encoding over a very tight laser communications beam. Such transmissions are almost impossible to intentionally intercept unless the position of both sender and receiver was known.

That binary signal was received by an installation just outside the Earth's orbital plane. The automated communications security installation encrypted and routed the data in digital packets to Corporate facilities on High New York and the headquarters of the Board of Corporations. The Board's censors would decide what news would be forwarded and to which news outlets, normally according to need and paid priority.

Only Board members, their staff and recognized business leaders, from whom operationally informed decisions were necessary, had unfiltered access to the most current information.

An Agent of the Board, dressed in a dark and costly suit, monitored the information as it arrived on his compact table monitor. He was displeased with what he was seeing. He was seated in the quiet of a restricted dining room at the Hathaway, an exclusive residential enclave on the orbital city of High New York. The light on his table linens and cutlery was bright, but in the rest of the room the light was subdued.

Wall-sized view screens displayed the night surface of the Earth in a 360-degree panorama around him. The planet's dark face was splashed broadly with the lights of North America's eastern seaboard. To the West, the Pacific was still enjoying dusk, and the thin film of the atmosphere there was still bright with remaining sunlight.

The only sound of cutlery on china was his own. As he finished his entree, he set his heavily silvered fork and knife side by side in the plate. He cleansed his palette with a sip of finely crafted ice water. The ice could barely be heard as it struck the crystal when he sat his stemware down. The trace mineral balance in the water was exquisite.

The agent was displeased with the performance of the Second Fleet. He was displeased in general.

Not only had a rogue news corporation disrupted the civil peace with an unsanctioned public report about the defeat at Dante system, but that company also reported to the public that a quarter of the Earth's basic food supply was cut off.

The commoners were fearful. Some had already turned violent. Several Nibbles distribution kiosks in Europe, Asia and North America had been wrecked. Many dispensers were nearing depletion, but not because of any immediate supply problem. Instead, the shortage was caused by people who were beginning to hoard food.

The agent lifted his linen napkin delicately to remove a hint of moisture left by the water at the corner of his lip.

Now the pride of Earth's Navy was running away from the fight. This news had best not get out.

The Trafalgar was now, for all intents and purposes, a multibillion credit deficit. Admiral Crow pointlessly wasted the forward two thirds of his ship, including four of the most expensive direct fire weapons in space. He had thrown it away in a futile, impotent gesture. Crow might not yet realize it, but his career was over. He'd be lucky if he retained his private assets.

A server approached the Board's Agent with his salad. He declined the shaved Parmesan but accepted a twist of the peppermill. The agent lifted a clean silver fork in his well-manicured fingers. He spent a moment appreciating the scent of freshly ground pepper accentuating those of basil, crisp romaine lettuce, freshly cut scallion and garlic infused vinegar. The faintest scent of virgin olive tied it all into one olfactory bouquet. The taste and texture of the first bite was appreciated. The crisp, faintly bitter lettuce was appropriate for the moment.

Despite all the money Corporate Earth had poured into weapons research over the years, only the rail guns were even marginally useful against this threat.

And now a damnable alliance of traitors, new faith scientists supported by unsavory thieves, were going to just swoop in and save the day. A successful, and unpaid Aldebari and Legion assault would seem cost effective, but in the long term it would be a setback for the Corporate Board's sociopolitical investments. Adjusting the public psyche to fit the changed general timetable would be costly.

If the Aldebari and Legion weren't successful, then... well, then there would be nothing between the alien ship and Earth. A plan must be provided for that contingency. Admiral Crow's speculation that the aliens would take no interest in negotiation was implausible. Admiral Crow was a loser.

Chapter 52: Spectators

The evening of news with Martin was becoming habitual for Steve and the kids, for Pat, and for Martin. Coverage of events in space on the common HoloNet was scant. The coverage for the elite was copious.

On the common HoloNet, the few news stories and commentaries about the approaching threat focused primarily on the troubles caused by panic. The hoarders, people who seized more than their fair share of nibbles and other supplies, were castigated for making a bad situation worse for everyone.

The elite, in contrast, had access to almost everything known about the situation, from the unit histories of the Aldebari Marines, to the known specifications for Legion military spacecraft.

New entertainment holos for Kathlyn and Stevie kept their attention isolated from the stress. Steve worried that he wasn't engaging with them as he should. Martin and Pat worried about the nearly invulnerable alien ship and what it might do if or when it arrived. Steve was with them, but his interests were divided. He wished to return his family to their home as soon as it was safe enough to make the trip.

It was ironic, almost ludicrous, to contemplate impending destruction over the amazing selection of fine foods and beverages from Martin's supply. There was always an engraved silver platter of cold cuts and cheeses on a beautiful walnut sideboard. Avery's wet bar seemed inexhaustible.

Tonight was special. Not only had the contract for modulinium through the Trondheim anomaly finally been inked, sealed, and dispatched without changes to Old New York, but there was a report circulating that the Aldebari Marines, covered by Aldebari and Legion fighters, were finally in position to board the Alien.

The evening began with a meal together in the employee cafeteria. Afterward they adjourned to Martin's suite. Steve and Pat assisted the children with popcorn and queued their holovids.

Steve had reservations about one of the holovids, a new release dramatizing the events surrounding the destruction of

Perry. In it, Steve's role was fancifully portrayed by an actor much more handsome than Steve felt he was. He wished he might review it before exposing his children to what might be an unrealistic dramatization.

Steve was acquainted with Auguste Tardieu, the producer of the film, from his first visit to Earth, shortly after he first met Pat. Mr. Tardieu had been an impressive man, a journalist, so Steve had hope that the holovid would be reasonably accurate.

The other holo on tap for the kids made no serious pretense. Its plot was archetypal, featuring the youth, played by Kelly Strange, nurtured and counseled by a wizened mentor and aided by an athletic romantic interest. They confront the embodiment of evil and, against all odds, emerge in triumph. Steve felt certain the children would be entertained by that one.

In hope that they fell asleep and missed the second show, Steve had queued the Kelly Strange title first.

As he joined Pat and Martin in the great room, he was thinking about the several different news feeds on the HoloNet.

"Martin, you said money was saved by eliminating meaningless variety and producing generic products. Why is it that there are still so many different vendors of the news?"

Martin looked at Steve with an evaluative eye. "There are several distinct personality types. Our behavioral studies in virtual reality have given us a good grasp of those varieties. Different news feeds are delivered couched in terms that will appeal to our people by type.

"We know that people will find controversy. There isn't a way around that. But we can usually decide what the controversy will be. By channeling different parts of the information that is reported to different personality types, we can plan out the controversy by feeding the right information to the right group. The content is framed by the interpretations and opinions of specialized spokespersons.

"The people will argue over something, no matter what. In our system, they argue predictably because we control what facts they will access that will form their view of the current events puzzle.

"The 'controversy' stays where the Board wants it to be, out of the way. The Corporate Board can then go about their business unimpeded by reactionary public sentiments. Public news is treated as a form of entertainment.

"People naturally tend to gravitate toward the vendor most suitable to their personality type. So even though all the news is fed by law through a single outlet, different parts of that information are fed by the corporate censors to the different vendors. It's all closely orchestrated. Does that make sense, Steve?"

Pat was mildly astonished by Martin's candor.

"So the Corporate Board essentially controls public opinion by controlling what information is released to which segment of the population." Steve summed.

"I'm uncomfortable with the ethics of doing that, Martin." Pat interjected.

Martin turned to Pat to explain. "The ethics were consciously decided by the corporations ages ago, Pat, but more importantly those ethics were in effect dictated to us by the people. When humanity kept reproducing, despite all the warnings about over-population, the choices the people made also dictated what the outcome would be." Martin replied. He turned back to Steve. "For a small state like your alliance, Steve, maybe it wouldn't be ethically right or fair. But for a world attempting to function with a population of eighteen billion people, we're talking about some pretty consequential ethics. We cannot afford the societal costs of uncontrolled socio- political passions wracking our populace. We must filter what information they receive. We cannot permit a civil war, and not just because we selfishly want to keep power. We are certainly, absolutely, selfish but we are also, in a way, enslaved by the responsibilities of power. A civil war here, among so many people, would be an inconceivably evil consequence. Failure to control socially mediated controversy in this context, to the extent such control is possible, would be irresponsible."

Martin held Steve's eyes, completely sincere.

Onscreen the Aldebari and Legion fighters approached the alien ship. They still had some distance to go before the aliens' point defenses should begin firing. The weapons of the fighters would be ineffectual until they entered beneath the shield envelope of the great ship.

"If anyone can pull this off, it's the Aldebari." Steve stated confidently.

Steve had experience with Aldebari naval assault. He had participated in hostile boarding actions with them. While they waited Martin asked him about his experience, and shared some recollections with Pat and Martin.

On the screen the Aldebari Marine assault shuttles had not reached the point of engagement, so Steve told them about the Aldebari marine assault he and Kyle had joined, along with Tibs and his pilots, when they captured Harden's last cruiser. That time, he had boarded with the assault and fought his way to confront Harden. He, aided by a timely intervention by Lieutenant Matsuo, ended up freeing Pat and the children from Harden's brig. The tale held his audience riveted, but he seemed unaware of the effect that his words had on them.

Pat hadn't heard that story from his perspective. Steve spoke of his part casually, as if his actions were only natural, practical solutions to some difficult problems. Pat found herself wondering whether his humility might really be some kind of unrealistic denial. She had been there, and she knew some of what he had done.

But for Steve, his actions were just matters of fact. Yes, in some events he had played a pivotal role, but what could have happened was shaped by the situation.

"I'm just glad you aren't out there today." Pat said to him at last, her voice in her goblet. Avery nodded his concurrence with serious eyes over the rim of his own cut crystal glass. They had raised their drinks in silent tribute, but Steve was looking toward the other room where the children watched their holovid and he seemed unaware of their gesture.

On Martin's large monitors it had grown evident that the point defenses of the alien ship had greater effective range than the energy weapons of the fighters. The fighters' ballistics, while of unlimited range in space, were also less accurate. The aliens' defensive weapons were like needles standing upright in a rain of projectiles that struck near, but seldom hit them directly.

Then the aliens' automated targeting system coordinated fire on single fighters, one at a time. All of the beam weapons were slaved into a single defensive superweapon. Bright needles of light burned constant, focusing steadily on each selected target in turn, no matter which way the pilot tried to evade.

There could be no effective maneuver. Beams of light are orders of magnitude faster than any fighter can move, faster than any pilot can evade. Energy weapons don't generally need to lead their targets within their effective range.

The normally invisible shields of each targeted fighter turned translucent almost immediately. Milky shields inevitably clouded until they became bright and opaque.

The violence of capacitor overload is minor compared to what happens when the electromagnetic containment of a ship's anti-matter loses power.

The alien defenses were faster and more effective than Naval intelligence had believed when the assault was planned.

As soon as a fighter was lost, the point defense beams immediately flicked to another target. There was no delay, no need to let the weaponry cool, and no time lost acquiring another target. The defensive fire didn't pause to celebrate victory. It was impersonal and efficient.

"Those weapons are controlled by artificial intelligence." Steve sounded alarmed. Pat and Martin looked at him expectantly, waiting for an explanation. He looked at them and tried to explain using urgent tones, as if they could do something if they understood. "There's no pause to acquire a new target. The beams coordinate fire too quickly to be manually controlled. The assault's fighter cover is being cut to pieces. Their attacks are ineffective. The point defenses aren't being eroded. The Marines should break off and withdraw while they can." Steve turned back to the monitor and wondered "What is their commander thinking? He should be on top of this!"

By the time the first fighters reached the alien ship they had already lost a third of their number. The aliens' point defense weaponry remained viciously unreduced. Its fire was unrelenting.

Steve turned his eyes away in dismay. "This will not end well." He looked at the audio receiver intently. "Come on, Command. Recall the assault", he demanded under breath.

They heard the voice comms from the fleet filled with urgent chatter. Many voices sounded professional and detached, but others were alarmed, requesting guidance. Then a louder, more distinct voice came from an officer, back with the combined fleet: "Marine One is down, medical. Stand by."

Steve gasped. "No! Not now!"

"What happened?" asked Pat.

Steve hesitated, hoping for a lucky break. Those people were dying for Earth out there. If their shields failed they might pod out, but the others... the rest were as good as gone. They wouldn't have had a chance to pod if their ships vaporized.

Sometimes skill and experience make no difference.

Steve's eyes filled with dread. "The commander of the assault is out of action. It's a medical emergency. Maybe he had a heart attack, I don't know. But someone should have immediately assumed command, and they haven't."

There was silence on Marine Command comms. Tactical comms were punctuated by urgent but increasingly scarce pilot chatter. The Legion and Aldebari fighter pilots wouldn't break off unless the Marines aborted. The Marines aboard the assaulting shuttles were following their orders, despite the destruction that was chewing up the Navy and Legion fighters all around them.

Marine command was still silent.

A senior Aldebari naval officer outside the direct chain of command recognized necessity, identified himself and ordered the assault shuttles to break off and return.

Five of the shuttles survived long enough to receive the command to abort. They tried to comply. They actually might have done better to continue into the alien launch bay as it was closer than safety. Two more shuttles were lost as they turned to withdraw. Only three emerged from the killing field.

The Marine commander in charge of the assault operation had suffered an aneurysm. Just as the first of the fighters were destroyed his blood pressure had spiked. A latent aneurysm burst, flooding his brain with blood. He was overcome and collapsed unconscious.

It was only because a Navy admiral outside the Marine chain of command was willing to risk his rank that there were any survivors from the failed assault.

Mike Billings was walking in a small oval, hands on his head. Pat gazed at her hands in her lap. Martin stared at the ceiling without seeing it. Steve's children had their movie.

Chapter 53: Luxury

Paul Harden sipped from the leathery shell of his egg and, even raw, it was good. He wished for salt. His belly felt better.

The crates of gear that the lizard-birds had stored in that air-lock had been stocked with supplies. They were probably intended to resupply their pilots.

One of the items he found was a small device no larger than his little finger. It was actually an amazingly miniaturized cutting laser. He had used it to cut the end from the leathery egg. Had he wanted to he could have used it to heat and cook the egg within the shell, but his hunger had been too great to spend the time.

He had gone through the containers and found about a dozen curious items that he didn't understand. He imagined possible uses for some of them, but never quite figured them out. He had built himself a mattress of sorts from several environmental suits, and he kept a case of water canisters.

Harden finished his egg while watching interior scenes within the ship on the screens. There seemed to be fewer bird-lizards walking the hallways, fewer than there had been. There were also fewer fighters visible in the hanger.

He felt much better and, though his full stomach urged sleep, he decided to first erase as many signs of his access from the airlock as he could, in case the lizards checked it. He worked to return all the containers into the airlock into their stacks. He tried to remember their original order, but thought the aliens were unlikely to think any disorder had been his doing. He had no way to reseal the opened boxes, so he put those on the bottom. When he felt satisfied that he had done all he could to allay suspicion, he closed the inner hatch and wedged the metal bar as it had been.

He wished for the grooming kit he had left aboard his launch so long ago. How long it had been he couldn't know. He sat back down on the seat in front of the display panels. His beard was growing long. He tried to stay clean, but he couldn't do much about his hair and beard except run his fingers through them the best he could. The little laser knife was too hot to use as a razor. Hair burns too easily and his skin was sensitive. He had no other cutting instrument.

He wanted badly to strike back at the aliens somehow, in particular that big one that acted like their leader, but he didn't want to lose the progress he had made making himself more comfortable.

Harden rose from his seat, and the screens went dark. Then he walked slowly and wearily to the pile of fabric pressure suits that offered him at last a cushioned sleep. He laid down to look at the ceiling.

It would have shocked him a year ago had he known he could fall so far from his privileged life. Such a simple, rudimentary convenience as a leather-shelled egg eaten raw, a ration of tasteless water and a makeshift bed of rags had become measures of success for him. Yet he had overcome so much, and been so fortunate, just to attain these basic essentials.

Paul Harden fell asleep.

Chapter 54: Utility

"Now what?" Martin Avery asked the ceiling before he turned toward Steve. "There is nothing left to stop the aliens in the solar system. Earth is naked. I don't know what they want with us, but I don't think we're going to like it. Admiral Crow said he thought their advance may be fueled by hunger. He thinks they want to eat us."

Mike Billings considered "The alternative is that they think we're a threat. That suggests to me that they would want to exterminate us. If they intend to use us as food, then at least they won't lay waste to the planet from orbit."

"Could they know how many we are?" Martin asked.

Pat reminded him "That ship Steve found out in Al Najid system was undetectable. They may already have scouted us."

Martin looked at her, then turned away. "If they *are* here because they are hungry, then at least we'll have a chance when they land to teach them a lesson about human beings. We don't have anything left to stop them from reaching Earth." He turned back. "I know there is at least one more battleship in the reserve fleet at Trondheim, but it isn't likely to do better than *Trafalgar*."

"The *Ariel*? It is old. It will be awhile before it can be manned and battle-ready." Mike objected.

Martin thought furiously. "If the surviving Navy ships made ready and they all tried to ram the alien we might be able to take it out."

"That would be asking the crews to waste themselves on a suicide mission." Steve objected. "Even if they tried to pod out before the collision, many of them would die and they still might fail. We need to think of another solution."

Steve paused. Nobody offered an idea, so he continued.

"If they want to destroy the planet we probably won't be able to stop them. But we may have a chance if the aliens do land, whatever their specific intention may be. If they all have personal shields, then our standard arms will be useless. But the alien mummy showed us they are vulnerable to slow weaponry. Perhaps we should start manufacturing spears, or maybe crossbows, and start setting up a distribution system."

Avery smiled slightly at Steve, approvingly, but like he knew a secret. "Crossbow quarrels would probably still be too fast, but we can do better than spears, my friend. Let's use the assumption that they will land as our starting point. It's the only scenario where our planning might do some good."

Steve nodded. "Right. But this is going to get complex. Many factors are involved. We need to find a weakness we can use. We should re-examine what we know about them."

Mike agreed with Steve's thinking. "It would be a plus to find their weakness."

Martin was talking to his wrist communicator, striding around the room making expansive gestures with his arms while speaking rapidly. He didn't lower his voice for privacy. He was seeking Corporate Board approval to activate a program he called 'Phoenix'. He urged whoever he was talking with to get the Corporate Board to evacuate High New York and get things mobilized on the surface.

The aliens hadn't destroyed the comm relay at the Earth/Aldebaran modulus, and communications had been restored through the Aldebaran/Dante relay.

Steve used Martin's distraction to compose a request to Perry Station for an update on what they knew about the aliens and the scout ship. He sent copies of the message to Councilor Lyman and to Kyle with his official news that the modulinium contract was signed and physically on the way to Old New York and the Station's lawyers.

Avery won clearance from the Corporate Board to make use of the Darknet, the old internet, for Project Phoenix comms and was tasked with control over the project's activation.

The HoloNet depended on satellite communications. As such it was especially vulnerable to an enemy in orbit. The Darknet was ancient, mostly underground, and on fiber-optic cable.

Earth had few formal land-based armed forces. They were

originally intended for the planet's defense, but when it became obvious that neither the Legion nor Aldebari were going to invade Earth, they had only been used to quell rebellions. It would be a gross misrepresentation to say that the Corporate Board was popular.

Avery had been pacing. When he disconnected from his call he paused, inadvertently dramatic. With hesitation he revealed to Steve and Pat the general substance of a previously classified military program called 'Phoenix'. Martin began to explain to them what the program was.

"If there is anything that the people of Earth are good at, it is virtual reality gaming. Many of our VR players have been pre-selected due to their skills. They were enrolled into the program, but we never notified them that the program even exists.

"They will use their HoloNet VR systems, visors and controllers, to guide 'drones', machines designed to be remotely operated.

"Every machine normally operated by artificial intelligence can also be remotely operated by a human pilot. Each was hard-coded during manufacture to respond to a unique digital key that will provide control of the machine to an authorized Phoenix pilot." Martin told them. "Machines controlled by select players will form irregular combat forces for their local geographic area.

"In exchange for their service these players will be granted social and economic advantages and perks, such as enhanced health care."

Steve saw some staggering implications. There was great potential, to be sure, but those potentials could play out in many different ways. Putting the world's automated machines into the hands of VR players sounded terribly dangerous, and not just for an invading army. Knowing about the proclivities of some people, he could foresee some serious problems. Players tend to want to *play*.

"Martin are you sure this is a good idea?" he asked.

"If we can avoid releasing the key codes until there is an identifiable threat on the ground we should be okay. But if we have to release the codes too early it is going to be a nightmare."

Global standardization meant common interfaces for common machines. Cars, forklifts and construction equipment offered a potentially vast number of remotely operable *ad hoc* combat units. The ability to override a vehicle's artificial intelligence had been a feature required of manufacturers by the Corporate Board's law enforcement agencies for decades.

The Darknet used a global network of hardwired telecom towers for operation. Telecommunications towers then broadcast signals to datalink local drones. The control interfaces were intuitive, designed for the gaming public. Almost all the people of Earth had grown up using similar interfaces in their online gaming sessions.

The Darknet, always the native digital realm of hackers and criminals, now gave humanity a medium in which to organize a resistance movement armed with machines, should that became necessary, a mechanized force that should come as a serious shock to any invader.

Avery directed Amanda to assemble a skilled team to run a select query against the central player database to secure appropriate player data for the implementation of the Phoenix program. He specified that the data should include contact information and the geographic locations of Phoenix candidates worldwide.

The existence of the program was going to first be made public to build morale. HoloNet activities were interrupted to inform the people about the program. Almost everyone knew that there was an alien threat, but they had been denied accurate information. Anonymously authored speculation was growing insane. The news of what was actually happening was frightening, but not as frightening as what was being imagined.

As word of Phoenix spread, public unrest began to measurably subside. Given a way to participate, even as spectators, and the provision of better information began to calm some of the of the hysteria. As bad as the real situation was, the imagined version was far worse. Fears that had been kindled by ignorance had become overwhelming for many people. When reliable and official information became available to regular citizens, thinking gradually supplanted panic, and social distrust began to give way to common cause. Community spirit awakened among neighbors. Project Phoenix assured the people that they weren't helpless, that there was something to be done, and that they might have the means to resist whatever might come.

Hopefully now the aliens wouldn't simply bombard the planet with asteroids. If they did that, all the preparation would be for nothing. But for the time being, humanity was coming together in determination, rather than collapsing.

Chapter 55: Contact

Tibs noted that the cargo hold of Harden's launch was stationary, open to space near the wreckage of an alien space craft. The launch's cargo bay was open and positioned to receive what looked like a large alien energy weapon. The weapon was still aboard the derelict ship, but disconnected from the alien wreck.

The alien ship's enamel looked seared. Its armor was scored and cratered. It must have seen fierce combat.

Unless the aliens had been fighting among themselves, then a third space-faring race had been present. Harden certainly hadn't defeated this ship with his pristine yacht.

It wasn't difficult to believe there were many self-aware species in the galaxy. Tibs had known it must be so since his childhood. He knew it then; with all the certainty a child can feel. He knew it now because of all that he had learned. It was a matter of chemistry, of physical law. Non-human intelligent species must exist. Maturity and education hadn't reduced his certainty, but bolstered it.

The moduli made it evident. Humanity was not the center of the universe, even if most people chose to ignore the odds to favor more comfortable, less challenging thinking. Too many people still flattered themselves that they were the crowning achievement of evolution in the universe.

Here was alien technology showing signs of combat. Warfare speaks of cultures and civilizations. Either the aliens had fought among themselves, or there were two alien cultures who found cause to do battle.

Tibs positioned his fighter near Harden's launch and stabilized there, preparing to investigate. His desire was to examine the alien derelict, but his duty directed his focus first onto Harden's launch. Harden was a wanted man, and justice must be served. Tibs' wing man held position nearby, ready to render assistance if needed.

Tibs commed to Master Kinkaid "Prepare the *Temple* to take these ships aboard. We can store them in my hanger. I'll stow my fighter to the side in the launch bay when I return. Await my signal to commence the operations needed. I'll make a record of my observations as I go."

Kinkaid acknowledged receipt "Very good, One."

Tibs sealed his helmet and tethered himself to a stanchion inside the airlock. He closed the inner door and cycled the air in the lock into his fighter's compression tanks. In near vacuum he began opening the outer door onto the magnificence of space. As the airlock hatch opened the remaining atmosphere rushed out, and the scant moisture it contained instantly froze into microscopic ice crystals, glistening from the light of the local sun. To port, on his left, the stars shone brilliant, like a spilled treasure of sunlit jewels in the darkness. To starboard was only fathomless darkness. Intergalactic space.

"*Jade Temple* have you identified this system's inhabitable planet? We will want to perform a survey." Tibs queried.

"Still scanning, One."

Beyond every modulus that had ever been discovered was a new habitable planet. Or there had been one in each, before Harden destroyed Perry in the Al Najid system.

The implication Tibs drew was that whatever species built the moduli were more like humanity than not. It was reasonable to assume that where the same chemistry produces life, then within a similar environmental context what evolves will be similar. There would surely be some interesting and educational differences.

The mummified specimen under study at Perry Station was a cautionary example. Tibs could easily see similar animals developing on Earth. Steve had noticed it too, so much so that he thought they might have been of dinosaur origin.

Tibs tucked carefully into a crouch and used his hands and arms on the two hand rails to either side of the airlock's outer hatchway. He reoriented his body to place his feet on the bulkhead behind him and pushed off, cautious to apply pressure smoothly and evenly to both of his feet. He launched himself gracefully out from the airlock through the emptiness, vast space falling away empty, falling forever far around him, in every direction. His infinitesimal, mortal body with his small beating heart traversed the interval to Harden's launch. His slender tether uncoiled smoothly and evenly behind him. He had been born in weightlessness, and his leap was natural to him. There was no up or down, there was 'here' and 'out', and out was inconceivably far. But there were places out there to move toward.

As he approached Harden's yacht he judged that his relative velocity was close to ideal. He should have no difficulty handling his inertia when he arrived. The direction of his leap had been unerring. During his approach Harden's open airlock suggested that Harden wasn't inside his ship. Had he been inside, the outer door would be sealed and the airlock pressurized. If he had someone with him, then that someone might still be aboard. Scans of the ship had shown only nominal power usage, as would be expected for keeping life support systems in operation.

His initial survey efforts from within his fighter had already included illumination of the open hatch and the cargo bay. The cargo bay had been empty. When Tibs reached the yacht's hull he pulled himself to the empty airlock just behind the cabin, on the port side, and entered. He used the tether's control switch to release the far clip from his fighter. He coiled and clipped the safety line to his EVA harness with practiced ease. Tibs then closed and sealed the outer airlock hatch.

When the airlock pressurized full cycle, he opened the inner hatch and entered the cabin, removing his helmet. He left his earbud and communicator boom in place to record his observations. There was an empty but uncleared food packet on the table of the small, well stocked galley, but no other sign of life. The packet was the same temperature as the cabin's atmosphere.

There was an expensive automedical station aboard. He downloaded the unit's memory and uploaded the data to the *Jade Temple*. Tibs checked around the cabin and noticed that Harden had left his personal kit. That suggested he hadn't intended to leave.

Tibs was in motion toward the ship's computer to retrieve the ship's log when both his wing man and the *Jade Temple* simultaneously said something in similar tones of professional urgency, rendering both unintelligible.

"Repeat, please." he requested. This time his wing man remained quiet.

"We have a visitor out here, One. You'll never forgive yourself if you miss it." The tone of Master Kinkaid's voice told Tibs he should be distinctly interested.

Tibs felt his heart pounding. He first secured his helmet and checked the seal. He hurried, but he was careful. He didn't want to miss whatever it was, but he didn't want it to be the last thing he ever saw.

The fastest and safest way to see whatever Kinkaid was excited over would be to use the launch's scanners, but his wing man was still in his ship, and possibly vulnerable. So Tibs headed straight back to the air lock. He would have to make the leap back prematurely, but if the 'visitor' was a threat he wanted to gain the protection and maneuverability of his fighter. And his wing man was out there alone. Well, except for the *Jade Temple*.

The airlock was damnably slow to cycle the air from the small chamber, but at last he gained a green tell-tale. He checked to ensure his tether was fastened and that the line was correctly coiled. An unintended knot or tangle would shorten the line's reach. The airlock's outer door slid open with a slight gust of residual atmosphere that threatened to take Tibs with it, but he was holding the rails ready for it.

He wasn't ready for the sight of another, very different alien ship.

"One, the *Temple* is being scanned. InfoSec reports that our computers' tripwire defenses are popping like firecrackers. The intrusion so far isn't overtly hostile, as nearly as we can tell, but it's so fast we can only tell where they are looking by the way our compartmental firewalls are being compromised. InfoSec says it is impressively skilled."

Beyond his heavy fighter was a strange-looking structure,

pentagonal in design. It hadn't been there earlier. It wasn't in relative motion but it had to be a vehicle, a spacecraft. Its architecture was unusual, to say the least. It didn't look like any spacecraft he had ever seen. Perhaps 'star' or 'pentacle' would be a more apt descriptor, since five arms radiated from a pentagonal central junction. Tibs could not avoid thinking it gave the term 'star ship' a new measure of humor.

The pentagonal core and five 'arms' were illuminated by a thin tracery of pale blue light, of similar hue as a modulus, possibly modulinium conduits along the arms. It glowed. It didn't look hostile, but it also looked so advanced that it might not need to be hostile.

"Understood, Master Kinkaid." Tibs acknowledged. "Avoid any sudden or overtly hostile actions if it can be helped. Naturally you must defend the *Temple* if it comes to that. Trace where in our computer memory's logic and file structure it is looking, as completely as you can. Watch for patterns in the search, because that could tell us whether or when it understands what it is looking at."

"Affirmative, One, but it seems to have already completed whatever it intended."

"That suggests we are badly outclassed here, Kinkaid. Don't do anything to antagonize the alien, but make ready to recover Harden's launch and salvage the alien derelict, especially that loose weapon. I'm going to return to my fighter and we'll go try and get a closer look."

Tibs gathered himself at the edge of the airlock, his feet shoulder width, and pushed off evenly toward his fighter. The speed and direction of his travel was committed.

The alien ship began to move.

"One, the alien ship is moving. Quickly. Too quickly." Kinkaid advised. It was unusual to hear Kinkaid sound alarmed.

"Thank you, Master Kinkaid. I am watching." Tibs replied more calmly than he felt. "Raise the shields but hold your fire."

"Already done, but..."

"I see it, Kinkaid. Evidence is prerequisite to good judgment, my friend. Don't jump to any unwarranted conclusions." Tibs assured Kinkaid.

The pentagon-shaped alien ship moved nimbly, with rapidity difficult to believe. It appeared to be propelled by devices on the ends of the five arms, but they didn't behave like thrusters would. Putting engines so far out on the projections would give it fantastic maneuverability if they were coordinated, and these obviously were. The promise of unknown technology was tantalizing. If there was anything Tibs felt greedy about, this alien presented it.

The alien starship swept around Tibs' fighter and then interposed itself between him and his intended destination. The star ship was large, but not overpoweringly so. The *Jade Temple* was larger than this star ship. A hatch opened smoothly in the central pentagon, easily large enough to admit him, exactly where his jump would take him.

There really wasn't enough time to gracefully overcome his forward momentum. It would be risky to try such a maneuver within the remaining distance. Tibs recognized that it was even more risky to enter the hatch it had opened before him. If he tried and did manage to stop his forward momentum, he might be able to pull himself back to Harden's yacht by the tether.

Yet Tibs didn't feel threatened, he felt invited. He spoke into his transmitter "Kinkaid," Tibs hesitated only a heartbeat. "I'm going in."

"I don't feel good about your decision, One." Kinkaid replied. "Acknowledged, my friend. But we don't receive invitations like this very often."

Kinkaid double-clicked his comm using a button on its interface for signaling receipt.

Within moments Tibs was inside, within a small chamber, an airlock. The chamber's interior was lit with that same tint of blue light.

Still two meters from the far bulkhead and coasting slowly, Tibs drew his legs up from behind him and pulled his arms back, which gave his body a slight backspin. When he extended once more, his feet were toward his destination and his arms were positioned to grab his tether. He had made a choice to follow the path offered him, rather than try to escape.

His feet and legs absorbed his momentum, and he went to one knee to avoid a rebound, letting the ship's mass accept the force of his leap. He used the tether's switch to detach the far clip and began to coil the line to his harness. The alien ship obliged his doing so, leaving the hatch open, which seemed to Tibs unexpectedly courteous.

"*This* is going to be interesting." he reported to his voice recorder.

"Affirmative, One." Kinkaid responded.

So his communications were still being received. Somehow he hadn't expected that to be the case, and he briefly described the interior of the airlock as he finished securing the coiled tether to his harness. As he did, the outer airlock hatch slid smoothly shut.

"Kinkaid, do you still receive my comms?" "Affirmative, One. If anything reception is improved."

"Fascinating." Tibs wondered aloud.

"Indeed it is, One. We will be standing by here." Kinkaid assured him.

"If you safely can, try to get those two ships aboard and get a start on identifying what Harden was up to and where he may have gone."

"Understood, One." Kinkaid replied.

An interior door slid aside.

Chapter 56: Status Update

Mackenzie looked across the worktable at Bobby, who was still reading a copy of Steve's request for a status update. Bobby's eyes looked weary. He was worried about his home planet.

The chief reflected on himself. He still held in memory an image, a personal myth of his home from his childhood. He knew his own childhood impressions were not well informed. The sentiments he associated with those impressions were hardly more than a fantasy. Or a nightmare. Reality invariably differs from recollection.

An engineer has to approach his work with both dark and light insight. Mackenzie conceded that any adult must ultimately do the same. Engineering does it with science.

Bobby looked up from his wristcom and his eyes cleared, as if he had made a decision.

"Thoughts?" Mackenzie asked.

Bobby took a moment. "If the alien point defenses are using artificial intelligence, and they also fly fighters, then their artificial intelligence must be able to distinguish between their own ships and ours."

Mackenzie nodded his head. "Yes, that is reasonable."

"We may be able to get into the alien ship using this one." Bobby gestured toward where the alien scout ship waited in the station's atmospheric dry dock, just outside Mackenzie's office.

The chief nodded again. "The question remains whether their AI will recognize the ship itself, or whatever signals it should emit. Even if the scout evaluates as friendly, we still wouldn't be able to do more than get ourselves killed once we got inside, Bobby." He gazed sadly at the young man. "Heroics," he added, "tend to get good people killed. Two men, no matter how brave, are not an assault force."

"I'm not thinking of staging an assault, Mack. What if we carried an explosive device and rigged it inside the alien's docking bay on a timer?" Bobby asked thoughtfully. "A really powerful explosive device?"

Against his better judgment, the chief felt a glimmer of interest. The prospect of setting a really powerful explosion in the alien ship was seductive. He recognized what it was that they were
actually talking about, but his emotional reaction to the idea sat
him back in his chair with an odd look on his face. It was incredible that he was still just a kid after all, infatuated with the idea of
setting off big explosions, but there it was. He wanted to do it.

He sobered himself impatiently, deliberating what they were
actually talking about. An explosive package powerful enough to
disable or destroy a ship of that size meant something on the order of an anti-ship warhead, even inside the armored hull. The
dimensions of any suitable warhead meant it would have to be
externally mounted. He would have to rig a timer for it, as there
would be no impact for the trigger, and a proximity fuse made no
sense if they needed time to get away. "We have access to an
AS-93c warhead, but it wouldn't fit inside the scout, Bobby.
There isn't a real cargo hatch, only the entry tube and airlock.
There isn't an external mount on the ship that we could use for a
payload like that."

"What about that big hexagonal hollow built into the scout's
undercarriage?"

"Too shallow, Bobby. I've been puzzled by that feature myself.
No use for it that I can think of, but it wouldn't be deep enough
for a 93c and the interior of the cavity is smooth as glass, nothing
to use to secure a payload." Mackenzie replied.

Bobby nodded back to him. "But what if we adapted the
antimatter containment systems from a few of the fighters on the
station? Take them aboard the scout individually, through the
airlock, and assemble them into a package when we get there?"

Mackenzie saw how it could be done. He looked at Bobby
askance, thinking the young man had an engineer's mind. He
nodded. "That might work, given enough time. Let me mull it
over."

Using antimatter containment systems would make the package something they could transport piecemeal and assemble *in
situ*... if he could keep the electromagnetic fields adequately

powered long enough for the trip. Magnetic antimatter containment systems use direct current. Battery backups don't have enough endurance. The scout, his engineering team had discovered, used alternating current, but... he could rig a direct current trickle feed from the alternating current of the alien scout. That should maintain sufficient charge in the backup batteries to do the trick.

Then Mack shook his head. "I don't believe the Station Council or ACM Command would let us do it, Bobby. The scout is too unique. It is too valuable."

Bobby's face suddenly transformed from that of a man too old for his years, back into a grinning kid again, young and mischievous. Mack was swept along in his boyish enthusiasm.

"So we don't ask them, Mack. This is one of those things that just has to be done. Unless the aliens are stopped, humanity on Earth may be extinguished. I think we might have a solution. It is our duty to try."

Mackenzie was considering it.

"Leadership requires authority." Bobby continued. "When action is required, inaction abrogates authority. It is our duty to do the right thing, whether the Council likes it or not."

Mackenzie considered the young man. Apprenticeship to Tibs had imbued Bobby with some of the old Aldebar's gumption. "As long as the action really is the right thing to do. Sometimes that isn't easy to know."

Mackenzie wistfully remembered across the years to his own mentor, old Abbas ibn Firnas, now long dead. He had been a leathery skinned North African who had a taste for distilled alcohol in contravention of his religion. The worldly wisdom that old Berber had lavished on Mackenzie ranged far beyond the scope of engineering. An image rose in Mackenzie's mind of the old man shaking his finger in warning, but the gleam in his eye spoke volumes.

In the time it took them to discuss the proposed challenge, Mackenzie conceived how they could maintain power to four deployable antimatter containment systems aboard the alien scout.

Four should fit and still give him room to be aboard. A few minutes with engineering's computer gave him the numbers he needed. It would be a tight fit in the scout, but the space was workable.

The weight would be a problem. Not for the ship, but for deploying and assembling the units. If they used portable antigravity fixtures the weight wouldn't be an issue, but the time it would take would add at least two minutes apiece to affix, power, remove, and return to get the next containment system. They would only have fifteen minutes to deploy the four devices before the first went off. They couldn't afford the time cost.

Bobby focused on securing the provisions they would need. Then he helped Mack wrestle four antimatter containment units from the station's stock onto the scout. They were as heavy as Mackenzie remembered. Bobby could move but not lift them. Mack would have to be the one down on deck. Bobby could move them to the airlock and lower them if Mack was there to help ease them down.

Chapter 57: Agent of the Board

The Agent of the Corporate Board strode toward the master communications console. His pale assistant walked behind him, watched closely by nearby guardsmen.

Martial Law had been declared globally. Only one in five Nibbles kiosks would be active and those would be under guard. Supply vehicles would have armored escorts. Rationing was in effect. The people were to shelter in place except when it was their rotation to move about. Hospitals were fully staffed and ready.

The Chairman was already *en route* to a secure installation, deep within a granite mountain in North America. The balance of the Corporate Board headed toward their own fortified facilities around the globe. Dispersal of the center of power was common sense under the circumstances.

With their staff, the board members had left in personal shuttles escorted by High New York's finest. The balance of the orbital city's population was evacuating as well. The other orbital cities followed suit.

As spacious as the docks were, only so many could board and depart at a given time. No matter how many complaints and threats of suit they filed, the Agent was determined that evacuation would be orderly.

Still, he was glad he wouldn't have to mix among them when he left High New York. The wealthy are no more considerate and understanding than commoners. Their complaints would be unbearable, and the Agent did not feel inclined to endure them. Every reply he made would be an opportunity for litigation. The bulk of his staff were already moving his most valued belongings to his shuttle through the executive terminal.

City maintenance functions were automated, of course, but a skeleton crew from engineering would have to remain behind to ensure everything remained in good working order. Security would also have to keep a presence in the orbital city.

Staff is wonderful. You need only ensure your team is the best and brightest available and the things that need doing will be accomplished effortlessly, often with compliments.

The loss of the *Trafalgar* was a serious setback. Earth had other battleships, to be sure, but they were older, some obsolete, like the *Ariel*, still powering up in Trondheim system.

The loss of the Aldebari Marines was regrettable. With them out of the picture the Aldebari fleet was significantly less formidable. It was possible that the Legion fleet, still intact, might decide the Aldebari were now weak enough to attack. Whether they actually would attack, despite the alien, was the larger question.

The alien *had* disrupted the balance of power in human space. Unbalanced, the triad of interests would know peace no longer unless all three were similarly degraded into some semblance of balance.

Contrary to popular belief, the great powers had not refrained from military action all these years for merely economic reasons. A triadic power balance is dynamic. Attacking one power would consequently expose vulnerability to the other. If one power is weakened, the others will pounce. Once the weakest has lost, the others will be at one other in no time.

Now the forces defending Earth were seriously weakened, at least until the reserves could be mustered. Activating the reserves would take time. The agent expected that this remarkable emergency alliance would fall apart in short order as soon as the Alien was removed from the equation.

How the alien could be defeated... well, all other problems in history had been overcome. It was unbelievable that this would be the exception. The finest minds were working all of that. What must be done at the level of the Corporate Board is foresee, shape and provide for the future.

To the agent's consternation, the aliens had failed to respond to appeals for them to negotiate. It was as if they were deaf. Perhaps Admiral Crow had been right to think that what they wanted wasn't negotiable. If it really was hunger that was driving them, then frankly humanity had no interest in negotiation either. Based

on that possibility alone, the Corporate Board signed off on Antarctic Continental's recommendation to implement plan Phoenix.

Phoenix had always been seen as the least desirable of all
homeworld defenses. It was never intended to be used, but until
it was used the solution was relatively inexpensive.

Standardization of products allowed a single software application to be built by the entertainment industry. Secure keys were
already incorporated into every automated device. And if there
was anything the common citizen could do, it was play a VR
game. VR is really all the commoners ever did, and some of
them had grown quite accomplished at it. So, as a system, Phoenix was inexpensive to prepare and implement.

The real expense had always only been a potential that everyone hoped would never be realized. Costs would accrue once
the system was used. Affording enhanced health care for the
participants would be quite expensive at a planetary scale, unless there were a way to reduce that impact

A provision was needed to restrict the incentive benefits to
only those who could prove that they actively engaged. To
merely be selected as a participant should be insufficient for reward. The agent's recommendation was that there should be no
extraordinary rewards at all. The reward should be survival itself.
Commoners did nothing but breed and make problems insoluble.

The agent scheduled time for discussion of the provision in
the next Corporate Board meeting's agenda.

The biggest problem with Phoenix would come afterward.
Once the public had control of those machines, getting the
equipment back into regular operation would be challenging. Further, system security would be irrevocably compromised.

The Legion and Aldebari weren't incompetents, so by now
they would know the program existed. That reduced viability for
the program's original purpose.

The agent felt frustration. He consciously kept his hands from
his face and refused to massage his temples, as those would be
tell-tales. They would telegraph his internal state. Outwardly, he
must appear as cool and professional as he had always been.

Chapter 58: A Trap

Kyle dropped by the Chief's office for the package he had requisitioned from engineering. He was pleasantly surprised to receive it from Bobby. Kyle had briefly seen Bobby at intervals during the young man's stay at Perry Station, but he hadn't had an opportunity to greet him personally.

When Bobby was first orphaned, Kyle had been the helpful deputy that found and took him in. Then only fourteen, Bobby was alone and bereft in a culture that must have felt utterly foreign. He was badly in need of good counsel.

Kyle had found Bobby behind some bins attempting to sleep. The boy had managed to escape from medical observation. His case was high-profile, since his parents died attempting to wrest control of the modulus from an ACM patrol.

His parents had been in the pay of Celestine Interstellar, Paul Harden's outfit. Bobby survived because his mother had the foresight to use an airlock as his emergency shelter. Steve Holbrook had boarded the disabled gunship and found Bobby trapped but alive in that airlock.

Now, after serving aboard the *Jade Temple* as Tibs' apprentice, Bobby was entering young adulthood as a remarkably bright young man. He had already gained a respectable reputation among the Aldebari. His native heritage was Corporate, but culturally Bobby had become a blend of Corporate, Aldebari and Alliance cultures. His biggest liability was that he attracted interesting problems like a magnet.

The package Kyle received from engineering was a handheld metal case. It contained specialized ordinance. Close examination of surveillance imagery revealed evidence that the aliens could communicate while their shields were active without any apparent use of comm devices. That meant sound waves penetrate alien personal shields. Obviously the aliens could see and were seen, meaning that radiant light would also bypass their shield defenses. Kyle concluded that concussive sound accompanied by a blinding flash of light might render the aliens incapable of resistance for a time.

The aliens were now known to be hiding in the hydroponics facility, so that area had been placed on lock-down. Ventilation requirements in the hydroponics facility were greater than normal with its humid environment, but there was no way for the aliens to access the air shafts. Even if they found or built a way to reach the air shaft and gain entry they would be stopped by air scrubbers that remove organic contaminants.

In preparation for his plan, Kyle directed that guards should enter hydroponics at the same time each day, every day. They would remain alert there and then leave, locking the door again when they departed. As the doors were locked, one of the guards would rap the metal of one locked door with a large wrench. The intent was to associate the clanging of the door with locking. Surveillance imagery had shown one of the aliens testing the doors after the guards left.

It was believed that, by this time, the aliens had to be hungry.

When everything was ready, Kyle used a sticky adhesive to set one of his flash-bang explosives onto the bulkhead just inside the hydroponics access corridor. When the guards entered and left hydroponics on schedule they 'forgot' to lock the door. They didn't rap the door with the wrench to simulate the sound of a lock.

"An alien is approaching the door, Kyle." Gabriella informed him by comms. He was using an earbud to hear her. She was at the security office monitoring a bank of surveillance screens.

Kyle held the remote detonator in his hand. He and his officers were behind a door in a room adjacent to the corridor. Matsuo and his Marines were further in and ready, just in case the plan went sideways and the aliens got past the trap.

Kyle had his fingers on the toggle of the controller. He was waiting for Gabriella, who could see on her monitor whether the alien was in position. She would signal when to trigger the flash-bangs. His men tensed at the door, ready.

Once the aliens were stunned, they would have to be restrained. The scientists who studied the physiology of the alien specimens told him that the way the aliens' shoulders were built disallowed restraint of their hands behind their back, but binding the forearms to their upper arms should be effective. Their legs bent in the back of the leg, like the legs of a bird. It was hoped that strapping their legs together would prevent leaping and kicking with their wickedly clawed feet.

There wasn't an easy way to bind their tails, but hobbled and bound they should be unable to put much power behind any whipping.

Kyle could think of only one way to prevent biting, and that was to bind their jaws shut with an adhesive fabric tape. The scientists he consulted objected to this measure. If an alien's snout was bound too tightly it might asphyxiate. The supporting structures of the snout were too supple to prevent constriction of the nostrils if the binding was too tight.

None of this had been done before. Kyle didn't want to kill the creatures if he could help it, but he wouldn't have a problem of conscience if they died. They had killed five of his people.

Figuring out how to feed them in captivity was going to be a headache for someone. Fortunately, the scientists would have to handle that.

In the time it had taken for Kyle to get the flash-bangs from Mackenzie and prepare his ambush, the scientists prepared a containment chamber for the aliens once they were captured. The scientists were keen to study live specimens.

Through the wall, Kyle heard the doors to hydroponics opening. Gabriella said nothing for a moment, until she whispered "The alien is suspicious of the open doors. It initially ducked back under the carousel planter after opening them. Now it is in the open again and edging closer."

"Stay ready, people." He urged his officers in a whisper. "The alien is being cautious."

They heard a quiet whistle in the corridor, like the call of a bird. After a moment Gabriella reported "Both of them are approaching the ambush."

Feeling like a sprinter tense in the blocks awaiting the start of a race, Kyle felt the blood coursing through his veins as tension built. At any moment...

"Go!" came the voice of Gabriella in his ear. He triggered the flash-bang. True to his calling, Mackenzie had made the charge well. A very loud crack went off in the corridor. The door that concealed the officers slid open and Kyle's security team swarmed out into clearing smoke in the hall to find the two aliens sprawled unconscious on the deck.

Their scaled skins were warm to the touch and their feathers were just like the feathers of birds. The necks and tails were limber but heavy while the aliens were unconscious. Lifting them was a challenge, as their muscles were dense. It was like trying to lift a very large snake.

There was some hesitation to touch the scaly skins of the creatures, but once that was overcome both creatures were soon bound. It was less simple to bind their snouts with adhesive tape, but they managed to get it done before the reptiles began to struggle and test their bonds.

Once the aliens awoke, they struggled mightily, necks and tails writhing, attempting to batter and lash. Their struggles were ineffectual. They quickly learned their efforts were both futile and painful. When they tried to open their jaws to bite, their breathing was impaired. The aliens learned quickly.

The aliens were taken on grav-assist stretchers through cleared corridors to the scientists, eager to receive the creatures into prepared chambers adjacent to the lab.

Chapter 59: Unrest

The period of social quiet worldwide that attended revelation of the Phoenix program was sadly brief. As soon as the alien ship became visible, a bright and growing speck in the sky, everyone who had been comfortably living in denial suddenly believed with passion. Ignorance was no longer an option, save for those who refused even to look to the heavens.

People were afraid, and they expressed their fear loudly. Some raged against whatever they associated with the threat, usually some corporate asset. Some brave few controlled their fear and sought to prepare for what they thought might happen next. Some grew quiet and cerebral.

Normally thoughtful people wrote dire predictions on the Holo-Net. Together their speculative sentiments fanned the flames of panic. Others agreed with them, and echoed the fear further. It was as if they were screaming into an echo chamber, creating a feedback loop, each amplifying the fears of every other before passing it on to the next. On the social channels of the HoloNet, the collective global panic grew powerfully.

Professional holocasters attempted to calm the populace, but were ignored. Everyone *knew* the professional media was only a corporate tool. Decades of tailoring the facts to serve preferred policy bit back hard at the Corporate Board. Across the globe, civilization grew shrill and incoherent.

A few reasonable persons stood, figuratively, in the path of an online stampede of emotions. They attempted to counsel reason, but were irrationally trampled. Those objecting to the panic were derided as fools.

Rather than prove how formidable eighteen billion people could be, the consensus seemed to be that their numbers only meant the aliens would grow fat.

For decades, subtle and not-so-subtle indoctrination had assured the people that they could do nothing alone to help themselves. Only the corporations could act effectively. The intent had been to keep the Corporate Board in power. That exercise of mass social control exacted a toll when cooperative interdependence was most needed.

Admiral Crow's opinion, that the aliens came because they were hungry, spread contagiously.

The alien ship approached orbit and began to destroy the satellites circling the planet. The HoloNet went down and remained down.

Most people, all over the planet, no longer had a way to know what was happening unless it was happening to them. Many reasoned that the HoloNet had been eliminated by the aliens. Some assumed that the net had been shut down by the corporations, and that the Corporate Board was trying to hide something.

The HoloNet was dead, its signal inert. A few of the most dedicated VR players finally realized something was happening in the real world.

To those in space, the Earth became ominously silent. The remnants of second fleet still had signal from a few ground stations, but command was shifted to the military's lunar facilities.

The great cities in orbit were deserted. Security and engineering maintained a presence to keep automated systems operating and property secure, but the cities were otherwise lifeless.

The alien ship fired on the first orbital city it reached, High London. It fired a powerful blast of energy that caused considerable destruction, but the evacuated city didn't respond.

Well above the planet's atmosphere, the orbital cities were so massive that destroying them would scatter debris into an already chaotic storm of navigational hazards. Left intact, the cities could be easily avoided. They might eventually be useful as conveniently positioned livestock pens.

The Skraa ceased testing the defenses of the high cities to focus on destroying smaller orbital satellites. On Earth, this meant satellite-dependent communications and navigation were gradually degraded, crippled and finally lost altogether. Most automated industries could no longer be operated. Supply became manual, more of a scavenging operation.

Pat had been cut off from a call to New York when the net

went down. She assumed the problem was with her wrist comm until she learned everyone was similarly affected.

Mike Baker was monitoring text conversations on Darknet. The destruction of satellites had eliminated the HoloNet, but hadn't affected Darknet or Milnet. These networks used antique buried fiber optic lines that had been lain centuries earlier, in the classical age.

The part of the Darknet and Milnet infrastructure most vulnerable to the alien was globally distributed. Hundreds of thousands of small wireless towers were spread across the planet. They were vulnerable, but they were many. Most of them remained intact. Some address blocks were lost when individual towers were caught by the destructive orbital fire of the alien, usually while striking other nearby targets, or when some coastal areas were flooded by the collapse of municipal seawalls. But the towers were so small and so many that, in themselves, they were almost beneath notice.

Milnet issued an advisory that the satellites that the HoloNet used had been destroyed. Mike saw the advisory and echoed it to Darknet. He shared the information verbally with the others around the conference room table.

The only working means of long-distance communication on the planet's surface were the Darknet and the Milnet. Data uplinks for off-planet communications were offline. No systems remained operational that had contact with Earth's defenders in space. Word on Milnet was that the military was working on restoring communications with the fleets.

Avery personally didn't have Milnet access, but he had Mike Billings. Mike would echo pertinent information from Milnet out onto the Darknet. On Darknet, inductees in the Phoenix program waited impatiently for their digital keys. For them, receipt of the keys would mean mobilization, a signal that the aliens were actually on the planet, where they could be fought. In orbit, the aliens couldn't be touched.

One of the Milnet infobits that were echoed to Darknet was a continuously updated list of installations that reported taking fire from the alien. The alien's great energy beam was powerful, but it wasn't as devastating as kinetic orbital bombardment would have been. While the energy was horrific, it generally didn't have great penetration. Underground installations were generally out of its reach.

It was believed that eventually the aliens would land. The question on the table for Martin was whether to release the digital keys now, or wait until a landing was confirmed. The probability seemed high that releasing the keys before targets were present would lead to increased chaos. Yet, if they waited too long, the Darknet itself might be lost.

Food production and residential areas generally weren't struck. Though the aliens weren't precise and did cause collateral damage, their weapon fire did not appear to be indiscriminate.

Food distribution systems and logistical transport were automated. They depended on global positioning systems. Loss of the satellites meant they no longer functioned. People were going to go hungry until someone figured out a way to move large amounts of Nibbles manually. Mike pointed out to Martin that the Phoenix pilots could solve that problem if the keys were released and they could keep from competitively destroying one another's drone machines.

Most people had access to water. Desalinization plants were usually small, widely distributed, and their delivery systems were often underground.

The alien ship was rapidly degrading humanity's infrastructure. It seemed clear that they were preparing to invade, yet there was no sign that they had begun to deploy. It was preposterous to imagine that a single spacecraft, no matter how large, could hope to successfully invade a planet of so many people, yet there was no other explanation anyone could imagine for the alien behavior.

Steve, Pat, Martin, and Mike were seated across from one another in comfortable chairs.

One of the last HoloNet messages that Steve had received, before the net went down completely, was a reply from Bobby Morrison and Chief Mackenzie, on Perry Station. It was a reply to his request for an update on the aliens and the scout ship.

Steve was a little surprised to find the reply had been sent directly from Bobby's mail because he hadn't been addressed. Steve had thought Bobby was with Tibs. Scrolling down to the previous message he found that Lyman had forwarded Steve's letter to Kyle and Mackenzie. There wasn't a response yet from Kyle.

Steve reread Bobby's message. "Bobby and Mack are going to try to destroy the Alien ship." he told the others. He glanced up to see Pat cock her head to the side.

Martin turned to him expectantly. "I could use some good news."

"How do they propose to go about doing that?" Mike asked.

Steve first told them about his friends to provide some context. "I don't think any of you, other than maybe Pat, have met him, but Bobby's a friend of mine, a bright young man who has been serving aboard the *Jade Temple* under Tibs.

"I killed his parents in a defensive action at the Al Najid modulus a couple of years ago and found him in the air lock." Steve began to explain.

Mike's eyebrows drew down. "You killed his parents, yet he's your friend?" he asked.

"He took time to listen to my side of what happened when his folks were killed. Revenge was his natural first reaction, but he didn't know his weapon. I disarmed him. But then I was reasonable in my response. He was only a kid, and I could understand where he was coming from. Remarkably, he suspended judgment on me in return, and actually tried to understand how it happened, from my perspective. I found it amazing of him to draw the distinction between intentionally killing someone and inflicting casualties defending yourself, even though it was his family we were talking about. And he *did,* even though it was his folks. He was able to forgive me. I'm not sure I could have. Then he directed his vengeance toward Paul Harden, the man who had so badly used his parents." Steve explained.

"Remarkable." Martin observed.

Steve nodded to him. "Frankly it would be scary, except that I've come to know him. He cares deeply about his folks. He blames Paul Harden with a passion."

"So how does this Bobby friend of yours propose to destroy a warship filled with aliens that just finished cutting its way through a modern war fleet, beat the stuffing out of the most powerful battleship in human space, and repulsed a fleet-scale Aldebari Marine assault?" Mike asked with an arched eyebrow.

Steve sat back in his chair, and then leaned forward again, his elbows on his knees as he explained. His hands grew expressive. "Remember when we found the first alien ship, the alien scout, out in Al Najid space? Had the mummified alien aboard?"

"You found it even though it was invisible, right?" Pat stated.
"Right. I didn't so much find as bump into it while I was out surveying. Chief Mackenzie got it back to the Station." Steve confirmed. "Anyway, once Chief Mackenzie and a guy working maintenance named Liam Green got it open they found the mummified alien and a cowl inside."

"Yes, everyone knows about your alien mummy. But what's a cowl?" Billings asked.

"It's something people used to wear on their heads, Mike. But, like, a drape instead of a helmet." Steve answered. "Anyway, according to Bobby's message, Mackenzie and his people were focused on figuring out how the alien ship works. There wasn't anyone with time to study the cowl, which turned out to be some kind of advanced alien device. The Jade Temple happened to be at Perry Station, and Mackenzie asked Tibs to loan him someone to study the device. Tibs chose Bobby."

Mike Billings seemed impatient, but Pat and Martin were focused and interested. Steve scanned the last part of Bobby's message to refresh his memory.

"Bobby says here, that they put the cowl on his head... and he discovered it was a flight control system for the alien scout. He says it works something like Aldebari implants. Bottom line, he says he can fly the alien scout."

"What I find most surprising," Steve continued "is that he somehow then talked Mackenzie into building an explosive device to sneak onto the alien ship." Steve gestured toward the ceiling, as if the alien ship were beyond it instead of half a world away.

"Bobby thinks the aliens' point defenses will hold fire on their own scout ship, which may give them a chance to slip an anti-matter device, rigged as a time bomb, into the aliens' docking bay." Steve explained.

Everyone was silent around the table. "It might work." Billings conceded.

"Will they be able to get away in time to escape the explosion?" Martin asked. Steve spread his hands to show he couldn't say.

Mike Billings thought about it. "They would have to use the scout's power supply for the trip, but once disconnected to place the antimatter containers aboard they would have use a battery system to keep the containment fields up. Fifteen to twenty minutes, tops, before it would fail. Once aboard the alien ship, they would have to offload and assemble them. That would take time. They will have to get away pretty fast."

Mike looked dubiously at Martin. "You know how many things could go wrong with that plan. I doubt they had any time to prac-tice the job. There's no way they can foresee all the problems. The odds against success look pretty overwhelming."

After his words everyone was quiet until Steve asked "How far away do you think they will have to get, Mike?"

Billings thought it out. "Well, it isn't like vacuum will communi-cate a shockwave, but annihilation generates a pretty energetic reaction. The explosion would push that energy, call it plasma, and wreckage of the ship outward radially, so the farther away they get the better.

"The safest path for their escape should be directly away from the hanger opening, since there will be less material there to push at them. The plasma should weaken at something like the square of four times the distance they can reach, times pi." Mike advised. "But if they are delayed at all, once they discon-nect, the odds against them increase at a similar rate because that delay will reduce the radius of the sphere when it hits them. There won't be the concussion they would have in an atmos-phere, but there will be an expanding sphere of violent energy produced as well as thrown debris. The power of the plasma in that sphere grows more attenuated the more it expands.

"But they will most likely be annihilated anyway as soon as they try to disconnect the power supply to deploy the antimatter."

"That isn't hopeful." said Steve in dismay.

Mike's eyebrows drew together and his brow furrowed. "The point of engineering is to avoid reliance on hope." He shook his head. "The magnetic bottles could be disrupted by any number of potential mishaps when they try to deploy the devices. The more antimatter they use, the greater the risk that something goes wrong." Mike Billings warned. "It will only take a single mistake to erase them, anywhere along the way."

"And they're going to try and do it alone up there." Steve observed. "They should have support. I don't think the Aldebari and Legion fleets are aware of the plan. If they see that alien scout they are immediately going to try and kill it."

He turned to Pat. "I want to be out there nearby. They should have someone with them who knows what they are trying to do. I doubt that alien scout has anything like a lifepod system."

Her eyes grew wide with concern. "Steve, no. Think of your children."

"Think of..." He objected. "I'm their father, Pat. But I'm not going to sit idle while my friends lay their lives on the line for us. If they get in trouble, there won't be anyone out there to help them. If they get in trouble, they're dead."

"What about Stevie and Kathlyn? What are they going to do when their father gets himself killed?" Pat asked pointedly.

"Please, Pat. Look, stay here with the kids for me. I can't ask Martin to babysit them, but they know you. They'll take comfort that you stayed with them. Explain why I had to do this."

Steve saw that Pat was upset with him, even though he was trying to do the best thing. The alien threatened not just Earth, but all of them, including the kids. It had to be eliminated.

"Steve if you want them to understand, then you damn well better explain it to Kathlyn and Stevie yourself!" Pat was more than just upset with him; she was afraid for him. "I don't understand what the hell you think you are doing, Steven. You're asking me to explain it to them when you go off and die out there and don't come back?" Pat turned away, furious, then spun back on him with an accusatory finger, trembling. "You have responsibilities, whether you like it or not, Steve. You can't just fly off and risk your life like that when you have children who depend on you."

Steve stopped himself in anguish. He wrestled with the conundrum of his conflicting duties. He couldn't leave his friends to die alone out there, but Pat was right too. He also couldn't just fly off, least of all without talking to the kids himself. He looked at Martin, who was looking back at him with a slow shaking of his head.

Steve tried to explain himself. "Pat, there isn't another way to communicate off-planet. Bobby and Mack will be flying an obviously alien ship. Someone has to get up there, to run interference for them with the Aldebari and the Legion, now, while they're still inbound on their mission. Someone has to be up there that will know they're not aliens. Whatever they might say over comms to explain their mission won't be believed. The first contact protocol gave the aliens our language. They'll be assumed to be aliens. They have to get to the target, but they'll be intercepted by our own forces. They will only have a chance if we give them that chance."

Pat grew pale. "You are willing to sacrifice the few for the sake of the many. But someone else you know was willing to sacrifice the few to save Earth. Do you know who that was? Paul Harden, Steve. Paul Harden sacrificed the people of Perry to try and save Earth. But, Steve, the people of Perry weren't his own children. If you die out there you will have sacrificed their Daddy on an altar to your own damn ego." She was visibly shaking, and her eyes were dark with rage.

Steve winced. "That's a low blow, Pat. I'm not putting anyone on an altar."

Pat lost her temper and flew at him, beating both fists on his chest. "You can't do this Steve!" she cried. "You can't! I've only just found you." She realized in an instant what she said and went pale.

Martin looked away at the ceiling, trying to not be there to hear this. Mike looked like he had heard about enough of the drama.

Pat loosed an exasperated sigh. She was weary of men. Her head bowed for a moment, dropping her beautiful eyes. Quietly she said "But you're willing to risk their future."

He lifted his hands to her shoulders. She raised her eyes to his once more, searching. "If it would save your life and the lives of those kids, I'd do worse than use a low blow, Steve." Pat assured him. "There has to be another way. You just have to find it." She pulled her shoulders away slowly from his hands and turned, looking lost. Her voice lowered. "You may not realize it yet, Steve, but you gave up the hero business when you rescued your children. And me. You aren't alone any more. Your responsibility is first for your family. As a father, not as a widower with little to lose."

Steve looked down at his hands. It was true.

"Pat's right, Steve, and you know it." Martin finally said. "I'll go up and run interference for your friends."

Pat heard his proposal with shock and spun on him. "Martin, No!"

Martin shook his head at her. "Steve is right, too, Pat. You're going to have to deal with that." Martin enumerated his points on his fingers, one at a time. "Someone has to get word to the fleets about friendlies incoming, but in an alien ship. It has to be someone with name recognition, someone that the admirals will find credible. They would have believed Steve. They would believe me. But as you point out, Steve can't do it. Mike, here, is unknown. And you aren't known either, not outside your client base.

"That leaves yours truly." he concluded.

"But..." Pat protested.

"But what, Pat? I don't have children."

"But I could do it, Martin." Pat said. "Your project has to come first. It's the best hope humanity has to overcome our overpopulation."

"Pfft." Martin dismissed her objection with the wave of a hand. "Mike already knows everything necessary, and he'll get the job done. Hell, he already does all the work. I just sign off on it. Look, Pat... before you two arrived with the kids I was drinking myself to an early grave. Ask Mike: he's been after me about it for months. Money is most valued by those who don't have it. My wealth gives me the unusual luxury of recognizing that it isn't the money that matters, but value. People matter."

Martin gestured at the main monitor. "I've got a feeling that my solution, those habitats in solar orbit, may not be needed unless someone, somehow, eliminates that alien ship. I don't know if Bobby and MacArthur can do it..."

"Mackenzie." Steve corrected him.

"...Mackenzie." Martin acknowledged with a nod to him before turning his eyes back to Pat. "...but if they do have a shot, then I need to do whatever it takes to let them take that shot."

"They have to get past our own forces."

Chapter 60: Star Ship

A stout bipedal creature stepped stiffly into the airlock. It was not taller than Tibs' shoulder. It motioned Tibs into the starship. Its two eyes appeared fully dilated, displaying huge pupils. Thin irises were visible around the edges. In the blue light, Tibs was unsure of the coloration, but the irises might have been golden. Its thick eyelids bore no eyelashes. The alien blinked, as if innocent. It was pale, giving Tibs the impression that the creature had evolved in a subterranean environment. Heavy skeletal features suggested that it was from a high-gravity environment, though the artificial gravity Tibs felt was close to Earth-normal.

Tibs quietly vocalized his observations using his pressure suit's comm recorder. His helmet encumbered his right hand. The alien ship was completely quiet, which Tibs found more reassuring than alarming.

His host didn't seem to have any hair, unless the bony, horn-like covering of its scalp was a kind of hair. It was wearing a drape of pale fabric, like a monk's wrap. Its hands were flat, with thick fingers, but there was an elegance of motion to those hands that suggested good dexterity when it beckoned to him.

When Tibs began to step toward the opening in response to the alien, the creature turned to lead the way. It was deliberate in its motions, but not especially slow. It turned its face and upper body away from Tibs, then twisted one of its short, thick legs without lifting its large foot from the deck. Once the first leg faced the direction it intended to go, the second leg turned until that foot was parallel to the first.

This being had certainly originated in a high gravity environment. It moved in ways that would minimize tripping or overbalancing. Tibs was surprised that it would stand at all, if it evolved on a high gravity world.

Once it faced the direction it intended to move, it shuffled its way further into the ship. The sound of its unhurried feet sliding carefully on the deck was loud in the silence aboard the ship. Its torso rocked gently side-to-side as it walked, and swung its arms like it was skating. It would surely be hard wired to avoid heights.

Tibs could not imagine what circumstances led its species to achieve space travel.

Tibs was fascinated. The creature was not at all fat, but its smooth skin seemed thick and leathery. Tibs didn't dare touch it to verify his observation. Smooth ropes of sinew undulated beneath its skin when it walked, suggesting great muscular strength and control. It used a rolling gait, the shoulder alternating its swing with the slide of the opposite foot.

It hadn't uttered a sound, other than the shuffling of its feet. They traversed a broad corridor, that was actually a tube. Five smooth walkways aligned in parallel on the deck, bulkheads, and ceiling of the corridor. They passed an intersection where five smaller tubes led off, surely into the star ship's radiating 'arms'. Tibs guessed that had he stepped from his current walkway to another, the orientation of his local gravity might have followed suit. The passage was cylindrical rather than rectangular, perhaps to avoid making the creature lift its feet to change passages.

They arrived at a chamber dimly lit by pale blue light. It was furnished at its center by what looked like a chair, perhaps an acceleration couch. In size it would fit the creature who led him.

The alien moved to stand next to the seat, and adroitly began making adjustments to it. It worked on the chair, then looked at Tibs again to re-evaluate. With odd half-steps and a partial torso twist, it estimated the length of his limbs and torso. Elements of the seat were extended to an appropriate size for Tibs, and then the creature stepped back from it. With simple economy it motioned with its open palm toward Tibs, then swept its hand toward the chair. It wanted him to be seated.

Obligingly Tibs stepped to the seat and sat down. There was a headrest that cupped to the back of his head, and the backrest conformed itself to his back and hips. The seat was comfortable, but Tibs felt something flat and cool moving at the back of his neck. He began to sit upright, startled.

The creature indicated with gestures that he should relax and sit back. Something about its eyes looked gently amused, and

Tibs tried to comply, albeit uneasily.

Tibs recognized how foolish he might be, obedient to a completely unknown sentient being. On the other hand, it was a non-human sentient being. The technology he had already caught hint of indicated that, should this alien have malevolent intent, there would be little chance to prevent the undesirable anyway. The behavior exhibited so far had seemed cordial, even caring.

Tibs recalled a similar choice from an old memory, when he lay awaiting the surgery that would implant his pilot augmentation, something every Aldebari pilot must endure. It was a moment of appropriately impersonal trust, when he underwent that medical procedure. Then, as now, there was no practical alternative to that trust.

Tibs' awareness was swept with a wave of disorientation. His alarm was mild. Blurred translucent images washed across his field of vision. To try and observe the images he closed his eyes. He heard a ringing in his ears. For a moment he smelled something acrid, like ammonia, and heat seemed to wash his skin.

Behind his eyelids there grew suggestions of light and dark that coalesced into what at first seemed the image of a human, but as it clarified, there were differences evident. The neck was too long, and the arms and hands were also too long to be human. It was clothed in a draping garment similar to that worn by the first creature, the short one that breathed softly nearby.

The ringing in his ears differentiated itself, gaining timbre and bass, but was still unintelligible as to content. He could distinguish facial features in the faint image which coalesced and became distinct. It was clear that, whatever it was, moved its mouth to utter what he assumed were words. As he watched and listened he was amazed to find that he was beginning to understand.

"Understand me you present? Now?"

Tibs replied "I believe so."

"This is good. I feel gladness. Ah, this contact of new mind pleases me. I promise quickly to good... well adapt. Split infinitive? Split infinitive. Ah! Thank you: I learn.

"I have wished to speak with your species member long time, but the rule is... strong? Not broken to be. Not alter course. Course must be your own..."

The creature paused a long moment. It was considering something and struggled mightily to learn.

"Your language is interesting, one of the more complete and complex languages I have found. A good metric of cognition. Accept my compliments."

Tibs was taken aback. That was fast. English is one of the most difficult languages to learn and, whatever this creature was, it may have approached mastery in maybe thirty seconds.

"Ah... Thank you." Tibs said, "We are proud of our language. And thank you for the honor of taking the trouble to learn it."

"Oh, while it is a pleasure ... to learn original? No, to learn new minds or languages, that is more difficult and gradual than what we are doing now, you and me. It is you who have the language we use. I'm am merely using your understanding of it to interpret my thoughts more closely and more quickly than I could... grow within your language. I appreciate your well-structured mind, Tibs. I apology, apologize for any clumsiness."

The image bowed. Its facial features seemed to ebb and flow with the moment.

"I am trying to represent myself in the image you see using the more appropriate of your expectations. Frankly, it is a poor representation so far, but likely more suitable than reality." it said, responding to a question Tibs hadn't quite asked.

To be fair to the creature, Tibs said aloud, for the sake of his recording: "The creature I see and hear in my mind tells me it is using my own brain to put its thoughts into our words. It is managing quite well. The grammar has improved remarkably in the elapsed moments since we began. I am not in distress, but I don't believe what it may say will be present on this recording unless I repeat its words, which may be disruptive to the conversation."

Kinkaid's voice confirmed in his ear "We are receiving your voice signal but not that of whoever you have encountered, One. Also be advised we are now bringing Harden's ship into the docking bay."

The creature appeared to wait politely for the inter-ship communication to finish before saying "I have interrupted your mission because we, this Beed and I, were the context of your... human... his capture by the Skraa. We would balance what was."

Tibs was taken aback. *Beed? The Skraa? Our human... Harden. Harden had been captured?*

The entity in his mind responded "The Beed, here, is your host."

Tibs opened his eyes to see the first creature who met him, the heavy-world being with the dark eyes. It was now wearing a scaled metallic cowl identical to the one Mackenzie had shown him at Perry Station. The 'Beed' appeared amused again, as it bowed. Tibs closed his eyes once more. "The Skraa are... predators from your own planet." the entity continued.

Tibs' heartbeat quickened. For the record he said "The aliens attacking our forces are called Skraa, and they are from Earth."

"We had a... very distant problem that neither we nor the Beed could resolve unaided. We found the Skraa, and knew they would be ideal for the resolution of our problem. Except our rules prohibit interference with less developed species.

"Yet we discovered that there was a large asteroid on course to possibly wipe all life from your planet. So what could we do? Some of us decided, unfortunately, that the situation was sufficiently unusual to allow them to pluck a sampling of the Skraa to use to solve our problem."

"Unfortunate? How so?" Tibs asked.

"The asteroid did indeed strike the planet with tremendous force after we took the Skraa aboard seven large ships we built especially for the purpose. Once we used them to solve our problem, and they succeeded, our intent was to bring them back to their point of origin for release. What was unfortunate, was that we found your world once again teeming with fascinating life, including your species.

"That meant we couldn't in good conscience release them there. We had witnessed their capabilities. Had we turned them loose on Earth it would have been an even worse transgression of our law.

"We were seeking somewhere else to let them go when they overcame their Beed hosts and seized the seven ships. There was little we could do, save only to lace into their computer libraries the information we had about the destruction of their homeworld, your homeworld, by the asteroid. We hoped that would lead them away rather than toward you, and it worked, at least until now.

"They had the cowls. They had the ships, and they went on a rampage through the moduli, consuming world after world."

Tibs was shocked at the revelation. "What is the reasoning behind your rule of non-intervention?"

"I intend to cover some of that, but in brief we need partners. We do not need dependents. That is why. Experience has taught us hard lessons."

Tibs wanted to hear more, but resolved to be patient. He was encouraged that the being would respond to questions. Tibs had many questions.

The alien continued, "The one you call Harden was unexpectedly near our course. The Skraa were chasing this ship. Your Harden was near an artificial heat source. The Skraa see heat, and they noticed and captured him. This was a regrettable complication."

Tibs' mind raced. His interest in Harden wasn't on the same scale as his interest in the aliens. The 'Skraa' were from Earth. That meant Steve had been right, but... "The birdlike lizards, these aliens you call the 'Skraa' that are from Earth... from how long ago?" he asked.

The image of the alien waved its hand. "We digress, but time is relative. It is difficult to say how long ago it may have been for them. It would have been a very long time ago for you, however. In the interval your species has evolved. Your culture appears to be reaching a crucial stage of early maturity. For them... the Skraa have, for many of their generations, had the ships they took. But it has not been so long if metered by the time that has passed for your planet."

Relativity. Time seems constant, but it isn't. Time elapses more quickly within a gravity well, such as on a planet. Time passes more slowly away from gravity. Time passes more slowly yet when traveling at great speed. All these occur at once. So if one person is on a high gravity planet, another is on a low-gravity planet, and a third person is traveling between them very quickly, each will age at a different rate. How extreme the difference may be being a function of the extremity of the context.

If Steve was right, and the Skraa were actually dinosaurs, it meant they were taken from Earth at least sixty million years ago. Depending where they went and how quickly they went there... the disparity suggested intergalactic travel, apparently at tremendous speed. It was incredible.

"Then the Skraa didn't build the ship they are using?"

"The Beed built those ships to help us. The Skraa rose up and seized them from the Beed long ago. Now, I would have your people hear something."

Kinkaid's voice came active over Tibs' headset. "We are receiving digital communication from the alien ship."

"Your ship will receive an official record of what I say now." the being in Tibs' mind said.

"You have reached a point in your development as a species where your technology can do all that you know you need of it. Normally at this point a civilization will enter a critical phase, where the only advances are simply refinements of what you already have, and discovery can come to seem mythical.

"To progress, humanity must find a way beyond the cognitive biases that evolution has shaped into your thinking. Those biases have practical uses, maintaining sanity for one, but they also channel how you think the universe works.

"Preference for linearity and symmetry is useful and comfortable, but it may filter out the asymmetrical and the nonlinear.

Those, along with a habitual disregard for temporal variance, are among your most significant cognitive biases.

"The universe does not conform itself to mortal preference. While linearity and symmetry are strong patterns in nature, they cannot properly signal equally true elements that are non-linear or asymmetrical. The patterns you rely upon work in your local reality more because it is local than because they represent anything like a complete set.

"Discovery differs from knowing. What has yet to be discovered cannot yet be recognized. Strive to compartmentalize your cognitive filters to ameliorate your developmental limitations.

"What you think of as reality is only part of the spectra that form the universe we share, and all its parts are integral. Bias filters and channels what we think, but not everything that exists fit such biases. Cognitive bias is like a comfortable cocoon, outside of which you expect to find monsters and treasures. But these are misconceptions. What seems complex viewed through filters may be simple in itself.

"At the extremes of understanding, you already have recognized that the rest of the universe, toward the micro, toward the macro, and similarly on other spectra, behave differently than what was locally sensible during your evolution."

The alien paused, as if to learn whether what it said was understood.

Tibs observed "You have grown remarkably adept in my language."

The being bowed slightly. "It is your mind that I use, after all, Tibs."

"Now: Go with our congratulations. Fare well." the being concluded.

"Wait, if you please." Tibs asked in concern. He had only just met this creature, and was not ready to be dismissed. "We could use your help with these Skraa."

"We have done what we can, possibly more than we should. We wish to not lose your potential." the alien replied.

"With respect, I should point out that this threat to us is a consequence of decisions your people made. Our predicament is a side effect of your error. You must assist us." Tibs attempted to persuade the creature. Their technology was at least advanced beyond what the Skraa enjoyed.

"To the contrary, we must not." the alien solemnly replied. "Seldom is one mistake corrected by its repetition. You have little idea what you are asking. Our responsibility is to refuse. We do wish you well, Human. If you can survive on your own, we need you. We do not need a dependent; however likable you might be. Go."

A thousand questions pressed urgently at Tibs. Some questions were ages old. Others were immediate but less enduring. So many times, since his youth, Tibs had dreamed of meeting this being, and of the questions he would ask. "A question, then, if you have time?"

"Time I certainly have, but understand that not only should I not tell you some things, but some things that I would like to tell you cannot be said well in your language. Languages are representations of cognition, and they filter what can be expressed and understood. Simplicity is often complicated."

Tibs chose a question from the many he had dreamed of asking. "Thank you. Have your people ever visited Earth since the time when you took up the Skraa?"

The alien cocked its head to the side, silent. It seemed to consider the question closely. "I am not sure now is the time, Tibs. Your culture must not allow the information of alien cultures to divert you from your potential." Then the alien seemed to listen to something Tibs couldn't hear. It reached a decision.

"Some time ago two of our researchers experienced a system failure. They crashed onto your planet, killing one immediately. The other was mortally injured. He made two dying requests of the local government, using your written language, which they had learned in their studies. That government was thoughtful enough to honor the requests.

"My sharing this with you now is in part to honor that honor your species afforded to one of our own."

Tibs was taken aback, surprised. "May I ask what the requests were?" Tibs asked earnestly.

"The first request asked that the findings of their research be broadcast in a specific digital format at a very specific frequency into the broad reach of space. This is how we learned their fate. Second, the researcher asked that our existence be kept secret, most especially from those who decide things for the rest of you. No, not your Corporate Board. They had a different name then. The second request was an effort, at death's door the best that the researcher could attempt, so that your people would continue to develop naturally, for the sake of much needed diversity among sentients in the universe.

"Your question tells me that their request was honored."

Tibs inferred that the being he was speaking with was also speaking with another. It had been that other who reminded this one of a debt of honor, and that debt had tilted the scales of jurisprudence.

"Why is diversity, specifically whatever you are calling our potential, important within this universal context?" Tibs persisted.

"Simply because we have learned so much. We cannot overcome all our own cognitive biases, Tibs. We aren't refusing to solve your problems because we think we are superior. We need *you* to win this. We need you to find your way, by your own native genius. We need partners, not dependents. And, fortunately, you are at a point in your development when we can share with you, as much as we have, without significant risk of diverting you from your natural course.

"Nature produces infinitely variable challenges. Our minds, our thinking, are sadly finite. This grows more evident the farther we progress. If you mirrored our ways of thinking, then you would reach no solution we wouldn't have reached ourselves.

"We are already who we are. We wish you to be human, to think like humans, and to solve like humans. Your position in the environment is unique. Ours is also unique. Together we may resolve challenges that neither of us could solve alone. We need you to be you, distinct from us."

Then the creature in his mind paused again, as if he were conferring with someone else who wasn't directly present to Tibs' experience. The being seemed to deliberate. Then the image of the creature in his mind seemed to turn back to Tibs.

"I apologize for the delay, but before we part ways I wish to point toward something that you already could know, yet apparently have not thought about. It may be of interest to you. Because you already know it, I can point out that your starship enjoys the technology to take energy from your overcharged shields to use in your offensive weaponry."

Tibs was alarmed. Very few knew of that technology. It was a closely held secret, shared between the Aldebari and the ACM Alliance. To the best of Tibs' knowledge only one other ship, Steve's gunship, could use it, at least until others were built.

"The Skraa also use that technology" the being continued. "Should your ship ever engage a Skraa capital ship, beware that you do not make use of that particular strength while your opponent fires energy in pulses, or you may be surprised."

"Farewell, Tibs. May we meet at a farther star." Tibs' jaw

dropped open.

Then he suddenly felt dizzy, as the neural connection of the chair released him. The creature's farewell was promising, and the warning sounded like an answer to his request for help against the Skraa. But Tibs was also disappointed to lose an opportunity to ask so many other critical questions. Curiosity was his weakness, his vice.

The discovery of aliens had been something he had desired since childhood. He blamed himself for asking only a question of curiosity, instead of asking something practical, like the tactics of the Skraa. And yet... it had said so *much*. He resolved to celebrate his good fortune, rather than blame himself for not gaining more.

The creature wished to not divert humanity, so what it said, its answer, would have been phrased to make no difference. Yet it told him straight out that the Skraa used the modulinium vane technology to bleed off excessive energy in its shields, and that firing pulses of energy... this was a question for a good engineer.

"Damn." he said aloud.

The Beed looked at him dispassionately with those deep liquid eyes.

"Affirmative, One." Kinkaid responded on comms. "As you are
fond of saying, every good answer deserves a better question."

"Can you understand me?" Tibs asked the Beed. The creature looked at him inscrutably from under its silvery cowl, gave a
slight bow, and swept its arm toward the way out.

Chapter 61: Incoming

Mackenzie and Bobby made their move during the night cycle in engineering. Their expectation was that the ACM Alliance and Perry Station Council would obstruct their mission if they discovered what was planned.

Though studies were ongoing, analysis of the alien scout had already inspired modest advances in shield, weapon, and materiel technology, even though those advances had yet to be realized in manufacturing. Because of the potential for further gains, the alien scout would be valued too greatly for the alliance and the station to risk.

Yet the alien scout ship was needed to get past the defenses of the alien ship that was ripping the satellites of Earth to pieces. It was a safe bet they wouldn't stop there. Three fleets had been unable to stop the aggressor who, it was believed, intended to use people as food.

Theirs was a greater cause than any career, and it was more important than any technological advance. If Earth fell, the rest of the planetary systems in human space would inevitably also fall.

Mackenzie could cycle the engineering bay's atmosphere to near-vacuum and open the bay door onto the splendor of space using his wrist communicator, despite its limited broadcast range.

As the Station's chief engineer, Mack had almost unrestricted access to Station systems. He received an automated query from ACM traffic control whether opening the doors to engineering's atmospheric bay was authorized. Mackenzie assured the system that he was conducting a flight test.

No alarm was raised.

Bobby wore the alien cowl and used its controls to maneuver the scout ship carefully from the bay's interior out into free space. He began to accelerate the scout toward the distant Al Najid modulus for the first leg of their journey.

The little ship handled responsively. It accelerated quickly, as if the little ship was a colt eager to feel her legs.

"How does she fly, Bobby?" Mackenzie asked.

"Nimble! It's disconcerting to pilot hands-free, but I think I'll get used to it." Bobby replied.

"What happens when you need to sleep? Will you leave the cowl on your head, or what?"

After a moment's consideration, Bobby replied "I hadn't thought that through yet, Mack. I don't think we'll be able to stop for a nap any time soon."

Bobby was in the pilot's acceleration couch forward, and Mack was sitting behind him on what the alien must have used in place of a sleep net. It was a small, nest-like dais, with a thinly cushioned, slightly concave upper surface.

Four heavy antimatter containment systems stood around the sleeping dais. Their electrical systems were attached to wires leading to an opened circuitry panel.

There was barely enough spare room for either of the men to stand and stretch his legs or offset the long hours of sitting with isometrics. The journey would be a long one.

"Once we get through the Al Najid/Cygnus modulus I'll set course and speed, then remove the cowl. We'll see what the ship does." Bobby proposed. The scout was up to speed and on course.

Mackenzie nodded distractedly, failing to consider that Bobby couldn't see him. He was bent over, checking the state of the antimatter containment systems on his instruments. He needed to verify that his handiwork was performing as intended. He felt anxious, and he was regretful that there hadn't been time to appropriately test the setup he had rigged. He would have preferred to at least make a dry run for the expected duration of the trip, using only the containment fields without a charge of antimatter.

Everything tested out, so far, but he was still uneasy. Antimatter containment was a reasonably mature technology, and there shouldn't be any surprises, but it is nearly axiomatic that anything man assembles will inevitably fall apart.

There wasn't much else to look at in the back of the scout craft. There wouldn't be much for Bobby to look at, even up there in the pilot's couch. Mack had noticed that the interior of the scout used some alloys that were unusual and distinctive. He wished he had thought to bring a copy of the metallurgical data and analyses his engineering department had generated for some interesting reading. It would at least be better than pondering anthropomorphic entropy.

"Where did you grow up, Mack?" Bobby asked.

Mackenzie considered his answer. "Never did grow up, Bobby." Bobby heard the smile in Mack's voice. "But I was born on Perry. Engineering school at Oberon. What about you?"

"Earth. On the west coast of North America near an old city named Seattle."

The alien scout was challenged on modulus approach by a patrolling flight of four ACM fighters. Bobby didn't know how to respond. He could hear them, but there didn't seem to be a microphone built into the cowl. There wasn't anything that looked like a microphone within reach of the pilot's couch. "Mack we have a problem. The patrol at the modulus can't identify us. I don't have a way to respond."

"Maybe I can use my wrist communicator." Mack proposed, and he gave it a try. The communicator didn't have the range.

"We're already in motion toward transit. I can boost shields to use the ship's stealth capability." Bobby suggested.

"My comm unit doesn't have the range to comm them, Bobby. Maybe if I go out the airlock..."

Bobby made a decision. "No, I'll handle this. We'll pass through using stealth."

Mackenzie had misgivings, but he wasn't the pilot. It would have been better to be above-board with the alliance. They would surely have seen reason. They might even have provided an escort that would see them through.

Bobby explained his thinking. "There isn't time to negotiate with every patrol we will meet at every modulus between Al Najid and Earth. Every second of delay is another second the alien will use to take Earth apart. There are more than our lives at stake." Bobby said.

Mackenzie thought taking the time to secure an escort would save time in the long run. Still, trying to negotiate for assistance carried its own risks.

Bobby prepared to maximize power to the shields. Behind them, the scout would become undetectable. The scout was already in motion, and inertia would maintain their forward momentum. He would otherwise be unable to maneuver, at least until he apportioned power once more to the engines and away from the shields. Diversion of that power would reduce the strength and scope of the shields, and the scout would emerge from stealth.

With the ACM patrol growing heated in their demands for a response, he made certain of his trajectory, shut down his inertial dampening and artificial gravity to feed that portion of power to the antimatter units and life support, and applied all other available power to the scout's shields. The scout vanished to the universe.

Invisible, the scout kept traveling in a straight line. The ACM patrol filled the comm channels with their consternation. The scout transited the modulus into Cygnus system undetected.

An ACM patrol on the far side received an alert from Al Najid space via the comm relay. The patrol swarmed the modulus seeking them but failed to discover the scout.

Bobby made use of a thin probe extending from the forward nacelle through the shield to passively sense their surroundings. The exposed tip of the probe was so small and slow that, if it was detected at all, its presence should be filtered from the data reported to the pilot's sensor interface.

Once Bobby and Mackenzie were beyond sensor range of the Cygnus patrol at the modulus, Bobby reduced shields, reoriented the scout toward the Arcturus modulus, and increased his thrust. Hopefully if the ship was detected by the ACM at Oberon station they still wouldn't attract notice. The scout didn't have a human transponder, so if their transit was in fact spotted, they might be flagged on ACM sensors for investigation. The only way they could shake such a flag would be to enter stealth once more.

Bobby didn't want to accelerate to such a velocity that he would be unable to avoid an obstacle, but the faster their transit the sooner they would reach their objective and the less time they would spend exposed. They needed to know what would happen if Bobby took a nap, because he couldn't remain awake for the duration of the journey.

"Okay, I am throttling back. I am going to remove the cowl to see how the ship responds. The ship should remain on course at the current speed." Bobby advised.

"Good. The sooner we understand the details of how the ship works, the better I'll feel. I'm already sacrificing my career for this gambit. Councilor Lyman won't easily forgive me even if we're successful. But you're right: the mission is necessary. It just damn well better work. I didn't do this just to die trying." Mackenzie stated.

Stealing the ship and defying the patrol had been suicidal as a career move. Mack had plenty saved for his retirement, but if the Station appropriated his accounts in compensation for his crime then, if he survived and wasn't imprisoned, he would still get awfully skinny without an income. Maybe he could make something writing a memoir.

Bobby looked back over his shoulder at the worried engineer with the best smile he could muster. "If I haven't said it, thank you Mack. You're putting it all on the line for my planet." he told him with sincerity. Mackenzie grunted.

Bobby turned back toward the bow and said "Now, stand by." Bobby didn't know if this escapade would divert his career or not, but he believed his mission was rightful, and that those who mattered to him would ultimately approve. He considered how fortunate he was to have his friends.

With that, Bobby removed the cowl from his head to observe what the ship might do without input. He was going to need sleep soon.

Without active guidance the ship behaved the way any object should and maintained its course and speed. Vacuum provides no resistance, so the speed remained constant in exactly the direction it had been traveling.

Without the interface provided by the cowl there was nothing to signal change. The ship was traveling in the empty depths of space. The only 'landmarks' were so distant that their relative positions wouldn't appreciably change in the time it took for the test.

It wasn't until he resumed wearing the cowl that he could use the navigation system to determine what the ship may actually have done.

Satisfied, Bobby suggested that while he slept Mackenzie should use the cowl to familiarize himself with the operation of the ship, just in case of mishap. Mackenzie had been thinking the same thing.

Chapter 62: Darkened Earth

When the satellites were no more than debris, the alien ship began striking strategic targets on the surface from orbit. Its great energy weapon burned down through the atmosphere and carved destruction across the face of the planet. Fires burned out of control. Chemical plants were destroyed, and the land and water near them was contaminated. Spaceports and air bases were seared into ruins. Concrete poured in the classical age spalled and cracked. Seawalls that had held out the risen ocean were breached and some old coastal cities were flooded beneath meters of seawater.

The aliens didn't know and didn't seem to care whether what they saw from space were military threats. Landmarks were misidentified and destroyed as if they were weapons emplacements.

Human forces in space were trying to find a way to counter or destroy the alien ship. They could survey the damage planetside wherever the alien ship was beyond the horizon. Word and visual imagery of the destruction went out to the stars. The fleets and planets were appalled and angered but the proximity of the alien ship to the planet frustrated them by preventing the battleships from firing their railguns. Railgun ordinance could have caromed from the shields and added to the destruction on the planet. Attacking with lesser weapons and smaller ships was repeatedly demonstrated to be futile. Such attacks only resulted in further losses.

The admirals could only conserve what strength they still had in hope of some unexpected break, an opportunity of chance.

The people of Earth had been stripped of their virtual reality cocoons. Men and women turned to face a newly hostile sky. Where the ship passed the power grid was sometimes extinguished. Where power was lost inventive scavengers and electronics enthusiasts emerged after the alien ship passed and went to work to restore the lights. Where the power grid had failed, it usually flickered back to life. Solar cells generated electricity, and the wind turned turbines. Inland hydroelectric sites were destroyed, but tidal generation installations beneath the ocean surface were uninterrupted. Humanity's methods of power generation were resilient with diversity.

Earth's banking system was preserved in stasis on auxiliary power and digital backups. While digital communications were at a standstill, the Earth's economy was in a state of suspended animation. Had the records been lost, civilization could have been lost with it. The interstellar economics of trade extended across human space. The politically distinct factions of Aldebari, the ACM and the Legion were economically integrated with one another, despite their differences. With Earth's money and accounts frozen, the galactic economy was disrupted.

The barter-driven shadow economy that had developed among the moneyless underclass of Earth emerged from the shadows to keep people alive. Imbalances in supply meant communities could only trade surplus goods. Shortages of food grew severe.

Communities stayed alive by pooling resources and sharing as equitably and fairly as they could, and the disparate personalities of ad hoc neighborhood leaders rediscovered the necessity of negotiation. Crippled by adversity, the extreme manifestation of Capitalism was comatose. The barter economy remained functional but scarcity kept it subdued. Criminals and gangs grew bold and emerged to exert barbarous strength. Burglary increased.

Artificial distractions were no more. Tempers were short, many were deeply afraid. Most had no idea what to do, except seek a place to hide as deeply as they could reach. Mankind began to hunger in the flickering darkness of the Earth, underground.

The people knew something needed to be done. There were people whose nature was to get things done. In the world that had been someone else would have seized the credit. As it was, leaders self-identified by their actions.

Some natural leaders were informally recognized by their communities. Interestingly enough, the training that they had once received in virtual environments adapted well to the disastrous reality.

People knew they had to work together to achieve success. The people would do the best they could with the resources they had, whatever they could find, and with whatever they could obtain.

People began to work collectively once more. They organized themselves to secure water, to secure food, to assemble supplies, and to work rooftop gardens or range afield into the croplands.

Emergent leaders organized the people by word of mouth.

These communities posted lookouts and located one another. In the absence of the HoloNet they reinvented couriers, and discovered among their number the members of the Phoenix program that still awaited command codes for their machines and word of an invasion.

The Antarctic Continental facility in the Ellsworth Mountains enjoyed its geothermal power generator, and the course of the alien ship had yet to bother with the south polar region.

"Mike, what is our status on the Darknet?" Martin asked. "Averaging about 60% coverage but it shifts. The aliens are
    still disrupting power. Darknet is constant, but destination
    addresses come up and go down in waves. Much of the
power grid is intermittent, but the Darknet backbone is powered separately." Mike responded. "Is there any sign of invasion? Should we release the Phoenix key codes?"

"I don't know, Mike, but I think maybe so. No word yet from the Corporate Board. Have your Milnet contacts reported any sign of aliens on the ground?" Martin replied.

"Milnet is mostly chatter about restoring mainland power outages on the continents and getting the main power plants back online so that the supply can gain better continuity. Some of those will be problematic, notably the nukes and hydroelectric plants. Everything we have relies on electricity. But the people seem to be organizing out there. We're seeing some encouraging signs about the populace attempting to pool resources and barter to balance resources between them. Darknet has seen a few mentions of phoenix candidates being incorporating into word-of-mouth communities." Mike reported.

Steve and Pat felt like they were on the sidelines. The kids were at the school, where a few of the techs had set up the local area network to replace the HoloNet. They installed a multiplayer

VR game on the server for the children, the same game Stevie and Kathlyn had played aboard the gunship.

"If the aliens land in the middle of a power outage it might be critical that the pilots already have the codes. They have people out there who know enough about electricity to restore the supply locally." Mike observed.

Martin considered. "The problem there is that, without a common enemy, those communities may try to use Phoenix against each other. The commodity in greatest demand will be food supplies. If those with surplus food realize their bartering advantage, and I'm sure they do, they may try to capitalize on it. It wouldn't take much for them to destructively compete instead of cooperate for the common good.

"Phoenix could end up exacerbating a thousand little wars between the haves and the have-nots if we activate the key codes too soon." Martin worried.

Pat spoke up. "If you don't give them the codes soon, what happens when you launch to help Bobby and Mackenzie in space, Martin? What if the aliens deploy to invade while you are out of position?"

Martin looked over at Pat. "Good point, Pat. I'd give Mike authorization authority if I could, but I can't because of some biometric authorization systems. I'm not certain that any of the other CEOs can connect to make authorization. I only barely got my authority before the Corporate Board went to ground in their bunkers."

Steve had been thinking. "What if the aliens have already begun their invasion but we simply aren't aware of it? We know their fighters and scouts have some sort of stealth capability. What if they are already down on the planet?"

Everyone in the room went silent.

Martin replied "We would surely have a report from someone on the Darknet if they had slipped a force through."

"I think that we have to let the people sort out the problems of power sharing themselves." Pat offered. "I don't think it will make a difference whether we arm them or not. If they decide to fight it will happen whether they have drones or rocks and sticks to fight with."

Martin considered the point. "Once I release the keys there will be no calling them back."

Mike argued for release. "If we don't release the keys now, we may be unable to release them later. We don't know whether you will even survive launch while that alien ship is in orbit. We don't know whether we will be alive here in the morning anyway."

Martin still looked reluctant.

Steve added "Look: either we trust the people or we don't. If we don't…"

"Alright already." Martin said, exasperated. I'll authorize release." He glanced at Steve "But it isn't a question of trust. The machines aren't their property. We won't easily get them back."

Martin turned to his assistant. "Amanda, come on. Let's go unleash the Phoenix."

Chapter 63: Mission Transit

Other than re-read one of the basic references that Mackenzie kept in the digital library of his wrist comm, there wasn't much else for him to do. They had far to go before they would reach Earth. Learning the cowl's controls was an attractive preoccupation.

When the scout approached the modulus to Arcturus system, Bobby set the shields to maximum, once more making the ship undetectable.

The flight was uneventful until they reached Dante system. There was too much uncharted debris left by the previous battle to let the ship travel unguided. Bobby could not allow himself to sleep unless Mackenzie was under the cowl. It was unlikely he would get much chance to sleep when they passed into Aldebaran, and then Earth's solar system as well, so they set their schedules to alternate pilot duties.

Mackenzie was a decent pilot. His age made him slow to react, but there really wasn't much to react to in the big empty. He wasn't in the same league as his young shipmate, but he could hope his experience and judgment compensated for it.

Learning to control the ship with the cowl didn't occupy all of Mack's time. He was curious about Bobby, for example what he recalled of his youth on Earth, and what he had learned while serving with Tibs and the Aldebari.

Long hours, waiting for obstacles to appear in their course, dragged on him at times. There wasn't much to keep him mentally alert and focused on piloting, so to pass the time he composed questions for Bobby as text messages. Doing this had several advantages. Bobby could respond at length during his time under the cowl, and he was able to include citations from his own wrist comm digital library. It turned out Bobby's library was more wide ranging than what Mack had brought.

In the ACM version of history that Mackenzie had learned, the Aldebari were scientists who managed to survive the wrath of Earth's empire. The Aldebari religion was viewed as a reasonable consequence of their unwavering devotion to science and the kind of skepticism that fuels the scientific methodology. It was thought that the object of their religion was the universe itself.

Some said the Aldebari believed the universe itself was a deity, but to Mackenzie, that seemed far- fetched and dissonant with scientific skepticism.

Historical accounts varied among the cultures. Each version had considerable supporting evidence. It was difficult for Mackenzie to decide which version of the Aldebari origin was more accurate. He wondered whether the truth might lie somewhere amongst them.

In the Corporate version, the scientists who became the Aldebari were rebellious religious fanatics driven mad by isolation, that the differences were the result of an attempt by the scientists to rewrite history in order to serve an imagined god.

The Aldebari contended that it was the Corporates who revised history. They accused the corporations of changing the language that the people on Earth used in order to control what people thought and talked about. Corporate revisionism was cited by the Aldebari as a core reason for their rebellion.

During one of Mackenzie's shifts flying the scout, he left a question for Bobby about the origins of the Aldebari conflict in a text message. By the end of his next shift, Bobby had responded, and included a quote from one of his digital reference books.

"Perhaps the most balanced view is that of the Legion." Bobby wrote. "In his study of the origins of the Aldebaran Conflict, Legion Strategist (Psych) William Gaines-Carver states:

"Cost-effective automation, not only of labor, but also of most professional vocations, inspired the Board of Corporations to supplant what had become a problematic work ethic with an alternative that was oriented toward virtual reality. In virtual reality, social status accrues from virtual wealth, rather than real. It became apparent that this radical cultural shift would entail replacement of classical ideologies with a more malleable surrogate.

"Reinvention of work-related values required an adjustment of the meanings embedded in the common language.

"Literature, both educational and other texts, was made legal only in digital format, where it was subject to instantaneous global revision, as needed. Non-digital texts, reference, fiction and non-fiction, were impounded or destroyed.

"There were forceful objections to such corporate revisionism, especially from scientists and academics.

"A rebellion against revisionism began at the scientific enclave in the Aldebaran system in 2794, and spread quickly."

~W. Gaines-Carver, "Ideological Genesis of the Aldebaran Conflict",
Ad Victorium Press, Canopus, 2nd Edition, copyright 3010

Chapter 64: Intervention

Martin Avery was aboard his spacecraft, a yacht, performing his preflight checks. Steve was aboard his gunship with his children and Pat. Steve also found aboard his ship a box filled with packets of seeds. Martin had remembered his request.

With Martin leaving to intercede for Bobby and Mack, the modulinium contract signed and in the hands of Perry Station's lawyers in Old New York, it was time to take Pat back to her home and the kids back to their lives at Perry Station.

The two ships would depart together to minimize exposure to the great alien ship while it was still over Spain and France. Steve hoped to make a landing at Brasilia to conceal the gunship on the surface, hopefully before the alien came over the western coast of South America.

Reports of destruction around the globe were gradually filtering through to them, relayed by Mike Billings. Sao Paulo and Marseilles were flooded when their seawalls were breached. There hadn't been word out of Old New York since it was struck heavily during an earlier orbit of the alien ship. Moscow was in flames.

Now that Martin had unlocked and activated Phoenix, his database system was dispatching key codes to Phoenix pilots one by one, worldwide, using the Darknet. Explanatory text prefaced the package. There were far too many addresses for manual input. Distribution had to be automated.

Martin Avery's personal spacecraft was a Vincenzo Sportsman, handcrafted at the Milan shipyards near High Rome. It had a nicely appointed interior propelled by twin high density antimatter containment systems. He didn't expect to be gone long, but Amanda had ensured that the Sportsman was fully stocked to include a respectable wardrobe.

Steve's gunship was slightly larger and much more utilitarian, but his four Aldebari light fighter engines gave him an even better thrust to mass ratio than Martin enjoyed. But then, his gunship had been handcrafted by Chief Mackenzie. When Steve arrived he found a box on his acceleration couch. The box was filled with packets of different vegetable seeds.

Tempting though it was, the two starships would not take the time to race. Steve had to get Pat back to New York and then take his children home to Perry Station.

Steve, Pat, and the two children walked casually through the now shielded dock facility to reach the gunship's berth. They stopped to watch Martin Avery's Sportsman lift off on antigrav and slip out the environmental shield toward space. Steve considered Martin's Sportsman a truly beautiful machine.

Chapter 65: Approach

Earth's solar system was open, and the modulus diminished behind them. Bobby needed the navigational calculations to complete before he could raise the shields once more to maximum, but he knew Earth was nearer the sun. Bobby began to accelerate sunward.

Then they were spotted.

"Morrison-Mackenzie flight, please respond." came a male voice on the alien scout's receiver.

Bobby was momentarily stunned. Hope, rather than fear rose in his chest. He desperately wished he could respond to them verbally. Mack wasn't wearing the cowl, so he hadn't heard them.

"Mack. Somehow... somehow they know this ship is us, instead of hostiles." Bobby reported to Mackenzie.

"No, lad, the ship isn't us, but I understand what you tried to say." Mackenzie replied. "So they know we are here. Steve must have sent them word that we were coming."

"What should we do?" Bobby asked. He felt afraid to hope. "We've got fighters coming up fast behind us."

"Well, if they are human, keep our course steady but waggle a bit to let them know you hear them. Then cross your fingers, Bobby." Mackenzie advised. He crossed his own thick fingers.

"Cross my...?" Bobby started to ask, but it wasn't a good time to get into whatever that might be about. Maybe something religious. He dipped port and starboard while holding course and then trimmed back to neutral.

A flight of four Legion fighters swept into position around them. The pilot to starboard gave Bobby a fist pump. Bright relief washed over the young man's face and heart. It almost brought him to tears. He felt recognized.

Human kinship is magnified by the immensity of cold space. He felt like a member of a brotherhood, and proud. Bobby saluted the Legionnaire in response, then somehow felt childish.

An impersonal female voice came over comms. "Alien flight be advised we will be unable to provide escort all the way in. Understood your intent to deploy a package aboard the target. Recommend course 6254.6.004. Use the sensor shadow of the moon. We can stick with you that far, but we don't want the alien to see us with you."

Bobby wished he could reply, but he set up a query for the cowl to pull onto his visual display a representation of the planet's position relative to its large moon. The alien ship didn't understand human navigational coordinates, but the idea of using the moon's mass to block sensors was clear. Bobby adjusted course to match the cowl's visual representation of an optimal path.

The Legion pilot continued. "Be advised we haven't seen any of their fighters since Dante, but we've been unable to degrade the big ship's defenses anyway. Repeat, alien defenses are not degraded. If your destination is his launch bay, it's on his port, repeat port side. Target's current location is over Western Europe, near High Berlin and headed Easterly. Will update position verbally until you have a visual.

"Before you come out of the lunar shadow we'll drop back. We want to establish that your ship is under attack, so if you will raise your aft shields and take evasive action we'll try to miss you when we fire."

Bobby rolled his eyes and told Mackenzie. When he looked back to see Mackenzie's reaction, Mack just grinned at him. "Canny. That's why we win, Bobby. Remember it."

The great alien ship was still finding targets on the planet for its powerful beam. It didn't seem to matter whether the target was a population center or a spaceport, or even just an old rural airfield, it kept firing down at targets on the planet's surface wherever it found an installation that looked like it might resist.

Urban fires burned worldwide.

The people hid from the sky when the alien was overhead. Where the weather permitted, the alien ship was clearly visible during daylight as it passed overhead, a pale blue lozenge moving in the sky. It was brilliant white in the black of night where it caught the high sunlight. Within the cone of the Earth's shadow, it blocked out the light of stars when it passed.

Humanity crept out from cover when the alien was elsewhere. They watched for signs of invasion.

People in regions under cloud cover couldn't tell whether it was safe to venture in the open. Beneath clouds there was no way to know until that terrible energy beam lanced down from the heavens in searing destructive fury.

When they dared to venture out, they sought nibbles or garden vegetables or filled salvaged containers with water.

No remote communications were working, except for an uneven scattering of people with access to the Darknet. From those few, word of mouth relayed every shred of news. People hungered to know. Couriers ran between communities to relay rumors and news.

Many of the Phoenix pilots waited impatiently for word of the invasion. When the power was struck down, neighborhoods mobilized to find and repair or route around the break to give the pilots the juice they needed to defend the neighborhood. Yet the invasion hadn't appeared.

Bobby would keep the moon between the scout and the Earth as long as he safely could. He began to accelerate once more, alert beneath the cowl. At first the moon looked small against the backdrop of the Earth. As he approached the moon's stark surface, it grew to block his view of the planet beyond. The scout skimmed just kilometers from the pitted lunar surface, so close to the dark side that he saw a web of light from a mining enclave there.

The Legion pilots dropped astern and Bobby raised his aft shields, just as the Earth was about to rise above the moon's horizon. The Legion fighters were joined by a following Aldebari flight.

When the fighters fired to his port he maneuvered starboard. When the fighters fired below him he rose. By increasing the tempo, they coordinated into a deadly dance that should have looked like the real thing, and presented a convincing appearance that should mislead their observers.

Naturally, such tight coordination produced mishaps. Even if the fighters had really been trying to destroy the scout they would have had to hit more often to bring the shields down. The display they presented was made more effective when the scout's shield flared translucent more than once.

The gambit was perilous. Bobby was soon drenched with

sweat from the stress but he kept up his simulated evasive efforts without complaint.

Mackenzie often swore aloud when hits registered.

Ahead of them loomed the beautiful planet. The hemisphere of night looked completely dark save for the red glow from fires. Europe and North Africa were in flames. South Africa appeared to have escaped notice so far.

Europeans watching the sky saw bright weapons fire in the heavens as the fighters fired at Bobby's scout, and the people cheered for the pilots defending them.

Then Old Moscow appeared on the horizon, engulfed in flame. Above it, the great alien ship was firing down into the wide suburbs. It was still moving east, a silhouette against the glare of the dawn.

~

"Scout incoming. Identity unrecognized, but she is one of ours. The animals are swarming her with active fire. She is maneuvering evasively at close to maximum thrust. No communication as yet." a technician reported aloud.

Sestrel turned his face to the huntress coordinating his weapons systems "Fire on her attackers."

Weapons station responded that the animals were still out of range.

"Fire on them anyway." the big male ordered. With an imperative trill he commanded "Now!"

He turned toward the display showing the desperate engagement out there, still out of his weapons' reach. She was flying with inspired grace, keeping her ship whole, narrowly avoiding the animals' fire with uncanny prescience. One of his huntresses, returning from the mission he harshly assigned as punishment to her and her sisters at the first system, the one with the destroyed planet. Sestrel felt sure of it. Her ship must have been too badly damaged for her to respond properly. His heart went out to her as she flew like inspiration incarnate.

This huntress deserves great reward, he felt. He turned to his idle flight coordinator. "Ready an emergency team for her. She may need medical attention. I will join you in the launch bay to personally welcome her."

Bobby hadn't realized just how big the alien ship was until he was in close approach. At first he thought the scout's instruments must be off. Surely it was closer than it registered. By the time he could finally see the alien ship's point defenses tracking him he realized that he just hadn't understood its size.

The alien ship's docking bay was amidships, and to port. The scout's forward display filtered the glare from the rising sun, but left the ship itself and the planet below clearly visible. The surface of the Earth was cloaked in early morning darkness, but the devastation of the city and the metropolitan area surrounding Moscow burned orange and red with flame below and behind them. Ahead were the industrial installations on the western slopes of the Ural Mountains.

"Are we ready, Mack?" Bobby checked.

"Let's get it done, Bobby." Mack replied. The backup power to the electromagnetic antimatter assemblies should hold good for fifteen minutes, once they were disconnected from the patch cords that had fed their batteries throughout the flight from Perry Station.

Once the battery charges were depleted, the magnetic fields preventing contact between matter and antimatter would fade. The particles they had contained would be loose, and they would find their way through the vacuum to contact the strong metal housing. When the first antimatter particle contacted any particle of matter, both would annihilate with a release of energy. The rest of the antimatter would be driven by the released energy and also annihilate. Since the first unit placed should be the first to explode, Mackenzie would place the other three units so that they would be thrown deeper into the ship as they went off. The power of the first explosion should act as a pressure wall directing the force of consequent blasts away from the direction of the scout's escape.

As Mack waited he considered that the explosion might throw the alien ship, like the thrust of a rocket engine. He tried to quiet the nervous energy that filled his skin with jumpy excitement as he waited. He tried to calculate how far the alien ship would be pushed southward. Since the ship was headed East and the landing bay opened North, the explosion should push the bulk of the ship toward the equator. But how far? He decided the answer really depended on how well the ship held together. "When it blows, I hope someone is recording the event." he said aloud.

"Entering the ship now, Mack. There is an atmospheric shield holding the ship's atmosphere from the vacuum." Bobby reported, interrupting Mack's calculations. Mack released his math and prepared to move the first unit. Bobby would open the hatch for him and then pass the second unit down. He heard the ship extend struts. He hoped his back held out. Then the ship touched down and the engines began to wind down.

Bobby triggered the hatch open using the cowl, and then moved with alacrity from his acceleration couch.

The hatch opened smoothly and the ladder extended down to the alien deck. The antimatter containment systems were large and heavy. They couldn't deploy more than one at a time. Mack held his breath and detached the electrical feed to the first anti-matter bottle. "Mark!" he said aloud, signaling that the first unit was now on backup battery. Bobby set the timer on his comm unit. They had roughly fifteen minutes.

It was fortunate that Mack had only been able to fit four of them into the little scout ship. Five would have taken more time to deploy than they had. He already felt pressed just to lift and move the first unit through the hatch. Moving one down the ladder onto the deck beneath the scout was an exercise in encumbrance. Mackenzie muttered to himself all manner of advice about what he really needed to do the next time he did this as he wrestled the containment system to the deck.

The docking bay was cavernous. Mack released the first unit and stepped back to the base of the ladder. He looked up feeling hurried and saw that Bobby was still struggling with the second unit. There wasn't room up there for both of them, so Mack took a quick look around while he waited. In his mind he visualized a timer counting down, but he hadn't an easy way to tell whether his count was fast or slow. He had expected to see alien fighters there. As he scanned the deserted expanse of the launch bay he thought of setting a timer on his wrist comm to sound a chime each minute, but the thought came too late to set up. He spotted motion: a distant doorway opened, but then Bobby was handing down the second unit. Mack looked up to receive it.

He had the second unit in his arms and was staggering to place it on the other side of the first when he heard a distant cry. It sounded like a human. Someone was calling out for them to wait. He distinctly heard a cry for help. It sounded like a man. Mack set the second unit down in position and looked up to see a human, nearly naked with unkempt hair and a badly trimmed beard running across the deck toward him. The man carried some kind of heavy tube or bar, and he was running in bare feet toward the scout ship from a distant hatchway. Other than a single strap over his shoulder he was naked from the waist up. His pants were rolled up to his shins. It looked like he had some kind of flimsy tail flapping behind him.

Mack stifled his curiosity. He had to get the third unit from Bobby. He couldn't afford the distraction, but, really he hadn't signed up for this. Bobby wasn't quite ready, so he glanced again toward the first door that had opened and half-ducked when he saw what must be aliens. They moved like they were stalking as they peered toward the scout ship. Then they began running swiftly toward him. One looked larger than the others.

"Mack!" Bobby called. Mackenzie reached up to take the load of the third antimatter unit. Bobby was struggling to lower it to him gently. The cowl was still on his head.

"We have company coming, Bobby! And there's a man coming too!"

Bobby couldn't believe his ears. "A man?"

"Wait for me!" came a man's distant voice. He sounded frightened.

Paul Harden called out to the big man he had seen emerge from the alien ship on the monitor in his safe room. He had excitedly run to open the unused airlock, hoping for a rescue. Now he ran gasping across the deck. The metal bar was heavy, but he didn't want to drop his only weapon until he was safely away. He had seen the lizards, and seen them running. He was deeply afraid. They were too quick. He could hear them calling to one another.

Ahead, Harden saw the bearlike man moving something

heavy from the small alien ship to set beside two others already on the deck. He might be setting explosives. Setting explosives out there on the open deck would be almost useless unless they were nukes, but at least they wouldn't leave until they were done.

Harden tried to put more push in his strides. He was desperate to get away but his legs felt like they were about to give out. He felt like he couldn't take enough air into his lungs. The heavy metal bar was slowing him down, but he wouldn't drop it. If the lizards caught him, it would be his only defense. He felt a stitch growing in his side but he had to get aboard before the lizards caught him.

Sestrel saw the escaped animal running toward the scout. He saw the other beast who tricked his way aboard in the scout ship and felt outrage. He looked again toward the escaped animal as he ran. That animal had been running loose on his ship, despite the efforts of the huntresses he had set to recapture it.

He commanded the females to recapture the stolen ship and take any animals there to the livestock pen for meat.

Then Sestrel changed course to intercept the escapee personally. He would rip it to pieces when he caught it. He would eat it there on the spot after ripping it to bloody ribbons.

Sestrel cursed himself for his optimism, for failing to arm his huntresses. He had thought the returned scout held part of his victory. Had he armed them, they could already have dropped the thief, instead of making Sestrel run.

He focused his fury on the escaped animal. He didn't need a weapon to kill it. It was bleating as it ran. He didn't want to kill it from afar anyway, he wanted to rip it apart. Sestrel was born to run. He was fast. When he caught it he would rip the creature apart and swallow its beating heart in view of its own dying eyes.

Harden realized the big alien was going to catch him whether he ran or not. It was much too fast. The metal bar he held was too heavy to swing effectively. It couldn't be thrown accurately. But he had visualized and practiced how to wield it, and he slowed down to focus, to catch his breath, and to find his feet once more. Timing would be everything.

The big alien raced forward on nimble clawed feet. Its snake-like neck held its head steady as it ran. Harden tried to not stare at the great cutting teeth in its smiling opened mouth or the claws exposed on its fingertips. Instinct guided his hands and arms as he concentrated. He tightened his grip on the heavy metal bar and prepared to thrust the end powerfully and precisely, just as he had visualized, directly into its onrushing head.

And he did. Perfectly.

He planted the end of the rod precisely into the creature's broad flat forehead, just above the broad scaled nose. Right between the eyes of the great predator he jammed the bar with all of his strength.

Sestrel's head carried his impetus and struck the heavy unyielding rod. The force of his momentum propelled the rod back through Harden's hands. The smooth steel was shoved back into the deck. The far end bounced, ringing like a bell.

The alien's body struck Harden powerfully, knocking him sprawling. The rod clanged end by end, away across the deck. Harden saw the big lizard was down, and he scrambled to get up and get to the ship.

The huntresses saw their male go down with alarm. The metal bar clattered across the deck beyond. The evil animal that hurt their male scrambled to its feet and scampered toward the scout ship.

There is nothing so precious to Skraa females as their male. He could give life to their eggs. He meant the future, and hope for their hatchlings. All but one of the huntresses diverted to try and rescue and protect their male.

Mackenzie and Bobby struggled to wrestle the last antimatter canister and its battery into position. They were running out of time, and they were already out of breath, but they had seen the man running toward them for all he was worth, yelling to wait for him, and they saw the aliens.

There was no time to waste, but neither Bobby nor Mackenzie could leave him there. Bobby climbed the ladder to wind up the engines. Mackenzie waited for the man, halfway up the ladder with his hand out to the wild-looking, filthy man racing toward him. "Come on!" Mack bellowed.

Bobby strapped into his acceleration couch, commanding the

cowl to prepare the maneuvering thrusters for launch. Then he anxiously waited for Mack to tell him to close the hatch and go. He glanced at the timer he had set on his wristcom. It was past time to go. "We have to go, Mack!" he yelled over his shoulder.

One of the huntresses was still in pursuit, undistracted by the fallen one. She could smell the beast. The wild animal smelled foul. It was almost to the ladder. She leaped forward with all the speed she could muster, her claws outstretched.

Mackenzie had hold of the wild man's forearm and pulled him up the ladder into the ship, but the man was suddenly jerked back, half way from the hatch. They still had to retract the ladder before they could seal the hatch and get away.

The huntress had her claws hooked deep in the animal's lower leg. She clenched her claws with all her strength and pulled, trying to reach his flesh with the claws of her other hand.

With a great groan Mackenzie pulled the screaming man's forearm powerfully, pulling him into the ship. The alien's claws were still hooked into his bleeding calf, and she was pulled with him. Paul Harden screamed again in pain. Her claws bit deeper into his flesh. Harden grabbed a handhold and used the pain to strain against her pull. His calf felt aflame and wet.

Mackenzie shifted his weight and kicked down hard on her scaled head. Her head twisted back on her supple neck and she released her grip, falling to the deck. "Close!" Mack yelled at Bobby. "GO!"

The ladder retracted and the hatch slid smoothly shut to seal. Bobby applied thrust without worrying about what his engines would do to the interior of the bay.

"Go! Go! Go!" Mackenzie yelled as the engines roared. Paul Harden was whimpering in pain and relief. "Hold onto something, man." Mackenzie shouted. The wild man stank horribly. Bobby commanded the cowl to raise shields and tried to initiate inertia dampening.

The battery of the first antimatter container faded lifeless, and the antimatter that had been held began to flow. A particle touched steel alloy. The pressure of the energy released in anni-hilation pressed the rest of the antimatter onto the metal cylinder wall and a small sun ignited there within the launch bay of the alien ship. A ball of pure energy expanded, faster than thought, throwing the other three containers deeper. There they became three more small suns expanding to merge into a great sphere of plasma that the alien ship could not contain. The ship disintegrated. The heavy interlocking armor expanded to its maximum and broke apart.

Too soon the speeding little scout was caught and thrown violently forward by the expanding ball of plasma, slamming Mackenzie and Paul Harden into a bulkhead. Bobby was secured in his acceleration couch. The detonation was stunning.

The pale shape of the alien ship distorted as it shunted unnaturally to the south before the links of its magnificent armor plates broke asunder around an expanding sphere of annihilation. The world beneath was starkly lit under the brief blinding light.

In space, a spontaneous cheer came from many Legion, Aldebari and Corporate comms. When the cheering faded, the voice of Avery Martin could be heard calling for a reply from the two men who had done what they had to do.

A tiny ship filled with journalists congratulated one another and checked the imagery they had captured, and then they listened for any response from the men from Perry Station.

A search for the little scout ship began in the skies northeast of Moscow.

Word came to Antarctica over Milnet. While the others cheered, Billings sent the news out to the Phoenix players. They passed word to the couriers who ran free, for once, to their surrounding communities.

Chapter 66: Destiny

It was the pain in his calf, where the female Skraa had sunk her claws, that roused Paul Harden to consciousness. He tried to sit up but his hands had been tied behind his back. He looked down and behind him to see his wrists were cinched with an EVA safety tether. The other end was tied to an airlock handhold. The knot looked well-formed. He turned to look at his captors.

At the sight of the cowl on Bobby's head, Harden began to panic.

"Just hold still." Bobby said to him. He had recognized the emaciated stinking man they had risked their lives to rescue, even beneath that ragged beard. Bobby's fletchette pistol was still holstered, with the safety strap in place.

"You don't understand." Harden told him in urgent, agitated tones. "That thing you are wearing will steal your mind!"

"It will not." Bobby told him with an impatient edge. "If I press the right sequence on the controls, I could upload my memory into it, but it won't 'steal' my mind." Bobby responded, pulling back from the stench of Harden's breath. The prisoner's wounds were cleaned and no longer bleeding. The chemical sutures were beginning to work with Harden's DNA to pull the gashes together. Bobby unstrapped his weapon and rested his hand on the pistol's butt, but he left it in the holster.

"You look familiar." Harden observed as Bobby stood up. "Do I know you?" he asked.

Mackenzie sat up. Bobby had treated him first for concussion and splinted the big man's left arm. Swelling made it difficult for Mack to speak, but he spoke anyway. "Harden, you arsehole," Mackenzie said with a growl, "we should've spaced you before we wasted the medpack."

Harden didn't know Mackenzie, but looking at Bobby realization dawned. The boy he had once tried to convince to join with him was now a man. "Bobby Morrison." he pronounced the name.

Bobby turned back to the open panel and returned the packet of chemical suture gel into the cabinet inside, wondering whether it could also knit bone. He had seen Quetzalcoatl use the panel

in the cowled memory, when she treated her wound before returning to space. Otherwise he might never have found it. If medical science could analyze and understand the substance it could
mean a significant advance for medical emergency tech. He
turned back to Harden, thinking what Tibs would say. He remembered Steve's admonishments about the law, and about justice.
That seemed so long ago, but Bobby decided Steve was right.
His personal vengeance would be inadequate to the man's
crimes.

"No, I won't space you if I can help it, Harden. I don't want to
solve your problems for you. I wouldn't want to release you from
your destiny. You are going to have to live through it yourself."
Bobby told him.

Mackenzie looked at Bobby and disagreed. "Yes, we should
have spaced him. He isn't worth the air he breathes. And he
stinks."

Bobby met Mack's gaze levelly. "Think it through, Chief. If we
snuff out his life now he will no longer have to face himself every
day, knowing that he killed half a million people, including
women and children, for nothing. My little desire for vengeance
just isn't adequate. It would feel good for a little while, but this
bastard needs real punishment. I'm not inventive enough to deliver it to him."

Harden was offended. He got his legs under him and stood
up. "For nothing? Don't be an idiot, Bobby. I was heroic. I did my
level best to save eighteen billion people. We had to have that
modulinium to do it! We can still save them, Bobby, if only you
will listen to reason!"

"Liar!" Bobby snarled and he slapped Paul Harden with his
open hand, making a loud pop. The slap left a reddening hand
print across Harden's pale cheek. Involuntary tears welled in
Harden's eyes. He recalled the face of his mother the last time
he saw her. She had slapped him, too.

"That felt too good, Harden. Don't tempt me again." Bobby
said. "There was no need at all to rip the modulinite out of the
planet, Harden, and you know it. You knew it then.

"The fastest way to get the modulinium needed, even for your
idiotic plan to ship those people off to die, was to push iron

through the anomaly into Trondheim system." Bobby continued. "You killed those people for no reason, whatever your intentions may have been, and no matter what lies you have been telling yourself." Bobby held Harden's eyes until his prisoner looked away.

After a moment Bobby looked back toward Mackenzie. "However, if he keeps lying like that we can put him in a spacesuit and tow him back to Perry Station by the safety tether."

The Chief smiled. He was growing to like this young man.

Bobby pulled his fletchette pistol from the holster and handed it butt first to Mackenzie, who took it with his good hand.

Bobby returned to his acceleration couch and, after a systems check, restarted the engines. He listened to his cowl for a minute, then turned back to Mack. "We have a legion escort to Perry Station. I'll let you know when I get tired, chief. Maybe we'll put him in the spacesuit out there when we need to sleep."

Epilogue

Kyle knew he had a chore in hydroponics, and he couldn't put it off any longer. It would be simpler if the leg bones of the assassin had also been eaten, but in that case his search would probably take quite a bit longer. He felt he had a pretty good idea where the aliens had hidden, so if the bones were in there they should turn up quickly. If the bones weren't there, well, hydroponics was a large area to search.

He walked toward the double doors and removed the 'crime scene' lock. He swung open the right-side door and snapped the lock back in place on the left door's latch.

The scientists were having trouble keeping the two aliens fed. Kyle was glad that duty was their headache instead of his. Importing beef from Mazzaroth was expensive, and the reptiles ate a lot of it.

The platform stood about a meter off the deck, held up by orange-painted steel beams. The nutrient solution perpetually gurgled in the elevated basin as it circulated to nourish the roots of young lettuce plants.

Kyle unclipped the focuslight he had brought, knowing there wasn't much light under there, and stooped over to shine the powerful beam into the darkness. He hoped to spot the bones before crawling around in there to recover them. Not only were the bones unsanitary evidence, but they should be kept with the rest of the assassin's remains, especially whenever the assassin's corpse was either cremated or spaced in the equivalent of a burial.

Kyle had a large evidence bag folded over his left arm, ready to use. His light didn't pick up any sign so far, so he moved to his right and looked again. He was about to move again to the right when the beam of his focuslight shone on something unusual. There was some kind of material stuffed under there. It looked like a large crumpled sheet of dark woven fiber stuffed among the orange support beams. He moved his light to a different angle and saw what was probably the end of a tibia, the largest of the pale bones he needed to find and recover.

Kyle turned off the light and unfolded the evidence bag. He whipped it in the air once to fully open it, then got down into a

squat to awkwardly climb under the nutrient tank and over an orange strut between the beams to get closer, trying to reach the
bone.

The dark fabric was the material used to bundle bales of plant
waste, like the roots left from harvesting lettuce, in preparation
for recycling. The remains of food vegetation were valuable. The
fabric had been bundled, surely by the aliens, into a makeshift
nest.

When Kyle finally managed to get close enough to get the
tibia he switched his focuslight back on and saw the eggs. He realized at once what the ovoid leathery objects must be. He only
had the one bag, so he first recovered the bones he came for,
placing them in the bottom of the evidence bag. Then he began
plucking the eggs one by one from the nest.

The eggs were warmer than the cool air under the basin.
They were leathery and pliable, and he felt the babies move inside a few of them, which alarmed him as he handled them. He
placed the eggs into the bag, counting eleven of them as he did.
He hoped they wouldn't hatch before he got them to the scientists. Since the baby aliens might already have their teeth, he
hurried. Once he had them all he clambered out from under the
basin. He used his comm unit to tell Gabriella about the eggs
and asked her to contact the scientists that were studying the aliens so they could prepare for them and hopefully send someone
to take them. He advised her that the eggs seemed about ready
to hatch.

About the Author:

Richard Romero retired from Federal service in July of 2015 after a career of measuring and analyzing business systems, errors and their causes.

He attended Cordova and McKinleyville High schools in California and American River College, Sacramento State College (now CSUS), and received a Bachelor of Arts degree (Integral Curriculum) at Saint Mary's College of California. Post Graduate studies were at Western Carolina University in Cullowhee, N.C. and Villanova University (online, Business Systems Analysis) in Philadelphia, PA.

Richard is proud to be the father of Eva, Jessica, and Logan. He lives in Philadelphia, PA with his sweetheart, Laura.

Photograph by Logan Romero

34329010R00212

Made in the USA
Middletown, DE
25 January 2019